A FATE OF

SHADOWS AND FIRE

MICHELLE ROSSA

Michelle Rossa

Copyright © 2024 by Michelle Rossa
Cover design by Michelle Rossa
Paperback ISBN: 979-8-218-44167-8

3

For those who have felt alone & in the shadows all their life, this one's for you.
And to Erik, I know you would be proud of how far I've come.

CONTENT WARNING

The material in this novel is for mature audiences only, and is not suitable for minors. Themes in this novel may be triggering, and should be read at your discretion. Themes of which include dissociation, depression, suicidal ideation, loss, trauma responses due to PTSD, attempted sexual assault, domestic abuse/violence, brief mention of rape, and explicit sexual content.

Themes in this book include hearing voices that are outside of your own. This is a work of fiction, and should be treated as such.

CHAPTER 1

"Awfully early to be out here all by yourself, darling."

My eyes remain closed as I face the rise of the early morning sun. It's been some time since I've been out here this early, but I find coming out here really helps me feel centered.

It seems like it's the only place that can give me that solace. When I come out here, everything feels right.

Although what *was* a peaceful morning is now being insufferably interrupted by a man who thinks that a woman sitting alone is automatically an invitation to approach her. Sighing internally because I already know how this is going to go.

"And what would I possibly need to be afraid of being out here by myself? You, perhaps?" I respond dryly, my eyes remaining closed.

Like oil against water, I feel the swift change in his energy at my dry and slightly cruel response. I can only surmise that he probably thought I'd reply with a more kind attitude. But I am hardly ever kind when men are pestering me when I *clearly* am not open to the company. I am also not naive, I can feel his intentions evaporating from his stance like incense wafting in the air.

"Fine, be a bitch. I was just trying to be nice."

When I do not feel his presence leave is when I finally open my eyes as my gaze falls onto the man before me. He appears to be in his mid-to-late forties, his scruffy beard has specs of cigarette ash in it.

Gross.

His brittle graying hair is wild and unbound, and his clothes are raggedy and smell strongly of musky cologne.

Gross, once again.

My gaze meets his, immediately noticing the hurt ego that drips from his expression. You would think if he knew himself well enough that if he was going to be this affected by a woman telling him no, then he should know better than to take the risk at all. Better yet, he should stay *far* away from women altogether if he thinks he is warranted a woman's time. "Yet, you're still standing here."

He clenches his hands at his sides. "Well, don't you got a fucking mouth on you. I bet it would be good around–"

"Gods, you cannot be serious." I say, lazily cutting him off. Spending another minute listening to this man yapping at me is definitely not how I envisioned my day.

His expression grows confused as he furrows his brows. I take that as my cue to explain, knowing it'll only aggravate him. But again, I'm not interested in being nice.

"I mean, look at you. Your confidence is alarmingly high if you think I would ever let you get near me. I'll pass."

His glare instantly pierces into mine and hardens with hostility as he clenches his fists. He takes a step toward me, hesitating when his fingers shoot up to his forehead. His eyes shut tightly as his mouth gapes open, stumbling back a step. He begins to grunt in pain as he rubs his temple viciously.

"Is something wrong?" I ask, a grin spreading wide on my face.

"My head it–gods, it fucking hurts! I–" In the next moment, his eyes spring open and widen as he stares at me. He shakily begins to back up when he trips and lands on his ass. Looking frantically around him as he begins clutching at his clothing, his hair, and then his face full of sheer terror.

"Wh–why aren't you afraid! Can't you see them?"

He begins screaming as he shoots up onto his feet, sprinting in the opposite direction as me. As he runs away I giggle to myself as the vile, and now frantic man dashes away before completely vanishing from my line of sight.

As I begin to feel my power draw back into myself, I breathe deeply in and out as I recenter myself.

Making people hallucinate and go mad is one of my few gifts I've had since I was young. I can manipulate the mind to see things that aren't there, such as spiders crawling all over themselves. But it's something that my village would not be compliant with, so the smart thing would be to not make my gift known.

Though this would be only the second time now that I've used it on someone. I know I should probably be a lot smarter about unveiling something that could potentially get me killed, but sometimes situations like these outweigh what's logical.

As I reclose my eyes, I ground into my surroundings. I feel the brisk breeze that brushes past my face, and the sound of morning doves cooing in the trees above me. It's the early morning hours into the first day of spring. I guess one would hardly call it spring though, as the temperature is hovering over a brisk chill that most wouldn't risk enduring unless necessary.

Now that I notice, it is pretty frigid out here. Yet a part of me doesn't care. Being in nature is my comfort blanket, my sacred space. A place where I can come and forget the incredulous demands of life.

As I sink further into the easy sounds of nature around me, I hear footsteps headed in my direction. As they get closer to me, I can smell that familiar sandalwood and musk cologne that I know too well. Hoping that if I just remain sitting here, he'll just leave me alone like he usually does. Though this time, I don't get so lucky.

I feel his calloused hand grip my shoulder and shove me forward, a motion that jumps me back to reality. If I could just simply escape my problems away by hiding out here, I would happily do just that.

But once again, I am faced with reality.

I swivel my head around to glare at the man hovering above me. My eyes glare into his as I wish I could show him how much I *hate* being pushed around, but for now I keep the anger simmered way, way below.

"Let's go. It's time for breakfast." He says, and I can see the impatience written all over his face. I turn my head around, and close my eyes as I take a deep breath in and out before standing up. I open my eyes and am greeted with the orange glow of the sun stretching over the canopies of the still-dead, lifeless trees. Soon, they will come back to life and blossom with the greenery that really makes this park come to life. But for now, they remain stalky branches.

As I begin to stretch my legs out from under me, I stretch upwards to a stance, glancing back at my father standing behind me.

"Goodorming father." I say. I begin walking ahead and he follows next to me, silent as we walk back home.

Our cabin is one of the only properties that is fortunate enough to be in walking distance from Hellen Park. The park has a trail that allows easy access for me to navigate to from the backyard of our home. So, it only makes sense that I come here as often as I do.

Being in nature has always been a feeling that can't be described nor compared to anything else I've experienced. Surrounded by the quietness of the wind brushing the trees, the faint noise of birds chirping, the occasional greeting from wildlife animals, it's like my connection for nature stems far deeper than surface level. I've never been able to describe it much past that, but regardless of my loss of words for the feeling, it's where I feel most at peace.

I turn my gaze around one last time toward the rising morning sun, allowing the warmth of the rays to drench into my pores one last time before I face forward once more.

My father and I walk mostly in silence, as that is a big part of what our relationship is. As we walk, I notice two women walking towards us, and a grin grows on my face as I overhear part of their conversation.

"Did you hear that man screaming? He was acting so strange! Probably was on something to make him act like that." One woman with short, fire red hair said. Her eyes shone like bright ocean tides against her hair.

"Did you see the way he kept pawing at his clothing? Gods, poor thing." The other woman said before they both giggled to one another. Her long blonde hair was half-up, half-down, and she kept fidgeting with a loose strand of it.

I do my best work of hiding the smirk that's crawling up my face, as my father is unaware of my gifts. Let's just say he would not be accepting of finding out I was the reason for that man's strange behavior.

Sebastian Khthor is the best handyman our village has ever had the pleasure of seeing. His love for fixing things has landed him to learn all sorts of trades. Trades ranging from plumbing, some electrical work, and other miscellaneous repair services he offers. As a family whose lives were not so financially advantageous, my father has done whatever it's taken for our family to survive. So if learning several trades is what it took for us to have food in our bellies, and a roof over our heads at night, he did just that.

Which meant he worked. A lot.

When I was younger I couldn't really understand this. He always had to work, so he couldn't dedicate more time to my sister and I. But as I grew older, the need to do what it takes for survival started to make sense. Especially since I too, had to learn what it took to survive and provide for my family.

After my mother died, the demands for work on my father became increasingly more necessary. Having to now raise two children on his own, he took pretty much anything that was offered to him. Which then inevitably only grew the divide that was already there between us, leaving me to raise Makaria for much on my own. At the age of twenty-five, I have a better grasp on what it entails to take care of someone now than when I started caring for my sister at the age of seven.

Makaria is three years younger than me, so when our mother died she was only four years old. I'll never forget her confusion as to why mother wasn't coming back home, and how since our father drunk himself to sleep every night trying to process his grief, I was left to be the bearer of news that no one should ever have to give.

If our father wasn't working, he was at home passed out drunk. This went on for the first two years, therefore I really had to pick up the slack to give Makaria everything she could need from a caregiver.

When we'd both get home from school, I made sure Makaria tended to her homework, as I would begin to prepare dinner for the three of us. After dinner, I would get Makaria setup for her nightly bath. Since our father knew basic electrical functioning, we were fortunate enough to have electricity. This really helped being able to just turn the hot water on in the bathtub, rather than needing to heat buckets of water by the fireplace.

I would've bitched and moaned about it if that were the case, but I would've done it anyway for my sister.

Once I helped Makaria get washed up, I would get her dried off and into a clean nightgown, ready for bed. Once Makaria was down for bed, then I was able to finally get to my studies, or let alone just cater to myself. Sure, there were many nights in those two years where I would only get maybe five hours of sleep, but I had no choice. After our mother passed, it was just the three of us. So, I did exactly this routine, for two straight years.

I did what I had to do.

Because though I had tremendous grief myself, and also empathized to some degree for my father's grief and how he chose to process it, I knew it was unfair that my younger sister should have to suffer anymore than she already has. Not to mention, at her age at that time she was completely unable to care for herself.

Though as I grew older, I realized the magnitude of how unfair it was for me to have had to take on that kind of responsibility. That now when I ponder over it, it creates a resentment within me that I'm afraid will never vanquish. Still, I took the lead. I feel taking on the role to care for my sister has allowed her to still grow up into the optimistic girl she has always been known to be, and for that alone it has made it worth it.

Even if it has led me to develop a cold distrust for anyone capable of doing the same for me. A steel wall that corners me on all four sides, that's slowly ingrained a conditioned mentality to believe that I'm all on my own, with no other way possible for me to survive.

As my father and I approach the back door of our cabin, I see Makaria through the window already seated at our kitchen table.

Our log cabin is enriched in a dark chestnut brown, connected with log corner posts on each end of the cabin. In our backyard, a small fire pit is situated with three green lawn chairs encircling it. Along the ground directly against the cabin's wall are bush branches that, once everything starts to bloom again, will spruce lavender. Our mother planted lavender bushes when I was just an infant, and Makaria and I have made sure to see them grown every year since her passing.

The rest of the backyard is filled with fern bushes and other foliage. In the village of Elzwin, it is very common to see various types of greenery on each family's property. As my father and I approach the back screen door, Makaria's gaze is on us once the screen door slides open.

"Gods, what took you two so long? I'm starving!" She exclaims as she turns back to eye up the pile of scrambled eggs, sausage, and assortments of fruit that our father laid out before coming to collect me.

"You know how your sister is, Makaria. Once she's in that damn park it's a challenge to get her to come out of it." Our father says, as he pulls out one chair for himself. I make my way to the chair I normally sit in, a few down from his.

During the brutally cold winter months, it's nearly impossible for me to enjoy being outside. So every year when I know spring is soon to approach, I am always counting down the days when it's warm enough for me to venture out to that park once again.

When I have an excuse to get a little time away from the house, and from my father.

Pulling myself from my thoughts I look up at my sister, who I've seated myself directly across from. She looks well rested, and almost like she has herself a special agenda for the day. After taking care of her it seems like I've developed this keen knowing of what my sister is feeling, something almost stronger then what a sisterly bond would encompass.

I've also noticed that though I don't need to as much anymore since she is now twenty-two, I still feel incredibly protective over her. It's as though I still have this motherly, caregiver instinct to make sure she's eating enough, or that she's getting enough sleep at night. Even though our father has been doing a better job of being the parent in this household, and taking a more active role in fathering

Makaria. I've come to just accept that the watchful eye I still have over her probably will never subside.

As I fill my plate with some of the scrambled eggs and sausage, I almost forget about one imperative part of breakfast.

"Coffee, anyone?" I ask.

Sebastian says nothing but instead holds his cup up, as if saying *"yes, please"* is too great a challenge for him. I find myself glaring at him and tentatively fill his mug. I glance over to my sister, who looks up at me. "No, I'm okay." She says as she grabs the pitcher of orange juice that's been sitting on the table, and pours herself a glass.

Makaria never really has been one for coffee, as Sebastian and I are the two coffee connoisseurs in this family. So, it doesn't surprise me that she declined to such.

As I sit back down, we all dig in greedily to our plates. One thing about the Khthor family is we love breakfast foods around here. There's even been many nights where we've said fuck it and had breakfast for dinner as well.

As the three of us are finished polishing off our plates, our father scooches his chair back an inch and stretches his legs out under the table, crossing at the ankles.

He sighs audibly and closes his eyes, as if he's about to take a nap right here at the table. He opens them a few moments later, looking straight ahead. As I'm still drinking my coffee, savoring the caramel creamer I splashed into my mug, our father uncrosses his legs and pushes out from the table once more. Already knowing he's about to get up and tell us he has to work.

Sometimes I feel like I know our father better than he knows himself. Normally, if he didn't have to be anywhere for at least a few hours, he would remain seated and at least ask us what our plans were for the day.

Well—more like he'd ask Makaria what her plans are and maybe acknowledge me with a glance. Instead, he's eagerly getting up to excuse himself. Which means he's got somewhere to be.

And the place he spends the majority of his time is work.

As he steps out from his chair to fully stand up, he looks at Makaria, completely unacknowledging me. "I have a few clients that need a few things fixed, I'm going to be gone for most of today. I should be home before dinner."

"Wait—it's Sunday, pa. You promised you would start keeping Sunday's free from work." Makaria says with the visibility of disappointment etching her face. Even though she's no longer a child, she still has trouble understanding why father has to work so much. I think it takes a bigger toll on her then it ever has me, mainly because the only time father pays any real attention to me is if I've done something to upset him.

"I know. I promise I'll make it up to you when I get home. What about smores over the fire?" Our father asks, and it's evident he sincerely doesn't mean to disappoint her.

Sebastian and my sister have always had a closer relationship with one another, then I and Sebastian have had. Maybe that's due to him trying to mend his absence from years prior, or maybe our father forgets that I'm not a caregiver but his daughter, too.

Makaria is literally the spitting image of Sebastian. They both share the same white-blonde wavy hair, accentuated by their honey-golden, soft eyes against their warm ivory skin. Thick, dark blonde eyebrows along with the most miniscule freckles that you can only see if you're standing right in front of them. They're basically twins.

Then there's me. Who came out looking far more like our beautiful mother, Persephone.

She had long, luscious wavy hair that trailed down her entire back, and glimmered the deepest shade of black. Her eyes were the most gorgeous shade of green you've ever seen. Like rich, emerald gemstones that shone like iridescent night stars. The fullness of her lips rested flawlessly along her defined jawline, all accentuated by the same warm, ivory skin.

She was the most impeccable woman I have ever known. My gut still churns when I think about how she was murdered and burned alive.

Our father really despises talking about it. I'm sure that is just how he decides to deal with the pain, by shoving it down and almost forgetting it exists. Whenever I would ask questions about why people would do this to her, he was always vague in his responses.

"She was murdered because of her gifts, Melinoë." He'd said one night when I came to him insisting on answers. He continued, *"Promise me that you will never*

go searching for knowledge on this, Melinoë. I forbid it. Just accept that she is gone, and move on." He'd said, staring at me as if he was mentally drilling this into my mind. I remember feeling utterly dumbfounded by his harshness of badgering me to forget, as if that wasn't his wife he lost. I remember him gripping both of my arms so tightly, that when he finally released me, there were faint indents into my sweater that remained where his fingers just were.

That was the first time my father proved his unreliability, and also the first that he showed the lash of his anger. When I demanded that he tell me more, he did not fuss with me.

He did not argue with me.

He only slapped me. The brunt whip of his hand across my face silenced me, from ever asking him questions again.

That was also the first time I learned he did not see me as his daughter, like he did Makaria. Because the way he treats her is far kinder than he has ever treated me. And before, I used to hate their relationship. Their closeness. Until one day that yearning, that wishing turned to numbness, and suddenly I didn't pine for a closer relationship with him.

I instead learned a man like that was not worthy of being close to me at all. So I tolerate him only when I absolutely need to.

My mother had the gift of communing with the deceased. I don't know much about how she learned to do this, or if it was just inherited through our family lineage. Neither my father or sister share the same gift, at least not that I'm aware of. Which creates all the more of a divide I feel from them both, as I share similar gifts as my mother.

And since my father forbids it, as it is not a safe space for me to express this with, I have no one to talk to about it.

The first time it happened it terrified me. I was sitting in Hellen Park, admiring the evergreen trees that circled around me. when suddenly, I heard someone speak.

"Pretty day, yes?"

I remember nearly jumping out of my skin. I had tried to make sense of it as it was definitely someone's voice I clearly heard, but it wasn't externally.

I heard it internally, in my head. A voice that was very clearly not my own. I thought back to our mother and what Sebastian said to me that one day.

"She was murdered for her gifts, Melinoë."

For a year after that, I tried to just forget that it even happened. I couldn't make sense of why I had that occurrence, but I knew that if my mother was killed for something as talking to the dead, then maybe I truly wasn't safe to learn more about it. But after a year, it began to happen more. Very far and few, but still. Always when I was at Hellen Park, or just when I'm alone at least.

Three years later, and now I'm more comfortable with it when it does happen. For the past few years I've been trying to research in secrecy. Finding myself asking questions like why are these spirits trying to talk to me?

Would I really be in danger if I told someone about this?

With the worry of what kind of panic I could ensue, I keep this to myself. Because in our village of Elzwin, the gift of communing with the deceased is something forbidden. Ever since the burning of my mother, along with others who claimed to have the gift, they've put bans on those trying to practice it.

So basically, I have no one to turn to for answers as I am once again, figuring things out as I go along.

Our father comes around and kneels down to Makaria, jostling me from my thoughts. He gives her a kiss on her forehead. "Have a good day, my sweet." He says as he turns to walk out of the kitchen.

"Bye, pa." Makaria says as she watches Sebastian walk to his bedroom to change into his work clothes. She looks back towards me where I'm standing at the sink, piling dirty dishes into.

"So what are you going to do today?" Makaria asks.

"I'm just going to clean up here, then I was going to walk over to the library and wander a bit. You want to come with me?" I ask, knowing it's probably a lot better than for her to sit around, drowning in her own sadness.

"Yes, I'd really like that." Makaria says. She pushes her seat back and grabs her plates to bring over to me. She gives me a wry smile, and continues "Can we also stop at the market to grab stuff for s'mores tonight?"

"Yes, of course." I say, meeting her smile with my own.

As I start to scrub the dishes, she awaits with a clean towel in her hand, ready to dry them once I've rinsed off the soap. We do this a short while until all the dishes are clean, and put away. Makaria heads to her room, coming back out with a folded clean pair of leggings and sweater. She heads into the bathroom to get washed up, as I head for my room.

I sit on my bed, waiting for her to finish since we only have one bathroom in our home. As I sit and wait, I begin to think of how I'm going to sneak what I want from the library back home today. My plan was to pick up a certain book I've heard about that shares knowledge about talking with the dead.

Even though they're topics my father has forbidden me from having access to, I'm still willing to risk going to great lengths in acquiring them.

CHAPTER 2

Walking through the village of Elzwin, I take note of the congestion of people that are wandering out and about today. Fully aware that this is only the case because it's Sunday, otherwise if it were any day during the week, the streets would still be quiet at this early in the day.

"So what book are you looking for?" My sister asks me. I can't tell her what I'm looking for as her innocence would most likely drive her to tell our father immediately. So instead, I lie.

"Nothing in particular, I just wanted to get out of the house for a bit." I reply, keeping my tone matter of factly.

My sister doesn't even question me why I would pick the library out of all places. She knows aside from being in Hellen Park, that it's my other favorite place to be. I began to grow a deep fondness for reading around the age of eight. Initially my main interest lay in folktales and fantasy novels, now I'll read almost anything. Yet in recent years, I've been trying to find as much about mediumship and necromancy as I possibly can, and the amount of books we have on that is very few.

Though our village has placed bans against those wanting to practice mediumship and necromancy, they have not banned any remaining books that we still have on the matter. The townspeople think that having the remaining books is a good way to educate people of all of the 'dangers' of such a gift, and will drive them away from wanting to dabble further with it.

Well, to their naivety it does the opposite for me.

As my sister and I walk the sidewalk I take note of a few shops that have their doors wide open. Since this morning, it has warmed up enough for people to be out in just pants and a sweater. It seems some of the shops are taking advantage of the decent weather and letting a little fresh air in.

Our village is very big on honoring the change of the seasons. The spring equinox is today and it's typical to see our people honor it by doing deep cleanings of their homes, shops, and even their appearance. For summer, many families will host big parties and gatherings to celebrate the longer days and shorter nights. Parties which include grilled food, alcoholic drinks, nuts, fruit, and more.

Elzwin believes that each season is a different transitional period in life. How fall brings cooler weather and the changing of the leaves, it's also believed fall is a time to turn inward and to harvest for the cold winter. Many of our huntsmen will hunt tirelessly to make sure we have enough meat for the cold winter when most animals turn to hibernating.

Elzwin is not a tremendously populated village, and we aren't a very wealthy one either, but we do alright here.

My sister and I reach the library and approach the vintage double doors that are already pried open. The library is the corner shop, connected to a stretch of four other shops. The whole building is laid with red brick, with half grid double hung windows lined on both sides. It's a really admirable, yet quaint building.

I walk in first with my sister following right behind me. It doesn't take long for my sister to find something that peaks her attention, and she walks away to a shelf of books labeled " YA ROMANCE ".

I chuckle to myself. Go figure, as she's always been one for romcoms on television, or finding herself venting to me about how she just read a new romance novel that she can't stop thinking about. I feel like my sister has always been one of those hopeless romantics that blindly believes in magical fairytales and grand happy endings.

That is one way she and I differ drastically.

Since my sister is preoccupied, I hurriedly head over towards the back by the history section looking for the section marked " OCCULT STUDIES ". I glance around at the five rows lined in front of me, searching quickly for it as I'm not sure how long my sister will be over there.

I've already read a few of their books here, but one in particular I'm looking for is—ha! Found it.

I grab the book and admire the gold lettering that displays the title:

"Mediumship: The Knowledge that Ensued Villagewide Panic"

The title alone makes me scoff and roll my eyes, and because of its already deemed negative connotation with the subject, I probably would've put it back. But I hear there's actually knowledge in here that goes unbiased. As I run my fingertips along the book, I freeze internally as my mind becomes clear with one thing.

I told my sister that I wasn't coming for anything in particular, and if I walk out with this book, her nosey self will be all over it.

Fuck. I definitely didn't think this through.

I glance around me, and notice I'm the only one over here. So, as an act of desperation to know what's in this book, I do the one thing I know would be frowned upon.

I decide to steal it.

I mean it's actually not really stealing if I'm going to bring it back as soon as I'm finished reading it, right?

Whatever, fuck it.

I hear the librarian's keys jingle as he's moving from the front of the store and now towards the back where I'm at. Thank gods I was smart enough to wear an oversized hoodie today.

I quickly shove the book under my hoodie, positioning it so that it's under my left armpit. I move my arm so it's secured against the book, keeping it in place so that it doesn't slip down from my side.

Definitely not noticeable at all.

Once it's secured, I decide to play it off and move over a few aisles so when Jester comes into view, it looks like I'm browsing around in the history section.

"Melinoë! It's so good to see you again. This time in the history section?" Jester says.

Yup, definitely what I was doing.

"Yes. I feel like I've read so much here already, that I need to branch out and widen my selection a bit. And please, call me Meli." I say to the librarian.

I've known Jester since I was a child, and even to this day he always calls me by my full name. It's not something that bothers me, I just hardly hear anyone call me by my full name anymore.

"Ah, that makes sense as you are one customer I have in here on a weekly basis it seems. Well, if you need anything at all just give me a holler!" Jester says as he gives me a wide smile.

He doesn't linger long after that, almost like he's trying to put as much distance between him and I as possible. But I know that's not the case. With him being the owner he's always hounded with work to be done around here. He's like my father in that way, always busy it seems. I begin to turn to move away from this section.

"I figured I would find you here."

Eiran Halverson walks towards me with a smirk on his face. His tall figure basically hovers over me when I stand next to him. His gorgeous bronzed skin and warm golden brown eyes contrast aesthetically against his sharp jawline and dark blonde short hair.

Eiran is my best friend, and well, probably the only man I'm tolerable of.

Our friendship is…different.

We've been great friends since we were both young, but over the last year things have progressed into something more. We aren't dating, but we definitely hook up once in a while.

The sex is great, and I care for Eiran deeply, but he knows where I stand with relationships. I'm grateful that he's never pressured me for more than what we are now, even if I know he'd love for us to flourish into more. Still, he never badgers me about it. It's not that I'm completely against being romantically involved with a man, I just like my independence.

Okay maybe the thought of being romantically involved with a man does create an uncomfortableness that I'm not willing to share aloud. But it's always been just me, and I've always been okay with that.

But if there's anyone that I have a soft spot for, it's Eiran.

"Let me guess you just got back from hunting?" I say as the stench of sweat seeps out of his pores and wafts toward me. I guess he thought skipping a shower would be a wise choice before coming out in public.

Eiran is also one of the village's huntsmen. When he was young, he used to go with his father hunting every chance he got. His father taught him everything he knew, which was a tremendous amount considering his father was the village's most skilled huntsman. At thirteen, both of Eiran's parents died in a tragic battle. Right after, he bounced around to a few shelters in the village until he turned seventeen and found a permanent living situation with another huntsman that he grew to be very close with. Ever since then, he's continued the legacy of hunting food for our village in his father's name.

He's even hunted privately for my family quite a few times when money was tight and we had to try to figure out how we were going to eat dinner for the next week.

In ways we've been able to bond over both of us experiencing the loss of a parent, or in his case, both. Many times when I've felt the pressure of taking care of Makaria, and the demands of life, he's been there for me and I'm eternally grateful for his companionship.

"Yeah we just got back. Easy to tell?" He says with a harmless wink. He tries to step forward into me but is cut off by the resistance of my palm pushing against his chest.

"Yes it's easy to tell, you absolutely reek." I say scrunching my nose, my head turning to the side.

"Aw, don't be an ass now." He says with a laugh. "I was on my way back home when I looked over and saw you standing suspiciously in the window."

Great, did he just witness me hide this book in my sweater? I've grown to trust him, so I know he will keep my secrets and support me. But it's hard for me to trust and open up to others.

So I won't mention it. For now.

"Suspicious is quite the descriptive word." I say, turning my head back into his direction. I keep my expression non readable, so as to not give away my poker face.

"Relax, I'm joking." He says with a laugh. "I was just coming to see you but since you've pointed it out so obviously that I stink, maybe I will head home instead."

He bumps his shoulder into my left one and for a second I feel the slightest shift of the book that is still under my shoulder. My eyes bulge for a second before straightening my expression out again. Without making another reaction, I ever so slightly fix the position of the book and laugh it off like he didn't just almost blow my cover.

I've got to get out of here.

"Yeah that's probably a good idea. But hey we're roasting smores tonight over the fire. For Makaria," I add. "Stop by?"

"Okay, I'll be there." Eiran says with a smile as his hand wraps around my head, bringing me in as he gives me a kiss on the top of my head. "I'll see you later then."

"Okay." I say before I pull away, and wander over to find Makaria.

I need to get the hell out of here.

CHAPTER 3

Once my sister and I get back from the library and the store, I put all of the s'mores ingredients in the kitchen and see our father is home. I thought for sure that I was going to have to prepare and make dinner tonight, but as he promised this morning, he is home before such.

"Hey, there's my girl. How was your day?" He says to Makaria, my presence is invisible as usual.

"Good! What are you making for dinner, pa?" Makaria asks, seeing her noticeable change in energy that father stuck to his promise of being home for dinner. Sometimes it's really enjoyable to see her light up as our father does something that doesn't involve letting her down. Even if sometimes it's a sore sight for me.

As long as my sister gets the caregiver that she deserves, I'll muster through it. I can take care of myself.

"I'm making pot roast with some carrots, celery, some mashed potatoes and ofcourse gravy. Give it another hour and she'll be ready. Why don't you both relax until then, okay?" Sebastian says, and comes over to give Makaria a kiss on the forehead, giving me a wry smile as he glances at me.

After retreating back to my room, I'm finally able to pull out the book I stole from the library.

I try to find somewhere to hide it and decide to put it at the top of my closet shelf, all the way to the back. Makaria and Sebastian never come into my room, thankfully. So the thought of either of them finding it doesn't worry me.

I grab a clean pair of jeans, underwear, and a sweater and set them on my bed before I head over to the bathroom. As I enter I'm immediately overwhelmed with scents of sandalwood and a strong musk-scented cologne, a familiar smell that belongs to Sebastian.

I walk over to the tub and turn the faucet on, setting it to just the right temperature. I begin to remove my clothing until my bare skin kisses the warm damp air. I eagerly step into the tub where I'm instantly greeted with the hot water. I exhale softly as I relax further into the tub, embracing the comfort it's bringing.

I sit here for some time, more eager to just enjoy this moment rather than rush right into washing up. I close my eyes and sit here for what feels like eternity.

Embracing the hot water that I know will turn cold if I don't—

"Your time is coming."

Startled, my eyes rush open and I'm instantly glancing around the room. Even through the warmth that still lingers in the water, a chill snakes down my spine.

Nobody is in here except for myself, or at least that I can see anyway.

"Who's there?" I whisper quietly into the nothingness, hoping not to have Makaria or our father hear me.

Remembering I'm naked in the tub, I begin to cross my arms over my chest in an attempt to cover myself. As if that is going to make me feel a whole lot more at ease. I listen for anything, for whoever that was to speak out again.

Nothing.

Frustrated by the silence, I decide that I'm going to wash up and carry on with myself.

I grab the lavender scented soap and start scrubbing my skin, removing any debris and sweat from the day. As I'm scrubbing my skin I can't help but find myself pausing every now and then, desperately trying to tune in to whoever just spoke to me. This is the first time in a while that I've been able to hear a spirit. Whenever it happens I always seem to struggle developing the communication any further, proving the challenge maddening.

Maybe there's something more I could be doing? Out of all people, what do they even want with me?

Bringing myself back from my thoughts, I start to lather the soap into my hair. After I rinse my hair clean, I pull the plug from the drain to let the water drain out. I go to grab the towel that's laid to my right, and for a moment I freeze. I become self conscious at the fact that I'm naked and some spirit just tried to speak to me. Are they going to watch me get out of this tub, naked?

Shaking my head at my roaming thoughts, I roll my eyes as a faint smirk grows on my face. I grab the towel and stand to dry myself off before rising out of the tub.

Fuck it, who cares if the dead can see me naked.

I weave the towel around my body, and walk out of the bathroom and back into my room. As I enter my room and close my door, I walk past my floor length mirror. Shedding the towel from my body, I watch it fall to the floor before my gaze meets mine in the mirror. For a long moment I admired myself.

My gaze trails from my arms, down to my waist. I bring my hands up my hips before moving up to my breasts. I've never been one to shy away from admiring my figure, and that's probably one solid staple I have going for myself. It also keeps me from being easily entertained by men who struggle to give even the bare minimum. I may have a hard time trusting others, but one thing for sure is I do love my body.

And it's a damn privilege to touch this body.

I am not always entirely pleased with how she may look some days, but I've spent so much of my life hating myself that one day I just decided enough is enough.

Enough with badgering myself on how my hips may sit a bit wider than other women I see roam the village.

Enough with being so concerned with whether my ass looks great or not in the leggings or skirts I wear.

Enough with all of the harsh demands of being a woman. It's debilitatingly exhausting.

Slowly over the years, I started picking less and less at myself, until one day I found that I was truly accepting of myself. Where I was truly happy with how I looked, for how I felt. That my worth ran far deeper than just how I looked. Because fuck what men think, and fuck the beauty standards.

I peer my gaze from my mirror and look over to my clean clothing laying on my bed. I reach for my underwear, slipping them on. Once I pull my jeans and sweater on, I realize I still have a little time before I have to meet my father and sister for dinner. I walk over to my closet door and reach for the book, finding it and pulling it out. I take the book and pad over to my bed, sitting on top of the covers.

As I sat there I began to wonder how I am always easily able to hear spirits speak to me, but then when I try to communicate back I get nothing.

Maybe the spirits just want to fuck with me. I mean, I guess I wouldn't blame them. I'm sure it gets boring after you pass over to the other side.

As I flip open the book, I instantly start reading through the first page I land on.

"Those with the gift of mediumship must first learn to become comfortable with the quiet. It is in great times of solitude and meditative state that one can further their ability to see and hear the dead."

Well that probably explains why I only ever hear spirits when I'm alone and not expecting it.. I continue to read on.

"One problem that most often occurs when one is having difficulty communing with the deceased, is of their own perceived fear of not only communing with the deceased, but also for fear of their gifts altogether."

I'm pulled from reading when I hear Makaria's bedroom door open, anticipating that she's coming to knock on mine. Instead, I hear her walk down the hall and out to the kitchen. I realize that I will have to resume reading this later on, but before I close the book up, I read one last section.

"For one to become confident in their gifts, one must become comfortable in the identification that is their own darkness. As more often than not, a true practitioner becomes proficient in their communication with the deceased through first working through their own shadow. When one suppresses the shadow within, one cannot fully surmount to their power that often than not comes deep from the depths. It is through great pain and grief that true power rises from."

My attention is redirected as I hear my father call for me that dinner is finished. I snap my book closed and hurriedly walk back to my closet to hide the book. As soon as I close my closet door, my father opens my bedroom door.

"You hear me, Meli? Time to eat." He says with a glance over at my closet, probably wondering why I'm just standing here. But he doesn't probe to ask me why.

"Yeah, I'm coming." I say and walk out of my bedroom for dinner.

As I ponder with what I just read, I hear the same familiar spirit speak to me, once again.

"You have no idea the power you hold. But soon, you will."

CHAPTER 4

At dinner I found myself distracted. I kept thinking back to one sentence in particular that I read in that book.

"It is through great pain and grief that true power rises."

So the only way you can stand in your power is if you experience pain and trauma?

That seems a little fucked up.

After dinner Makaria and our father went out to the backyard to get a fire started. While they did, I began putting away the leftover pot roast, cleaned and put away the dishes, and wiped down the kitchen counters.

Our father sure knew how to cook, and he sure knew how to make a mess too.

After cleaning up, I grab the s'mores supplies and head outside to join them. As I close the screen door behind me, I turn around to find that Eiran is sitting in the chair beside them. He turns his head towards me and flashes me a sincere grin.

Since we only have three chairs, I fully intend to sit on the grass. But before I can finish taking a third step towards them, Eiran stands up from his seat.

I wave a hand at Eiran as he approaches me. "I don't mind sitting on the grass."

"What kind of a guy would I be to let you sit on the ground?" He says as he grabs some of the s'mores supplies out of my hands. "Sit."

I look at him as he shuffles some of the items out of my hands. He grabs things until all I'm left carrying is the measly box of graham crackers. He looks up at me and smiles, unaware of the rush of emotion that's currently clogging my throat.

It's not the gesture of letting me sit in the seat that has me feeling emotional, but the fact that he's always been the one person that's never made me feel like I didn't matter.

He's always made me feel seen.

Even if part of being seen involves just someone trying to help lessen the load of things I'm carrying, or even just acknowledging that I'm here at all.

I know that my father has done so much for us just in order to keep Makaria and I fed, clothes on our backs, and a roof over our heads. But it doesn't excuse his rash, or mostly avoidant, behavior towards me. Though I don't care to develop a relationship further with him, I can't deny the brand on my heart that reminds me everyday that I mean little to him.

And that is a pain that I think will haunt me to my grave. Makaria is his whole world and I'm just a stranger occupying it. A vessel that he gets to unleash his anger and disappointment onto.

Shakily exhaling I shove all of those feelings way, way down and walk over to the chair, as Eiran now sits on the ground next to it. I glance at him and my love for him ignites like an ember in my broken heart. His friendship is the one thing that grounds me, keeps me sane. He reminds me that there is someone who does care very much for me.

I take a seat and try to just engage with whatever current conversation my sister and father are chiming in about.

"She falls in love with a man who can shift into a what?" My father says, looking ever so perplexed at Makaria. I can tell in his facial expression he's trying to understand but is having a hard time with it.

"She falls in love with a man who can shift into a drago! I've read much about them and people say that they're just make-believe stories, but I believe they're real!" My sister says nearly shouting in her seat.

Our mother used to tell us stories when she was still alive, about mythical creatures and ancient goddesses that walked this world well before us. She used to tell us stories about the Draghi. Stories about those who could take the form of a drago, a fire-breathing creature with wingspans that spread well over thirty feet. Shifters who could tear whole villages down in one swift blow of fire from their mouths. Makaria, as she got older, still believed much in the stories our mother shared. I, on the other hand, think it could've been real at some existence in time. I think it's hard to believe that creatures like that still exist in our world today.

So, I believe that they're just cute stories to tell.

"That sounds frightening." Sebastian says, nowhere near matching Makaria's same enthusiasm but still engaging anyway.

"Maybe… but I think it's romantic!" Makaria chimes.

I roll my eyes as I shift in my seat, hugging my knees up to my chest.

"Don't believe that people can be monsters and still have a good heart?" Eiran says to me softly when he catches my expressive reaction.

I look over at Eiran. "I believe that people put too much of an emphasis on finding 'true love' but often neglect to look at the reality of the person they're sharing their time with."

"Hmm, quite the pessimist aren't we." Eiran says, playfully nudging his elbow into my side.

I roll my eyes again, this time followed by a smirk. "I think you are confusing being pessimistic with being realistic."

Eiran gives me a wry grin as he gazes at me. Instead of probing further, he deters the conversation and grabs the chocolate bars and graham crackers.

"Okay well, I don't know about you guys, but I'm ready for smores. Makaria?" Eiran asks my sister, holding a metal poker out for her.

I turn my head to see both Makaria and Sebastian glancing at me. Makaria has a somber look on her face, like she can't be oblivious to our fathers neglect towards me, though the subject is too sensitive to bring it up.

I don't expect her to. That's not her responsibility.

Makaria shifts her gaze to Eiran. Forcing a smile on her face, she grabs the metal poker.

I meet my fathers gaze and he averts his eyes, like the thought of looking at me would bring far too much discomfort for him. Like the thought of Makaria knowing how he is towards me when there isn't an audience would be a truth that he can't handle being revealed.

I brush it off and grab a metal poker myself, putting a marshmallow at the end. As I guide the marshmallow into the fire, I find myself enchanted by the bright orange glow. I stare aimlessly into the fire, forgetting I'm outside for a few seconds. My mind numbing, begins to conjure up scenarios of what it would be like to not be invisible to your family. Of what it would be like to have a parent who values you, respects you.

I wonder if Sebastian was a better man to our mother. My memories of when she was still alive are so hazy, I can hardly recall a thing. The only memories I can distinctly recall are the sounds of her voice, the brush of her lavender scented hair when she'd wrap me in her arms. How I wish I could smell the scent of her hair one last time, experience her unending love one last time.

The sorrow of feeling like such an outcast to everyone except myself causes me to sink deeper into the void of the fire. My aimless staring sinking deeper, and deeper. The fire feeling like a blanket of escape that maybe wouldn't be so bad to—

"Get up!"

Jerking from my seat my attention is back on the present moment, and I realize I've burnt my marshmallow to a crisp. Not only that, but everyone is looking at me like I just broke my damn neck.

"What?" I snap, trying to shrug off the fact that a spirit just tried to talk to me, again.

"Nothing we just…we were trying to get your attention to tell you you were burning the shit out of that marshmallow there." Eiran says as he points to the crispy bit that can hardly be called a marshmallow anymore. "But it was like you weren't there, or weren't hearing us or something. I said your name like four times, Meli. You just kept staring off into the fire, unmoved."

I look at Eiran, a hint of skepticism on his face. Great, these people are going to think I'm insane now. But how could I explain to them that I too, have no idea what just happened.

It was like I was here, but I wasn't. I was zoned out…elsewhere. Not to mention I heard someone try to communicate with me.

Gods, who was that this time? And why can't it ever be at a normal time, where I'm given more than just a "Hello" or something random. Bringing myself back from my thoughts, I shrug my shoulders as I sit up a little straighter.

"Sorry, I think I'm just a bit tired." I lied. "I was watching the fire and completely zoned out."

I look at my father and try to gauge what he's thinking. His expression seems pensive, almost worrisome. He stares at me for a few moments, and I could've sworn for a moment a flash of fear hinted in his eyes.

Trying to brush what just happened off, I decide to just skip on the marshmallows tonight. Thankfully, when I set the metal poker down in the grass, I noticed my father stretching his arms and legs out, followed by a wide yawn. Knowing he's about to get up and go inside for bed.

Like clockwork, my father stands up and sends himself off to bed. Before he does, he kneels down to Makaria and gives her a kiss on her forehead. Lighting up from the show of fatherly affection, she tells him goodnight. Sebastian comes around and pats Eiran on the back, telling him to have a good night and thanking him for stopping by.

Sebastian looks at me with a forced smile, then heads back inside.

Makaria stays outside for a little while longer, until she too is yawning and rubbing her eyes. Shortly after she gets up to go inside.

"Goodnight." She says as she wraps a hug around me from behind my chair. I lift my left arm up and give her arm a gentle squeeze.

"Goodnight."

Once she's inside the kitchen and closes the screen door behind her, I look at Eiran.

"So you really tried to get my attention? And I wasn't budging?" I ask, since nobody is out here now I feel like we can actually talk about it.

"Yes. It wasn't just like you were lost in the fire, Meli. I can't explain it. You just weren't there for those few moments." Eiran says, as he gets up to seat himself in the now open chair next to me.

Eiran has been my best friend for as long as I can remember, and he's definitely earned his trust with me. Though I can't shake the nervousness that plaques me about confiding in him about my gifts, and about the experiences I've had that come with them.

"Not to mention, when I saw you at the library earlier today, I saw you hike that book under your sweater. I didn't say anything because I figured you'd tell me one day if, and when you were ready to. But I was surprised because I know you. You're not a thief." Eiran says and my cheeks start to flush.

Shit. He saw me steal that book.

"And now this—I don't know what to even call it. This thing where you're in a trance or something and nobody can shake it out of you, even if for only a few moments. What's really going on with you?"

My mouth pulls into a frown as I realize that I know Eiran genuinely cares about me, and only wants to know so he can help in any way he can. It's just hard to accept help when you've learned to do everything on your own most of your life. The mere thought of someone *really* being there for me, without having any intentions of them getting something out of it in return feels far and few for me.

As my eyes swell up with tears, I realize that the need to confide in someone has possibly been weighing heavier on me than I let myself believe. So, I decided to push past my fear of trust for now.

"Remember when I told you how my mother died? And why?" I ask, fidgeting with my fingers.

"Yes, I do." He says.

"Well…I have some of those same gifts. And for the past year or so, they've been growing and becoming stronger. Like I can't avoid them any longer."

"Does that frighten you? To be able to have gifts like that?" Eiran asks, his expression calm yet intrigued.

"Honestly…no. My father doesn't ever talk about our mother or her gifts, and he's gone so far as to forbid my sister or I to ever learn more about it. He thinks mediumship and necromancy are dangerous, he thinks that's why my mother died. That's why I have to keep this to myself, because I'm not sure what he'd do if he found out I was a lot more like my mother than he thinks."

I nervously bring my attention from the fire and to Eiran. He watches me in wonder and not at all what I expected. When he makes no effort to interrupt me, I continue.

"So, the book you saw me grab earlier was about that. How to better tap into my gifts. I had to steal it because I can't risk Makaria finding out."

"Do you not trust your own sister to keep your secrets?"

I give him a knowing look, like he should know me better by now to know that I certainly trust no one. His expression smoothes out as he averts his gaze towards the fire. He runs a hand through his hair, audibly exhaling. After a few moments, his gaze is back on me as he responds.

"I think that makes sense, why you would want to know more about it. Regardless of the risks of your father finding out."

I find myself sagging into my chair as relief overwhelms me that he doesn't think I'm crazy. That he's really listening to me, understanding me.

"So I'm the only one you told about this?" He asks.

"Yes. I've thought about telling Makaria a few times, but since she's so attached to our father that she may run and tell him. So I've always just kept it to myself, until now." I say, as another wave of relief washes over me that I finally shared this with someone. Feeling some of the bouldering weight fall off my shoulders.

"So what do you think he'd do if he found out?" Eiran asks.

My mind immediately paints a haunting picture of my father using his anger against me. My mind tumbles between scenarios of Sebastian beating me into submission, or some other form of malicious punishment. But I don't tell Eiran that. He knows Sebastian and I don't have a good relationship, but he doesn't know the depths of what his anger can do.

So I lie. "Honestly, I have no idea. I'm twenty-five. It's not like he can ground me or imprison me in the house. But using the gifts is how he lost his wife, our mother. So I know it would be drastic whatever he'd try to do." I say while looking at the fire.

At my age, I should surely have my own place by now. But since I was seven I've cared for my sister, and somewhere along the line I found myself still taking care of her even as we both grew into adults. Whether that's by taking her into the village to get food, or helping out around the house. Not to mention that as a family, we make only enough money to get us by. And work comes very scarcely in Elzwin.

Eiran pulls me from my thoughts as he brings my hand into his, drawing my attention to him. I look at him and watch how his golden eyes are amplified from the glow of the fire.

"Anything you ever share with me will always be safe with me."

My bottom lip slightly trembles as I smile softly at his words. "Thank you. I appreciate you more than you know."

Eiran's smile matches mine and suddenly I yearn to close the distance between us. Pulling my hand from his I stand up from my chair as Eiran's gaze remains on me. He watches me intently as I stand in front of him and begin climbing into his lap. I don't even ask if I can curl into his lap, knowing that he would do anything to make me feel safe to begin with.

And right now, I just need to feel close to him.

As I curl myself into his lap, Eiran brings his arms around me and holds me close to him. Surrounded by the warmth of him, I shamelessly allow myself to be suffocated by it. Nudging my nose into his jacket, I inhale deeply.

"You smell much better now than you did earlier today."

Eiran chuckles softly, the vibration of it striking me. He brings a hand up to my head and begins running his fingers through my hair. He doesn't say a word for a short while, and doesn't question my wanting to be near him. He just strokes my hair and lets me curl up against him.

"In a world where it seems like nobody stands behind you, know that I am *never* far from your side."

My heart swells as he tenderly runs his fingers through my hair. My eyes begin to rim with tears that I desperately try to fight against.

Sometimes I think he knows me so well that he knows exactly what to say to me, in the exact moment that I need to hear it. It's a connection between us I've never experienced before, one that I can't quite explain. How even though we're just friends, he is the very thing that keeps me grounded to this world.

In a world where I feel like I can only rely and depend on myself, that he's the exception. A constant reminder that I'm not entirely alone.

CHAPTER 5

"This way, child."

My attention is drawn when I hear someone far off speak to me. I look down to see my bare feet on– cobblestone? Confusion arises as I jerk upright, taking in my surroundings. I'm in a village, one that is vastly unfamiliar.

This isn't home.

I notice there's not a single person in sight, and an overwhelming part of me feels like I'm being watched, though I'm not afraid. I find myself walking forward, my bare feet hitting the cobblestone road with each step. The coldness seeping into the soles of my feet.

That's when I noticed her.

She's standing at the end of the street, watching me as I walk towards her. I try to make out any features, to see if I recognize her. Her head is down, buried underneath a long amethyst robe. I turn my head back to where I was. Glancing up and down at the buildings that stretch on each side of the road. Walls lined with black and gray brick, the street lights casting a luminescent glow on them. Deep green vines creep through all of the crevices, as if the greenery is swallowing the building whole. I realize that the building hosts a variety of shops. When I look to the other side, it's the same scenery. I turn my gaze back around and I startle in place.

The woman that was in front of me is gone. I pick up my pace until I'm nearly jogging. There's no way she just got up and disappeared.

As soon as I made it to where she was standing I looked around. My head whips from each direction, as if I'm going to catch her dodging from my sight. My breath hitches.

Now I find myself afraid.

"Do not fear, child. You will understand when it is time."

My body stills, and goosebumps raise the fine hairs on the back of my neck. Frantically now, I search around me, but it's the same as just a few moments ago.

It's just me here.

"Wh-who's there?" My voice trembles as I speak out loud. When suddenly, the same woman reappears a few feet in front of me.

"That is not important right now. What's important is that you do not fight the urge to act. To search."

"What are you talking about? What does that even mean?" I ask as I try to make out who this woman is. I noticed something strange though. She's standing only a few feet away from me, but yet her voice sounds like it's far off. How does that make sense?

"Listen to me, child. Do not fight your instincts. We have watched you for far too long, have watched you ignore them. Now fate must take the reins. It is the only way, before it is too late."

Baffled by what this woman is talking about, and doing my best to hear everything clearly since she sounds so far away. Growing frustrated, I steady my voice and speak again.

"I don't understand. Why don't you just tell—"

"It is time. Listen to your inner knowing. Listen to the voices. We will guide you. Open yourself up to us. It is time, child."

Before I can react with a blast of hot frustration and confusion, my sight begins to fade as everything begins to slither out of definition. My surroundings, the street before me starts to slip away like fog when suddenly, everything's black.

Not even a full second after, I'm awake in my bed.

Stunned, I immediately opened my eyes to take notice of my bedroom. As if needing reassurance, I grab for the blanket that covers my now ice-pricked skin. I feel the soft, worn-out plush blanket that lays on top of my body. I grip the material, my fingers curling tightly inward as I desperately try to ground myself in the present. I loosen my grip, and my gaze wanders to my closet. I take notice of the flimsy door knob that occupies it. My gaze is now averting to my bedroom window, the same window I've seen every day since I was a babe. My breathing slows as I fully comprehend that I'm in my bedroom.

I must've been dreaming. There's no way that was just a dream, though. Everything felt so vivid, so damn real. I remember being able to feel the soft brush of the air. Walking on the cobblestone ground and how I *felt* the cool ground seep through my bare feet. That's…not possible.

You're not supposed to be able to feel sensations in dreams.

And that woman. Who was that fucking lady? I'm sure it would've helped me to have a better guess if it weren't for her voice feeling so far away. Not to mention the creepy cloak she was wearing that, of course, shielded herself.

I immediately think back to some of the things she was saying.

"We will guide you. Open yourself up to us. It is time, child."

Maybe she knows who's been trying to talk to me for the past year or so. It can't be her voice though, only because it has always been a male voice that's presented itself to me.

She said *they* have been watching me. Who's they? And if they've been watching me, what's the reasoning for that?

As I obsessively worry myself with questions, I realize that the woman confirmed one thing about me that I always struggled to understand. That my intuitive yearning to learn about mediumship is not without a reason, regardless of the potential risks that it may involve. That understanding it further cannot be avoided any longer.

CHAPTER 6

When I awake again, I lie in bed for a while. Going over the *dream* I had last night, as if to make sure it doesn't jog from my memory. I find that I remember every detail, word for word. I lay awake, nestled in my blanket, contemplating how I'm going to learn more about how to nurture and use these gifts.

I realize that I said gifts as if I'm confident I have them. The skepticism that normally lingers, no longer there.

Pulling myself from my thoughts, I stretch up and out of bed. I must've laid around for longer than I expected, because I am greeted with the smell of french toast and scrambled eggs.

Gods, do I love breakfast in the morning.

I walk over to my closet and grab my black plush robe that hangs on the doorknob, wrapping it around myself before I step out of my room. I walk towards the kitchen and see Makaria and our father already chowing down on breakfast. Makaria looks up, our father following suit.

"I opened your door but you were still sleeping. I didn't want to wake you." Makaria says, with a subtle guilty look in her eyes. I'm usually the first one up each morning, so I'm sure she was just surprised to see me still sleeping.

"Coffee's in the pot." Sebastian says, only glancing up for a quick second in between mouthfuls of his french toast.

Wiping the sleepiness from my eyes. I grab a mug and pour coffee into it, steam rising from the mug as I do.

I top the coffee off with my favorite caramel creamer, and take a seat at the kitchen table. There's already a plate set out for me, so I pile on two thick pieces of french toast along with a helping of scrambled eggs. Since I just got up, I take a few moments to enjoy a few sips of my coffee first. Taking in the flavor, I sigh with contentment as a soft smile greets my face.

"Are you going to the stable today?"

Using my fork to stab at a piece of french toast, I meet my sister's gaze. "Yes, I'll be going this afternoon."

"Well, I'm sure Alastor will be happy to see you."

Alastor, my horse that I adopted. Well–adopting would mean you spent money, money that our family doesn't have. Three years ago I saw an adoption poster in the deli market for a horse looking for a new owner. When I saw the poster, and saw Alastor in all of his sleek, onyx glory, I knew I had to meet the stable owner to inquire about him. When I met Terry, I asked him if there was any way that he would negotiate for taking half of what he was asking.

It was a long shot, but it was worth a try.

When I told him of my situation, that I just needed some time to come up with the money, he started asking me questions like "Where you gonna keep him?" and "Have you ever owned a horse before?"

I couldn't even blame him because he was right. I had nowhere to keep Alastor, and I never actually owned a horse before. But I can't explain what it was that drove me to want- no *need* to know this horse. After I thanked him for speaking with me anyway, Terry looked at me for a long moment. I'm not sure what he saw in me, but then he gave me a deal.

"Alright I'll give you a deal. You come here a few times a week to do my dirty work, and I'll let you spend time with Alastor while you're here. But don't grow too attached now, can't guarantee he'll be around long."

I happily and eagerly accepted his deal.

So I cleaned stalls, fed the horses, turned them out to the pastures, and I spent as much time with Alastor as I could. I know Terry said not to grow attached, but I couldn't help it. Alastor and I just clicked.

After some time Terry said he'd notice Alastor begin to act strange if I hadn't been there in days to see him, like not seeing me for a while would cause him to become depressed.

After eight months of still no one showing interest in wanting to adopt Alastor, Terry ended up taking his adoption poster down. He came to me and told me Alastor was mine, and all I had to do was just help him around the stable, and Alastor could stay housed there.

Three years later, and here we are.

"Terry has a new horse that he just brought in so a lot of his attention has been on her as of late. I'm sure Alastor will enjoy the attention from me." I say, taking another sip of my coffee before taking another bite of french toast.

"I'm sure he will appreciate the visit." My sister says with a wide closed-mouthed grin.

After a few moments of silence, Sebastian wipes his calloused fingers with his napkin before plopping the napkin onto his plate. He pushes his chair back. "I'll be working late tonight. Meli, you'll need to cover dinner. I'll be home shortly after." My father says dryly.

"Anything in particular I should get?" I ask, my attention still on my food.

"No. Just get whatever."

I nod gently in response. As I bring my gaze up to his, Sebastian is already standing up from the table. He leans over my sister and gives her a kiss on the top of her head.

"Have a good day." He says before he's off to his bedroom to get changed for work.

He doesn't even try to be subtle about it anymore. He makes it known each and everyday that I'm nothing more than a maid around the house. As if our blood doesn't tie us to one another, and we are no closer than a man that goes to see his barber.

Coming to him only when he needs something.

My attention fixates on the un-surprising amount of dirty dishes Sebastian has left on the table. There's a visceral part of me that feels quakes with anger that he always expects me to clean up after him.

Sometimes I wonder to myself what would happen if I were to just leave his mess there one day. Instead of resorting to being an obedient daughter- no, housekeeper, if he'd grow angry at my defiance. I find myself thinking back to when our mother was alive and if he was always like this, but my mind always draws up blank. Since I was only a child when our mother died, my memories of her are somewhat foggy. Though certain things I remember vividly. Memories such as her tucking us in at night for bed, and the way she used to wrap me in her arms. The feel of her nose against my cheek as she smiled against my laughter.

Back to a time when things were much more simple. There's nothing I wouldn't do in order to get that back.

Grabbing mine and Sebastian's dirty dishes, I walk over to the sink. After putting them in the sink, I walk over to Makaria. My hand gestures to her plate. "You done?"

"Yeah, thanks." She says with a thoughtful smile. I take her plate and cup and bring them to the sink, and turn the faucet on.

After the dishes are done and the kitchen counters are cleaned up, I walk to my bedroom to get dressed for the day. Since I'm going to the stables, I pull out my brown boots, a thick pair of black leggings, and a gray sweater. Once I'm dressed I open my bedroom door to find Makaria just standing there.

"What are you doing?"

"I was just coming to see if I could borrow a sweater from your closet. All of mine are dirty."

"Yeah, that's fine. Go ahead." I say, but a few seconds later Makaria is heading into my room towards my closet, and I freeze.

Shit. That book is in there.

Even though it's up on the top shelf, and there should be no reason why she should look up there as all of my sweaters are hanging, I internally panic. I turn around to face Makaria. "Actually, I have one in mind for you. Are you wearing leggings?" I ask, trying not to sound on edge.

Makaria narrows her chin slightly, squinting her eyes at me. "Okay you know what, yes. Pick something out for me."

I rummage through my hanging clothes, pretending to really put some thought into this. I figured if I just pulled out something randomly, she'd be suspicious.

"Okay, how about this one?" I ask with subtle enthusiasm, holding up a maroon colored hoodie for my sister.

She eyes it up, tapping her pointer finger against her lip. "Hmm, I like it."

Relieved, I hand her the sweater. I watch her slip it over her head, and give me a quick smile before she heads back to her room.

I have got to finish reading that book so I can get it back to where it belongs.

⸻

The sun is high in the sky when I make it to the stable. Thankfully, it's not far from where I live, so I'm very capable of walking on foot to get here. When I arrive, I walk into the barn to see Terry in one of the stalls grooming Dayla.

Terry is an older gentleman, pushing his late forties. His cropped short black hair, almost always covered by a worn green baseball hat. His rich brown skin pleasantly accentuates his chestnut brown eyes. His thick black brows rest against his oval face. Terry has always been kind to me, and he's always been good company to talk to.

Dayla is an off-white mare with gray markings, and she's been here even longer than Alastor has been. When I walk into the barn, Terry looks up from Dayla.

"Hey kid, how was your weekend?" Terry asks.

"It was decent. Yours?"

"Oh you know, I was here taking care of these mares." He says, though without an ounce of sarcasm. Terry has been in the equestrian business since he was just a teenager. So he really loves and takes care of these horses well.

"Well, I'll get started on mucking the stalls. Is Alastor outside?"

"Yeah he is, I swear it's like he knows you'd be coming today. Just sitting out in the pasture, like he's waiting for ya."

My heart warms and before I start cleaning the stalls, I decide I have to at least say hello to Alastor first. And sure enough, when I step outside by the paddocks, there he is. Just standing there, waiting.

I walk over and he instantly greets me with a whinny. I step up to open the gate, closing it behind me.

"Hey, you miss me?" I say as I run my hand over his neck, giving him kisses as I do. When I pull my hand away, he immediately nudges it with his nose. A smile grows on my face at his response.

"Wow you did miss me didn't you?" I say as I go back to petting him for a moment longer, before I head back into the barn to clean the stalls.

I spend the next small portion of the afternoon mucking the stalls, and since he lets a few other owners house their horses here, there are quite a few of them. Once I'm finished I take my bucket of grooming brushes and go back out by Alastor.

As I groom him, I talk softly to him. I know he has no idea what I'm saying, but it's comforting to just have that outlet to let all of my thoughts out to someone–or something–that can't repeat it back to anyone.

I talk about the weird dream I had last night, the book I stole but plan to return back, I tell him about the weird occurrence I had in the bathtub. Through it all, he just listens. It seems like sometimes he's the only one I can talk to. Well, him and Eiran.

After I give him a good grooming, and give him some more love, I say my goodbyes until I'm back in a couple days.

"Don't miss me too much, okay?" I say while running my hand through his mane once more. He gives me one more whinny, lowering his head towards my chest. Whenever he does this, I tell myself it seems like he's trying to give me a hug.

He's my sweet boy.

I put Alastor's grooming bin away and say goodbye to Terry, who's got a notebook in his hand and a pen between his fingers. Assuming he's doing inventory.

As I walk the distance back to my house I take a slight detour and stop at the market. Grabbing some beef, potatoes, onion, carrots and a loaf of bread, I realized that Sebastian didn't throw me any money for food. Pulling out the money Terry slipped me today, I paid the clerk. Walking home with the bags in my hand I notice Eiran on the street walking towards me.

"You have in your hands exactly what I'm going to get." He says while he looks at my outfit, knowing I would only typically wear my boots if I were at the stable. "Did you go see Alastor today?"

"Yeah, I did. I loved seeing him, per usual." I say, already missing him.

"Well I don't blame him. What's not to love about you." He says with a sheepish grin.

"Such the poet aren't we?" I say, raising an eyebrow at him.

"Among other things." He says as my stomach flutters.

"Well I've got to go and get started on dinner. Sebastian is working late tonight, so I'm cooking. But before I go, I need to tell you something." I say. I step in closer to him, and glance around me.

"Okay, what's up?" Intrigue written on his face as he grins.

I then tell Eiran about the dream I had last night. Trying to tell him all of the important parts, but also keep it somewhat brief as I don't want to carry these groceries much longer. Eiran must've noticed my arm getting tired because he takes the bag from me and we begin to walk.

My heart warms at the gesture.

After I finish telling him, he looks at me with wide eyes. "That's wild, I have never heard of anyone having a dream where they were able to *feel* things. The only time I've heard of someone having a similar experience with sensations it wasn't a dream."

"What do you mean? What did they say it was?"

"Have you ever heard of astral projection?"

I know what astral projection is. Why didn't I think of this? I've read up on it that it's basically when people enter this 'dreamscape' where they know that they're dreaming, and can therefore change the trajectory of what they're dreaming. In one book I read a while back, it said that when one can successfully astral project that they can come into contact with non-human entities. Yet in that same book, I read that it's not very often that those who succeed at astral projecting actually feel real sensations. Maybe this is something else entirely.

"You think that's what I experienced? I–I've never experienced that before."

"Possibly. All I know is that what you experienced last night was not some typical dream."

I take what Eiran says and ponder over it. When I remember another important detail. "The woman in my dream said she had been watching me for some time. The interaction was pretty short as I woke up not long after."

Eiran's expression peaks with wonder as he stops and turns toward me, halting me in place. His gaze finds mine as his head tilts slightly, his eyebrows raised. "I...think you connected with the dead last night."

CHAPTER 7

Shortly after continuing my walk home, I thought over what Eiran said. Did I really come into contact with someone from the other side?

Was I truly astral projecting?

All of these thoughts halt from further interrogation when an overwhelming feeling of unease starts to ensue. Beginning from the depths of my abdomen, slithering into an all over body awareness.

Something feels wrong.

As I approach my cabin's front door, I reach for the handle when suddenly I hear a voice.

"I'm sorry, it was the only way."

Stilling, I try to clear my mind to see if the spirit continues further. But I'm, like most times, left with nothing. Shaking it off, I decide I'll worry about it later, and head inside. Only to be greeted with exactly what the spirit was talking about.

"What is this, Meli?" My sister demands, a biting franticness dripping from her tone. The confusion of it all only lasts half a second before my gaze is coaxed to what she's holding in her hand.

That damn book.

She must've gone snooping around in my closet after I left and found it. Fuck.

"It's a book." I drawl like a sarcastic ass, hoping that my lack of interest will keep her from thinking I care much about what's in it. I *really* don't need her running to father about it.

"Well no shit. I mean what are you doing with *this* kind of book? And if it's *just* a book, then why was it tucked all the way to the back of your closet shelf?"

I really don't have a fighting argument. But because I'm trying desperately to keep things from escalating, I try anyway.

"It's just material I found at the library, and I was interested in reading it. That's it. And with father so against this stuff, I didn't need him finding it and making such a big fuss about it. It's no big deal, Makaria."

"No big deal? And making a big fuss about the very thing that killed our mother? Are you so fucking insensitive!" Makaria is nearly screaming at this point, and with somewhat good reason. I guess I could have worded that better.

"I didn't mean that mother dying is no big deal, of course it is. Every day without her here is the greatest void in my life. But mother's gifts aren't what killed her, *people* did. People that burned her body alive. Murdered her because they saw her gifts only through a fear-based, closed-minded perspective. And that fear is what drove them to kill her." I say with the stern bite of my words.

"And so what, you think that because you're different that people won't do the same to you? And—wait. You hear dead people?"

For a long moment, I contemplated whether or not I wanted to lie to my sister. Most people would've vented to their siblings by now about it, but our situation is complicated. Our mother died because she was expressive with her gifts, and I knew if the day ever came that I finally told my sister about it, her fear for my safety would override any concrete judgment. But at this point, she found the book. It's out in the open now, so I decide to tell the truth. I'm getting so tired of limiting myself for the sake of others.

"Yes. I do. I could use a bit more practice with it, though." I purposefully leave out the part that I can manipulate hallucinations and fear into peoples minds.

That can be aired out a different time.

"I knew that you and Sebastian would react strongly so I kept it to myself. This village is banned from anything to do with mediumship, so I have zero guidance in the matter. I started reading the very few resources we have on it from the library, in hopes that one day I could teach myself. But at the end of the day, I'm all alone in this. And quite frankly, it sucks."

Makaria's gaze softens to an extent, though the fear in her eyes is still ever so potent. It takes her a dreadfully long minute to respond, and during which time I'm shifting my weight between both of my feet. This could go horribly wrong, where she still tells father, and then who knows how he'd react.

Or maybe she'll decide to just keep it between us, holding compassion for my feelings, as I am trying to with her. Regardless, the silence leaves me incredulously anxious.

"So, what is it like? When the spirit—or whoever talks to you?"

An immediate relief washes over me at my sister's words, her response nearly causing my knees to buckle. The suffocation of her silence crashing away, and I audibly sigh as I relax into myself.

"It varies. I can't control it—yet. It's always been at random moments, and it's never more than a few words. It frustrates me to no end as it never really makes sense, either."

As I finish that last statement, I freeze internally.

"I'm sorry, it was the only way."

My mind is frozen for a few moments on the memory of hearing that right before I entered our home. Someone was trying to warn me, or rather apologize. Did they nudge my sister into snooping through my closet, knowing she'd find that book? Well, so much for any books I've read stating that spirits only ever want to be helpful to the living.

"Do you ever…hear mother?"

Makaria draws me back from my thoughts, and I figured this was the first thing she'd ask. I mean, if I were in her shoes it'd be my first thought, too.

"No. I'd recognize her voice if she ever did try to communicate with me. I'm hopeful one day when I can learn to become better at it."

Noticing Makaria's faint desperation fade into disappointment is identical to how I've felt since my gifts started arising. I thought for sure that our mother would be the first one to come forward, hoping that she would've seen my struggle to understand and therefore guided me.

But still, no sign of her. Maybe I'm just not advanced enough yet.

"I know that this may be wrong for me to ask of you, Makaria, but please. Do not tell father. I know you two are close, believe me do I ever know how much closer you two are then father and I ever will be." That truth causes sadness to clog my throat before I shake it off. "But I ask of you, *beg* of you even. Keep this between us. Please Makaria, I've never asked anything of you."

As I plead with my sister, her gaze adverts to the ground. She lifts her gaze back to the book, turning it to inspect it before responding. It takes her awhile before she responds, and in those moments of silence I grow increasingly worried that I just made a horrible mistake by unveiling so much of myself to her. Which is an incredibly sad, and bizarre statement to even ponder over considering I should have no issues trusting my own flesh and blood, my sister.

Though our father has proven time and time again, that blood means nothing when it comes to respect.

Maybe that's where I went wrong. Maybe I just assumed that Makaria would react negatively to knowing that I have gifts, like our mother did. Maybe I misjudged our bond because…I'm terrified of putting my trust into anyone else that isn't me. Therefore, I didn't even give her a chance to hear me out first and just be honest with her.

This I recognize is something that I can openly admit, that maybe I need to work on. I'll do that much for my sister.

"Okay, just put this back in the closet, and get rid of it as soon as you can."

Feeling relieved that, though she doesn't seem entirely on board or fully understanding of this yet, she's at least willing to keep this between us. And that's all that matters for now.

I rush over to my sister and wrap my arms around her, my eyes closed tightly against the tears fighting against my eyelids that successfully stream their way out.

"Thank you, I know I am asking a lot. But please understand, you have no idea what this means to me."

I feel Makaria's initial stiffness relax as she brings her arms around me into a full embrace. We don't say much for a few moments, but when I pull away I notice that Makaria's red eyes match my own.

What I said about her and father being noticeably closer must've struck an emotional response in her. Though she is very fond of our father, she can't be naive to the way that he treats me. I just hope she doesn't feel guilt for having a closer relationship with him. I never want my sister to feel like she is caught between the crossfire of Sebastian and I.

I never want her to be burdened with the weight of his neglect towards me.

Tears slip down her cheeks as she gives me a cheeky smile, before she hands me back the book. I watch her fingertips gently tremble as she brings them to wipe under her eyes. She brings her hands down to her sides and for a moment her body tenses up. Like she's resisting her emotional reaction.

In the next moment, Makaria turns on her heels and leaves my bedroom.

CHAPTER 8

After I hid the book back in my closet, I decided to get a head start on making dinner. Since I knew our father wasn't going to be home until after dinner, I figured Makaria and I could still enjoy it in his absence.

After dinner was finished, I called out for Makaria and shortly after she joined me at the dinner table. Tonight I made roast beef sandwiches, with sauteed onion, steamed carrots, and roasted garlic potatoes. As Makaria and I sat at the table, we both helped ourselves to our plates. As we hungrily wolfed down our food, we both sat at the table for some time. Swirling the red wine in my glass, I look up at Makaria.

"We still have quite a bit of firewood, and it's supposed to rain tomorrow night. Want to have a fire?"

"Sure, but I don't think I can stomach any smores tonight." My sister says with a nervous laugh as she rubs her belly.

"Agreed." We both share a laugh, and sit for a few more moments before I polish off my wine and begin to stand.

"Don't. I've got the dishes this time." My sister says as she nearly jumps out of her seat. She flashes me a quick smile, before she goes to grab both my dishes as well as hers. It's always been my job to clean up after dinner, so Makaria volunteering to clean up is a bit of a shock, but nonetheless I'm grateful for her generosity.

"Thank you." I say as I match her gaze. "I'll go ahead and go start the fire then, and meet you out there."

Having Makaria be the one to clean up after dinner, you'd think I would be more than okay with the gesture. But instead I'm confronted with a challenging mix of emotions. The first being this sense of guilt. Why would I feel guilty that my sister wants to help out? I don't mind keeping the house clean, or preparing dinner for us when father is working late, I've done it for as long as I can remember.

But for a moment I'm overwhelmed with this feeling that if I'm not the one doing dishes, then I'm doing something wrong. Conflicted, I decide to shake it off and save it for another time to anxiously ponder over.

Heading out to our backyard, I grab the remaining logs we have left and toss them into our fire pit. After getting the fire lit, I pull one of our lawn chairs forward and sink into the seat. It's a cool spring night, but not cold enough to deem a blanket around me necessary. I shimmy my hands together and I let the friction warm my palms.

Sinking into the chair, I let the wonderful heat envelop my body. As I stare into the flames, I watch the vibrancy of orange and yellow dance together in the darkness of the night. I begin to close my eyes and relax into the moment.

Until I hear my father yell for me, the anger evident in his voice.

I fling my eyes open and immediately buck out of my seat, turning around to see my father whipping the screen door open. The door bangs against the wall and it's a surprise that he didn't shatter the damn thing. My breathing halts as I watch my father stride towards me, frozen in place by his wrath. My eyes fixate on what he's holding, and a nervous chill runs along my skin.

He's holding the book.

My whole body feels like it is cemented into the spot I'm standing in. Standing just to the side of my chair, but close enough to feel the burn of the heat from the fire, yet all I can feel is cold dread.

"Melinoë! What the fuck is this!" Sebastian roars, the fire that's in his eyes palpable enough to make the hairs on the back of my neck stand up. His body posture leaning ever so slightly forward, his hand gripping the book so hard that I can see the pages *inside* of the book crinkle.

After I lose all ability to speak, my father closes the distance between us until he's standing directly in front of me. My gaze shifts to my sister who is standing behind him, near the screen door. Her hands are folded tightly up to her chest, as she fiddles with her thumbs nervously. Her expression leaking of severe worry, as she is only able to mouth two words to me.

"I'm sorry."

My blood runs cold. Regardless of how remorseful my sister appears right now, I *begged* her to keep this between us. I thought I could finally trust someone other than myself just this once.

Regretfully, I was wrong.

I redirect my gaze onto my father who I realize has been screaming at me this whole time, but my mind has been altered elsewhere to even register. I force myself back into my body and finally have the courage to speak.

"It's just a book! I just wanted to read more about what it entails to have the gift of mediumship!"

"I don't give a fuck *why* you have this, Melinoë! I forbid you and your sister from coming anywhere near this shit, and I will not have you defy my wishes!" My father roars in my face.

I can feel spit fly from his mouth, it lands on my cheek as he's screaming at me. I bring my hand up to wipe it away, my fingers trembling slightly from his rage. I bring my gaze back to my father, and I want to shrink into myself by the anger that flames to life from his posture. But I won't let myself shrink this time.

I'm trying my hardest to see from everyone's perspective here, but I can't ignore the desire to tap into this side of myself that demands I stand up for myself.

Regardless of what it costs me.

"I'm sorry that I went against your wishes, but I wanted answers! Answers that you won't give me! And you know what, that's fine. I understand. Mother died because she was fearless enough in her expression over her gifts, and I am so sorry that you lost the love of your life because of it. But I have the same gifts, and I have many questions. I just want to understand myself better." I plead as the nostrils in my fathers nose remain flared, with not a hint of remorse in his features. The sight of it weighs heavily on my heart that it's evident he won't understand me, once again.

"You're right, look what it cost your mother. I am only protecting you Meli!"

"No, she didn't die because of her gifts, she died because people couldn't understand her. And instead of giving her a chance to become understood, she was murdered."

In an instant, I feel the harsh smack of my fathers palm strike across my cheek. I don't even register it until I hear my sister gasp in shock, followed by her screaming at our father for his reaction.

Suddenly my mind feels disoriented.

My hands begin to tremble as shock courses through my body. I place a hand gently on my cheek, and wince at the pain. Tears swell in my eyes and now it isn't my hand that trembles, but my whole body. My breathing begins to quicken scarily, and for a moment I feel like I may pass out from how labored my breathing is.

"You will obey me, Melinoë. That is an order."

I peer my gaze up to my father staring at me sternly, not an ounce of sympathy visible in his expression. For a moment I wonder if I'm dreaming, because the thought of our father hitting me isn't what stuns me. It's that he's always been careful to never show his anger towards me while Makaria has been present. Yet tonight, he let his facade slip away as if he never cared to uphold it in the first place.

That now I live in a reality where he no longer hides his aggression, and instead unleashes it regardless of our audience. Though when has reality ever been kind to me to begin with.

I glance behind me to see Makaria holding her hands up to her mouth, tears streaming down her face. I slowly avert my gaze back to my father, and my body runs cold. I've done nothing but pick up his slack while he drunk himself to sleep every night, unable to take care of Makaria.

I clean up after *him*, a grown man who is capable of doing it himself.

I spent my childhood after my mother died being the parent, when what I desperately needed was a loving father. A seven year old girl taking care of her sister, and I'm repaid for it by becoming invisible to my father. Only when the brunt swipe of his hand meets my face does he decide it's necessary to pay attention to me.

My mind fades to a shallow nothingness as my mind falls on a recurring thought.

He has never hit me in front of Makaria before.

I—

Suddenly, my body feels like it can move again. I don't feel the weighing blanket of despair that hangs over me, and my mind tunes everything out. Every thought of what just occurred vanishes, and my gaze trains forward lifelessly.

Before I can even register it, my body feels like I'm being pulled forward towards the screen door, through the kitchen and to my room. I realize that I'm walking, but I feel so disconnected from my body that it feels like my legs are doing it for me. I realize I've reached my room and shuffle through my closet, grabbing a sweater to throw over my torso.

I can't believe this is my reality.

Not now, my mind tells me. *Shove it down, we need to move.*

After donning my sweater, and pulling on my boots, I look up to see my sister and father are both standing in my doorway.

Why is Makaria still crying?

Doesn't matter, we need to move.

I shuffle past them as I see my fathers lips are still moving, but I can't register anything he's saying. But as I try to walk out of my bedroom door, my father steps in front of me. I'm still unable to fully concentrate on what he's saying, but I finally manage to speak a few words. When I do speak, my tone is lost of any spark.

"I'm going out."

I push myself past him and thankfully he just lets me go. I feel this unwavering drive to leave and keep walking, away from my cabin. I watch myself grab the doorknob to our front door, and pull it open. As I step out, I notice a crumpled can trailing along the ground from the bellows of the wind. Yet if it weren't for the sight of the can, I wouldn't have even noticed that it was windy tonight as I can't feel anything right now.

I begin walking, letting my body guide me as it runs on autopilot. I feel the weight of my body, but my mind feels desolate. I decide that right now isn't the time to wonder what I'm feeling, but to keep walking.

It's not until I come up to a familiar home, that is another cabin. I stand there noticing the detailing on the door.

Did I knock already? I can't seem to remember. Maybe I should knock again because I–

Before I have long to wonder, the door opens and I am greeted with a familiar face.

"Meli, what happened?"

Eiran immediately steps out of the doorframe and cups his hands gently under my jaw. I realize he's turning my face so he can get a better view of the red mark my father left.

His jaw clenches visibly as fury flames to life in his eyes. A moment later, he's guiding me inside and sitting me down on the familiar dark cherry leather couch in his living room. It's only then I'm able to distinguish the immediate change in temperature. I feel Eiran sit me down on the couch as he finally lets go of me, acting as if I'm going to slip away. My gaze is trained forward, noticing the intricate detail of the fireplace that's before me.

Did his family always have this fireplace?

I take in the ash that's leftover, realizing they must've had a fire at some point today or last night-

Fire…the book.

My body is disturbingly still while my fingers resting on my lap are tapping at a wicked pace. Eiran is walking back toward me, though I don't see him and only know because I feel his presence. He's handing me something hot, wafting toward me is the smell of lavender.

He made my favorite tea for me.

I notice now that he's speaking to me, but it's incredibly challenging to decipher what he's saying. The only thing my body has room for right now is to just remain where I am, with my gaze peeled forward. After a few moments, I feel him gently wrap his arm around me as he brings me in closer until my head is leaning on his shoulder.

Eiran whispers softly atop my head, though his voice sounds pained. "It's okay, I've got you. Whenever you're ready to talk, I'm here."

My head begins to fall limp as does the rest of my body, as I fully allow it to rest on Eiran's shoulder. The gentle contact begins to bring me back to the moment, as I fully internalize that I've left and found myself in Eiran's arms.

Memories resurface of my father finding the book, and that he was so angry that he hit me. With no remorse etched into his features to follow. As the pieces of tonight congrue back together, I realize something that I don't even remember witnessing.

My father tossed that same book into the fire, burning it to a crisp. Making sure I can never have access to it again.

My throat begins to feel like it's on fire as emotion creeps up my throat. The earlier need to shove everything down and just move begins to melt away, as the need to feel overrides my dull mind. Tears stream down my face, and I finally feel safe enough to relax. My body begins to tremble violently as I sob into Eiran's arms, as the feeling of being wronged overtakes my body.

He wraps his other arm around me and holds me tighter. I bring myself to curl into his lap as he rubs a hand through my hair tenderly. The feel of his gentle fingers running through my black hair begins to soothe me. He leans his head down to nestle on top of mine as he quietly speaks to me.

"You're safe here with me. I'm right here, Meli."

CHAPTER 9

For a long while I didn't have the words to bring myself to share what happened. All I could do was just sit there, with my body resting against Eiran. And for that long while Eiran held me, his fingers never stopped stroking back my hair.

In a world where I feel like I'm all on my own, I am truly grateful to have him in my life to remind me otherwise.

Once I felt myself come back into my body entirely, I finally wiped away my tear stained cheeks.

"He found the book." I say as I bring my head up from Eiran's shoulder. "He found the book I told you about and he hit me because I disobeyed him."

I look at Eiran, and I see him clearly for the first time since I've arrived here. His eyes are on fire, his jaw clenched so tight I would be surprised if he didn't break a tooth. He averts his gaze back to me and looks at my cheek.

He brings his hand up, hesitating for a moment as if wishing not to startle me. His eyes look sad and pained, as if he somehow thinks that he could've prevented this. His hand softly grazes my cheek, as his fingers push a strand of my hair behind my ear.

"There is not one justifiable reason for how he handled his anger tonight." He says, the gold in his eyes churning wildly. "You did not deserve this."

"I know." Is all I can say, the hollowness still lingering. "I just want to forget it even happened. I don't want to deal–"

"Don't do that."

I furrow my brows at his sudden change in tone. He watches me for a moment before he continues.

"You always just want to forget, shove it all down and act like it's not there or that it didn't happen. Which I'm not saying is always a bad thing to do, but I've watched it cost you in the most self-deprecating ways. Where he does something that bothers you, hurts you–" Eiran turns his head for a brief moment, eyes closed shut, as if he's trying to rethink what he's trying to say. He turns his gaze back to me as I watch him exhale slowly, his voice regaining calmness. "Instead of giving yourself permission to feel disrespected and hurt over it, you decide to shove all of the pain down. Just to make it disappear. He doesn't deserve that mercy."

Eiran's words hit me like a blade and I feel the stab everywhere in my body. I want to deny what he's saying, even let myself get mad at him for accusing me of such a thing. But he's right.

Tears well up in my eyes and I don't know if I'm capable of keeping them in this time. But to my surprise, only a few slipped free. As they sweep down my cheek, Eiran's thumb presses against my cheek, wiping them away.

"Regardless of what you see in yourself, or what your father makes you believe, you are by far the most selfless woman I have ever met, Melinoë. And by far the most resilient."

I let Eiran's words sink in as heat floods my eyes. I'm not naive enough to not notice that I put my needs on the back burner so I can help keep the house together and take care of Makaria while my father works. I'm also not naive enough to not wonder what my life will look like in five years if nothing changes.

I'll still be here, letting myself fade away as I remain mute so I can keep the peace. I'll still be here, cooking dinner for Makaria and I, night after night when father is working too late to do it himself. I'll still be here with no real idea who I am because my father forbids me to learn about my gifts. Which I'm beginning to think is a major part of who I am.

I know that nothing will drastically change unless I make it happen, but I can't help this overwhelming feeling of guilt of how Makaria will manage without her sister around to check on her, cook dinner for her, or even just talk to her. I'd be leaving her behind and I don't know if I can do that to her.

As I bring myself from my thoughts, I look at Eiran who's still watching me.

"You're right. I do put my needs on the back burner." I say while I twist my fingers in my lap. "But you don't understand. Besides my father and Makaria, I have no one. No other family that is." I say quickly as to not give Eiran the impression I don't consider him someone important in my life. If it weren't for his unending loving support, I don't know who I'd be today.

Or how I would've survived this long.

"So even if I finally say fuck it, I'm going to start living my life, I'll fall up short because I have no idea what my ideal life looks like for me. And what am I going to do? Where would I go? I've only ever known taking care of my sister, I've never known any other life than being a caregiver and basically a maid."

As I release some of the things I've for so long kept harbored to myself, my embarrassment for the vulnerable display causes me to nervously bite my cheek. I glance at Eiran, and notice his eyes have softened as his mouth forms a soft smile.

"I think you have a better idea of what your ideal life looks like, more than you're willing to let yourself believe." He says as he gently moves me to the side as he gets up and grabs my empty mug from the side table. I completely forgot I even had a cup of tea when I got here.

He tilts the mug toward me, gesturing if I'd like another round of tea.

"No, thank you." I say softly.

He walks to the kitchen, setting the mug in the kitchen sink before coming to seat himself back down next to me. "I think once you become honest with yourself on what type of life you deserve, then you'll be forced to realize how drastically wrong the life you've been living now is. And I think you know that, and it terrifies you because it means you will have no other choice than to choose yourself. And part of choosing yourself is admitting that you've been abused, and it should rightfully anger you."

As I let his words sink in, I realize he's right. I'm upset, but I'm not angry enough, and that makes me worried that I will just want to forget it happened altogether and move on from it. But I shouldn't give Sebastian that kind of satisfaction. I should be fuming at the blatant abuse and it should *enrage* me to be treated that way.

As for Makaria, I understand why she might've felt justified in her reasoning to tell father—

No.

I trusted her with this. As someone who doesn't trust anyone other than herself, her telling Sebastian hurts deep. I think I'm actually resisting coming home to see my sister more than I am our father. Our father has disappointed me many times before, so the sting of rejection and hurt has long faded its initial weight.

But I never expected this from my sister.

Eiran must notice the resistance I'm facing with going home, so he reaches over to the side table to his right, pulling out a deck of cards. Instead of asking me if I want to play cards, he immediately starts shuffling them. As he does, he diverts the conversation by talking about the new huntsman that has joined his group. He tells me of how he's only seventeen, and says he reminds him a lot of himself when he was that age. He goes on to tell me about how the new huntsman has little to no experience hunting, and I get lost in the story as he begins laying out the cards.

I watch him in awe at how he can understand my need for company, but still resistant to fully sharing my feelings. How he doesn't shame me, but rather shows he's still here for me when I'm ready.

I realize that while my father may never see through me, and Makaria may never understand me, I have always had one very genuine person in my life who has never failed to show me I'm someone worth getting to know.

After spending a few more hours at Eiran's, I finally decided I can no longer hide from my father or Makaria.

So I made my short trek back home.

As soon as I reach our front door steps, a nervousness fills my energy. Immediately it's like I feel the sting of my father's hand all over again, and my palms begin to dampen.

No, we have nothing to feel guilty about.

My mind tells me, as though trying to remind me that what happened earlier tonight was not my fault. That no matter if I disobeyed my father's wishes, I still didn't deserve how he reacted. So with that, I lift my chin and open our front door to head inside.

Most of the lights are off, and at first I think that considering it's past midnight, everyone is probably asleep. I close the door behind me, quietly so I don't wake anyone up. I walk through our living room and before turning down the hall to head for my room, I see Sebastian sitting at the kitchen table, with a bottle of whiskey in front of him.

"I figured you'd be back home at some point tonight." He says as he takes his glass—no, the whole bottle, and takes a swig of the whiskey.

Of course he's drunk. I should've expected nothing different.

"Thought if I just wait up, I'd catch you in time before you went off to bed. But over the course of the night, well, I'm sure you see yourself." He says. His back is towards me as he faces towards the screen door. I'm beginning to feel increasingly more uncomfortable and can't seem to find what to say next.

Be brave.

"Yeah, I went over by Eiran's to calm myself down after you thought it was appropriate to hit me."

He doesn't even stand up at my remark, he remains in his seat. His back is still facing me as he takes another swig from the bottle.

"Come sit with me Melinoë."

I really do not want to just sit and talk at this hour of the night. My mind is exhausted. My body is exhausted. I just want to get a good night's rest and quite frankly never speak to him again. But considering my father has been drinking this can go either one or two ways.

Either he would become very emotional the minute I decide on otherwise. Or he could become angry. But I am so tired of shrinking myself around here and letting the mistreatment slide. So I reel in any remaining boldness I have in me, and I defy him once more.

"No."

At that, my father stands up from his seat and strides over to me, surprised that he didn't bring the bottle of whiskey with him. He strides over to me until he's right in front of me once more, and I have to remind myself that I'm not some vulnerable child anymore who can't defend themselves. I'm a grown woman, and I won't silence my voice any longer.

As he stands in front of me, I fully expect him to yell at me once more. Instead, he chuckles and his cold stare makes my skin prick. He begins to slowly pace in front of me.

"I always wondered if you would grow to have the same gifts as her one day. It's only fitting since you are the spitting image of her." He says as he gives a lazy chuckle.

"I prayed that day would never come. Because I knew if it did, that I would have to reveal a side of myself I fought to hide."

Sebastian averts his gaze away for a few moments, but when he turns his gaze back on me it looks unfamiliar.

His eyes are…sinister.

My blood runs cold as the energy begins to palpitate around the room. My breathing hitches as I feel a throbbing sensation prick my skin, clear enough for me to feel but too dim for me to pinpoint the location.

He stops pacing and stands directly in front of me. He stares at me for just a second before his arm shoots out and I feel the grip of his hand around my throat. His rough fingers grip into my throat and my fingers begin to claw at his wrist. My nails embed into his skin, but that doesn't even throw him off. I keep trying to claw my way out of his grasp anyway.

"I am sorry for the way I reacted earlier tonight, and well, how I'm reacting now. But I must make one thing clear." Sebastian says, his cold sinister voice causing panic to erode within me.

"If I ever catch you in possession of something like that again, I will destroy it. Another word of any of this again, and I will strip you dry of your gifts."

He releases his hand as I fall to the floor, coughing and gasping for air. My hand shakes violently as it wraps around my neck, and I'm terrified to meet my fathers gaze. Strip me of my gifts?

"H-how?" I rasp, my throat working desperately on a swallow.

Sebastian just stares at me, his gaze void of any compassion. He curves his mouth into a smile as he tilts his head. "For me to know, and for you to fear."

Suddenly, fury rages inside of me. I'm no longer trembling from alarm, but now from the rage that fills my blood. As I am still kneeling on the ground, my palms flat on the ground before me. I would normally try to shove the rage down.

Except this time, I don't want to fight it. Instead, I choose to welcome it.

I slowly bring my gaze up to my father, and I stand up as if he wasn't just choking me a moment ago. As I straighten myself out, I watch as my fathers sinister expression does not falter. And instead of being afraid of it, I challenge it.

A wicked and cold smile grows on my face, and for a split second I see my fathers expression falter.

In a voice that seems unfamiliar to my own, I speak steadily through words of promise. "We will see about that."

I focus on Sebastian. My gaze digs its nails into his as I concentrate on penetrating his mind. It doesn't take me long to bring what I want him to see to his vision. His eyes widen as he rubs a hand over his eyes, as if trying to wipe away what he's seeing. I manipulate him into visualizing me melting, my limbs pooling to the ground in heaps of thick oil. The color of my ivory skin, my emerald green eyes, and my onyx hair molding together as one on the ground. I watch his fingers tremble for a brief moment before he steadies them again.

Suddenly, his head is cocked to the right, and then to the left. He's jerking his head around so rigidly and fast, that I'm surprised he's not getting whiplash. His hands come up to his ears as his eyes shut, trying desperately to drone out the high-pitched screaming I've manipulated his ears to hear. He shakes his head as he groans in pain for a few minutes until I halt the illusions. His eyes shoot open, and slowly move his hands away from his ears.

His gaze moves to mine. Sebastian goes mute and rigidly still as a smile grows on my face. I turn on my heels and walk towards my bedroom. Before I close the door behind me, I turn around and see Sebastian is still standing there, unmoving.

I close the door behind me and lean up against the door for a few moments, feeling the adrenaline of power flowing through my body. I realize that I just unveiled a part of myself I swore I would keep secret.

But the adrenaline coursing through my veins feels empowering. Feeling far from small and much more in control then I ever have before, and watching the look on his face made it all worth it. I'm tired of being taken advantage of. I don't want to sit quietly anymore, I will unleash that power that is festering inside of me.

No matter what it costs me.

CHAPTER 10

The cool breeze of the night air gently sweeps my hair over my shoulder. It's eerily quiet, as if I'm the only one in these streets. My feet feel cold against the hard ground, I look down and notice—

Cobblestone.

Suddenly I realize I'm dreaming again, back in the same exact place that I was last time. Awareness shifts over me as I turn my gaze to scale the now familiar black and gray brick walls, with the shops that line it. The beautiful green vines that nearly cover it throughout. As I take in my surroundings, I realize that I'm not alone.

Before I even turn my gaze ahead, a chill runs down my back as tiny hairs on the back of my neck prick up. Like an utter knowing that I'm not alone. I turn my gaze to find her.

The same woman as before.

"You." Is all I manage to escape out of my mouth as I immediately begin to close the distance between us. As I walk towards her, she stands there so still that I would've mistaken her for a statue if it weren't for her deep purple robe flowing in the wind. I tense up, afraid that as soon as I get close enough she will vanish from sight. Her head is still tilted down, hands folded in front of her lap.

Once I'm only a few feet away from her, she finally looks up.

I try to get a good look at her, but with the darkness of the night around us, and the shadows that block her face, I see nothing.

"Why am I here again? Why do I keep coming to this specific place?" I ask her. For what seems like a long moment, she doesn't say anything. But then she finally speaks.

"You venture here because your soul seeks to bring you here."

As if that wasn't the most vague answer I've ever heard in my life. "What do you mean 'my soul' seeks to bring me here? Where even is here?"

Before she responds, she unclasps her hands, and walks towards an iron bench that sits right outside one of the shops. I follow her, and take a seat after she does. I sit there waiting for her to explain all of this. As I glance over, I notice she's not looking at me but straight ahead.

What is up with this strange woman?

"Though you may not know what this place is in this lifetime, yet," She says, pausing before she continues. *"Your soul recognizes the familiarity of it. It is a place you have been to in many of your past lives."*

I have heard about past lives before, so that doesn't really throw me for a loop. But what she's saying about being here before, that's what gets me.

Because a part of me feels like she's right. Though I have no idea where I am, I have this keen sense of knowing. Like a part of me through the confusion feels like I belong here.

The woman continues. *"As you awaken into yourself, you have felt a desperate longing to understand more of who you are, yes?"* She asks, as I slowly nod.

"This I know, child. I have watched you for many years. I have seen you torment yourself with obligations that do not need to belong to you. I have watched these past few years specifically, as you've tried to understand your gifts better, but always feeling like a blockage keeps you from further understanding."

I can't even argue with her. She's not wrong in her assumptions. A little freaked out that some strange woman has been watching me, yes. But also intrigued to better understand who she is. With that thought, I bring myself to ask her my first question.

"Are you a ghost?"

She laughs and I just realized that last time when she spoke to me in this–strange dream, I could barely hear her. I could hear her enough to make out what she was saying, but her voice sounded off in the distance. This time, I can hear her clearly. Her voice sounds warm. Powerful.

Like her intentions aren't to hurt me, but rather to inspire me. I'm not sure how I'm able to gather this from just her voice, but I trust myself anyway.

"Not quite."

So she's not dead. Okay, that leaves me even more confused.

"So you're a figment of my imagination then? Because how can you not be dead, but still be spot on with the details of my life? Not to mention you said you've been watching me. So that's it…I'm imagining all of thi--"

"You are not imagining this. This is all real."

Before I can argue her statement, she turns her head slightly towards my hands that rest in my lap. She reaches out with one hand, lightly placing it on top of mine. As soon as she does, I *feel* it.

A gentle buzzing sensation that flows first through my hands, and then generates throughout my entire body. I gasp, jerking my gaze from my hands to her. Even though I still cannot see much of her, I can do nothing but sit there and gape at her as this sensation continues.

I gaze back down at her hand, and notice her skin is a gorgeous shade of rich, deep brown. Her manicured, medium-length nails the color of red wine. She wears several golden vintage rings, each ring with a different colored crystal. I recognize some of the crystals as black obsidian, amethyst, and moonstone.

I look back up and see that she's turned her head back to looking straight ahead again. Another second later, and the buzzing sensation begins to dissipate from my body, until it recedes altogether.

"What was that?" I demand, frazzled.

"That my dear, was me showing you what energy feels like."

My mind races with astonishment that this woman was able to manipulate energy enough for me to *feel* it that intensely. So she's not dead, knows all of this stuff about me, and has the power to manipulate energy. My breath hitches as I realize she must be–

"We don't have time for getting into all of that right now, dear. I will explain everything to you soon. But for now, listen to me very carefully. What I tell you next will not make much sense, but you must trust what I am saying. Do you understand?"

Still not having any idea who this woman is, I should probably take whatever she says next and let it through one ear and out the other so I can wake up from this dream. But a part of me feels like I need to listen to whatever it is she tells me. I nod my head.

"The place you are in, that we are both in right now, is the village of Vulir. It is a place that not many people know about, and for good reason. Only those who seek good intentions with our people may have access to entering, for everyone else, we remain an unseen village to them."

At the mention of Vulir, I feel an instant yearning that doesn't make sense. I've never heard of this place before so how could I possibly feel drawn to it? I wait for her to hopefully make a bit more sense.

"But you, my dear, know the way here. It is a knowledge that has been passed down from your mother."

My mother—

"How did you know my mother?"

How could she have known this place but have never said anything to Makaria or I? A brief sting of emotion arises at the mention of my mother, and also at the mention of more of my mothers past that apparently I truly have no real understanding about.

"I knew your mother for many, many years. She was a dear friend of mine. A fearless and brave woman might I add. I see that same fearlessness and bravery in you now."

I bite my inner lip at her kind words. I've never received recognition from my father, so hearing her say that is like having a part of my dignity restored. A tear slips down my face and I can feel the cool brush of it as it slips down.

She gives a soft smile. *"One's current circumstances hardly denote who they are internally, dear. You taking an active role in the household and for Makaria's care, standing strong even in the face of an abusive father, doesn't tell me of someone who is afraid, but rather tells me of someone who just hasn't found enough fire within to make the necessary sacrifices for a better life for herself."*

Her words sit heavy in the pit of my stomach as I, once again, can't argue or deny what she's saying. I've always wanted more for myself.

I've deserved a lot more for myself.

And after everything that has happened between my father and I, I find myself caring very little of what pleases him and a hell of a lot more on how I can execute a life that's right for *me*.

"She knew that this day would come, where you would begin to have a glimpse into the magnitude that are your gifts, child. A glimpse into the truth. Nonetheless, it's time for the path you're currently on to be intercepted."

"What do you mean intercepted?"

"The life you are living now is not your true calling, Melinoë."

As the woman says this, I feel my surroundings begin to gradually slither away. Panicking, because I know this means that I'm about to wake up and I still have many questions. The woman must sense this because she places her hand on mine again, pulling my attention back.

"Listen to me very carefully. You know the way to Vulir. Pay attention, as the spirits will help guide you. But most importantly, listen to your intuition. It will guide you most of all."

I take in everything she's saying and though I want to ask a million questions, I know I'm about to run out of time. I nod and let her continue for as long as I have with her before I do wake up.

"Start through the Sephyra Forest. Head west and bring food, shelter. As the trek here is strenuous from where you are now. Remember, trust your journey here, let your intuition lead the way. When you arrive, you will be met with Charon. He is the gatekeeper of Vulir. He is the

one who knows all, and sees all, and the one who grants access to the village. I will be waiting for your arrival, where we can officially begin."

"Begin what?"

She finally looks at me and I am finally able to get a glimpse at her eyes. They glow ferociously like golden pools of sunlight. Her eyes I've–never seen anything like them before.

She looks at me, her golden eyes churning brightly. *"Begin your ascension into your true calling."*

CHAPTER 11

As I'm sitting at the kitchen table, I can hear the muffled morning chatter that's occurring between my father and Makaria. My mind is too distracted from my dream to join in their conversation. Not that I have any desire to do so anyway.

My father is acting like nothing happened between us.

From last night when he hit me outside, to when I got home and he wrapped his hand around my throat, siphoning the breath out of my lungs. My jaw clenches as I sit in his presence and all I want to do is put as much space between him and I as possible.

The only thing I'm grateful for in this situation is that he didn't leave any bruises on my neck. Which greatly surprises me as his strength was evident as he gripped my neck. How inconvenient that would be for me, to have had bruises on my neck from my *father* and have to explain that—

My internal rage builds as my fingers are tapping my mug. I'm trying to reel all of my anger in, to save it for another day. That's when I remember how I manipulated his mind to hear and see things that weren't there. My anger settles to some degree as a smile grows on my face.

Makaria has barely looked at me at all this morning. Every now and then when my head is turned down, looking at my plate or my coffee mug, she gives a subtle glance towards me. She must think it's subtle and I don't notice.

I do, though I just don't have it in me to fight with her right now. Because though my sister isn't the main target for my hurt, she is still someone who broke my trust.

And that still hurts like fucking hell.

So instead, I give her the satisfaction of thinking that I don't notice her glances.

She has no idea what happened last night after she went off to bed. I'm not sure I'll ever tell her.

Feeling out of place and anxious, I excuse myself from the kitchen table, grabbing my plate and mug. Carrying them to the kitchen sink, I realize that the morning chatter between my sister and father has ceased, and now there's only a stretch of silence that fills the kitchen.

"A—are you going to see Alastor today?" my sister to my surprise softly chimes in, probably to break the uncomfortable silence. And also most likely out of a weight of guilt that she's desperate to alleviate.

"Yes, I'll be going soon." Is all I say, before I walk out of the kitchen and head for my bedroom.

When I enter my room, I close the door behind me. Standing with my back against the door, I'm not sure what comes over me but I quietly sob to myself.

I wasn't feeling very emotional this morning, so this reaction stuns me. Nonetheless, instead of trying to shove everything back down, I feel an inclination to feel whatever it is that's coming to the surface.

So I let myself feel it all.

The despairing loneliness that has ensued my entire life. The abusive critical demands of my father that weigh heavily over my own autonomy. The deep unfulfillment that lingers much below what I project on the surface. I feel it *all* churn inside of me. I have been shoving everything down for so long that it feels like I'm bursting with thoughts that I've overlooked for my whole life. Like I'm being reacquainted with darkness herself.

I feel like I have done everything, and received nothing in return. I…deserve so much better.

After allowing myself to sob everything out, I take a few deep breaths and begin to feel like everything is caving in. My breathing picks up until I feel like nothing is entering my lungs. Sinking down against the door, I sit on the ground with my legs brought up to my chest. Holding my legs, I squeeze my knees and begin taking deep breaths.

In.

And out.

I do this for a few minutes until my breathing becomes much more regular. Once I feel steady again, I slowly begin standing up from the ground. Wiping underneath my eyes, I take a few last deep breaths before I head to my closet.

Ruffling through my closet I grab a black sweater, and black leggings. I sink into the softness of the sweater once I pull it over my head, letting my body feel comfort in the soft texture of it. I pull on my boots, and I'm walking out of my bedroom door. As soon as I open my door, my sister is standing there.

She really has to stop doing that.

"Can we talk, please?" My sister asks, with a sad longing in her eyes.

"I have to go by Terry's, so I can't right now." I say, as I shove my way past her. Before I can make it to the front door, I stop. Turning back around, I see my sister with tears welling in her eyes.

My heart is wounded. I wanted desperately for my sister to keep just something between us, and her betrayal hurts deep. But as I look at her now, even through my own pain, I can't help but to sympathize with her. I look at her now and I wonder how she must be feeling to have seen the father that talks sweetly to her, hit me. How she must be processing the disturbing truth that Sebastian is a lot more awful to me behind closed doors. Even through my own heartache, her relationship is one that I never want to dwindle, and because of that I will always give her a chance.

I sigh. "But I'm open to talk later."

The tears welling in her eyes nearly vanish as a smile grows on her face. She nods her head in agreement, and walks off to her room.

There are some sacrifices I'm willing to make. Repairing the relationship with my sister at the sake of her betrayal is one of them. Because besides Eiran, my sister is all I have.

I have no one else.

Once I'm at Terry's, it's not long before I venture over to check on Alastor. He's out in the paddocks, grazing the grass. Soon, his ears turn backwards as he hears me approaching. Immediately, he lifts his head and walks over to me.

He immediately greets me with a whinny and nudges his nose in my hand. Such a needy, but sweet boy.

"Hey. I missed you." I say as I begin to pet his neck and let my fingers brush out the little bits of grass from his mane. "You've been rolling around out here, haven't ya?"

He responds with another nudge. I continue to run my hand down his neck, until I walk back into the barn to start mucking out the stalls.

I see Terry in there and we shoot the shit for a bit. He tells me how someone adopted the new horse he brought in a while ago, and that they're coming by tomorrow to meet with her. He says that since he's been spending so much one on one time with her, that he's actually sad to see her go. But he says that she's going to a good home, to people he knows well.

"Yeah damnit, I've grown very fond of her. Sort of like how fond you've grown on Alastor." Terry says.

"I couldn't imagine not having Alastor in my life. But none of that would've happened without you. I don't think I thank you enough for keeping Alastor here. Keeping him here for me."

"Oh don't go all soft on me now, kid. But you're welcome. Hey, I'm afraid if I didn't, that damn horse would keel over from depression. He's grown very fond of you." He says.

After Terry gets back to—whatever it is he was doing, I get back to mucking out the stalls. As I do, I ponder over my dream again. Well, I guess it's hardly a dream anymore if this lady is supposedly a real person. I think back to what she told me about needing to go to Vulir, but that nobody would know what Vulir is if I asked around because it's a village that's *unseen* to most.

So basically, it's some magical but invisible village. Got it.

As I ponder over it, it seems as though it's beginning harder and harder for me to resist the message that woman gave me. It seems instead that I begin to feel more and more interested in what exactly this place is. She made it also seem like going there is where I could begin to finally understand what my gifts are.

Understand better who I am, and what my potential is. I suddenly remembered something she said to me.

"Your birthright as it was once your mothers."

She was definitely talking about my mothers gifts. Which makes me feel validated in my chronic need to understand myself more.

Maybe I could make the journey there? I could always come back?

But then who will really watch over Makaria?

"Oh for fuck's sake she's twenty-two, Melinoë. She can take care of herself."

I pause mid-mucking a stall when a spirit speaks to me. Hardly phased anymore by the interaction, I know that it won't extend much further than a few words. Instead of being spooked by it, I find myself intrigued.

I speak aloud. "I know. But what if I leave and it wrecks her? What if the absence of her sister, her basically main caregiver is too much for her? I don't want to be the cause of her suffering."

"There you go again. Worrying too damn much about everyone else! She'll be fine. Sheesh, she's not a child anymore."

Surprise flashes as I'm making real conversation with them, past the usual few words before everything goes mute. Normally they say a few words and disappear altogether. Right now, I can hear him clearly.

And he hasn't disappeared yet.

How I'm casually just having a conversation with a spirit right now. I can't see him, but I can clearly *hear* him speak to me. What's different this time?

I push my questions aside for a minute while I try to get to know who I'm speaking to. "What's your name?"

"Nikolai. But that ain't what's important right now. What's important is that you get prepared."

My brows furrow as I peer around, before setting the shovel against the stall wall. "Prepared for what?"

"To leave, you silly woman!" Nikolai all but shouts. It doesn't take me long to realize that he's talking about me leaving for Vulir. And it doesn't take me long to realize that I think I actually want to.

And that drive to go terrifies me.

"I don't know if I can. It's a big decision to make considering that I have no idea where I'm going, or how to find this place." I say, sorrowfully.

"Well if you'd only trust yourself more than maybe you will find you can actually find the way there. But I guess we'll never know if you just sit around wondering what if."

For a spirit that seems like he's trying to help me, he sure does it in a cut-throat, straight to the point kind of way. Maybe his bluntness serves its purpose with this. Because I can't help but think that he has a point. How do I expect to truly understand myself if I spend my whole life wondering *how* rather than actually *doing*. How do I expect to change the trajectory of my life if I won't actually take any action to do so?

My palms begin to sweat mildly with anticipation as I ponder over the possibility of actually going.

I mean…what's the worst that could happen?

If I hate it there, I can just come back. Though the thought of that instantly creates a stiffness in my belly, followed by a feeling of resistance. A resistance that shows me that this place hasn't served as my place of home in…a long time. And that tells me everything I need to know and the decision I need to make for myself. Opening and closing my hands, I fight the nerves that are plaguing my body currently.

"Okay, I'll do it. When should I go?"

"Tonight. The sooner the better."

Feeling a little taken back by his hurried response, the thought of leaving right away fills me with panic that maybe I'm not actually ready for this. But something in the pit of my soul also feels like if I don't act quickly on this, while I'm still angry about the recent injustices from my father, that I'll never feel the necessary push to actually do it.

So fuck it, I'm going to take that leap. A reckless, wickedly insane leap.

"I must note, the Sephyra Forest is supposed to be a safe haven for the creatures that reside in it. Most people are oblivious to these creatures, but there are very few who know of them, and therefore hunt them. These poachers are ruthless, and you must stay clear of them."

"Creatures? What creatures?" I begin to worry about what kind of creatures I'm about to be faced with. In Elzwin, the only creatures we have are your normal wildlife. I've only ever heard of mythical creatures in stories, so some of them are…real?

He gives a chuckle before he continues. *"You have nothing to fear with them. They will recognize you."*

Recognize me? What is he fucking talking about? Whatever, let's worry about that later. For now I stick with the basics.

"How long is the trek there?" I ask.

"Expect your travels to last three days. Bring food and water accordingly."

Three days? Well, surely by then my father and Makaria will have noticed I've left. That's also a long distance for someone like me who doesn't get out much to begin with. I've never traveled anywhere else before. But I can't deny the overwhelming adrenaline that's coursing through my body that tells me that I *need* to do this.

"I must go. Go home to prepare. And remember, listen to your intuition. She is your most trusted guide."

Right after that, I hear Terry walk back into the barn. I realize that I was standing right outside the stall while this conversation went on, and I've been standing in one place the entire time. Immediately I'm glad that Terry wasn't here to witness this. He'd probably think I've gone mentally insane.

"What're you doing?" He asks. Caught off guard, I say the first thing that comes to mind.

"My back started getting stiff. So I thought I'd take a few moments." I say smoothly.

Terry looks at me, and I'm relieved when he starts laughing. "Yeah, well that'll happen." He starts walking away and is still laughing.

I finish mucking out the last two stalls before I put everything away. I head outside to see Alastor before I make my way back home. He's standing near the gate, and I walk up to him. Normally, I would enter the paddock, but since I know I'll be back tonight to get him, I don't bother.

There's not a chance I'm going to Vulir without my horse.

At the thought of taking one of Terry's horses, my palms begin to sweat. Wondering how Terry will react when he wakes the next morning to find Alastor is gone leaves me with a nervousness I can't shake. The poor man will probably think someone stole him. That is unless Makaria sends word to him that I've left. In which case, he'll know I was the culprit.

I'll be back after my travels anyway, which at that point I will probably sorely pay for abducting Alastor.

Alastor, acting like he can read my thoughts, nudges my chin with his.

"You're coming with me. I can't do this without you."

He gives me another nudge, as I pet him for a little longer before I head out. But before I head back home, I decide that there's one place that I need to venture too before I can plan for my departure tonight.

I start heading for Eiran's.

CHAPTER 12

"I'm coming with you."

"No, you're not. I need you to stay here."

Once I got to Eiran's cabin, I explained to him everything that's going on, and what I'm about to do. He was quiet for a long while. I wasn't sure if he was quiet because he was afraid if he said something, that it would come off as unsupportive. Knowing how little I receive support at home. Or if he was quiet because I told him I need him here, to keep an eye on Makaria for me while I'm gone. Though it should've been no surprise that he insisted he come with me.

"Look, I know you're worried about Makaria's wellbeing while you're away. But she's *twenty-two* Meli, she can take care of herself. She might not know how to cook since you are more than generous enough to do it all for her. But tough luck, she's just gonna have to learn then."

Eiran's words are not shared in an aggressive manner, but he is being blunt nonetheless. So what he's saying doesn't sting me because of that.

They sting because he's right.

"I don't mean for this to sound insensitive, but there's a difference between taking care of someone because you *have* to, like when they're children and can't fend for themselves. And then there's enabling someone, such as Makaria. Whose twenty-two years old, again might I add."

Flinching as if Eiran just splashed water on my face, I look at the ground. Twisting my fingers I feel so conflicted with what Eiran is saying. On one hand I've always been more than happy to take care of my sister, especially since our father is away at work nearly all of the time.

But even through my selflessness, I'm not naive. I can admit that it's quite possible I've been enabling Makaria when I shouldn't. I can also admit that I've taken on a lot of the responsibility of looking after Makaria because Sebastian has made it my duty to, even if I never fully agreed to it.

Eiran distracts me with my worrying thoughts as his hand cups my chin, bringing my gaze onto him. I know that everything he's saying is with love and worry for *my* well being, and sometimes it brings me an edge of discomfort to have someone care so deeply for me like that. When all I've ever known is to sacrifice my own needs for the sake of my family. To be invisible.

But the earnest worry that's etched into his eyes tells me that he's not going to let me do this on my own, and he'll fight with me hard on it. The thought brings a sharp twist of ache in my heart.

"I know. I realize that I probably have been enabling Makaria, but sometimes I feel like that's all I'm good for. And it haunts me that I even feel that way. That the best that life has for me is to be a damn caregiver to a family who hardly notices me. A family who I can't even count on to be there for me. A father who—" My words cut off with a choke, and tears swell in my eyes. It's rare for me to announce aloud how I'm feeling, or to anyone for that matter. So coming to terms with the things that have been rooted deep in the darkest depths of my heart, is hauntingly terrifying. Yet releasing them also feels good.

I close my eyes, trying to shut the tears away and all that ends up happening is I help the tears escape down my cheeks. Opening my eyes again, Eiran is looking at me. His soft gaze never leaves mine, as he gently wipes my tears away.

"You are worth a life that is infinitely better than the one you're living currently. And if you think going to this Vulir place will help you find that for yourself, then I'm with you every step of the way. But if you think I will let you travel there by yourself, then you truly do not understand the depths of my care for you."

I want to beg Eiran to stay and watch Makaria anyway. To forbid him from coming with me, to possibly tell him I don't want him to come with me in hopes it'll entice him to actually stay back. But his words cause a flutter sensation in my belly that is impossible for me to ignore. A sensation that pries my heart to swell as a result of his care for me.

I sigh audibly. My discomfort immediately displaces from fear of the journey itself, to fear of Eiran leaving everything behind for me. Fear of if he would later regret his decision. Or worse, resent me for it.

"You would really drop everything? To venture with me to a place that I'm not even sure is entirely real. And leave this life behind, even if it's just temporarily?"

His gaze searches mine for a few moments. His gaze is stern, yearning, like he doesn't have to think twice on his answer. "There is nothing I wouldn't do for you, Melinoë."

My gaze searches his as I see two things come to life in his eyes, clearly for the first time.

Love and devotion.

My heart swells as the praise in his gaze is evident, intensifying the fluttering feeling in my belly. I realize that maybe I don't have to do this on my own. That I should have someone by my side, supporting me along the way. And who better to join me on this journey than my best friend. A man who I deeply admire.

I think I have always felt something for Eiran, but my inexplicable resistance to commitment has always swayed me to stay just friends. And I have greatly appreciated his respect for that. But maybe I've been wrong. Maybe my own fear for more is just getting in the way of something good. Maybe my own fear of genuine, real love is preventing me from realizing I have that right in front of me.

Bringing my hands up to his, I nod and smile softly.

"Okay. But we leave tonight."

The sudden relief I see in Eiran's expression is evident, leaving goosebumps to raise on my arms.

"How are we getting there?"

"I planned on taking Alastor. Terry is probably going to be upset when he wakes to see Alastor gone, but when we get back I'll explain everything to him. And I will definitely have to make it up to him when we're back."

Now that Eiran is coming with me, I realize we'll have to ride together. It's one thing to take Alastor with me, but stealing another horse is too risky. I'm not bonded well enough with the other horses like I am with Alastor. They may not come willingly at all.

"We can only risk taking Alastor. We won't be able to risk trying to take another horse for you, so you'll have to ride with me."

"Do you know how long the trek is to get there? What were you going to do about food and water?" Eiran asks. I might be inaccurate in my assumptions, but for a second there it seemed like Eiran was actually excited about this journey.

"I was told it'll take three days to get there. For food I was just going to bring what I could. Bread, nuts, crackers, fruit, and a water flask-" My memories flashing back from the conversation I had with Nikolai, remembering what he said about the Sephyra Forest. "We'll have to hunt before we reach the Sephyra Forest."

"Why's that?" Eiran asks, confusion sparking from his voice.

"I was told that the Sephyra Forest is home to creatures that I guess us humans don't know about. That it's supposed to be their safe haven from hunters and poachers. And that we're basically not to hurt them."

I watch as Eiran ponders silently in his head, until it's evident he's thought of a solution. "Okay. Do we even know what these creatures are?"

I bite my inner cheek as I softly shake my head. "No idea."

Eiran rakes his hand through his hair, clearly thinking of a different way for him to hunt food for us.

"There's an area that me and the other huntsman have hunted in before, it's a large open field that's right before you enter the Sephyra Forest. It's about a day's ride out from the village. We'll stop for me to hunt, and camp there for the night. We'll just have to eat good that night, and then eat whatever you bring with you. I have water flasks at home, I'll bring two for us. There's fresh water that runs through that landscape."

As Eiran goes over our plan, I can't help the bubbling of excitement that's rising its way through me. The confirmation that this is really happening is both nerve wracking and also exhilarating. "That works."

Eiran must notice the rush of overwhelming emotions I'm feeling from the way I'm twisting my fingers. He steps up to me. "What is it?"

"I don't know. I know this is something I have to do, and to be honest, I'm excited. But I can't help but feel—"

"Guilty?" Eiran says, finishing my sentence showing me once again that this man really does know me far greater than I sometimes believe he does.

"I know what you're going to say, that guilt is the last thing that I should feel. But I've never been away from home before. Been away from that cabin. This is all moving really fast and all a lot to take in. What if–"

"What I was going to say," Eiran says, turning my gaze back onto him, drawing me from the mass worrying I was about to embark on. My breathing starts to slow to a less rapid pace. "Is that I think what you're doing is *brave*. I think as someone that tends to think about others a hell of a lot more than she thinks of herself, it doesn't surprise me that you're filled with uncertainty now that you're finally choosing you."

Eiran's thumb gently swipes over my cheek as he gazes at me. I'm not sure I've ever seen this level of intimacy between us and for the moment, I'm going to push away any unease that this type of closeness usually brings me. For a moment, our eyes remain locked and I'm for once not sure what's about to happen here.

Eiran has always been my best friend. Sure, we've hooked up. A lot.

Though we've never crossed that friendship boundary. But at this moment, it seems like it's more than just what it's been. And I can't help the anticipation that weighs on my caged heart, wondering if this is meant to be something more.

I've known him almost my whole life, so I trust Eiran. I know his integrity, and his intentions are never to pressure me into anything. But if he were to kiss me right now, I would allow it. Fully knowing that it would be something that meant a lot more than just friends.

Pulling me from my thoughts, Eiran clears his throat, as he slowly pulls away from me. His eyes remain locked on mine.

"If we're to leave tonight, I need to tie up some loose ends. I'll meet you at the stable, okay?"

Feeling a sudden rush of disappointment, I realize that he's trying to respect my boundaries. I realize that if this is really what I want, I have to express that to him. Otherwise, he'll continue to respect my want for us to remain friends.

I'll save that for another day. For now, I need to focus on preparing for our departure.

"Meet me at the stable at midnight. Terry isn't usually in from the barn until late, so we can't meet until then."

As I turn to walk back to my cabin, already planning every little detail, Eiran calls for me.

"Meli."

I turn around to face him.

"Bring your dagger. I know I'm coming with you, so I'll be armed. But we can never have too much protection."

I know that he just wants us to take every safety precaution possible, but my heart sinks to my feet at the thought of someone trying to attack either of us. I really hope that Eiran and I can make it to Vulir as smoothly as possible. Not to mention that I have to trust my intuition to get us there. Which begs the thought.

Eiran must have *a lot* of trust in me. To know that that's how we get ourselves there, and for him to not even question it. Gods, I really appreciate him and his unending support.

Before I turn on my heels to head home, I give Eiran a nod and a smirk draws up my face. "I was already planning on it."

Once I get home, I immediately check the kitchen, the backyard, and then Makaria's room to see if she's home. Once it's clear that she's not, I rush to my bedroom and grab my black duffle bag and start piling in the necessities.

As it tends to get chilly at night, I decide to pack two sweatshirts, a pair of sweatpants, some clean socks, and clean underwear. I can always buy clothing in Vulir when we're there.

At that thought, I pull out my jar of cash I keep hidden in my dresser. I count how much I have left from my shifts at Terry's barn. I come out to one-hundred and twenty-six dollars. Not terrible, but it definitely won't last.

I have no idea how long Eiran and I will stay in Vulir, but it could end up being a while. If I'm going to go there and meet this mystery woman, whose name I still don't know, I can't accurately judge how long it'll take for me to find the answers I'm seeking. We could be there for months, which means I will need to pick up work while we're there.

I walk to the bathroom to grab my toothbrush, toothpaste, hairbrush, a bar of soap and deodorant. Walking back to my bedroom, I place them in my duffel bag and walk over to my closet. I pull out a rolled up sleeping pallet, and my dagger that's been shoved into a wad of extra blankets. Since my sister and father don't know about my dagger, I've hid it here in hopes that they'd never find it. It's a beautiful dagger that Eiran gifted me a few years ago from our local bladesmith.

Its double-edged blade is sharp and forged from stainless silver. The hilt is heavy against my hand, but also light enough for me to wield comfortably. Eiran had a small crescent moon etched into the blade, a small detail that I cherish greatly.

I hid it on the bottom of my duffel bag for the time being. Before I'm ready to leave, I'll sheathe it to my thigh.

Before I head into the kitchen, I take another look around just to make sure Makaria still isn't home yet. Immediately, I go to our kitchen pantry and grab small ziplock bags and fill them with dried fruit, nuts, crackers, and I hoard a half loaf of bread into my duffle bag. Since Eiran said he'd bring along water flasks, I don't bother packing any. Which, I must say, was a great idea because my duffle bag is nearly full now.

I triple check over everything that I have and once I'm positive I didn't leave anything out, I hide the duffle bag in my closet, and plop my anxious body onto my bed.

In just seven hours, I'll be leaving to head to the stable. Where I'll meet with Eiran to get Alastor out of the paddocks and onto the trail that cuts through the woods. As I lay on my bed, anxious but excited all at the same time, I find it difficult to close my eyes. My father should be home within the hour, so I'm grateful that I don't have to worry about making dinner tonight.

That leaves one last worry off my plate.

Since we're going to be riding through the night, I should shut my eyes and let myself sleep for a couple hours, until father calls out for dinner. As I shut my eyes, trying to get my body to relax enough to sleep, all I can see in the imagination of my mind is riding through the Sephyra Forest, with Eiran at my back and Alastor guiding the way. It's like I can already feel the breeze of the air whipping past my face, the smell of the tall pine trees.

All I can imagine is getting out of this village, once and for all. Even if it's just temporarily. All I can imagine is that finally, I get to choose me.

CHAPTER 13

I'm woken up by my father's call for dinner. I pull myself out of bed and slip on my slippers and head out into the kitchen. Feeling a lot more restful, and a lot less anxious for the moment, I realize that could all change the minute I sit with Makaria and Sebastian.

Get it together Melinoë. You can do this.

Ignoring any etched in worry for how they will react once they discover me gone tomorrow morning, I enter the kitchen and find Makaria and our father already sitting at the kitchen table. They both have their plates already piled full with tonight's dinner, which consists of seasoned baked chicken breast, green beans and dinner rolls.

As I walk into the room, my sister peers up and forces a smile. My father glances up, though he doesn't even try to fake a smile.

I'm going to get through dinner, I'll need a little liquid courage to ease any anxiety. I head over to the cupboard and grab a bottle of sweet red wine. I sit down at the table with it, and pour myself a generous class of it in my mug. I normally would grab a wine glass, but tonight it's the furthest thing from my mind. Because all that I can think about is that this is the last time I will eat dinner at this table for a while.

I put the wine bottle down, and take a generous drink. Makaria eyes me for a moment before training her attention back to her plate. I begin to pile my plate with a helping of each, and I waste no time digging in.

Knowing that I won't be eating a home cooked meal for a few days, I'm savoring what I can right now.

"So I was thinking," my sister begins. I can see she's still not entirely confident with approaching me yet, considering she was the one who told father about the book and most likely still feels some guilt for it.

"That tomorrow we can go to Hellen Park? It's supposed to be nice out. We could even bring a basket of snacks. You know, make an afternoon out of it."

My gaze finds Makaria's as I battle between feeling guilty that I won't be here tomorrow, and also feeling determined to leave. Gods, I can just feel the guilt ooze its way back into my thinking on all of this. But I can't let it. I have to remember that Makaria is more than old enough to take care of herself now. No matter how harsh it may feel to admit that.

Since I can't let them know my intentions of not being around, I lie to my sister. It pains me to do it, to get her hopes up in spending time with me tomorrow. But one day, maybe she will understand this wasn't about her.

"Yeah, sure. That sounds fun." I say, trying to compose a nonchalant face so as not to give any indication that somethings up.

I think what makes me feel guilty is that I can tell that my sister is trying to make amends for what happened, but when she realizes that I'm gone, there's a good chance she'll feel like she could've done more. But I can't let the weighing thoughts of "what if" keep me stuck here anymore. I have to make this journey to Vulir, and hopefully get the answers that I need about myself. I need to grow more in my gifts as they are an ever-evolving part of me.

Makaria gives me a generously wide grin, and begins to talk about how excited she is for the flowers to begin blooming. She talks of how soon it'll be warm enough outside to go swimming in the lake, one of her favorite things to do. For once, I don't feel bothered by the fact that my sister is rambling on and on, not leaving much room for me to chime in. This time, I take it all in and enjoy this last moment together. At least for a while, that is.

I watch the excitement light up in Makaria's face as she talks, noting how my father is watching her in the same way. Makaria has always had such a bubbly and bright personality, which has always made me strongly believe that two people can come from the same mother, but be totally different in more ways than one.

She believes in fairytales, magical endings, and romance. While I believe in practicality, responsibility, and stability. Sometimes I wish I had her same enthusiasm for life, and who knows, maybe that will change someday. For now, I'll soak in the enthusiasm she's emitting at the table right now. Holding on to that version of her, instead of wondering how she'll become once she realizes that I'm gone.

I won't sit here and wonder how it may drastically affect her, or even not affect her at all. All I'm going to do, is just be in the moment. Drink my wine, and listen to my sister talk her head off.

Before I leave, and everything changes.

After dinner I decided to take another nap. We're going to be riding until tomorrow late afternoon, so I want to be as rested as I reasonably can be.

After waking up, I look at the alarm clock on my nightstand, which reads ten o'clock.

Only an hour and a half before I leave.

Since I have a little time, and also since my nerves are starting to get the best of me, I decide to utilize our bathtub for one last time. We're going to be traveling in the woods for three days, so it's likely a wise decision for me to wash up now while the option is still available to me.

Gathering some clean black leggings, a brown long sleeve shirt, clean underwear and clean socks, I head out into the hall to our bathroom. Peering up and down the hallway, it's dead quiet, which means everyone should be sleeping.

Perfect.

I enter the bathroom and close the door behind me, locking it. I turn on the faucet for the bathtub, shutting it off when enough water has filled it. I strip off all of my clothes, and step into the tub.

Instantly, I relish in the hot water as it relaxes not only my body but my nerves, too. I sink in the water until my whole body is covered, save for my head. I let myself sit here for some time, before I begin to scrub my body with my lavender soap.

As I scrub my skin I take in the aroma of the sweet scent, framing it to memory. Then I lather it in my hair, doing my best work to lather out any dirt and debris. Once I feel like I've scrubbed myself clean, I stand up as I watch the water slosh down my body. After leaning to pull the drain stopper, I grab the towel I laid out and pat my skin fully dry. I then take the towel and wrap it around my hair. After pulling my clean clothes on, I walk out of the bathroom and back to my bedroom.

I gaze at the clock and notice a half hour has passed by. As I sit here letting my hair dry a little longer before I brush it out, I feel like I'm forgetting something.

Suddenly, it dawns on me.

I walk over to my nightstand drawer and pull out a few pieces of paper, and a pen. I sit down on my bed, leaning over the nightstand and begin to write a letter to my sister:

Makaria,

By the time you read this, I will be long gone. Please do not worry for me. I will return. Eiran is with me, so rest assured I am not alone. I don't expect you to understand, but know that this is just something I had to do. But for now, take care of yourself. I may not be around for a while to watch over you, but you are strong. It's time to learn how to rely on yourself now. I love you.

All my love,

Meli

As I finish writing my letter to Makaria, I contemplate on whether I'll write a letter to my father or not. I fall short on what I would say to him.

"Thanks for never supporting me, but see ya when I get back."

"I won't be around to watch over Makaria anymore, or take care of the house, so good luck."

I realize that a part of me doesn't think he's worthy of receiving a letter explaining why I've left, and I don't feel considerably obligated to give him one, and I'm finally honest with myself about why.

He's never supported me. Never given me the respect that I deserved when I've done nothing less than try to appease him. Hardly ever showed me any thanks for taking care of Makaria when he was too drunk to be able to. He's hit me. Strangled me. Manipulated me into doing something that only benefits him.

I'm done playing nice. So, I decide to write him a very brief, promise to him:

"Father",

Your abuse is potent,
It burns my skin like wildfire.
But where damaged skin peels away,
New skin is replaced.
With power wrapped in rage,
and soon, you will see the wrath of it.

Melinoë

After finishing his letter, I fold both of them up separately and keep them on my nightstand until I'm ready to leave. I look at the clock as it reads eleven-fifteen. Fifteen more minutes before I make the journey with Eiran to Vulir and it's really settling in that I'm actually leaving.

I grab the notes and stand up from my bed. I shake off any feelings of anxiety of whether or not Makaria will see me slip into her room or not, and just trust that I have to be quiet enough for me to pull it off. Sebastian I'm not worried about. That man could sleep through a damn car crash right outside the window and never even flinch in his sleep.

As soon as I drop the letters off to both of their rooms, I don't want to waste any time lingering around here. So I'll come straight back to my room, grab my stuff, and head out as quickly yet quietly as possible.

I walk nearly on tip-toes as I walk to Sebastian's room first. Since I know he's the heaviest sleeper, it makes more sense to drop his note off first. I slowly open his door, prying it open, I peer over at Sebastian sprawled out on his bed. His blinds shut so it's pitch black in here, save for the alarm clock that's on his nightstand.

I creep silently over to his nightstand, slowly tucking the letter under his alarm clock, and pause. Once I see he hasn't moved in his sleep, I quietly make my way out of his room. Once I'm nearly out of his room, I turn back around towards him and take one last look at him.

I bring my hand up and silently give him a vulgar gesture. No longer feeling remorse for him and his actions. No longer willing to abide by his abuse.

Once I turn around and step out of his room, I pull his door mostly closed. Walking slowly down to Makaria's room, I notice her door is closed all the way.

The slowest I think I've ever moved in my life, I gently twist her doorknob until it clicks open. Quietly, I pry her door open enough for me to slip through her room. Makaria's back is thankfully towards me, as she lies facing her bedroom window. I walk over to her nightstand, setting her letter down when she shifts in her sleep.

Fuck.

I stand impeccably still as she stretches her legs some, slightly arching her back. Cursing in my head, I dare not to move a damn muscle until she stills.

Once she stills, I walk slowly back to the door until I'm out of there. I take one glance back at Makaria, and silently mouth a farewell.

"See you soon, sister."

Closing the door behind me, I walk to my room to gather my duffle bag. I pull my dagger out of my bag and sheath it to my thigh, feeling the weight of the blade against my leggings. I hike my sleeping bag over my shoulder, with my duffel bag, and I'm heading out of my room.

I make it to our front door and take one last look at our home.

I've never been away from home–

Feeling stumped, I can't even bring myself to call this place home as I've never actually felt at home here since our mother died. I begin to hope that someday, I can find some place that feels much more like home.

Who knows, maybe I'll feel that way with Vulir.

Without another thought, I'm out the door and walking away from my cabin, heading to Terry's to meet with Eiran.

CHAPTER 14

Walking up the gravel road to Terry's stable, I see Eiran standing off to the side of the barn, waiting for me. As I walk up towards him, I notice he has his sword strapped to his back, and a dagger sheathed to his thigh.

A sword that has been passed down from the male bloodline in his family, from generation to generation. Since it's one of the remaining things he has left of his father, he cherishes that sword greatly, and only ventures with it on rare occasions. The criss-cross pattern of the ash colored grip, adjoined by a ruby crystal in the center of the bronzed pommel. A beautiful blade.

He's wearing cargo pants, a black sweater, and hunting boots. Hanging over his shoulder is a hunting bag that I'm certain is carrying the two water flasks, along with some clean clothing. As I approach him, he closes the distance between us.

"You ready for this?"

I nod. "I'm ready."

I take us quietly around the barn, out to the paddocks. Usually Terry keeps all the horses out in the paddocks at night, but I definitely didn't want to test my luck by going through the barn and spooking the horses.

As we make our way around, I look out to the paddock that Alastor is usually in. I lock onto him as I see him grazing the grass.

He loves the damn grass.

As Eiran and I near the gate, Alastor's ears twitch toward us, and his head jerks right up. Once he sees it's me, his body relaxes as he starts walking towards me.

I whisper to Eiran. "Stay here. I'm going to just go in the paddock quickly to get him saddled up. Keep an eye out for me."

Eiran nods his head, and immediately keeps his eyes trained on the tiny house that's near the barn.

Once I'm in the paddock, Alastor is right in front of me, already nudging me. "I know you want all the affection in the world. But I need you, buddy. I need you with me for this."

As if he understood what I was saying he gives a shake of his head and angles his body so it's more accessible for me to put his saddle on. I give him neck rubs every so often so he feels appreciated. As I'm saddling him up, I notice a couple of the other horses in this paddock look over curiously.

"No, *please* stay over there." I whisper.

Sure enough, they start to walk over. Damnit.

As I try to finish getting Alastor saddled up, two other horses approach me. One gives me a whinny and I immediately look over to Eiran.

He looks over at me, whispering. "Hurry."

Trying to hurry as fast as I can, one horse nudges into me with her muzzle. Alastor reaches his head around and gives a whinny at her. Alastor is not a temperamental horse, but because he has grown very bonded with me, it's possible he's protective of me.

The other horse gives another whinny, flicking her tail around. She starts pawing at the ground. I realize that since it's dark out here, she may not recognize me, and may think I'm trying to steal Alastor. Because I don't know how temperamental this horse is, I figure my best option is to just get this saddle fastened and get out of this paddock.

Any other horse and I would try to approach it, but this one I'm not familiar with. I realize that's because this is the newer horse Terry's been tending to.

With the saddle fully fastened, I grab Alastor's lead rope and get ready to guide him out of the gate.

I look over to Eiran. "I'm done. I'm going to guide him out, but since these two other horses are right here, I need you to close the gate right after me."

Eiran nods as he moves over to the gate, opening it. As I guide Alastor out, sure enough the other two horses are trying to come out. I guide Alastor out a little quicker, and as soon as I'm out Eiran closes the gate behind me, nearly closing it on the newer female horse.

"Sorry you two, but only Alastor can come with me." I whisper to the other two horses.

I grab a small rubber water bowl for Alastor. I put it in my duffel bag, in case at any point we're not near fresh water for him to drink. We begin walking down to the end of the paddocks, where we are met with a wall of trees. Through these woods is a trail that will take us straight to the Sephyra Forest.

"Alright, this is our starting point. I'll swing up first, then you after me. And then we're off."

I hand Eiran my duffle bag with my rolled up pallet, and swing myself onto Alastor. Taking a few seconds to see if he becomes antsy, I'm relieved when he stands there like the good boy he is.

Eiran hands me my things back, and swings himself onto Alastor behind me. As he settles himself, I feel the brush of his muscular arms rub against me. Since we'll be riding fast to start out, he'll have to hold onto me to keep himself steady.

Eiran wraps an arm around my waist, bringing me flush against him. The feel of his hard chest against my back causes my stomach to flutter even more than it already is. I take a deep breath in and out, my hold on the lead rope tightening.

"You ready?" I look over my shoulder, as I ask him. His face not showing an ounce of doubt in his decision to come with me.

"I'm ready."

Gripping Alastor's reins, I give a gentle squeeze with my heels, and Alastor begins the trot through the trail.

We've remained at a steady pace for the remainder of the night. I figured if we could get to that open landscape by late afternoon, then we could stop there to rest for the night.

I'm not quite sure what time it is, but with the soft glow that's beginning to break up the night sky, it's probably around five in the morning. It was only until a little while ago that the trail ended. From that point, I geared Alastor through an opening through the woods where we've been making our way through.

Right now is the easy part. Nikolai said that I just have to make it through the Sephyra Forest, but from there I'll have to rely on my intuition to guide us all the rest of the way to Vulir.

So for now, I'm feeling confident in our trek there. But I imagine I'll feel differently once it comes time to rely on nothing but my intuition to guide us.

It'll be fine, I keep telling myself.

We'll make it there.

As the sun's glow makes its rise into the early morning sky, I figure now is a good time to make a quick stop to give Alastor some water, and maybe for us to have a snack.

"Let's rest for a few minutes." I tell Eiran over my shoulder. He gives a quick nod.

I shift Alastor's reins to the right, over by a flattened terrain and motion for him to stop. We're completely surrounded by tall pine trees, and the chirping of birds is everywhere. After Eiran swings off first, he raises his hand for me as he helps me down. Gripping his hand, I lower myself to the ground when I stumble into him. Eiran steadies me as our bodies hardly have an inch of space to separate them. I take note of the feel of his hands, how roughly they sit inside of mine. After a moment, I pull away and go over to Alastor and give him a few good neck rubs. Trying to fight the tension that saturates the air between us.

We have a long trek ahead of us, and now's not the time to get distracted.

"I know you're not used to traveling this long. But you're doing a great job."

Alastor leans his muzzle into my hand as I give him some much deserved affection. After running my hand along the bridge of his nose, I turn around towards Eiran. "Do you have that water flask?"

Eiran goes to open his hunting bag, grabbing one and throwing it towards me.

"Thank you." I catch it, and twist the top off. I greedily gulp a few drinks for myself, and then I pour some in the bowl that I grabbed for Alastor. It's not a very big bowl, but it's something for him until we get to fresh water.

I pour a generous amount into the bowl, setting it down for him. He wastes no time lowering his head and drinking the bowl dry. I pour him some more, take a few more sips for myself, and twist the top back on.

I walk over to Eiran who's taken a few gulps from his flask. Handing him my flask, he takes it and puts it back in his hunting back.

"So, can you hear anything out here other birds?"

It might've seemed like a stupid question, but considering he's one of the best huntsman our village has ever seen, I've always been curious if he—

At the thought of our village I become anxious as I realize it's morning. Makaria is probably reading my letter right now, or if not, will very soon. I wonder what her initial reaction is going to be.

Sebastians I genuinely couldn't care less about. He probably won't lose any sleep over my absence.

"It's not so much as hearing but seeing. I guess it's more like I can see things that maybe you'd overlook or wouldn't notice unless you had the right practice." Eiran says, pulling me back from my thoughts.

Eiran takes his gaze off of me, and begins walking a few steps forward, not straying far. He's taking in every direction, when he looks down. Bending down, his fingers gently press over the soil.

"See here," he says, tilting his head to the ground. I move over to kneel next to him, looking at the animal print that's faded into the soil, "That's a deer print, but you can tell by how faded and dry it is that it's not fresh. My guess is this was probably from sometime early yesterday. But it looks like she's headed the same way we are."

I look at the soil in fascination that he's able to tell that from just an animal print. But hey, I'm no hunter so what do I know?

"Well I'm glad I brought you along with me after all." I say with a playful smile. Eiran meets my gaze and nudges his elbow into me.

I take in the smile Eiran is giving me and the way his eyes sparkle against the approaching sunlight. For a moment, I just admire him and how lucky I am to have someone like him in my corner. How I've possibly overlooked what we could be this entire time, and how much I suddenly want to close that distance between us. But we still have a ways to go, and I can't let myself get distracted right now.

I avert my gaze over to Alastor, breaking whatever tension is lingering between us at the moment. Eiran clears his throat before he speaks. "Well, if we want to make it there by late afternoon, we'll need to leave now." He stands up from the ground, holding his hand out for me with a smile on his face.

I take his hand as he pulls me up, the force of it pulling me right into him. I gasp at the contact, my hands finding themselves against Eiran's chest. Eiran watches me, still holding my hand, his eyes piercing mine. We stand there for just a moment when Alastor gives one of his famous whinnys.

I look at Alastor and back at Eiran, who's eyes haven't left my face. He swallows and drops my hand, forcing a smile. He holds his arm out, towards Alastor, and we walk back to him.

Once we're back I swing myself up onto Alastor, with Eiran following right behind. He wraps an arm around my waist, and before it didn't give me the kind of reaction it's giving me now. Before I didn't notice the weight of his arm around me, but after just a moment ago, I sure do now.

I can feel the tension in his muscles, almost as if he's fighting with himself about this too. Shaking the thoughts away, I squeeze my heels in and Alastor begins jogging.

We traveled straight through from there. The ride was long and at some points the ground wasn't as smooth as we were so blessed with earlier, creating a bumpy journey.

After a while I felt myself getting tired of sitting straight up, and eventually rested myself into Eiran. He didn't seem to mind, and his arm never left my waist.

We traveled through endless miles of trees and foliage. Once we made our way through the woods, we came out into an unending land of grassy terrain. I felt Alastor even shake his head at me a couple times, and I knew it was because he wanted nothing more than to graze the endless amount of grass around us.

As we ride through, I see ahead of us what looks like a field that has a stream of water that runs into a treeline.

"Right up there, that's it." Eiran says and I couldn't be more relieved to finally get off this horse. I love Alastor and I'm entirely grateful we did not have to walk this distance, but my thighs feel like boulders.

We ride for a little while longer until we're about to approach the field.

"Let's dismount now." Eiran says.

Nodding my head, I pull Alastor's reins over; he slows his pace, as we pull off to the side. Once he's fully stopped, both Eiran and I dismount and walk the short rest of the way with Alastor. Once we get to the field, we travel into the shaded area surrounded by trees and dump our stuff there. It's right next to the field, but in a ducked off area where we won't draw much attention to ourselves.

I highly doubt anyone lives out here, but you just never know.

Eiran wastes no time venturing off to hunt for us. While he seeks out dinner, I bring Alastor and I over to the nearby stream of water. Alastor greedily drinks from it, while I fill up our water flasks. Taking a few drinks from mine, I refill it and twist it shut. Once Alastor finally stops gulping down the water from the stream, we head back over to our spot for the night.

For a while I brush my fingers through Alastor's mane, picking any dirt out of it. I talk softly to him as I do. "I have to say, I don't think I would've been able to do this without you." I rest my head against the bridge of his nose, taking in the moment that we've started our journey out here.

I begin to wonder what Makaria is doing, and how she is reacting to the letter. Is she in shock? Or maybe she is even happy for me?

I hear Eiran walking up the field. In his hands, I see him holding by a line three large trouts.

As he approaches me, his gaze meets mine. He holds up the line. "It's pretty quiet out here, not many animals moving along. But this will do for now."

After foraging for some wood and branches, we start a fire and roast the fish over it. It's not the greatest dinner I've had, but like he said. It'll do for now.

From my duffle bag I pull out the bags of dried fruit, nuts and crackers I packed. I pull out the half loaf of bread and rip it into a few pieces. I hand everything to Eiran and he takes a little of everything.

"So once we get to the Sephyra Forest, how will you know which way we go?"

As I nibble on the dried fruit, I ponder over Eiran's question. "I'm not sure. I guess I'm just going to have to trust myself and lead us whichever way feels best." I say, through bites of our food. "Are you worried at all?"

"No. I trust you."

His reassurance strikes a chord in my heart.

After dinner, we leave the fire going for as long as it'll go. Alastor is right next to us, rolling around in the grass as he loves to do.

Since it's starting to get late, I've already rolled out my pallet and noticed that Eiran didn't bring one with him. My brows furrow as I look up at him, who's sitting near me, his gaze trained on the fire.

"Where's your pallet?"

His gaze doesn't waver from the fire. "I don't need it. I don't plan on sleeping while you're asleep. I'll stay up and keep watch."

"You're going to need to sleep at some point, we've been riding since midnight last night. You need the rest too if we're going to ride all day tomorrow."

Eiran then looks at me as if he knows I'm right, but still has resistance etched into his features. "The risk is worth it if it means that I get to make sure you're safe."

His loyalty. His kindness. He'd rather risk him getting hardly any rest just to make sure I'm safe throughout the night. I'm moved by his gesture, but I need him to be well rested.

"We have Alastor, who will get spooked at any indication of something nearby. You have to get at least a few hours of rest, otherwise you won't be alert for when we get through the Sephyra Forest, a place that neither you and I have been in before. Where we have no idea what lurks in there."

Eiran clenches his jaw, and looks straight ahead for a minute. Finally, after a few moments he replies.

"Fine, you're right."

Feeling satisfied with his answer, I wrap myself into my pallet, Eiran tentatively nuzzling himself behind me. He lays on his back for what seems like forever, and I know he's just trying to be respectful. Which I love. But it's pretty chilly out here and so I wouldn't mind snuggling up a little.

"You know, it would probably help dealing with the cold weather out here if you let me use you as a body heater."

Eiran lets out a deep laugh, one I haven't heard in awhile. He turns himself onto his side, facing towards me. He wraps an arm over me, pulling me right into him. I shamelessly embrace the warmth his body is reverberating, and lay my arm over his. I can feel his heartbeat beating a mile a minute, and wonder if he can feel mine too.

As I let go of any worries of how things could be affected by us, or how I normally would not let myself get close like this with someone, I just embrace the moment. I begin tracing circles around Eiran's forearm, and I feel him relax even more. He leans his head a little lower, and kisses my cheek. The intimacy is more than just our normal hookups.

Everything just feels like…more.

Maybe Eiran and I can be more.

"Eiran."

I feel him re-position his head above mine, his voice vibrating my body when he responds, eliciting a thrill through me.

"Yes?"

"Thank you. For coming with me."

He gives me another kiss, this time on the top of my head and I'd be lying if I wasn't swooning over this affection. He pauses my fingers from trailing circles on his forearm, and brings my hand into his.

"Like I said, I would do anything for you."

Pondering over just how deep his feelings are for me, I am interrupted by the feel of his thumb lightly stroking my wrist. Before I can ponder further on it, I lose to my own exhaustion and fall fast asleep.

CHAPTER 15

I wake up to being firmly wrapped up into the pallet, not an inch of my back exposed to the chill morning air.

Sheepishly opening my eyes, I see Alastor grazing just a few feet away from me. I rub the underneath of my eyelids with my thumb, trying to rub away my tiredness.

And also my awakening anxiety.

Today, we'll arrive at the Sephyra Forest, where afterwards we will only have my intuition to guide us the rest of the way.

With that thought, I do not relax in the least.

It's not that I'm distrustful of my instincts, but when I'm being put to the ultimate test of whether or not I can trust them enough to guide us successfully to Vulir, well you could say the panic is surely starting to ensue.

As I rustle my way out of my pallet, Alastor lifts his head towards me in response. He walks towards me until he approaches me, and nudges his nose into my chin. As a tired smile grows across my face, I reach up and rub my hand down his neck. Soon after I hear footfalls coming up over the grassy plains.

Turning my head, I see Eiran walking towards us with what looks to be our breakfast. Hanging from a line are two large trouts.

"It should hold us over until we make it out of the Sephyra Forest and finally into Vulir." Eiran says, as he drops the line of fish down by my pallet. He kneels over by the pit we created last night and begins laying a small amount of wood and twigs.

"So from here on out until we're in Vulir, we'll have to survive on what you've brought."

Even though according to Nikolai's directions, if he's right and we only have less than two days until we make it to Vulir, I can't help the worry settling deeply in my stomach.

Re-examining in my head what we have left I recount that we still have left a little less than half loaf of bread, as well as an ample amount of nuts, dried fruit, and just a handful of crackers left.

Oh gods, what if we get lost and starve out here?

No, that won't happen. I can trust myself to get us there in time. I have to.

After Eiran has cleaned and gutted our fish, he cooks them over a small fire. After I manage to bring myself out of my pallet, I walk over next to Eiran and sit by the fire with him. Once they're both cooked, he hands one to me that is noticeably bigger than the other one. I frown at his generosity as I wonder if his is enough for him.

He's a pretty muscular man who weighs more than I do. I can't imagine that little fish is enough for him. Still, he says nothing and we eat eagerly.

Once finished, we both waste no time to put out the fire and get ready to start our journey once again. If Eiran is right, we should make it to the Sephyra Forest by midday today.

Rolling up my pallet and grabbing my duffel bag, I walk over to Alastor who is polishing off his water bowl that I set out for him. I whisper gentle words of appreciation to him, and give him some generous neck rubs.

I can feel Eiran's eyes boring into my back, and though I know he's trying to be respectful so as to not rush me, I know that we do have to get moving.

Reaching down to grab Alastor's water bowl, I shove it into my duffel bag. Turning to Eiran, I try to fight the nervous energy that's exploding through my body right now. Suddenly, I feel like the pressure to know how to get to Vulir is weighing on me, and I'm having a moment of what feels like pure suffocation.

"Meli?" Eiran's expression grows concerned as he closes the distance between us. His hands are on my shoulders and it's only at that moment I realize I was trembling. The gentle pressure of his hands holding my shoulders brings my body to relax.

I stand there, roaming his face. His expression balances both the look of worry, and also the look of admiration. "We will make it there. I know you can do this.

"But how do you know that? What if I end up taking us the wrong way? Or what if my intuition fails me and tells me nothing while we're—"

"Your intuition will not fail you." Eiran interrupts, his hands moving to my cheeks as he focuses my frantic gaze back onto him. "You just need to relax, and listen. Trust yourself, as much as I have always trusted you."

As I keep my stare on Eiran, I begin to slow my breathing and notice my body feels less and less frantic. Breathing deeply and slowly, in and out, I close my eyes for a few moments.

In those moments, I remind myself of how right this journey to Vulir has felt regardless of my worrying mind.

I remind myself that I don't get to do this journey alone, either. That I'm blessed enough to share this journey with someone who *truly* sees me. Someone who has always believed in me even when I have been too broken to see the strength within myself.

I open my eyes, and I decide to let my instincts guide me from here on out. Starting with this moment right here.

I press my lips to Eiran's as I bring my hands up to his. I feel his whole body still, as if he's not sure how to react to this.

In the next moment, he relaxes fully into the kiss. The kiss quickly becomes frantic as he wraps his arms around my waist pulling me closer into him. It quickly becomes apparent to me that I have not been the only one who feels something evolving between us. Eiran explores my mouth as if he's trying to map out how every corner of my mouth aligns with his.

After a while, Eiran finally pulls away with his hands still wrapped around my waist. His gaze roams my face as if he is trying to savor the moment.

He gazes at me as if he's trying to figure out what to say, but instead of speaking, his lips press against mine again. My lips part as the kiss deepens.

As my tongue clashes with his, he pulls me closer into his body where I can feel his arousal. As I press my hips into him, his fingers grip into my hips as he rocks against me, and he groans softly into my mouth.

Eiran's mouth suddenly pulls away as his gaze meets mine. His hands loosen their grip as one comes up to push a strand of hair behind my ear.

"I'm *thoroughly* enjoying this, but if we want to make it to Sephyra Forest by midday, we have to get going." He says, through an expression that tells me *but if you want to say fuck it and continue I'll be happy to oblige.*

No matter how much I want to eagerly continue this, we have to stay on track. I hesitate for a few seconds, and then pull away entirely.

"You're right. Let's go."

As I walk over to Alastor to swing myself up, I look over my shoulder at Eiran who is trailing right behind me.

"Besides, there's always later." I say with a grin and a wink.

I notice Eiran stiffen for a quick moment as he clears his throat, a grin forming his mouth.

As he swings himself up behind me, he pulls me flush against him. Instantly, I feel his hard cock nestling in my back. It fills me with an eagerness that makes me want to do more than just kissing right now. I feel the featherlight brush of Eiran's finger as they trail some of my hair away from my ear. It causes my breath to hitch as he leans in and whispers against my ear.

"Then I guess for now, you'll just have to feel what's waiting for you later."

The sun is high in the sky now, which means it must be around noon. Hoping to make it to the Sephyra Forest in a couple of hours, I'd say we're making good timing.

We've been riding through the forest since we started our journey this morning. Alastor's pace has remained at a quick canter, so Eiran has kept his arm firmly around my waist.

Meaning I've been rubbing up against him for hours.

Ugh, this is not helping my sexual frustration.

Eiran must feel the same way, as he's made a few grunts in the beginning of our trek out. But now, he calmly sits with me firmly against his torso.

This man has some serious restraint. Impressive.

We ride for another three hours when suddenly the forest seems to…change.

The change happens so quickly that I have to confirm with Eiran that he's noticing the same things as I.

"I see it too. Something is…different. We must be here."

I turn my head back from Eiran as I look far above me at the trees that hover over us. They look like normal luscious evergreen trees except there's a thin curtain of iridescence to them. I squint my eyes, hoping to better understand what I'm looking at when I see it.

"It looks like they're…breathing."

Taking in the trees I can see them *moving*. It's ever so subtle, but when you truly pay attention, it's there. Along with the subtle breathing the trees are also reflecting this soft glimmer that I feel myself enchanted by.

I've never seen anything like this.

I feel Eiran looking up with me as he takes it all in. After a short moment, I feel his gaze lock back onto the trail ahead of us. I feel his chest expand as he takes a deep breath in.

"Meli—-you've got to see this."

Fixing my gaze back forward I gasp.

Ahead of us, we meet with a vast array of wildlife that roam the forest. Animals that range from deer, rabbits, wolves, foxes, squirrels, and even racoons.

"How? How is this possible?"

"I–I don't know." Eiran says, and I don't have to turn my head to know he is just as astounded at this as I am. "The wolves—how are they just coexisting? With the deer?"

Ahead of us, we just silently stare at all of these animals roaming amongst one another. Not only that, but there are so many of them. They all look well fed and happy too, no signs of malnourishment detected.

My attention is then dragged to the tapping of a woodpecker on a nearby pine tree. I take note of all the birds that are perched in the trees next to us.

"Look!" I gasp, dragging Eiran's attention to what I'm fixated on.

On the same tree that the woodpecker is on, we both see a couple of ravens, along with a hawk perched at the very top staring down at us. As I turn my head to the other side, I see that more trees house these beautiful birds.

"It's...beautiful."

I lose all sense of speech as I stare amazed at all of the wildlife that gathers here. At the fact that they are all coexisting.

The forest itself gives a certain ambiance of liveliness and enchanting beauty. Without thinking twice, I gently pull on Alastor's reins urging him to stop. I pull us over by a tree and I swing myself off. Eiran swings himself off after and I think he too, is so baffled by the beauty that this forest brings, because he doesn't even begin to harp on how we just stopped in the middle of a forest we're both unfamiliar with.

I take a few steps forward, completely losing all sense of logic and find myself nearing a wolf. I freeze, immediately hating myself for being so careless. I can feel Eiran still behind me and quietly call for me to remain still.

As I hear him slowly unsheath his dagger, I keep my eyes trained on the wolf.

"Don't. They made it clear this is a safe haven for them."

"A safe haven—Meli. A wolf is eyeing you up right now. If I have to choose whether to stand by and let you be attacked just because this spirit told you there's a no killing policy here, or if I have to risk bending the rules to save your life, I think I'm going to risk saving–"

"No, please. It's alright."

As I keep my eyes trained on the wolf in front of me, I hear Eiran curse to himself. But something begins to wash over me.

The next moment, I feel a tingling sensation in my body. It's a soft buzzing sensation, the same sensation I felt with—

"Remember, trust yourself."

I'm brought back to what that woman in my dream said and—

My gods. I've felt this same buzzing sensation before.

"Shit."

"What is it?" Eiran's voice begins to trickle a sense of franticness in it.

"I think I'm feeling this wolf's energy."

As I keep my sights trained on the wolf, I take in everything I'm feeling. I take note of how it makes me feel.

I feel…welcomed.

As I focus harder on the wolf's energy, he begins to approach me, slowly and deliberately. I expect my palms to start profusely sweating, or for this wolf to be able to smell the fear ricocheting off my body.

But I feel calm, even with this predatory animal closing in on me.

A few agonizing seconds later, the wolf is directly in front of me. He sniffs the air as he takes one more step towards me. I slowly reach my hand out, unsure of what the hell I'm doing and how I could be so careless. I reach out, and the wolf meets my hand with his snout. Sniffing me, he nudges my hand.

I think he wants me to pet him?

I timidly brush my hand across the top of his head and down. I still when I hear him make a low growl, but I keep my hand steady so as to not show this animal I'm afraid.

His nose nudges into my hand again, and then he's licking my hand.

I begin petting him again, realizing that the low growl was not a signal of danger for me. It was just his way of communicating with me. He continues licking my hand and I begin to see his tail wag, showing he's happy.

What the fuck is happening here. This thing should be wanting to eat me.

The wolf howls, and a few moments later a pack of around eight other wolves descend out of the tree line. They walk towards me and mimic the same behavior.

As they close in, they sniff the air around us. But after a few seconds, they fully approach me and they welcome me.

"What the fuck is happening." Eiran says behind me. I hear him make a very slow descent over to us, and a part of me is terrified these wolves are only accepting of me.

But I'm surprised when the wolves begin to welcome Eiran as well.

"This is fucking crazy." I say looking over at Eiran who is petting a few of the wolves. They start licking his face and he has a nervous grin on his face.

"This definitely should not be happening."

Some kind of forest this is.

Where Eiran and I are being loved on by animals who should be trying to make a meal out of us.

As more animals start to approach us, I notice something from the corner of my eye sprinting across the woods.

Immediately, I look over trying to find what it was. When I can't pinpoint it, my gaze meets Eiran's. "Did you see that?"

His brows furrow at me as he looks behind him. "See what?"

Fervently glancing around, I desperately try to spot whatever it was that I saw again. Discouraged, I look back down at the wolves in front of me.

"Meli."

Disliking the rigidness that's dripping from Eiran's voice, I freeze. Looking up, a scream tears through my throat.

Before me is a creature that's not an animal, but I'd say is the closest thing related to a human. It has skin like humans do, but with pointed ears and disturbingly wide set eyes. The whites to its eyes are nearly gone, leaving only black voids in its wake.

Looking behind it I notice wings that stretch tall but are not very wide. They almost look like they can shrink into themselves. The same color as their skin, an olive tone that shines with a soft glimmer from the sunlight that peeks through the trees.

Its hands have claws for nails. Gasping, I notice the claws are absurdly long and very sharp. I am not sure what this thing is but I only have one guess as to what it is.

"Are you…a fairy?"

The creature looks at me for a moment, then gives a terrifying laugh that reminds me of wind chimes. "Oh dear, fairies are made up. But us, yes we are real.

I furrow my brows in confusion. "So…what are you?"

"I am what is referred to as the Fae."

Inhaling a sharp breath in that seems to go nowhere, I still. The Fae in front of me begins laughing again, and takes a few steps forward.

"Forget your worries. I'm certain I'm not the most frightful thing you've come across."

What is he talking about? The Fae man stands there as if to wait for me to agree, but when I'm left gaping at him he waves his hands at me.

"Oh, I see, I see. We'll get there."

As soon as I'm about to ask what the fuck this guy is talking about, I hear Eiran approaching us. "Who are you?"

The Fae male exchanges a few glances between Eiran and I before finally answering. "The question is not who I am, but who your friend is as she seems to have not discovered that yet."

Does he know about my gifts? But how would he know that?

"Vulir is closer than you think. A day's ride, give or take." The Fae male interrupts me, and before I can even get a chance to respond, he begins to gallop away.

"Wait!" I shout after him, because though it's only been a few brief seconds, he sure can make quick distance. The fae man turns back to me, cocking his head as he assesses me.

"How do we get to Vulir?"

The Fae male doesn't respond for a few seconds, and as he opens his mouth to speak, he halts.

For half a minute, he stands there with his gaze averted to his right. He stands there as if he sees something, and before he turns his attention back to me, he gives a cheerful laugh.

"Ah yes, Vulir. Well, I'm told you have this already underway. And that you actually do not seek my help, but seek validation you are going the right way."

I mean, he's not entirely wrong about—

Wait.

"Was a spirit just speaking to you just now?"

"Why of course, you silly girl. Did you really think I was just speaking to thin air? Unless—"

The Fae male in the blink of an eye is right in front of me once again and I stumble back at how quick this thing is. I watch as curiosity stretches across his face. "You can't see them yet, can you?"

I realize that he's referring to seeing the spirits.

I shake my head. "No, I can't. I'm having a hard time getting past just the few interceptions of words that I hear. That's why I need to go to Vulir."

"Ah, interesting. Well—"

Once again, the fae man makes an abrupt stop in his speech to talk to thin—no, not thin air, to a spirit. If I were a normal person, I would probably be mortified with this whole thing. But I'm actually quite jealous he seems to be able to see them so easily.

He turns back to me. "Well, it seems you shall find everything you are looking for." He says with a wink. Before he turns on his heels to gallop away, he gives me a final statement.

"Follow this path for another twenty miles. Camp for one night, then follow straight through to Vulir tomorrow.

Follow the signs that present themselves to you, Melinoë. Follow your intuition."

Eiran and I ride the entire time without stopping, both at the fact that we want to make it there before nightfall, and also because I think we're both still in shock over everything we just witnessed in that forest.

The sun begins to set and we ride until we reach a ducked off area in the forest that's secluded enough for us to rest for the night.

Once I swing myself off Alastor I grab my duffle bag and glance over at this small hill that dips down steeply, noticing that there is a small cave at the foot of it.

Eiran and I walk over there, as I guide Alastor with us. Thankfully, there's a stream of fresh water running by, in which Eiran goes to top off our water flasks. When he gets back, I immediately grab the food we have left and we rest for a moment to eat. Taking a very generous drink of my water, I look at Eiran who's going to town on his pieces of bread.

I reach my hand into the bag of nuts and pull a small handful out, savoring the salty taste of them.

After we eat, we don't bother starting a fire. This is unfamiliar territory to us, so the least attention we can attract to ourselves the better.

Unrolling my pallet, I pat my hand down for Eiran to once again let me use him as a body heater. He grins and slides into the pallet with me. He positions his body so his back is towards the back of the cave, so both of us are looking forward to the opening.

He pulls me in close to him and snakes an arm around my waist.

"So when that Fae was talking to the spirit like that, is that what it's like for you?"

"Well I can't physically see them, if that's what you mean." I say.

"No, I mean like how he was able to just hear them. But we couldn't. Or—could you? Hear whoever was talking to him?"

"No…I couldn't. But when it is actually happening for me, yeah it's basically like that. I hear them mostly through my mind, that's the best way I can explain it."

I begin to nestle myself into Eiran a little more as I shamelessly embrace his warmth. He wraps his arm around me tighter and begins tracing his fingers along my forearm. I relax into the comfort it brings me.

"That sounds slightly terrifying. But also intriguing." Eiran says with a chuckle.

I laugh as I run my other hand over Eiran's arm. My fingers brush gently along the ridges of his muscles. Goosebumps begin to form under my fingertips and things feel right. Even though we're traveling to a village that we have no knowledge on, and all of the encompassing worries that come with that, I know that I'm safe through it all.

Because I've never felt this level of safety with anyone before, save for when I'm with Eiran.

"Eiran?"

He makes a noise that doesn't escape his lips, and the vibration of it rumbles against me.

"Do you think things are meant to be different between us?"

I feel his fingers cease their tracing of my skin, and he doesn't move for a few seconds. His body relaxes as his fingers continue tracing circles into my forearm. "I think I'm happy no matter how our relationship evolves. As long as I have you in my life, then I have everything I've ever wanted."

My heart swells as he—

"But," He says as he interrupts my thoughts. "If you were interested in us becoming more than friends, then that's something I wouldn't take for granted"

At Eiran's proclamation, I turn my head towards him. My lips mere inches from his as my eyes roam his lips. I take in what he's saying and it moves something inside of me. My heart feels like it's floating in my chest as I stare at him.

He moves his hand up to my chin, as his thumb caresses my cheek. "Melinoë, tell me what you want from us. And it will be yours."

I've always resisted being more than friends with Eiran because I was afraid of what would happen if things progressed, and it later on ruined our friendship somehow.

I admittedly, have also been afraid to love.

I've always told myself I'm better off on my own, that the only person I can count on for anything is myself.

But that logic doesn't ring true with Eiran. He's been here since the very beginning.

Though my chest feels as though it's caging in, I steady my voice anyhow. "I've known you my whole life, Eiran. You know me better than I know myself sometimes. But I'm not the happy-free-spirited girl like my sister is. I'm dense. I trust no one, save for you and myself. How could I be fit to give my time to someone like that when I am who I am?"

Eiran gazes at me softly while I pour my darkest thoughts to him. He trails a strand of my hair behind my ear. "Yes, you are all of those things. But you are also *brave*, and courageous. And the effect you have on me is astronomical. Your eyes like the lighthouse that guides me from my wandering thoughts. Your laugh is like silk against my rough skin. You have no idea about everything *else* that you are. I have no desire to fix you, or change you. As I have accepted you exactly as you are, since day one. And I will continue to accept you from here forward."

My gaze does not falter from Eiran's as his words reach through the deepest depths of my broken soul. The depths that have known violence, and loss, and have drowned in it for years. But through the darkness, I have always found myself gravitating to Eiran's light to bring me back home. And it wasn't until this moment, that I realized he's been everything that's been good about my life.

I bring my hand up to Eiran's jaw, my fingers ignited by the heat emanating from his skin. I watch his eyes narrow to my lips before they meet my gaze once more. I do not run from this moment, I do not hide.

Instead, I welcome it.

I bring my lips to his. A deep, languid kiss that I feel down to my toes. We kiss like this for a while, until he pulls away. His gaze mapping out my face. "Then more is exactly what I will give you."

Suddenly his mouth is on me again, this time more greedy in his exploration. His tongue pries my mouth open as I lap mine against his. Eiran pulls me flush against his chest, where I can feel his hard cock. I grind my ass on him in which he gives a satisfied grunt, as he grips my waist.

As our kissing deepens and our tongues clash, I continue grinding into him and he meets my movement. His hand moves to my navel as he slowly trails his fingers in circles. As he slowly makes his way down further and further, the anticipation is almost boiling over for me and I grow impatient.

Grabbing his hand, I try to move it further down, but he holds it in place.

"Not so fast." He says as his lips move against mine. He trails his head to my neck and gives me a kiss, causing me to arch my back in response.

He descends his hand lower, nearly right on my pussy. I moan in anticipation as he whispers into my neck. "I'm going to take my time and enjoy *every* second of this."

That's all I get before he moves his fingers in between my thighs, lightly trailing my clit with his thumb. The touch is so featherlight. He continues trailing my clit, driving me absolutely mad. I smile as I realize that two can play at this game though.

I move a hand behind me and place it on his cock, outside of his pants. I slip my hand low enough that it's cupping his balls, and his whole body jerks.

I slowly move my hand up his pants, pushing his pants down just enough for me to slip his cock out. I rub my thumb over the tip, reveling in the way that Eiran's body keeps jerking into my hand.

His desperation begins to show as he starts running a finger through my pussy. He doesn't slip it in, but just teases me by rubbing around my entrance.

I moan in response, as I free my hand from his cock, bringing it my wetness. Eiran stills for a moment as I touch myself, before I slip my hand back down to his cock. His whole body jerks in a feverish way. He moans into my neck, before he kisses my neck again.

Moving my hand up and down, he meets my feverish need with his, and slips his finger fully inside me. As I stroke him, Eiran moves his finger in and out of me and gods, I'm already close.

But I know he won't let me finish yet. As he said, he wants to take his time with me.

He flips me onto my back and his lips meet mine. He's hovering over my body now, thrusting into my hand as I work his cock. As it starts to bead at the top, I rub my thumb over it and Eiran jerks forward.

I really love the way his body reacts to me.

Eiran begins to slide another finger in and I gasp at the contact. He begins to finger me faster while his thumb circles my clit. I'm shamelessly writing beneath him as I can feel myself coming close. I begin grinding my hips against his hand and I can feel Eiran smiling against my mouth.

Our tongues clash violently and hungrily together as we both work each other deliciously. It's a frenzy I've never felt with another man before, and maybe I feel so comfortable with Eiran because I've known him for so long.

I trust him.

Eiran pulls away from my mouth as he looks at me, before he lowers his head. His mouth is on one of my breasts as his tongue swirls around my nipple, his eyes never leaving mine.

"Keep your eyes on me, I want to watch you come undone."

I do as he says and keep my eyes on him. I normally would be uncomfortable with this much intimacy but with him, I'm the most comfortable I've ever been with a man.

Writhing against him, my moans become louder as I'm about to climb over the edge. I watch his tongue as it swirls around my hardened flesh and I begin working him faster. As soon as I feel like the ecstasy is too much, Eiran slips his finger out as he grabs my hand. He positions himself with his cock at my entrance and immediately thrusts inside of me.

I cry with pleasure as Eiran thrusts deeply. My arms come up to his neck as my cries intensify. His hands snake around my head, protecting my head from banging into the ground as our bodies move the pallet around.

"Fuck." I curse. I begin matching Eiran's thrusts and there's nothing gentle about us right now.

"I want to hear you scream my name as I feel you cum around my cock." Eiran says as he groans into my neck. He's kissing my neck and it only amplifies the pleasure I'm chasing.

My body begins to tremble as the orgasm rocks through me. I give Eiran exactly what he wants, his name a pleasurable cry from my lips. I ride my orgasm until Eiran is bucking against me and I can feel him cum inside of me. His body jerks as he groans into my neck.

After we both ride our waves of pleasure, Eiran lays down next to me. Both of us lying limp, trying to catch our breaths. After a few minutes, Eiran sits up to grab a washcloth from his bag. After cleaning me up, he cleans himself before folding it up and tossing it to the side.

With how fast I can hear his heart beating, I'm sure he'll wait until the morning to rinse the washcloth off.

Eiran leans over and cradles me against his chest, wrapping an arm around me. I embrace his closeness and its familiar weight. I lazily smile to myself as I realize everything is changing, even my relationship with Eiran.

He reaches his head down to my cheek and kisses me, and I sink into his arms even deeper. We begin to talk about the rest of the journey there, and what we both wonder what Vulir is going to be like. I bring up ways we could earn money while we're there, in which he tells me not to worry. That everything is going to work out.

We lay like this for a while longer, when I've almost fallen asleep.

"You are my life, Meli." Eiran begins, and I listen to his words as I fight with my eyes to remain open. "You are my heart, and my soul. And I will never let you forget it."

Smiling at his words, I find myself failing the battle against staying awake. Before I fall asleep in his arms, I manage to sleepily muster out a few words.

"As you are mine."

CHAPTER 16

"Melinoë, get up!"

My surroundings are hazy but I can automatically recognize where I am. With the grass sinking between my toes, trees in every direction.

I'm standing in the Sephyra Forest. Except it's clear I'm not awake.

"Melinoë, listen to me!"

My attention is jostled as I try to locate whoever is speaking to me. I glance ahead of me, to my right, to my left—-

The hair on the back of my neck stands up as I can feel someone standing right behind me.

Slowly, I circle around until I'm facing a man. Except his figure is…different. The detailing in his body, his face is all fairly clear. But it's this innate knowing that tells me he's not alive.

My attention is immediately directed to the familiarity of his voice. He sounds just like—

"Nikolai?"

My excitement rises as I can actually see the same man who gave me directions to get to Vulir. Though my excitement quickly vanishes as his fraught energy fills me with worry.

"Yes, it's me. That doesn't matter right now though. You need to wake up! You and Eiran need to leave NOW!"

"What—I don't understand—"

"Melinoë, please. Poachers are nearing the cave, and they are not good. You must get out now!"

Frozen in worry, I begin to stumble over my words. The next second, the man has his hands on my shoulders. His grip shocks me not because his expression reads frenetic, but because I'm able to even feel his palms digging into my skin.

"Now!"

In the next moment, I startle awake.

My body freezes internally as I have no intention to deny what this man was saying is true, but I'm overfilled with an unnatural amount of fear for what's coming our way.

I don't second guess it for one minute, and I'm rolling over to shake Eiran awake.

He startles awake, looking around until his eyes are on me. He must see the worry sketched into my face, because without question he's jolting up into a sitting position. "What is it?"

"I don't have time to explain, but we need to get going. Now."

His face for a brief moment searches mine, and I can tell he's trying to understand what kind of perceived danger we're in. He looks forward, towards the opening of the tent. I grab his face back towards me, drilling his gaze onto me.

"Eiran, do you trust me?"

It only takes him a second to nod in agreement, and we're both jumping up out of the pallet.

We near the opening of the cave, Eiran in front of me with both of our belongings hanging over his shoulders. I watch him peer out on both sides, making sure nobody is approaching the cave. When he looks back at me, he nods his head curtly. As I walk up to his side, his gaze tracks mine.

As we meet each other's gazes, there's this unspoken knowing that needs not explaining out loud. He reaches for the dagger he's sheathed at his thigh, and pulls it out. He hands it to me, and I take it without questioning what he's insinuating.

If we get ambushed, we fight.

Quickly rushing out of the cave, but controlled enough not to spook Alastor, we start hauling our bags onto Alastor. With Eiran's dagger in my hand, and my other one sheathed in my boot, I feel the cool weight of them like I never have before.

Once we get everything settled, a crunch of a twig draws our attention to our far right. When Alastor gives an anxious whinny himself, we know that we aren't imagining things.

We're not alone.

Eiran immediately stands in front of me, and reaches for his sword strapped to his back. The ruby crystal gleaming against the early morning sunrise. With Eiran at my front, and Alastor at my back, I'm sandwiched between them.

Eiran scopes out the forest, trying to see if he can see any movement in the tree line. If someone we're out here, I have no doubt that Eiran will be able to—

My thoughts are ambushed when Eiran backs into me. Panic starts to arise as I can't see much in front of me, until I see it.

A steel-tipped arrowhead piercing straight through his left shoulder, staring directly at me. I watch as his blood covers the area and begins to spread around the wound.

No.

"Meli, get out of here! *Now!*"

"*No*, I'm not leaving you!" I say sternly.

My hand instinctively goes to the arrow in his shoulder as I inspect it. In response Eiran shouts in agony.

"We have to move."

With determination to get us both out of here and to safety, I turn around to swing up onto Alastor. As I brace my left foot up into the stirrup, I feel the sudden loss of Eiran's body heat, as if he was flown from just where he was standing not even a second ago.

Turning around, I see he's squaring off with a man, his grip fastened on the hilt of his sword.

"Well, well, where do y'all think you're goin'?"

My breath hitches as I spin around to face two other men walking towards us on the other side of Alastor. Their clothes look dirty and frayed, like they've been out here in these woods for far longer than we've been.

I take in both of the men that close in on me now. One of them has a coarse, dark brown bread that falls almost halfway down his neck. His beard matches his dark brown cropped hair, though it's apparent it's grown out some. His brown khaki pants are frayed at the bottom, and his black rain jacket is covered in dirt and grass stains.

The other man has sandy brown hair that's pulled back into a bun. By the looks of it, I'd say it's a little longer than shoulder length. His beard is patchy, and resembles more of a bristly goatee, and I notice there's a miniscule cut that sits right above his jawline. His outfit resembles the same as the other guy, brown khaki pants and a black rain jacket.

As the two men close in on us, Alastor begins to start pacing in his place. I try to hold his reins, but realize that if something happens to us, I don't want to see Alastor go down with us.

But as I let go of his reins, he still doesn't leave my side. I watch his jaw clench tight and his ears begin to peel fully back, and I know in an instant that Alastor is going to retaliate against these men.

Before Alastor can shift his body to kick outward at these men, I hear a pained shout. My head whips around to see Eiran stumbling off, but remaining on his feet. My eyes search for him and I realize that he's gripping his arm, the same one that has the arrow embedded into his shoulder still.

Leaving that arrow in Eiran's shoulder I know is causing him an excruciating amount of pain, but pulling it out without assessing the wound could cause him to bleed out.

I look at the man he's defending himself against as a nasty wound that slices across his torso begins to drench his shirt. But that's not the only wound Eiran's sword has inflicted.

My gaze slightly lowers and I see he also has a massive wound on his lower abdomen, and my gods is it bleeding fast.

He's dropped to the ground as he holds his abdomen, blood now pooling out of his mouth.

I need to get to Eiran. As I whip my head back around I notice the men aren't there anymore. Alastor is still very uneasy as he paces in place, but the men are now gone.

In an instant, I hear the loud clink of a sword hitting the ground. I whip my head back around as I realize it's Eiran's sword.

The two men who were just approaching me now have Eiran on his stomach with his arms pinned behind his back. The man with the long beard has his knee shoved into Eiran's back, as he's wrapping his hands behind his back. The goatee man is walking towards his sword, ever so slowly like he has no fear for any retaliation.

Eiran is very athletically built, so with any other man he would probably have been able to resist this guy's hold.

But even as Eiran bucks hard against the man pinning him down, this man is more than twice his size.

Eiran needs me.

I look over at Alastor quickly. "I need to help Eiran, so I need you to stay here. But if something happens, you leave. Okay?"

Holding Alastor's gaze, I doubt he understands what I'm saying. He responds by giving a nervous whinny, and with that I turn back around.

My body trembles as I know I am outnumbered here. I have the dagger that Eiran gave to me, as well as my own, but if this man tries to square off with me with a sword, I'll be sorely bested.

This is exactly what Nikolai warned me about, the dire frenzy in his voice that was clearly trying to warn me is all playing out before me. So I realize my only other option is to use my only advantage against him.

I stand there focusing on infiltrating the goatee man's mind. My emotions are all over the place as my gaze keeps wanting to wander over to Eiran's—

Focus, Meli.

Inhaling in and out again, I refocus my attention on the man. My gaze bores into his skull as he is too busy looking at his friend. I push my way through the barriers of his mind, pushing, pushing–

Nothing.

Snarling, I quickly try again. Eiran needs me, I have to make my way into his mind and cause this man to hallucinate long enough for Eiran and I to get away. As my fists clench and I strain myself to enter his mind, I force myself to push through. Pushing, pushing—

Nothing.

Panic suffocates my entire body and my eyes widen. W-why isn't it working? Knowing I can't afford to sit here and beg the question why, I realize I have to succumb to a different plan. One that I would never be caught succumbing to.

But for Eiran, I would happily set aside my pride to do it.

"Stop!"

I shout at the men who now have Eiran up on his knees, his hands tied behind his back. My body is trembling with a sickening worry that these men are going to kill the one person I've ever grown to bond with. I have to give everything I've got if I'm going to fight for Eiran's life.

Even if it means getting on my knees and pleading.

I stride over to the men, feeling the weight of the dagger that is in my boot.

"Oh yes, I almost forgot about you. My, what a pretty thing you are." The man with the goatee says, eyeing me up in a sick gaze that makes my stomach churn. He now stands before Eiran's sword and I realize I need to think of something fast.

"Just take what you want. But don't hurt him, We mean no harm."

"Oh, but you see, he meant harm when he injured my partner here." The man looks over at the man Eiran was squaring off with, who you can visibly see is bleeding out and dying.

"He wouldn't have had to hurt your partner if he didn't shoot an arrow at him! Your friend is dying, just take him somewhere so he can get some help, and we'll leave like nothing happened."

My voice is calmer than I expect, as I try to will my hands to cease their shaking. I watch the man in front of me keenly, trying to gauge how this is going to go.

I look over at Eiran, and he's mouthing four words to me.

Get. Out. Of. Here.

I shake my head at him, refusing to leave him here with these poachers. The man with the goatee now forms a grin on his face, as he bends down to pick up Eiran's sword. He weighs it in his hand, turning it around to slowly inspect it.

"Well, you see the truth is," he says as he walks slowly over towards the man who lies on the ground. "In a few minutes, he will be dead. So what kind of friend would I be if I didn't just...put him out of his misery?"

In the next second, he's looking down at his friend. In a voice that is too quiet for me to hear, I watch his mouth form the words to his dying partner.

"I'm sorry, friend."

I watch as he swings Eiran's sword through the man's neck, cutting straight through sinew. A terrible wet sound follows as I watch the man's head separate from his body. A quick and painless death.

I immediately lean over to my side, where I retch and vomit. When I finish, my body is visibly trembling. I watch my hands tremble, my breathing panting heavily as I just witnessed someone get their head decapitated off their body.

This man is going to kill Eiran.

I peer my gaze at the man with the goatee, I timidly walk forward as I force my hands back at my side. Now just a few feet away from them, I fall onto my knees. An excruciating hopelessness fills my entire body and my gaze locks onto Eiran once more.

They cannot take him from me.

I move my gaze back onto the man. "I'm sorry for your friend. I'll do anything, name your price. Just don't hurt him."

Before I know it I begin to cry, pleading in my head and now out loud that this man will spare Eiran's life. "He's all I have, please I'll do anything."

The man looks at me, tilting his head with that foul grin now growing in size. Bile rises in my throat as I can only imagine exactly what this man is thinking about.

"You see, the three of—well, now the two of us," he says as he gives an insidious look at his dead friend. He continues. "have roamed this forest many, many times. Since this forest is nowhere near any villages, it's very rare for us to come across other people. Unless…"

He trails off as he continues to stare at me, with his head cocked to the side like he's imagining a scenario in his head. "Unless you two are out here in search of Vulir."

My body freezes as my crying dissipates.

He begins to walk towards me, his silence stretching on as he takes deliberately slow steps. It's evident this is a game to him, one he's getting off on. As he approaches me, his body seems to relax as he inhales, and exhales dramatically.

"You know where Vulir is, don't you?"

He knows about Vulir, but he doesn't know *where* it is. I realize this gives me the upper hand, and use this to my advantage. My body begins to cease its trembling as I meet his gaze.

"That depends. Agree to free him, and maybe I will share my knowledge with you."

Bringing my chin up, I try to fake a demeanor of confidence even though I still have no idea how to get there. I can't let him know that though if it means keeping Eiran alive.

He studies me curiously, as he brings a hand up to his chin and begins tapping his beard.

Gods, how I want to kick that fucking chin in.

Trying to reel in my anger that begins to rise, I wait for him to answer as he purposefully takes an excruciating long time. I look over at Eiran, who's eyes keep glancing from mine to the guy. His eyes read both fear and an undeniable rage. Finally, my attention is drawn as he speaks.

"I'll tell you what. I'll take you up on your offer, the one where you say you'll do *anything* for him." He says with a wink, and I nearly vomit again right then and there.

My skin goes cold and clammy.

"You show us to Vulir, as I know that we are close. I have scoured this forest for months, but dreadfully we're always coming up short. I have a particular…interest with something Vulir has."

I have gone completely numb, mainly for the fact that I am not ready for whatever this man plans to do to me. I look at Eiran and his jaw is clenched so damn tight the veins in his neck bulge. He's bucking against the guy who has him pinned still.

"Meli, don't! I'm not worth the trauma, don't do this–"

The guy moves his knee so now he's burrowing his neck into the ground, cutting Eiran off from speaking. I just want these people to stop hurting him. I want to go back to how things were, or how things were seeming to progress with us. I will do anything for him if it means keeping him alive.

I ignore Eiran and look up at the man who still looms over me. I shove every ounce of nausea and unwanted imaginations of what this man is capable of. He's agreeing to my deal, which means Eiran will be alive.

And I…

I will survive, one way or another.

Gritting my teeth, I respond. "You've got a deal. Now untie his hands."

The goatee man smiles, but it is far from genuine. His insidious nature looms behind it, and I begin to wonder what he's got planned for me. He begins to walk slowly over to Eiran and his partner, where he's going to untie his restraints. Hope starts to spark within.

He's letting him go, this is good.

Let's just get these fuckers to Vulir, and then we can be free of them. I'll have Eiran by my side, he'll help me process through the trauma. I won't have to do it alone.

He reaches Eiran, and motions for his partner to stand Eiran up fully. His partner gets up, dragging Eiran up by his bound wrists. Holding him there, the man with the goatee looks Eiran in his eyes.

"You have some *friend* there, willing to do anything for your behalf. It's just a shame."

I freeze and everything goes completely numb.

Everything around me goes unnaturally silent. The only sounds I can focus on are the words coming out of this man's mouth, and the quickening of my heart beat.

No.

"A shame that regardless of any deal she makes, I will still seek revenge for our fallen brother."

I watch immobilized as the man raises Eiran's sword, an heirloom passed down from generation to generation. I watch as it now pierces down on Eiran, straight through his chest.

CHAPTER 17

A dreadfully continuous, high-pitched scream crushes my eardrums. It's agonizing and difficult to hear anything else other than the profound screaming.

Screaming that I realize is coming from me.

For a few moments I can't seem to focus on anything other than the suffocating hollowness that overwhelms my entire body. How I can't seem to pull my body up from the damp ground. As I sink into myself, I hear the footfalls of a man walking towards me.

Eiran is…dying.

I spring back into awareness as I jump up onto my feet. I begin to dash to Eiran when the man responsible for his staggering breaths grabs my shoulder, blocking me from running to him. I was being docile before, as to hopefully better my chances of protecting my best friend. My love.

To better contain myself so I wouldn't risk setting these men off, so they would hopefully take my deal.

But I am no longer interested in being docile.

I swing my dagger up towards his chest but he knocks it out of my hand before the blade can even knick his skin. I swing my hand out and punch the man in the cheek. When he instinctively pulls his hand up to touch his cheek, I dash over to Eiran.

The other man who had his knee in Eiran's back, sees me fastly approaching and just stands there. I can tell by the look on his face, he's thinking to himself *"It doesn't matter, her friend is dying anyway."* But he is unaware of the other dagger I still have in my boot.

As I close in on the man, I reach for my dagger at just the right moment. When I reach down, there's a split second where the man's expression changes. I smile at his change in expression

"You'll be lying next to your friend real soon."

Taking all of the built up rage that's currently imploding inside of me, I grab my dagger and buck up so that I'm shoving the dagger straight through his neck. He immediately begins to reach for the hilt to try and pull it out, so I do the honors and pull it out for him.

Where I then drive it straight into his chest, right into his heart.

In the next second, his face begins to turn slack as he falls down to his knees, and then to his feet. Catching him off guard was my only advantage, and I know I won't have the same advantage with the other guy. But I'll surely try.

At that thought, I turn to see the other guy charging for me, still with the sword in his hand. I need to get him to drop that sword–

My thoughts flush as my gaze darts towards the bow and arrow. I look over to see it near the guy that Eiran killed–

Eiran…

Meli, focus.

Shaking my mournful thoughts away for now, I rush to the bow and arrow laying on the ground. Quickly picking it up I knock an arrow. The guy with the goatee has his enraged gaze set on me, the sword wielded in the air ready to strike. If I don't act now, he's going to close in on me and I'll be disadvantaged.

Knocking the arrow back, I release and it misses.

Fuck.

The guy is nearly closing in on me, and I realize I have one shot left. Pulling another arrow I immediately knock it.

I have to make this one count, I think to myself.

For Eiran.

I release and it strikes true. I was trying to aim for the guy's chest, but instead it aimed for his thigh. The man shouts as he stumbles onto his side, dropping the sword as he clutches his thigh.

Sprinting to Eiran's sword, my knees slam harshly against the ground and I manage to grab it before the man can crawl close enough. I stand with it now as now I loom over him, a dark rage washing over me.

Cold vengeance takes over my mind, injecting itself through every vein. For my dearest friend, my love. It courses through my bones, and seeps out of my pores. The rush of pure darkness overwhelming but a sinful promise of retribution.

And I allow it to coax me.

"How the tables have turned now." I say in a voice that stains of murderous delight.

The man doesn't even beg for mercy, like he's too proud to plead for his life. He smiles at me as he spits at my feet, his ignorance provoking the darkness within. "Well, don't be shy now. Do I—"

I bear the sword down on his chest. He must've had a slight doubt about my willingness to actually follow through, because for a split moment his eyes bulged out, a surprised expression painting his cruel face. I remove the sword as blood coats the blade, dripping onto the ground. He brings a hand up to the wound, as his eyes wildly roam my face. I smile at his discomfort.

"Don't worry, your death will be far more agonizing than your friends."

I bring the sword down onto his arm, watching the severed limb fall to the ground. An agonized scream fills the air around us as the man cries, and I find that I'm far from uncomfortable from the blood that's gushing from his wound. It fills me with great satisfaction.

I bring the sword down firmly on his other arm, and then swipe it across his chest.

The sword swipes through him again, and again.

Until I realize that I am now matching his agonized screams with my own. My eyes burn as tears stream down my face, mixing with his blood splattered across my cheeks. What is left of the man is now nothing more than a butchered bloody mess.

My body is wracking violently as grief implodes through me. Grief that they took the only person from me that truly loved me.

My shaky legs tremble as I rush over to Eiran lying on the ground. I feel like I'm in a fever dream and that I'll wake up any minute now, and know that this was just all a horrible nightmare.

How just last night Eiran and I were nestled together in that cave.

And now he lies a dying man.

I rush to his side and see he's struggling to keep himself tethered to stay alive. I realize that no amount of anything I do will keep him alive, and that he'll be gone within minutes.

Eiran looks at me warily, as blood is beginning to trickle out of his mouth. My hands move to his handsome face, as I level his gaze with mine.

"I'm here. I'm right here." I choke as tears continue to stream down my cheek.

Eiran opens his mouth as if to try and speak, but I interrupt him when I notice he's struggling to do so.

"Don't speak. I won't leave you, you hear me? I'm—" I choke on a painful sob before I can continue. "I'm *right here.*"

I move my hand over his chest, where one of his hands lay. I grab onto his hand so tight I think I may break his hand. I grab onto his hand almost to prove to myself that if I just hang on tight enough, he won't leave me.

"I—" Eiran says, pulling my gaze from his wound back to him. I watch him work on a swallow that seems entirely too uncomfortable, but he continues nonetheless. "I love you. I—I always have…"

As if the bleak silence around us wasn't already jarring enough, life goes even quieter at his confession. Eiran and I have told each other before how much we love each other, but that's been different. More of like a deep, genuine friendship type of love.

But he *loves* me.

My heart shatters inside my chest and my mouth trembles violently as I sob. I bring his hands up to my lips as I kiss them, my tears falling over his fingertips.

He…*loves* me.

The pain of hearing those words cracks me wide open and I can't think of anything other than the fact that I won't experience what it's like to be deeply loved by Eiran, an honorable man and friend. That I never got a chance to let myself be open to his love, even though it was right there in front of me. And now, I never will.

I realize that this is not the time for me to resist whatever I have felt for him, and truths spill out of my lips like honey.

"I love you. I—I'm so sorry I couldn't love you sooner. I—" My lips quiver as my body quakes violently with grief. "I was afraid. I'm so sorry. I resisted anything further between us because I thought I was better on my own. But

I won't be fine! Because *your* love is what keeps me sane. *Your* companionship is what's kept me going."

My head burrows into the crook of his neck, without a care if I'm getting blood on me or not. I'm sobbing to the point of hyperventilation and clutch onto Eiran's sweater so tight that fabric burrows underneath my nails.

This isn't supposed to happen like this.

He's the only person who has ever made me feel seen and appreciated, when I've grown up my whole life feeling useless to the people around me.

He's everything to me, and now he's going to die.

I pull my face up to meet his softened gaze. I stare at his handsome face as it begins to relax, and I watch as he begins to form a slight upward curve to his lips.

"Ah, I…get it."

Confused by his statement, and petrified by how relaxed his body is becoming, I shake his hand to look at me. He gives a weak squeeze in response, as if to tell me he feels my presence still.

"Eiran, please don't leave me. I can't lose you, please!" I plead with him through my tears.

He slowly looks at me, the color beginning to drain from his face rapidly. He opens his mouth one last time.

"I…am always…here…for you."

I watch as his face goes completely slack and all the life vanishes from his face. I watch the very second that it's evident his soul has left his body, and the torment of knowing shatters me.

"Eiran!" My voice screeches on a cry. I squeeze his hands, trying to get him to mimic the same gesture.

When I feel nothing, I feel the heavy burden of knowing flood me.

Eiran is dead.

For a long time, I can't bring myself to close his eyes. Feeling like the moment I shut his eyelids closed, I shut him out from this lifetime.

A lifetime where he can never come back to me.

Lost to me for good.

I sit there next to Eiran and cry for a very long time. It's not until the sun has reached the highest point in the sky when I realize that it's been several hours. The amount of crying my body purges does not ease up and my lips begin to dry severely from dehydration.

Alastor at some point has returned to my side. I'm not sure exactly when that was, but as I finally pull my gaze away from Eiran, I realize he's laying next to me.

As I look down at my hands I take in the blood that's sprayed upon them.

Blood that belongs to the men who killed Eiran.

I can't even bring myself to look at the men right now, though the heat from the suns peaking rays reminds me that they're still here.

My gaze falls somberly back to Eiran, with my hand still cradling his own.

Taking my other hand I lightly trace my fingertips over his full lips. I begin to tremble at the fact that these are lips I was just kissing not even a full day ago. The same lips that spoke words of admiration to me.

Tears stream down my face as I stare at my beautiful friend, who I had just agreed to become something more with, and I feel the crushing weight of despair sink heavily onto me. My stomach begins to rumble, but I can't bring myself to get up to get the little bit of food that we have left.

I can't bring myself to leave this spot.

I can't leave Eiran.

I begin to lower myself next to him, cradling myself into his lifeless body. He's still warm, but I know soon that it will no longer be that way. I take his arm and drape it over me, frantically needing to feel an ounce of his warmness soothe the gut-wrenching pain I feel from his loss. Instead, I am reminded that he will never kiss me again.

Never be able to laugh with him again.

My mind goes numb, as I feel every ounce of optimism excavate itself out of me.

The hope in finding Vulir.

The excitement for a new life.

The bravery to fight.

Now, all that's left is a gaping hole that infiltrates my whole body.

I feel nothing. I am numb, and I do not have the desire to fight it.

CHAPTER 18

It must be late because the sky around us is completely dark now. I don't think I've slept at all, I think now is just the first time I've been coherent enough to notice.

My body is here, but my mind isn't. Every now and then, I sink my fingers into Eiran's clothing and I'm reminded that he's still here.

My stomach growls again and this time, the hollowness I'm feeling has accompanied another terrible sensation: starvation. The last time I…the last time Eiran and I ate was yesterday sometime. Judging by how dark it is, I'd say we're following into the late hours of the night, possibly nearing the brink of dawn.

I want to stay right here though.

I need him.

I cannot leave him. Not yet.

Alastor nudges me and I think he worries for me. He can't be hungry because there's grass all around us, even if that's not an adequate diet for him. As if my body is moving itself for me, I find myself at my duffel bag scouring for food. My mind can't wrap itself around how I even managed to get here when all I can feel is the coldness of Eiran's body.

I pull out a little bit of nuts and a few pieces of bread left. I bring everything over to Eiran, including his hunting bag. Immense sadness clogs my throat as I bring everything over, sitting down next to Eiran once more.

I stare at the food in front of me, the drive to eat scarily evading me.

I'm hungry, but I don't want to eat. My thoughts darken as I wonder:

"Maybe if I starve myself, I'll eventually die too. Then, I can be with him again…"

But I know that's not what Eiran would want.

Taking what's left of the food and gingerly eating it, it's not nearly enough to fulfill my raging hunger. But I can't leave his side right now. He's the only loving presence that's ever been in my life, and I'm not ready to let that go yet.

Once I polish off what's left of the food, I cradle myself back up next to Eiran. I bring my hands to grip his sweater, beginning to feel his body grow more and more cold. I clutch the fabric in between my finger nails, and I tightly shut my eyes.

"I'm not ready. I'm not ready." My lips quiver as I mumble to myself. With my nose burrowed into Eiran's chest, I inhale deeply hoping to have the smell of his cologne—-anything sink itself in my nose and bring me some comfort. Instead, all I smell is the metallic blood that pools around him.

That pools around us, as I lie in it with him.

Tears once again stream from my eyes as I cry into his arms. And eventually at some point, I do manage to fall asleep.

"Meli."

My eyes break wide open as I hear a familiar voice call for me.

"Eiran?" My voice cracks as I find myself yet again, standing in the forest. The grass seeping in between my toes, as I look to see him standing before me. My breath hitches and I instantly break out into a dash as I run towards him.

I can tell right away that I'm dreaming.

I rush into Eiran and I can *feel* him.

None of that matters right now as Eiran is in my line of sight. I grab onto him but the shock causes my knees to buckle as I fall to the ground, nearly pulling him down with me.

I sob violently as Eiran kneels down to reach his hands out to reel me into him. I can feel his body as he holds me and it only makes me shake and sob even more uncontrollably. He holds me like this for what seems like a long time, but I know better than to think that these types of dreams last long.

Before I pull myself away to look at him, I feel an intense buzzing sensation rack my body. It's so potent, that I almost question myself if I'm actually dreaming or not. I pull myself from Eiran, looking at him as he stares at me with a calm smile on his face.

"H—how? I can *feel* you?" I can't help but stammer with my words.

"It's my energy. You're feeling my energy."

I let what he says sink in as I think back to that one time with that woman. She did the same thing with me, except it was much gentler than it is right now with Eiran. Realizing I don't know how much time I have left, I lean in and kiss him.

Oh, my gods I can *feel* the kiss.

He meets my same franticness and kisses me deeply, as the energy between us pulses and spreads. I break away from the kiss, taking him in as I gaze at him. "I can *feel* that. Actually feel your mouth on me. Can you?"

"I can." Eiran says with a smile as his hands come up to wipe away the tears from my eyes. He gazes at me, an innocent longing in his eyes before he speaks again. *"Meli, listen to me. I love you, and I will always love you. I told you I would do anything for you, and I meant it. None of this is your fault. I would've done it all again, if it meant to protect you."*

Tears stream down my eyes once more.

"I know you don't want to leave me, your will to want to keep going is...weakened, I see it here on the other side. But promise me something."

"Anything." I replied without hesitation.

Eiran gives me a look as if I'm going to resist what he's about to ask me. *"I need you to bury my body, and keep going to Vulir."*

His words make my heart sink so low I think it's going to fall out of the soles of my feet. I can't go to Vulir, I can't leave him here—

"No. I can't! I need to be here with you. Who's going to look out for you? Who's going to tell your–oh my gods. Who's going to tell your roommates you're—" I can't even bring myself to finish the sentence.

Instead, Eiran brings my gaze back to him. *"Meli, I get it now. I've become clear of what my path is, I'm not going anywhere. You'll understand soon."*

Confusion tampering all of my thoughts. "What do you mean 'your path'? So what, your path was to just *die* for me? And no, you won't be here because you're *dead*! How will you be here for me?" I begin to sob as it feels like my heart can't take anymore crying, but yet it still keeps coming.

"Meli, think about it. I'm here right now, talking to you. Touching you. Don't you see? My purpose is to be a guide for you. Both in the physical world and in the spiritual. Our bond just makes it so much easier for you to communicate with me."

For a moment I stop crying as I take in what he's saying. He is right, other than with that one lady, I've never been able to have such encounters with other spirits.

My mouth gapes open at him. "So, you're now a guide for me on the other side?

"Yes. But I'm not the only guide you have over here. Meli, you have so many spirits that stand behind you. I know you can't see it but, you have an incredible team over here that is willing to throw down for you."

I have a *team*? On the other side?

The thought of having people—spirits, anything really supporting me clogs my throat with immense emotion. I've felt so alone all of my life. So misunderstood.

But knowing that I have what sounds like a whole lot of love and support on the other side, makes me more eager to nurture my gifts.

"I'll be here for you as you travel to Vulir, and I'll be here for you as you further your gifts, I'll be here for it all. I'm not going anywhere." Eiran says as he interrupts my thoughts. *"Everything...is going to turn out for you. Everything."* He says with a genuine smile that warms my grieving heart.

Even with his admission, I can't help but still feel a pang of guilt begin to cloud my energy.

"But...what if I just want to stay with you. For just a little while longer? I don't know if I'm ready to leave you just yet."

"I'm afraid you don't have much of a choice, Meli. You're all out of food, and you need to eat soon."

Eiran grabs my hands, my eyes glancing down at our joining hands that I very much feel. His energy is still reverberating through me. I meet his gaze again as he stares at me with pure admiration.

"It's okay to bury my body, and leave me. You aren't doing a disservice to me, as I will see you again soon anyway. This is the part where I need you to put your needs first. Find food and water, and get to Vulir. You're so close, Meli, you don't even realize it. I didn't when I was alive."

Suddenly my surroundings begin to slither away and I know exactly what this means.

I begin to panic as I desperately want this moment to last. I just want a little while longer with him. To feel him, to touch him.

Eiran grabs my face, giving me one last kiss that I feel throughout my entire body. When he pulls away, he looks at me. *"Go. Trust me, I'm not going anywhere."*

Before I can respond, everything turns black.

I spring awake, and he's gone.

With his lifeless, physical body lying next to me in his place.

CHAPTER 19

As I lie next to Eiran's cold body, rain begins to fall. It starts off as a gentle rain shower, but soon turns much heavier. I've been awake for a little while now, and I know Eiran would want me to get up and do as he wished.

The despair that weighs on me seems to keep me anchored right next to him. I haven't eaten since yesterday, and my stomach feels like it's caving into itself. If I don't want to starve myself, I'm going to have to actually get up and get moving.

The grief of leaving Eiran's body floods me.

Sitting up, I realize I am a bit weaker than I imagined I'd be by this point. My head hurts and my insides feel like chalk.

I need to find water and food.

I reach over to my duffel bag where my water flask is, uncapping it as I down the rest that's left. Grabbing the water flask, I stand up and head over to the water stream that's nearby. Alastor trails behind me, assuming he's thirsty as well. Or maybe he can just tell that I'm weaker than normal. I'm sure I look like shit.

The ground is beginning to become muddy from the rain, so every now and then as I walk I nearly slip on my ass.

Once we get to the stream, I fill my water flask up as full as it'll let me. Taking a few minutes to allow Alastor to get his fill from the stream, I sat thinking to myself about something Eiran had said.

"You're so close, Meli, you don't even realize it. I didn't when I was alive."

As I trail my fingers on my lips, I vividly remember how it felt to kiss him. My fingers begin to tremble as grief plows through me again.

If I wasn't so wrapped up into my own shit with my family maybe I would've noticed my growing feelings sooner. Where maybe we could've had more together, before it was too late.

If I hadn't sought out this trip, Eiran would still be alive.

Tears welcome my red and puffy eyes once more. I'm not used to crying this much, but I also realize I'm not nearly used to allowing myself to show this much emotion. I'm used to putting on a tough face, and handling everything while shoving every emotion down in the process. But this time, the grief and terrible sadness has conquered its tumultuous place, and it demands my attention.

I have no choice but to surrender to it.

Wiping the dampness from my eyes, which doesn't seem to help much considering the rain that's pelting my face, I try my best to clear my mind. I take a few deep breaths in, and exhale slowly, trying my best to save the interference of depression for later.

Think, Meli. Eiran says that we're close to Vulir. I look all around me, and in every direction nothing stands out to me. There's probably hundreds of trees that fill this entire forest, with no distinguishable landmarks that stand out to me.

But that's not what will stand out to me.

"Trust your intuition, it will be your best guide."

I begin by closing my eyes, trying my damn hardest to center myself. When nothing comes to mind, I open my eyes and look back over at Eiran.

Getting up from the muddy ground, I travel back to where Eiran's body is with Alastor next to me. Before I sit next to Eiran again, I turn to Alastor.

"Okay buddy, I need you to be my eyes and ears for a moment. I need to meditate and figure out how we get ourselves to Vulir. Okay?"

Alastor gives me a whinny and as I move to sit next to Eiran, Alastor stands right next to me, his attention alert and focused.

I swear this horse understands me.

Sitting down in a cross-legged position next to Eiran, I look down at his lifeless face. I give a pained smile, as I place my hand over his once again.

"I'm not sure if this will work, but it's worth a shot."

With my hand on Eiran's, I close my eyes and take a few deep breaths.

Trying to focus on the feel of his hand to keep me grounded, I focus on how his energy felt to me last night. As I sit here, eyes closed, I try to focus on my surroundings without opening my eyes. For a while, everything is pitch dark as nothing materializes. This is what I get for not meditating much more frequently.

Focusing on my breathing, I let my body and my mind relax. After a while, I begin to feel tingling in my body.

I follow that feeling, and suddenly my surroundings begin to materialize in front of me. They materialize in my mind.

I can see the green begin to paint the tall trees, the mud thickening on the ground around me, even Alastor who's standing guard next to me.

Then, I see him.

I first feel his energy radiating near me, and as I walk forward towards it, I find his handsome self standing there.

"See, now you're getting it." Eiran says with a wink.

I run up to him and wrap my arms around him. It takes me a few moments before I finally let go. When my gaze meets his, I see a smile on his face. It gives me comfort to see him acting so…relaxed even though he just died not even two days ago.

"I didn't think that would work. I just had a thought to try it, and holy shit it worked."

"That's because you're finally listening to your intuition. It guided you to do this, to help you, and you listened."

He's right, I listened to the nudge that told me meditating would help me seek out Eiran, and would then help me find my next step to getting to Vulir.

For the first time in days I feel the upward curve of my mouth as I smile hard. Realizing I don't have much time, I get right to asking what I need from Eiran.

"What do I look for? What can you tell me about where I need to look next?"

"From here you need to ride north, just four miles out. You'll come across a part in the forest where a set of trees will form a crescent moon. There will be a small opening in between the middle of the trees, that's your entrance."

"Okay." I say, feeling a little more confident now with knowing that information.

"Look for the glimmer, only those who seek pure intentions with Vulir will be able to see the glimmer. Approach it and speak these words out loud: I wish to grant access to Vulir. You'll be invited in."

My entrance is through some damn trees? Through a mystical…fog? This sounds like some fucking crazy folktale shit, but Eiran wouldn't lie to me.

"Okay, I got it."

Eiran is smiling at me so big, the sight slightly uncomfortable for someone who just died. It makes me wonder if he truly has found peace through his death, and is at peace with his end. The thought saddening me for some reason.

"You'll meet Charon. He's the gatekeeper to Vulir, he will tell you where to go. You've got this, Meli. You're so close."

"I just wish you were here to experience it with me." My smile forms a frown as guilt seeps into my chest. Eiran doesn't falter his smile even at my admission. Instead, he tilts his head slightly, giving me a look as implying that's not the truth.

"I told you, I'm here with you every step of the way. I've got your back, just over here now." He puts his hand on my shoulder, and immediately the energy pulsates between us. *"I'm not going anywhere."*

I lift my hand up to meet his, and the energy begins to electrify. The shock it brings to me hasn't gotten familiar quite yet, and my breath hitches in response. I look at Eiran, whose admiring gaze falls on mine.

"Go. There's an incline by the water stream that you can bury my body in. The rain will have made it easier to bury me. But then you must go, Meli."

Tears welling my eyes, I bite my bottom lip as I nod in agreement.

Eiran brings me in for a warm embrace, and I cherish the energy that I can feel radiate off of him. As I embrace him, I feel his energy slip away, until in the next moment he's gone.

I open my eyes and decide it's time to finally give Eiran a proper burial.

Eiran was right. There was an incline down by the stream that made burying him a lot easier considering I have no tools to assist me.

After I opened my eyes, I hauled Eiran's body down the incline. Thankfully, it was near me so I didn't have to drag his body far. He's quite heavy, and I hardly have the strength left in me to be doing any heavy lifting.

Once we reached the incline I began to dig out his grave. At this point, I'm undeniably covered in mud from my soaked pants that kneel in the mud, to my hands and up to my elbows from digging his grave.

It's almost as if the gods initiated this rain so it would help make it much easier to dig out here. I'm sure that's just crazy thinking, but whatever. It's surely fucking helping right now.

There's a few times where I have to take a break and catch my breath, ever so often feeling a dizziness begin to take over. I grab my water flask and slam a few gulps of water down, but that hardly seems to help any longer. Because what my body is begging for now is food. But I won't leave until I have Eiran buried.

After a long time, when I finally have something deep enough to drag Eiran's body into, I grab him by his feet. Before I do, I take one last look at his now rain drenched face.

"I wish we could've done this at home, you know, not covered in rain and mud. But this is what we have for now."

I trail the back of my hand across his cheek, knowing that he's no longer in there anymore but still painting his face to memory. I shed a few more tears for him, giving him a kiss on that same cheek before I dragged him into the hole.

It's not a very deep hole, and that's mainly because I'm too weak to dig much further, but it's deep enough to be able to get a decent layer of soil over him where the only way he'll be seen is if someone goes digging around over here.

As I cup handfuls of muddy soil to cover his body with, I mutter loving final words to him. I mutter things like how much he has helped me through moments that I felt powerless. How he's never questioned me and always made me feel understood. How his kind heart is what I loved most about him, even when he himself had troubling circumstances as a child that could've turned him cold.

I tell him how much I love him, how his friendship and love has always meant everything to me, and how lost I would've been without it. How lost I will be without it.

I lastly thank him, for risking his own life for me to protect me, and how I will spend the rest of my life proving to him that he didn't risk it for nothing.

I vow to him, and to myself, I will start to live my life for me.

After he's fully covered, I place my hand over his new grave, and I whisper to him once more.

"I will make you proud."

With that, I stand as I take one last glance at the grave I just dug for my dear Eiran, and I walk back to where our things are. When I grab my duffel bag, I come face to face with Eiran's hunting bag. For a moment, it really sets in that I've just buried his body and he's truly dead. His things still remain.

I decided to take his bag with me. Finding the dagger I sheath it onto my thigh, then I grab his sword.

My feelings immediately range from grief as this was the sword Eiran died by, but also sorrow as I don't know if I can part with it because it was *his* sword. Conflicted with what I want to do with it, I try to think of what Eiran would want me to do. And what my intuition is telling me, is that Eiran would want no one else but me to have it in his honor. Even if it's the weapon that so regretfully brought him his death.

I move to strap it to my back, and bring it along with me.

As I swing myself onto Alastor, with both mine and Eiran's bags strapped onto my steed, I take one last look around. I look over to where the three men still lay, two of them dead by my hands. If it weren't for the rain, the blood would still be there, dried from their wounds.

As I look at them, I imagined I would feel at least a sliver of revulsion for I've never killed someone before.

That bile would rise in my throat that one man lays butchered and it's all thanks to me.

Instead, I feel revenge. I feel rageful power.

As I turn back around, I gently squeeze my heels into Alastor, and we're off.

Eiran said to travel about four miles north, which doesn't take us long as Alastor moves at an uncomfortably fast pace.

Uncomfortable as I'm beginning to feel tired and all I want to do is just lie down. I feel my stomach rumbling and I swear it's loud enough for the wildlife mingling around to hear. I'm beginning to feel light headed when I feel like I need to lean over to vomit.

Fighting back the urge, I steady my breathing and keep telling myself we should be there soon. That as soon as I get through Vulir, I'll figure out a way to get some food in me. Also get some food for Alastor as well.

Almost an hour after weaving through the forest, I see the patch of trees Eiran was talking about. I see the formation of the crescent moon, and I immediately pull us to a stop.

As I swing myself off Alastor, I stumble to the ground. At first I blamed it on the fact it's still raining, and that the mud has made the ground too slippery for me to bear. But when my vision starts to feel fuzzy, and my breathing begins to pace, I realize it's not because of the muddy ground.

We're almost there, Meli. Get up.

I push myself onto my feet, my legs feeling scarily shaky. I grab Alastors reins and guide us closer to the tree formation. As I get closer, I try to find this glimmer that Eiran was talking about. He said it would be right in the middle of the tree formation. Looking, I don't see it.

As I approach right up to it, Alastor begins to sniff the air in front of us. His ears begin to twitch from front to back.

"What is it? Do you feel or hear something?"

I look straight ahead. It should be right here—

Suddenly, I'm on the ground again and I'm having a hard time keeping myself up. I'm reaching my body's limit. I just need a little longer.

I hear Alastor begin to give a nervous whinny as he nudges me as if to tell me to get up.

I…almost there. Get….up.

My vision begins to fade as I force my head to look up and–

There it is.

It's so subtle, and translucent so it blends with our surroundings. But right up close, it's there.

I begin to feel myself fading in and out of consciousness.

No.

Without wasting any more time, I speak. "I…wish to grant access to Vulir…"

I'm barely holding myself up from the muddy ground, waiting for something to happen. I slip as I can't hold myself up any longer.

Fuck. No, no, no. I did not come all this way to just pass out right here.

Steadying my voice, I try again. This time a little louder. "I wish to grant access to Vulir–"

My voice cuts off as I fall to the ground, my arms no longer able to hold me up as I tremble ferociously.

I tried. I'm here. But I'm just so damn…tired.

I begin to slip into nothingness.

At some point, I can feel myself floating. Why would I be floating? I can't be dead though. I didn't go without food and water for that long…

Yet instead of fighting it, I just let myself slip further, and further until I lose consciousness again…

At some point, I come back to consciousness again. I can't seem to pry my eyes open and I assume I'm too weak to do so. I take note of how the brisk air feels as it whips against my body. I feel something cradle my body upwards, as my head rests against a rough texture. It feels like someone is carrying me.

My delirium assumes it's Eiran carrying me to the afterlife. And so, I let him as I let myself slip back under once more.

Ready to spend an eternity with him in the afterlife, rather than an existence without him...

CHAPTER 20

I'm conscious once more, this time laying on something warm and dry. My mind brings me back to my last conscious memory.

I was in the mud, in front of the gate to Vulir but I passed out before anyone could hear me and let me in. Well someone must've heard me because I'm definitely not outside in the pouring rain anymore.

Groggily peeling my eyes open, I lie on my back as I stare up at a ceiling. It's dark in here, so all I can make out is the soft glow of something that illuminates a section to the left.

I turn my head towards it and see the orange glow that is emanating from a fireplace. My body begins to register the heat emanating from it. The mantle has beautiful detailing in it, definitely not something that someone with little to no money would have.

Did I make it to Vulir?

Whose room is this—

Panic begins to ensue as I realize I am in a *bedroom*. Jerking upright into a seated position, my gaze begins to scour around as I take in my surroundings.

Next to the fireplace is an open door that leads to a bathroom. I can't see much from the bed, but what I can make out is a porcelain white clawfoot tub. There's a window that's positioned right above it, with a dark cherry-colored wooden rack that appears to have different arrays of soaps on it.

Sliding my attention back to the room, right in front of me is a large dresser. The wood is the same color as the rack in the bathroom, and there's not much that sits on top of it, other than a mirror that hangs on the wall. Catching myself in the mirror I begin to crawl out of bed and move closer to the mirror and–my gods.

I look like shit.

My hair matted down from the mud I trekked in, my clothes darkened from the blood I was lying in. My face looks slightly sunken in, like the evidence of starvation is prevalent in my features. Yet, I don't feel so hungry anymore?

Did I eat already? Whose room is this?

I look back towards the bed. It's a beautifully large, old-fashioned canopy bed with four posters at each corner. The wood is a deep midnight black, but no curtains hang from it.

I trace my fingers over the silken black sheets, running my fingers over the noticeable sweat stains that I've left in my wake. As my gaze turns to a chair that sits right next to the bed, I notice all of my things are perched on it.

My duffel bag along with Eiran's.

I immediately rummage through it, and everything is there. Except for one thing.

Eiran's sword.

Fury blasts through me as it's clear that someone took it since last I remember I had it strapped to my back. Instantly at that thought, I check and notice another thing is gone.

My dagger.

Instead of fury now panic racks through my body. Not only am I in someone's room, I am also defenseless in unknown territory. The thought jostles me as I have no idea if I'm truly safe here or not. I begin to look around for something, anything I can use as a weapon.

Searching around the room, I grow wary as I can't find anything other than pillows, blankets, and a few two-branched candelabras.

I'm fucked.

I decided to settle with the candelabra. After grabbing one I can feel the surprising weight that clings to it, and grow a little more at ease because of it.

I begin to hear footsteps coming from the hallway outside of the bedroom door. As they grow closer, I realize I don't have time to hide. I'll just have to catch them by surprise.

I hurry over behind the door, standing next to it so when it opens, I can strike. I decide that I'm just going to give it my all and fight like hell.

When the footsteps stop right in front of the door, they take a few seconds before they actually open the door.

When they do, at first it's slow as if just to peak inside. When they see I'm clearly not in the bed anymore, they open it all the way. That's when I make my move.

I step out from behind the door and wail the candelabra over their head. I don't even think twice about it or wonder who this mystery person can be. I hear a grunt as the man stumbles, holding his head.

Gripping the candelabra in my hand, I rush around him and run to exit out of the room. I'm quickly interrupted with the weight of his arm wrapped around my shoulders, right below my neck. His other arm swings out as he grabs the candelabra, tossing it to the floor.

"Sorry little spitfire, but you're going to have to do a lot better than that with me."

His voice is deep and his tone drips with a coldness that seeps through my bones. My breath hitches as he has me pinned against his chest. I buck against him, my arms wailing as I try to land blows anywhere I possibly can on this man. Since it's evident I won't get my way out of his arms by fighting, I decide on a different, more crafty approach.

I move one arm behind me, moving down as my hand scales his hard abdomen. I move my hand lower until it rests on his waist, my fingers playing with the buttons on his jeans. I feel his tall body stiffen and his arms unfasten the slightest, and take that as my cue to act. I spring out of his arms as I run out of the bedroom, having no idea which way is the way out of this damn place. It doesn't matter, I will keep running until I'm someplace safe.

Before I can make it halfway down the hallway I feel the crushing weight of the man slam into my back, bringing us down. Before we both slam onto the ground, he shifts us so he takes the fall, pinning me to his chest.

"Get the fuck off of me!" I scream as I thrash against his hold. I do not know who this man thinks he is, but he will know who the fuck I am.

I cease my movement as a smile curves up on my face. Closing my eyes, I focus on the man underneath me. I focus on infiltrating his mind, and once I've felt myself succeed, I let the darkness override his mind.

I feel his body go stiff behind me, and I take satisfaction that it's doing what I intend for it to do. I want to drive this man who kidnapped me utterly mad. And when I feel his arms loosen this time, I won't give him the opportunity to re-capture me. What I visualize in his mind is possibly cruel, but I'm in no mood for being pleasant right now.

I visualize the room around us turning to ash, flumes of smoke wafting all around us. I visualize the people that he loves nothing more than crisp, decaying bodies. All of them coated in maggots, feeding off of their entrails. I visualize him covered in blood—

Suddenly he twirls us over until I'm on the ground and he's pinning me down with the weight of his body. I open my eyes and confusion floods me.

Nobody has ever been able to resist my hallucinations before.

"And you have tricks, too? Now I'm thoroughly curious." He says as he gives me a wicked, cold grin. I gasp at his reaction and fear that this man not only will kill me now, but also knows my secret.

Fucking damnit.

"I guess you didn't hear me the first time, but I asked you to get the fuck *off* of me!" I protest as I squirm against him, trying to free myself from his hold.

"I can do that. Under one condition—"

"*No*. You don't get to make conditions with me." I seethe.

He looks at me with his head tilt, a grin still plastered on his face. "Has someone ever told you it's rude to interrupt someone when they're speaking?"

My brows furrow as my anger scalds within me. I take a deep frustrating breath in and release it raggedly.

"What I was going to say, is I will release you if you just let me explain how you came into my possession first. You know, before you try escaping again."

My breathing quickens as I realize I loathe this man that has me caged down, and how badly I want to kick his fucking teeth in. Realizing that his stubbornness won't let me go any other way, I clench my jaw as I hiss through my teeth.

"Fine."

The man begins to stand up, bringing me off the ground with him. Once we're both standing, I finally get a good look at him. His medium, wavy hair perfectly matches the color of the midnight black sheets that I was just laying on.

His hair is thick, and a few strands hang above his dark brows. The color contrasts vividly against his warm ivory skin tone. His eye color is reminiscent of the moon and the sea, both tied together into one shade.

His sharp jawline is accentuated with a pair of full lips. He's much taller than me, so I have to look up at him just to meet his gaze. And when I do, I find that he's gazing at me. His head is slightly tilted as the grin is washed off of his face.

Irritated, I roll my eyes. "What?" I demand.

Suddenly, a slow grin forms his lips once again. Instead of responding, he moves to the side as he gestures for us to continue walking down the hallway. I begin walking as he trails right next to me. I keep as much distance as I can between us, until I'm nearly walking into the wall. As we walk down the hallway I take note of the antique paintings that hang on the walls. How brass candle holders hang on the walls with white taper candles filling them. My gaze adverts to my feet as I finally realize I'm walking on stone flooring covered by black detailing.

I lift my gaze to his, and find he's staring straight ahead. "Who are you? Why did you bring me here?" I demand.

"My name is Reimus Kallias, but you may call me Rei if you'd like." He says as he walks—no, strides down the hallway. He evaporates a certain power to him that no matter how infuriated I am by him, it's hard to disregard. "I was told we had a visitor trying to enter, but that they had fallen ill. I came to investigate the situation, and now here we are."

I stop dead in my steps, my mouth gaping open. "I'm…here? I'm in Vulir?"

Reimus turns around with a quizzical look on his face. "Well, that is where you were trying to go wasn't it?"

"Yes, I was. But I passed out…"

"You did."

I stand there as I realize I passed out in a strange man's home, or wherever I am. I begin to look around me, before my gaze trains on him again.

"Where am I?"

Instead of answering right away, he turns on his heels and continues walking. I stomp my foot as I wail my hands in the air, and follow him. Once we turn a corner, we are greeted with a staircase that travels to the floor below us. As we wind down it, I take note of how he still hasn't answered me yet.

When we made it to the bottom of the stairs, I thrust my hand in the air. "Hello? An answer would be fucking great any day now."

When he still doesn't answer me, I grow irate. Before I can unleash my anger on him once more, we come to a room that smells—

Oh, my gods.

Walking into the room I realize we're in a dining room. A long table stretches down the middle of the room, and I notice immediately all of the food laid out on top of it. I almost lose all sense of rationality and nearly run to the table, but instead I keep my chin held high as we walk to the table. When we reach a chair, Reimus pulls it out for me and I give him a look.

"I will answer your questions. But you look like you haven't eaten in days." He says as his hand gestures to me to sit down.

I tentatively take the seat, as he pushes my chair in. He goes to take the seat at the head of the table, two seats away from where I'm seated. As soon as he sits down, he gazes at me. He sighs as he nods his head at the array of food, gesturing for me to go ahead.

I look ahead and take in everything that's laid out here. Judging by the food selection, I'd have to assume it's the evening hours of the day. Before me is a hefty serving of roasted turkey, mashed potatoes, grilled asparagus, buttered rolls, and a platter of cantaloupe, mango and strawberries. I meet my gaze with his, and cross my arms over my chest.

"And you expect me to willingly eat? When I'm unsure of *who* you are, or *what* you may have done to the food?" I say as I seethe through my teeth. It's at this moment I'm thankful that my stomach didn't growl, giving away my eagerness to want to dig in. But I don't know this man or what his intentions are here. So I fight my hunger until proven otherwise.

Reimus stares at me for a few moments, before he grabs a plate and fills it with a little of everything. I watch him as he doesn't say a word, but instead takes a small bite of everything laid out. His gaze never leaves mine as he does so, and it causes me to want to sink into my seat and run from the fierceness in his eyes.

But I do not run. I stay firmly seated.

After he's taken a bite of everything, he looks away to take a napkin and wipes his mouth. After he sets it down, he meets my gaze once more. "Hopefully that was proof enough that I'm not trying to poison you."

My gaze wavers then to look at all of the food left out on the table. I want to be stubborn and still resist his offer. But once I realize he isn't keeling over from the food, my stubbornness loses the battle.

I begin to take a serving of everything, and I waste no time before I dig in. The turkey is perfectly seasoned and I softly moan at the decadent flavor of it. I take a little of the turkey and begin mixing it with some mashed potatoes, uncaring of how I may look right now.

As I wolf down the food before me, I peer up at Reimus who's watching me. He doesn't seem repulsed by my behavior right now, but more curious. I swallow my bite of food and reach for the water set out in front of me. I gulp the whole glass down until it's empty. Once I set it down, and I begin to feel less ravenous, I look up at Reimus. I motion my hand for him to talk, rolling my eyes.

He chuckles, and a smile lifts. "To answer your question, you are in the Guardians Palace."

"Guardians Palace? You mean like…Guardians of Vulir?" I ask after I pick up a buttered roll. I bite into it and am overly pleased with the flavor of it.

"The Guardians' purpose is to protect the people of Vulir. We have a duty to keep our people safe."

"Is it just you here?" I ask.

"Now, it is just me and another that live here."

Suddenly fear rolls through me as there is someone else in this palace other than just us two. My mind also hyper focuses on how Reimus said *now*, as if to insinuate there were more of them that lived here at one point. "Who are they?"

"His name is Dimitri. You probably won't see much of him as he spends most of his time in the village doing surveillance."

"Oh." I say. My mind ponders over the exact duties of what a Guardian is. "And have you always been a Guardian?"

His gaze softly bores into mine. "I didn't come into my role until I was old enough to, but it's been my path ever since I was born."

"And how old are you?"

"Twenty-seven."

I nod my head. I begin to feel my belly expand as I pick at the last few pieces of fruit on my plate. When I look at my empty glass, Remius calls out for someone by the name of Aven. A man walks out in cream colored clothing, followed with a strained apron. His blonde hair is wild and messy, the stubble of his beard visible. He definitely looks older than me, I'd assume he's around his mid-forties. As he approaches me, he has a wide grin on his face. Like he wouldn't possibly wish to be anywhere else than here right now.

"May I?" He asks, holding a glass decanter of clear liquid that I can only presume is water. I nod my head yes. He fills my glass cup up and then steps back.

"Thank you." I say.

"You're welcome!" The man says delightfully.

I watch as he nearly gallops out of the dining room, amazed by how energetic and lively he is.

"That is Aven. As you can see he thoroughly enjoys being here."

My gaze whips back over to Reimus as I grab my glass. "Surprising. I thought for sure anyone would loathe working for you." I take a sip of my water.

He laughs at my snide remark, and I watch as his hair ruffles in front of his forehead. Instead of responding to it, he instead asks me a question.

"Tell me what brings you to Vulir." He says rather than asks. Unwilling to share much personal information with this man, I try to keep it as brief as possible.

"I'm here to meet with a woman."

"And who might this woman be?" He asks.

"I'm...not sure."

"You traveled all this way and you have no idea who it is you're meeting—"

"I know who I'm meeting." I say as I shoot up from my chair. Getting annoyed with this fuckers sarcasm, my anger causes me to show a physical reaction. I watch as Reimus stares at me, not an ounce of fear visible in his expression.

I take a deep breath in, and slowly lower myself into my seat. "I have only seen her in dreams, but she knew things about me that she couldn't have possibly known. I *felt* her."

Reimus raises a curious brow. "Felt her how?"

"I felt her energy. I didn't believe that she wasn't a spirit, so she proved that she was alive by showing me through her energy. I don't know how to explain it, okay?" I say as frustration lurks out of my tone.

"What did she look like? What was she wearing?" He asks, his tone stern but calm.

"She wore a lot of gold jewelry, and wore a long rich purple robe. She—"

Reimus stands up while his gaze remains on mine, interrupting my sentence. He begins slowly walking towards me and I begin to tense up as I'm not sure why his mood visibly changed. He approaches me and takes the seat next to me. "You're sure she wore a purple robe?"

Skepticism clouding my tone as I answer. "Yes, I'm sure. Why is that a big deal?"

Reimus immediately stands up, and pushes his chair in. He stands there gazing at me, when he slowly nods his head. "Aven." He calls out.

Aven comes out with that same damn smile on his face. "Yes, my Lord?"

My—what?

"Please take Melinoë up to her room, and show her to the restroom. Where she can bathe and rest. I will be back shortly."

"Yes, my Lord."

"Wait, you're leaving? Where are you going?" I demand. I don't even know this man and he expects me to just bathe in his—

Wait.

"How did you know my name? I didn't tell you my name." I rise from my seat and push my chair out, feeling weary that this man knows more about me than I thought.

Reimus just watches me, before he turns on his heels and walks away. "Bathe, Melinoë. Trust me, you need it. We will talk when I am back."

Reimus walks out of the room and I am left standing with Aven, who is collecting my used dishes. "I will set these in the kitchen and be right out to take you up to your room."

My room?

Aven carries my dishes into the kitchen and I'm instantly fidgeting. How did he know my name? Why did he act like that when I told him about the woman? Aven comes back and approaches me calmly. He gestures his hand for the door. "Whenever you're ready." He says with a smile.

I hesitate as worry caves in. Aven doesn't strike me as a violent person, but you can never be too sure these days. I would very much like to bathe, though. I sniff at myself and realize that I do stink. So, I nod my head and we walk back to my room.

When we enter, I stand off to the side as Aven walks in. He motions his hand for me to follow him to the restroom.

I follow him in and immediately spot the pearl while clawfoot bathtub that I noticed earlier. Off the far wall is a stand up shower that is large enough to fit around five of me. It's surrounded by charcoal and off-white colored tile walls, with see-through glass doors. My gaze wanders over to the marbled sink and the large vanity mirror that hangs above it.

"I'm going to grab you a fresh towel, and try to find some clean clothing. I'll be right back."

I nod my head in agreement, and stand there in the same spot until he gets back. In his hands he carries a soft white towel, a pair of gray sweatpants, and a hoodie. I can tell by looking at the clothing that it's definitely mens clothing, but I don't argue as I'm shamefully desperate to get out of these soiled clothes and into something clean and dry.

He walks over timidly, handing me the towel and clothing. He nods to the wooden cart near the bathtub. "There's soap and a brush in there for you already. Feel free to use either the bathtub or the shower, take as long as you need."

I look over to the bathtub, and look back at Aven. The thought of being completely left alone in a place I'm unfamiliar with fills me with anxiety, and I begin to fidget my fingers. Aven looks at my hands, and his expression smoothes out. "There's a lock on the inside of this door." He says as he walks over to the door and points with his finger, insinuating that's an option if it will make me feel safer. "Okay?"

Well, if he really wanted to do vile things to me or hurt me, I don't think he'd be trying to comfort me right now and tell me that I have the option to lock myself in. It doesn't completely set me at ease, but it helps relieve some tension.

I nod in agreement, and he turns on his heels to walk out of the bedroom door. I hurriedly walk over to the bathroom and close the door behind me, locking it. I wiggle the doorknob as it feels very sturdy, so I try to remind myself that it's locked and no one can get in.

I plop the towel and clothing near the bathtub, and I glance between the shower and the bathtub. I decide on using the bathtub.

Dragging off my filthy clothing until I'm bare naked, I lean over and turn the faucet on. I run my fingers through the water, and I exhale at the comfort the hot water brings my hand.

The water is still filling up as I sink into the tub. The water reaches higher and higher until it reaches my shoulders, when I then turn the faucet off. I sink in and immediately ravish in the way my body is greedily taking in the warmth of the water. I let out a soft moan of appreciation as I rub my hands over my face, scrubbing away the sweat and dirt that clings to my pores.

I don't rush washing my body or my hair. Instead, I let myself sit here for a while. And after what was a tumultuous past few days, I let my body for the first time rest.

And I let myself cry.

I cried uncontrollably at first. All of the grief that swells me when I remember watching that man drive that blade through Eiran. I cry at the fact that though he tells me he's still here for me on the other side, I know that it will never, ever be the same.

I cry for the fact that I finally made it to Vulir, but I don't have my best friend here with me to celebrate. Not only that, but I also have nothing familiar to grasp onto while I'm here.

I'm all alone, once again.

Even though being alone is what I'm used to, I don't always want to be alone. That makes the depression of losing Eiran all the more painful. As I sit and sulk in this tub, I do what I normally don't allow myself to do.

I fully allow myself to feel my feelings.

Every single one of them, no matter how annoying or gruesome they are. I decide that I'm allowed to feel afraid, that I'm allowed to be scared for what's to come next. I also made this huge leap to travel here to learn more about myself, but now I feel afraid that I might not find what I'm looking for.

I unintentionally think back to Eiran's final moments, and my mind is frozen there. For a moment it's like I'm back in that same forest, my knees folded under me in the ground as I watched. I see the look on Eiran's face as he takes his last breath.

I feel the soil beneath my fingers as I grip them inward. The smell of the forest air as my knees dig into the ground.

"Please, no!" I scream as the blade drives down onto Eiran. I'm shaking profusely, I lock eyes with the man who is responsible. The look on his face is—

My breathing is staggered and I'm finding it hard to get air in as it moves at a more rapid pace. I focus on trying to get my breathing steady, but I'm beginning to feel lightheaded and feel like I need to get myself out of this tub *now*.

I nearly jumped out of the bathtub, water sloshing everywhere. Now that I'm out, I'm on the floor steadying my breathing once more. My fingers try to burrow themselves into the tiled ground, so I can try to convince my mind that I'm here and not there.

In. And out.

Once my body has calmed down, I find I'm a little more coherent and begin to regain much more control over my breathing. I slide myself back into the tub, and begin to wash my body. I look over at the cart with all of the soaps and find one that smells like lavender.

My favorite.

I scrub my body with it generously, then move onto my hair. I take in the sweet floral scent and it helps calm my body even more. I bring my hands up to the sides of the tub, and I squeeze the hard surface as I try to self-soothe myself back into the present.

I'm right here.

I'm in the bathtub.

I remove my hands and I pull the drain plug and let the water begin to drain. I grab the towel and wrap myself in it as I step out of the tub. Letting myself embrace the softness of the towel, I grab the brush on the counter and begin brushing out my tangles. My hair is down to nearly my waist, so it takes a few minutes to work them all out.

Once I shed the towel I pull on the sweatpants and the sweater. Since my bag is damp from the rain, I know my underwear inside won't be clean anymore, and I really don't want to put my dirty ones back on, so I just wear none under the sweatpants for the time being.

As I walk over by the fireplace, I nestle myself into a lounge chair. I lay on my side, as I bring my knees up to my chest. I begin to wrap my mind around everything that's happened since I've woken up.

But at some point, I find myself falling victim to my exhausted body, and I fall asleep in the chair.

CHAPTER 21

"Wake up."

Startling awake, I open my eyes to see Reimus standing over me. Before I have time to ask questions, he's hauling me up from the chair.

Once I'm on my feet, I push his hands off me. "You know I would've gotten up on my own, no need to *man handle* me." I seethe, my eyes glaring at him.

Reimus looks thoroughly annoyed. "Are you done yet?"

I scoff angrily. "No, I am not done yet. How about you tell me where you rushed off to? Or whose room this is? Or why you—"

"This is a guest room. And if you follow me to the dining room, I will show you why I left." He says with a drip of frustration in his voice.

"Fine." I say as I storm out of the room. I don't even bother seeing if he's following me, or keeping up. I stride down the hallway, down the staircase until I reach the lower floor. My annoyance growing at this insufferable man who won't just give me straight answers.

As I rage into the dining room, I jerk to a halt. I feel Reimus after a few seconds walk in behind me. He says nothing as he walks towards the woman standing near the table. The same woman who has sought me in the astral realm, nudging me to come to Vulir. Wearing the same rich purple robe.

"Hello, Melinoë."

"You."

Understanding floods me that she truly wasn't a ghost, and indeed is a real, *living* human being. My palms begin to sweat faintly as I stand in her presence, one that drenches of power and authority.

"You may call me Hecate."

My mouth gapes open at her and I forget how to function like a normal human being for a few moments. I watch as Hecate pulls out two chairs for us, and motions for me to sit. My gaze darts to Reimus who is intently watching me, his expression unreadable. I slowly walk over to the seat she's pulled out for me, and I shakily sit down. My gaze never leaves her as I can't process the reality that I'm seeing this woman in real life right now. This is the first time I'm seeing her without the weight of the hood of her cloak to hide her face.

She is…flawless. From her rich brown skin, to her long wavy midnight black hair, to her honey golden eyes. Her lips are a bright cherry red, and the color accentuates her gold adornments well. Just looking at her I get this distinct feeling that I'm about to find out just how powerful she is.

She seats herself next to me, a soft smile painted on her face. "I'm sure you have many questions for me, one of which is why I sought you out in your dreams, yes?"

I slowly nod in response.

"Well, as I told you before, I knew your mother very well. She told me of you, and one thing your mother had a gift for was prophecy. When she saw visions of her fate, she met with me and promised me to look after you. Of course, I was limited as to how I could watch over you if your village prohibits witchcraft and mediumship of any kind. So, I watched you the best I could. Until I knew it was time."

"Time for what?"

"For you to come into your powers."

A chill of awareness runs through me at her words. The urge to become more of my true self has overwhelmed me as of late, and I wonder what exactly are these powers she speaks of? She must be referring to my mind manipulation, though I feel like I have that gift mostly developed already. Before I can ask for clarification, she continues.

"Your gifts, they are becoming louder and louder now, yes? Almost as if the more you keep ignoring them the louder their demands of attention get."

"Yes…that's why I came here, so I could better understand how to use them. I have no one to lean on about this back home."

Hecate keeps her gaze pinned on me, and the power that exudes from her makes me shift in my seat. Her palpitating energy is strong, intimidating even. I get this overwhelming feeling that she has been doing this for a long time, and that it would be an honor to learn even a fraction of knowledge from her.

She stares at me for a little while longer, and for a few seconds she seems to have tuned out from us. I notice she's still staring at me, yet when I look into her eyes she seems to not be *here*. As if she's fully engaged in another conversation at the moment. Or is tremendously lost in her thoughts at least. Finally, her focus comes back and she begins to smile.

She reaches to grab my hands, and I jolt at the surge of energy I feel immediately from her. She sits there and just holds my hands for a few seconds before she speaks again. I can feel Reimus staring at us, surprised that his annoying mouth hasn't started yapping yet.

"Oh, my dear. You've been through more than most could even imagine, and yet you still stand here today. They are so very proud of you."

Tears begin to well in my eyes as she grips my hands a little tighter. I shake my head as confusion clouds me. "Whose we?"

Hecate smiles at me. "What you lack in the physical you flourish in the spiritual. One day soon, you will see that you have an army of support behind you, watching over you."

I can't even hold it back as tears begin streaming down my face. My arms begin to gently tremble thinking that I have been told twice now that I have support in my life, even if it's from spirits that I don't know yet.

One of which I know is my mother.

"Why do I struggle to connect with them? Am I doing something wrong?" I can feel the desperation in my question to know how I can better communicate with them. Because if there is anything I desperately want, it's to feel connected.

"Because you have not been ready, dear. A part of you has blocked out your gifts due to shame and distrust in yourself. But you are beginning to step into your power, and soon you will release the blockages that keep you from fully aligning with your gifts."

Blinking back the tears, Reimus is so quiet that I forget he's even there. Not sure if his lack of words is due to his own surprise in all of this, or rather his respect for the moment. Regardless, this is all still a lot for me.

"So how do I get started? What am I missing?"

"Well, we need to get back to the basics first before anything. How often do you meditate?"

Already knowing that I am horrible with sticking to a routine, I hesitate on answering her. I avert my gaze away, and that must tell her all she needs to know because she nods her head.

"Okay, well we're going to need to start there then. Which doesn't surprise me as the moment I took one look at you, I could see that there is much pent up energy that needs to be addressed. Have you ever come face to face with your shadow before?"

Hesitating for a moment, I shake my head.

Hecate takes a sudden breath in and chuckles. "Oh girl, well we have much to do then. This will be very interesting. Okay, well I assume you are staying here awhile then?"

Stay here? As in *here* with *him*? Oh, that's not going to—

"She is."

My head whips towards Reimus as anger pools in my veins. "And who says I *agreed* to this?"

Reimus looks unaffected by my disagreement on the matter. Instead he walks over to a credenza cart where there is a glass decanter of amber liquid, followed by a few whiskey glasses. He grabs one, and pours some of the amber liquid in it. He turns around with the glass in his hand. "Whiskey?" He asks both Hecate and I.

"I'm fine, thank you." Hecate says, her eyes never leaving me. I can't believe this prick is asking if I want whiskey when he just decided for me I'm staying *here*. Stomping over towards Reimus, I approach him and swat the glass out of his hand. The liquid goes flying as the glass breaks against the hardwood floor.

I am seething with rage at this point. My gaze bores into Reimus as he couldn't look more relaxed than he does right now.

"Well, if you didn't want one you could've just said that." Reimus says dryly.

"I am *not* staying here with you!" I roar.

Reimus closes his eyes. He takes a deep breath in, releasing slowly. Opening his eyes again, he looks thoroughly annoyed. "Where else will you go? Do you have friends here? Anyone?"

I don't say anything as he has a point. But because I'm hard headed, I lie. "I might."

"Oh spitfire, I can see straight through your lies. Now," He begins as he walks to grab another glass, filling it with whiskey. "I have a guest room that you can easily stay in. If you quit being such a stubborn ass and accept it. Otherwise, sleep on the streets. Your choice."

My breathing is ragged as I watch him bring the glass to his lips, and take a swig of the whiskey. His expression is neutral and calm. Gods, I want to drive my dagger into his throat everytime he calls me—

Wait. My dagger. Eiran's sword. If Reimus was the one who brought me here, then he has to have my weapons. The thought of parting with Eiran's sword brings a heaviness in my heart that I can't bear to feel right now.

I'm already feeling too much.

Taking a deep breath in, I exhale slowly before I respond. "I may consider your offer. If you tell me where my weapons are."

"You mean the dagger and the sword? I do have them. And your horse is here too, if you are curious."

My breath hitches. I thought for sure that Alastor would've ran off, and that I would have to go looking for him. But the thought of him being here.

My voice trembles slightly as I choke back a cry. "Alastor's here?"

"He's out in our pasture. I can take you to him."

Trying to reel my anger in, now that I know that Alastor is alive and here with me has me considering my initial resistance. If he has Alastor, and he has Eiran's sword I think about how I can tolerate living with the imbecile long enough to learn from Hecate. I only planned on being here temporarily anyway, and maybe I will only be here for a couple of months. So, what's a couple of months if it means I get to keep something special of Eiran's? And I get to have someplace for Alastor to stay?

"Fine. I will stay here. But I stay in the guest room, *alone*. Don't even think for a minute I'd *ever* be interested in you. I want to make that perfectly clear."

Reimus now looks amused and he gives a soft laugh. "Your message is heard, loud and clear, little spitfire."

"And *stop* calling me spitfire." I seethe.

"That I cannot promise." Reimus says with a grin.

Gods, I'm going to sever that grin right off his face with my blade one of these days.

"Okay well," Hecate begins to stand out of her seat. "This was interesting." She says as she laughs to herself. She turns towards me with her hands folded in front of her waist. "Tell you what, meet me at The Ravens Claw everyday say…one o'clock. It's right in the village, I'm sure Reimus can be a gentleman and show you." She says as she gives a look towards Reimus. "I will help mentor you there."

"Wow, thank you so much, but I'm not sure that I can accept that. I…don't have any way to compensate you for your time." I say as I bite my inner cheek.

"Consider this a debt that I'm paying your mother from long, long ago. Don't worry about money, just help me keep the shop tidy if anything. Deal?"

Feeling immensely grateful at her proposal that is more than fair, I nod my head eagerly. "Deal. Whatever you need around the shop, I will be happy to help."

"Great. Well, I must be going now. I have a client in an hour. I will see you tomorrow." Hecate says as she smiles before she excuses herself, and walks out of the dining room. After she leaves, I try my best to ignore Reimus. But I have many questions about how he knew I was talking about her.

"How did you know? That it was her?"

"Because Hecate is the most powerful witch we have seen in a very long time, and when you mentioned her infamous purple robe, I knew it had to have been her astral traveling to meet you."

"You know what astral traveling is?" I ask.

Reimus watches me confusedly as if I had just asked him what color the sky is. "I do."

Not understanding his confusion, I ask another question. "Can you communicate with spirits too?"

"As Guardian of Vulir, yes. I can see spirits and I can hear them. It's not at every given moment of every day, but rather just when a spirit wants to make contact. Mostly though, the spirits rest, unless they feel a particular protectiveness over someone who is still earthbound in which case they may make themselves known much more frequently."

At that thought I instantly think about Eiran. I wonder if he's still earthbound, for me. I want nothing more than for him to be near me, but I also want him to rest. Gods, he's been through enough. That's the very least he deserves.

"But not everyone in the village has the same ability. After the burning that occurred in Elzwin, many witches and mediums sought our village out as they heard we were a safe place for those with gifts. Some can see spirits, some just feel energy, some can only hear them, everyone's gifts are unique to their own."

At the mention of the burning of my home village, the burning that included my mother, my heart sinks. I knew that the likelihood of other mediums being burned was high, but my father never told me stories of the others who had been burned alive.

Well, to be fair he didn't really share anything with me.

My heart hurts for the women who were just trying to be their authentic selves, in which case they were murdered for it. Yet, the eagerness to learn more about this place is even more potent now. What it sounds like Reimus is saying, is that Vulir is really meant to be a place where people can be themselves without fear. It makes me wonder what else they do for their people here, and it makes me wonder if this is why it felt right to seek this place out.

"Wow that's…amazing."

As I process everything, that's all I can manage to say at the moment.

"Amazing?" Reimus asks.

"Yeah. Where I'm from we don't have that."

"You are from Elzwin, is that correct?"

Feeling my face heat as I freeze internally. I guess it was easy for him to put two and two together.

"Yes, I am."

Reimus watches me for a moment before he takes another swig of his whiskey, before he sets it down on the credenza tray. Feeling uncomfortable with the silence, I ask what I really want to ask.

"Why are you doing this?" I ask, twisting my fingers in my lap.

Reimus watches me, his expression unreadable. I begin to fear that he isn't going to respond to me until he slowly strides forward. He takes a few steps closer to me, until he's right in front of me.

"Because you remind me of someone I used to know. And I think Vulir can help you find what you seek."

Feeling perplexed on how this man knows nothing about me, yet is able to remind him of someone he knows. Or knew, rather. I watch as a half grin curves up one side of his face. "Would you like to go see Alastor?"

Immediately I'm nodding my head eagerly. I want nothing more than to see my boy right now, and let him know I'm alive and well. Or as well as I can be right now. Before we venture out of the dining room, Reimus raises a finger.

"I would like to make one thing clear," he begins. I grow slightly nervous at the coldness from his tone. "as

Guardian of Vulir, I see far more than most. And what I cannot see, the spirits see. And they never fail to warn me."

I blink at his threat.

"So should you seek harm against me, it will not bode well for you, little spitfire."

CHAPTER 22

Reimus does as he promised and takes me out to see Alastor. When we step outside, I am met with acres of spacious land. As we walk across the grass, I turn my head in every direction trying to spot any shrubbery or flowers at all. When I find that there is absolutely nothing on the ground except for grassy terrain, I scoff.

"What is it now?" Reimus lazily inquires, annoyance evident in his tone.

"You have all this land out here, but nothing to show for it. No foliage, no flowers, it's so…bare. Such a shame." I say.

"And I'm assuming you have an idea of what you'd plant out here?" He asks.

As I scan the terrain I imagine how I'd curate the perfect garden. "Well I would definitely have some lavender planted, as well as some hyacinth, asphodel, and I'd have many ferns and shrubs along the exterior walls." I move my gaze over my shoulder, looking back at the door we just came out of. "I would probably even put a small area for me to sit and read right by the entrance there, " I say, turning back around. "And I would definitely have a few feeders and a fountain, for the birds."

I look over at Reimus and see him staring at me. My gaze meets his and I think he's actually paying attention to the details. I break the gaze and look forward again. "But obviously that will never happen. Considering this is not my home."

As if Reimus snaps himself out of whatever the fuck he was doing just now, he clears his throat and trains his gaze forward. "Obviously."

A weight suddenly pulls my heart down to my stomach as I think about Makaria. I begin to wonder how she's doing. Guilt pours over me as I try to remember that she's grown now, that she can take care of herself. Because if I don't remind myself of that fact, I'll drown myself in miserable shame that shouldn't belong to me.

As we continue walking we come into view of a stable that's connected to a pasture. It looks like it's relatively new, and well maintained. The stable itself is pearl white with black doors, with black ranch fencing around the two pastures.

When we come up to the stable, I take note of the pastures that branch out. There's only two of them, so I wonder if not many horses are housed here. Considering Reimus said it's just him and Dimitri, I would guess not.

"He'll be right in here. We've tried to let him out to the pastures a few times now, but he won't leave this stall."

We enter the stable, and immediately I see him.

My sweet Alastor. Who must've heard me coming because his eyes immediately lock onto mine. He begins to whine and pace anxiously, and I waste no time closing the distance between us. I rush up to his stall, and once I'm face to face with him, the tension in his body begins to severely relax. My poor baby was probably out here thinking I died or something, and probably worried sick about me.

"My boy, look at you."

I slide the stall door open, and step inside giving Alastor a hug. Tears begin to fill my eyes. "I'm so glad you're safe."

At this point, I'm full blown sobbing. I wasn't expecting a reaction like this, but considering Alastor is the only familiar anchor I have to hang onto at this point, seeing him alive and healthy really hit me emotionally.

Once I've composed myself, I wipe my eyes before I turn back around to Reimus, knowing full well that he's been standing here this whole time and definitely heard me just have a breakdown. I'm thankful he didn't feel inclined to say anything as I've had my moment, but he doesn't need to just stand there.

I quickly wipe my eyes before I turn to face him. "Could I take him out to the pastures?"

"Of course. I'll grab some grooming supplies for you."

I open the stall door and Alastor comes right out. Reimus walks us out to the connected pasture, opening the gate as Alastor and I walk through. I turn to look at Reimus, expecting him to come in with us and just stare at me again. Instead, he sets the bucket down and takes a step back. "I'll give you two some privacy. I'll come back in a little while."

I nod, and Reimus turns around and heads back the same way we came. For a long while, I spent some much needed time with Alastor. I talk to him while I brush him, stopping every now and then to give him lots of neck rubs. I brush off any dirt that clings to his fur, as well as his mane. He stands there and just listens, like the goodest steed he is.

I tell him about Reimus, and the deal I made with him. How I made it only so that we could both have a place to stay while we're still here. Occasionally, Alastor lowers his head into my chest and nudges me softly. I smile in response, and I feel grateful that I still have him alive.

At that thought I think about Eiran, wondering if I buried his body appropriately. I wonder about when the next time I will talk to him is, or if he's with me right now and I just can't feel him. I like to think that he is.

Suddenly I hear Reimus approaching us. "We tend to keep our horses out in the pastures overnight, but if you feel more comfortable putting him back in the stall we can do that."

I look over at the next pasture over and see two horses grazing over there. They've raised their heads every now and then to watch me, but otherwise they've been grazing this whole time. I turn my gaze back to Reimus. "I'd like to keep him out here then. Thanks."

Reimus gives me a curt nod, as his gaze lingers on me for a few brief moments. I give Alastor another neck rub as I whisper sweet words to him, and then I part ways with him for the night to head back inside.

As I walk with Reimus, I'm reminded all over again how tall he is. Tonight he's wearing a pair of black jeans, with a gray shirt. He smells like…a mixture of patchouli and cedarwood. His midnight black hair is like a gaping void against the glow of the sun as it sets for the day.

"So what does that all mean, anyway. To be a Guardian of Vulir?" I ask.

Reimus continues looking ahead as we walk to the door. "We vow our lives to protect the people that live here, and also to protect the spirits. We keep a close watch over the village, and work closely with Charon who's the gatekeeper of Vulir. He lets us know if there's any disturbance outside the shield, newcomers, things like that."

"The shield?" I ask.

"It's the protective border at the entrance to Vulir."

"Wait, you mean the glimmer?" I ask.

Reimus chuckles. "Some call it that, but it is properly known as the shield. It is an energetic boundary that keeps a field of protection around Vulir's entrance, only recognizable to those deemed worthy of passing through. Though, as time goes on, there's been a few ill-intentioned individuals that have come to find a way in."

"And I'm assuming that's where you come in?"

Reimus keeps his gaze trained forward, a sureness evident in his tone. "You'd be correct."

"What would you do with them?"

Reimus doesn't answer for a few moments, and I grow wary at his silence. When he finally responds, his voice fills the air around us like dark smoke. "We take care of them."

Quick alarm fills me as I'm not sure what exactly he means by that, and it only makes me want to find my sword and dagger that much more. I don't show fear though, I keep my chin raised as we near the palace door.

"So what would happen, if someone wanted to be granted access but their intentions were not pure?"

"Then they wouldn't have been able to see the shield. It would've been completely concealed from their eyes."

"So what keeps the shield there? How was it even created?" I ask, curiosity peaking my interest.

"The King of the Underworld maintains the shield with his magick."

I've heard of the Underworld, but again, living in Elzwin leaves you with no material for reference on basically anything. All I know is that he is a god that doesn't make his presence known very much. He rules over the Underworld, and over the dead that reside there.

Anytime I've ever talked to someone back home about death, or anything of the like, they always get wigged out. Like I'm speaking a foreign language or something. After a while the stares continued, so I stopped bringing the subject up altogether. I'm not sure why people fear talking about death so much. I mean, it's going to happen to us all some day. Not to mention, death isn't just in the literal sense. Death in a metaphorical sense is something everyone goes through, numerous times in their life to be exact. The death of old habits, relationships that no longer serve you, ancestral healing, the loss of a loved one—

The thought brings me back to Eiran and I instantly wish I could talk to him right now. I hope that he visits me again soon. I want to tell him about my first day here so far, tell him about meeting the woman from my dreams. Though, if he's with me like he says he is, I'm hoping he's experiencing everything with me.

I must've been zoning out because suddenly we're right in front of my bedroom. I turn to look at Reimus. Without wasting another second, he nods his head as he steps away.

"Get some rest. I will meet you in the dining room tomorrow for breakfast."

"Thank you."

He stops himself from turning around, his gaze meeting mine. "For what?"

I meet his gaze. "For saving my horse."

Reimus' expression flashes to understanding, as he nods his head again and turns around to walk down the hallway.

I go inside the bedroom, locking the door behind me. I immediately scour the room and bathroom, making sure there's no one hiding in here, just waiting for me to be alone so they can murder me in my sleep. Once I'm convinced the only person in this room is myself, I shuck off my clothing from the day and find that a pair of pajama pants and a short sleeved shirt have been laid out for me on the chair.

Did Reimus put these here? Did Aven?

I put the clothing on and shimmy over to the bed. Noticing the bed has been made, and the sweat-drenched sheets have been replaced with clean ones. Crawling under the covers I bring the silken sheets up to the base of my neck and inhale deeply. Lying on my back, I stare at the ceiling above me as I exhale slowly.

My life has changed so drastically in the past few days. How I suddenly went from essentially being this stay at home nobody, to leaving that life behind to come to Vulir. To how my best friend was murdered on the journey here.

I place my hands over my chest, deeply wishing to myself that I'll see him again soon. I know it's not the same as having him alive, but if I'm able to have the closure of seeing him as a spirit, it would help to some degree.

What would he say about me being here?

Would he say this is an irresponsible move on my part? To be honest, it might be. But nothing about any of this is familiar or normal.

I'm going to just have to make do with what I've got. I won't let myself give up on the overall goal, no matter how uncomfortable the changes are. No matter how much I dread even existing without my best friend by my side to anchor me down in that lovingly, familiar way of his. I'll fight through my grief. I'll do it because I refuse to have gone through everything that I have to just quit now. I'll do it for younger me who has dreamt of being something infinitely more than what she's been.

I'll do it for Eiran.

CHAPTER 23

When I awake in the morning I meet with Reimus for breakfast. As I enter the dining room, I notice the table is already set and Reimus is seated in the same seat he's sat in since I got here. I walk towards the seat with an empty plate on it, and I pull my seat out. I look over to Reimus and see he has a mug that's steaming from the top. I look at his calloused hands as they hold the mug, and notice he's not wearing a shirt. Just a pair of gray sweatpants that hang low on his hips.

Gods, he's insufferable. I roll my eyes.

"I hope you didn't think I would be foolish enough to be easily captivated at something as trivial as you showing your bare chest." I say as I seat myself in the chair.

Reimus doesn't even look up at me as his gaze remains pinned on the newspaper in his hands. He takes another sip of his coffee, the veins in his arm jutting out. "I didn't think of you at all, actually. At least not until you interrupted my quiet morning just now."

I glare at him as I grab the butter knife that lays next to my empty plate. I fantasize about stabbing him with it, the thought filling me with intriguing satisfaction. I slowly release my hand as I look at the coffee pot in front of me. I grab it and hold it over my mug as I smile. "I can guarantee my absence from your thoughts will be jogged the moment I dowse your body with this. Maybe next time you'll think twice about not wearing a shirt."

Reimus peers his gaze from the newspaper up to me, and a wicked grin forms his face. "Do try, little spitfire. See where it leads you."

"*Stop* calling me spitfire." I seethe. I set the pot down as I bring the mug to my lips, letting the coffee's rich aroma distract me.

"I think I'll pass."

I scoff as fury overwhelms me. I'm going to definitely stab this man before I leave Vulir, and it will fill me with sinful delight.

I begin to ignore him and fill my plate. This morning there are trays of scrambled eggs with cheese, buttered toast, sausage links, and a tray of grapes and cherries. I load a little of everything onto my plate and angrily begin eating. My fork jabs into the scrambled eggs as I try to ignore him.

"I imagine you are picturing me as the eggs." He says, now having put down the newspaper as he begins to fill his plate.

I chew a mouthful of eggs, opening my mouth to respond when I've swallowed. "I guess I'll leave it to your little imagination to figure it out."

He smirks as he picks his fork up. "I can assure you my *little* imagination would be fascinated by this fact."

Rolling my eyes, I finish my breakfast in silence. Once I've finished, I wipe my mouth with a cloth napkin that's been laid out for me. And I push my chair out as I begin to stand.

"Leaving so soon?" Reimus asks.

"More like getting the fuck away from you. I need to shower, I'll be down in an hour so you can show me to Hecate's shop." I stand up and step out of my seat, pushing my chair in. I take one more gulp of my coffee and set the mug down. I begin walking away when I hear Reimus respond dryly.

"Can't wait."

Reimus and I walk towards the village in silence. I thought for sure he'd have some smart ass remark for me, but thankfully he hasn't said a word. As we near the heart of the village I stop in my tracks.

"Something wrong?" Reimus asks.

I'm at a loss for words as I'm taking in my immediate surroundings. My gaze roams along the streets, before my gaze lands on—

Cobblestone.

"I've been here before." My voice trails off as my gaze lifts up. Before me are shops lined up along a long brick wall. The bricks alternate from black to gray, as green vines nearly suffocate the entire building. I gaze back up at all the people roaming around, searching further down the street until I see the same familiar bench.

"How?" Reimus inquires.

"I've been here before. It's how I first met Hecate, in the astral realm. We'd always meet on this same street." I say spreading my arms out.

Reimus steps in front of me, his silver blue eyes widening slightly. "Really?"

Am I speaking French to this man? I roll my eyes. "*Yes, really. I thought it was just random scenery, but now I know it was completely intentional.*"

Reimus stares at me for a few moments. "I didn't know you could astral travel."

"Neither did I until recently."

As we walk down the street we approach The Raven's Claw. Before I step inside I hesitate. I turn around to Reimus. As if he already understands what I'm about to say, he interrupts me. "I'll see you when you get back. Are you okay walking back by yourself?"

"I'll be fine." I say, and Reimus nods his head and turns to walk back to the Guardians Palace.

I step inside and I'm immediately overwhelmed with a surge of energy. Not used to the intensity of it, I have to take a few breaths before I proceed further. After a few moments, Hecate walks out.

"Hello, dear. Please, follow me."

Hecate wastes no time and directs me to the back room. The room has several tables that all line the walls of the room. Intricately placed on the tables are crystals, candles, spell jars, miniature statues, and herbs. Lots and lots of herbs. I go to seat myself at a circular table, before Hecate stops me.

"Actually, we will start here today."

She points to a section on the floor that's sprawled out with pillows, some of which are set against the wall. I go to take my seat, resting my back against a pillow against the wall, with my knees bent up to my chest. Hecate then seats herself just a few feet in front of me.

"How did you sleep?"

"I slept alright." I say.

"Good." She says. She's wearing her same robe today, and I wonder to myself if there's ever a day that she doesn't wear it. I wonder to myself if it's an heirloom, similarly to how Eiran's sword was.

"So before we get started, I want to make you aware of what you're getting yourself into. Some of the exercises I'm going to have you perform can be...physically draining at first. But I promise, it's for the best. Though at any time, if it becomes intolerable, we can stop for the day. Understood?"

Feeling a little unsure now about what I got myself signed up for, I try not to worry and just trust the process of it all. I nod in agreement. "Yes, understood."

"Perfect. Well, as I said yesterday, we need to start with some of the basics. So today, I just want us to sit and be still."

I furrow my brows at her response. "That's it?"

Hecate's expression is calm as she speaks. "That's it."

She just wants me to sit here today? For how long? I really hope that I didn't get myself involved with a false medium. Gods, how awful would that be to have gone through everything just to be seduced by a fake witch. And what exactly am I supposed to do while I sit here? What's the purpose?

Confusion unfurls deeply within me, along with a little disappointment in how I thought today would go.

"Please don't take offense to this at all, but I really thought we'd be starting off strong. You know, jumping right into strengthening my gifts. But instead I'm just…going to sit here?"

"This is a part of strengthening your gifts, child. Part of which begins with you centering into yourself. Listening."

"Listening to what?" I ask.

Hecate forces a smile that doesn't ease my worry of the situation. "You'll see."

Anxiety begins to twirl through my body as I'm feeling really unsure now. She jolts me out of my thoughts as she places her hand on my shoulder, drawing my attention to her. "Just relax, and listen. That's all I want you to do today. Okay? Remember, I'm right here"

"O-okay."

Her expression softens as she lowers her head. "Close your eyes."

I do as she says and close my eyes.

"Now pay attention to your feet. Feel them connecting to the cold ground, how they dig into the rug. Use that as your anchor."

As my knees are bent up towards my chest, my feet lay flat on the ground. Wiggling my toes, I can feel the soft touch of the rug. I pay attention to how it feels. After a few minutes, Hecate speaks in a calm and gentle voice.

"Good. Now relax your body. Remember, you are in a safe place here."

Breathing in and out slowly, I begin to physically feel my body relax.

"Good. Now, just listen. Do not fight what comes to the surface. Let it through."

As I sit here, breathing in and out again, I continuously try to further relax my body. I'm not sure how long it's been, but after a while I forget that Hecate is seated right in front of me. I'm not sure what exactly I'm supposed to listen for, but I still wait.

And wait.

Until suddenly I'm standing in front of my cabin. I begin to see myself walking through the door, until I come face to face with my father standing a few feet away from me.

He's carrying something in his hand—

I realize it's the book.

Why would I think of this—

"Focus, child. Do not fight whatever it is that's coming up right now."

Hecate feels like she's far away even though I know she's right in front of me. Doing as she says, I allow myself to go further. I can feel dread course through my body as I walk closer to my father, my palms beginning to sweat. I walk towards him and eye the book that's in his hands, noting the anger that paints his face.

I suddenly feel like I'm not wanted here, that I'm in trouble.

"I told you about this shit, Melinoë!" My father throws the book on the ground as he walks towards me.

"I'm sorry, I just wanted to—-"

My head flinches sharply to the side. Bringing my hand up to my cheek, tears well in my eyes. I can't tell if they're welling in my real eyes or if it's just perceived. Regardless, my cheek stings from the brunt of his harsh hand.

"You are a good for nothing little shit, you can't even listen to me! You are worthless!"

I begin to start breathing faster as my fingers are gripping into my hands. I can feel the pit of my stomach churning wildly with desolation and rage.

"I do everything for you! And you do nothing in return for me! What about me? What about me!"

I begin to feel myself shrinking into the floorboard. I look up and it seems like my father is dozens of feet taller than me. His ginormous figure towers over me like a tree hovering over a mouse. I begin running, out of the door and away from the house. I keep running until my feet land on grass and I see trees—

Suddenly I'm in the Sephyra Forest, where Eiran is on his knees with a sword pointed at him.

His sword, and it's held by his assassin.

My breathing picks up and now I'm trembling, I begin to start fighting myself awake—

Until I feel heat on me. I—I can't focus on where exactly the heat is originating from, but I begin to hear Hecate's voice.

"You're doing so well, child. I'm right here. You are safe. It's okay to feel this. I'm with you."

Attention immediately refocuses on what's in front of me. Eiran is on his knees, and he's about to be murdered. My body yanks against itself and I feel myself running, but it's not fast enough. I pump my legs faster, and faster but it doesn't seem to do anything.

Screaming, I grow frantic and frustrated. *"Why can't I get to him faster!"*

I see the man with the goatee circling him, with a vile grin on his face. He's taking pleasure in the fact that I can't run fast enough. He taunts me with that grin, and he knows it too.

My palms begin sweating profusely, and I finally make it to Eiran. Terror courses through my trembling body as I witness the blade of his sword pierce through his flesh.

I nearly vomit at the sound of his wet flesh tearing. I look over and see the sick grin plastered on the goatee man's face, watching me fall, fall apart at the slow death of my beloved.

I scream as Eiran falls down, my face feeling hot from the strain on my throat. I crawl to Eiran as my knees scrape against the rough soil. I cradle him in my arms as I look at his beautiful strong face.

"I'm so sorry. It's my fault you're dead. If you never came with me, you'd still be alive. I ruined your life!"

My hunched over body racks violently as I'm uncontrollably sobbing. Rocking Eiran and I back and forth I keep him tethered to me as long as I possibly can. *"You were everything to me, and it's my fault I lost you. You were the only one who ever saw me, and I needed you more than I ever let myself know. I am all alone. My own father never loved me the way you loved me. I'm sorry Eiran. I'm so sorry—"*

"Melinoë, wake up dear!"

Jolting awake, my eyes rock open. My throat is raw and it's evident that my screaming was not perceived, but real.

My cheeks soaked from the tears that dampen my face, and my skin feels cold and clammy. I sniff myself and realize I've been sweating. My wild gaze bores into Hecate's as she softly gazes at me.

"You are safe dear, you are safe here. Let it all out."

Next thing I know, Hecate is wrapping me in her arms, cradling me against her chest. The warm contact shoots me straight into emotional overdrive, and suddenly I'm a small child seeking comfort from her mother.

Except my mother is dead.

Eiran is dead.

And my father always treated me like an unworthy outcast.

He's abused you. He's manipulated you—

"Stop! *Stop, stop, make* it stop, please!" I scream at nothing and no one as my mind plagues me with the overwhelming truth I have tried so long to disregard, shoving far down for it to never reach me. To never hurt me. The daunting truth that has hooked itself onto my bones, but I have tried to ignore anyway.

Everything overwhelms me as I rock against Hecate.

For a long while I sob into her arms. She has no reason to be so kind to me, yet here she is. Holding me in her arms as I unload all of my emotional burdens onto her.

As I cry, I face feelings that I've suppressed for a long, long time. Feelings of unworthiness. Feelings of shame.

For so long I've shoved everything down in hopes that it would all go away on its own, and most of the time it did just that. For a while at least.

Little did I realize that I had been keeping everything unhealthily bottled up instead of coming to terms with what I'm feeling is valid. That I'm allowed to feel like I've been this burden of a daughter ever since my mother died. That I've done everything for my father and in return he's done absolutely nothing for me. No generosity, not even a thank you. Instead all I got in return was a smack to the face, and a grip to my throat.

I've felt used and underappreciated and I've let it go for so long because I desperately wanted him to one day decide to do better. But in the process of hoping he'd turn out differently, I only hurt myself in the end. Instead of coming to terms with the reality of how things really are. Realizing that I shouldn't have taken on as much as I have, and because I did, it's no wonder I can't trust anyone to be there for me.

Like I feel like I have to do everything on my own.

My mind begins to drain rapidly with all of these daunting thoughts and I become hollow inside.

"I…don't want to feel this heaviness." I say into Hecate's shoulder, my voice ending on a rasp.

Hecate rubs my hair and the gesture is soothing. "I am so sorry for everything that you have been through, dear. The pain of coming face to face with your shadow for the first time is excruciatingly painful. I just want you to know that there is nothing wrong with you, you understand? I need you to know that you are a brave young woman, and there has *never* been *anything* wrong with you."

I begin to cry once more at Hecate's generous and much needed words.

"This is the hard part dear. I'm so sorry we had to start things this way, but your shadow has been begging to be freed from suppression. Only then can you truly come to terms with the trauma, and truly come to terms with how it has hurt you. So then, you may make the necessary boundaries. So you may really take back your power."

As I let Hecate's insightful words sink in, I let the pressure of her hands around my shoulders soothe me. As I let myself curl in this woman's arms, I don't let myself think about how strange this must be to be cradled in this kind woman's arms.

I decide to just let myself be cared for, for once.

After I compose myself and have allowed myself to sob, Hecate pulls me away from her and looks at me. "Feeling a little better?"

At her words I notice a huge difference in my body already. Even though I'm feeling emotionally heavy, my body feels…lighter. I feel like I just released a jarring load off my soul.

I wipe my eyes, and look at her. "Yeah, a little. I—I feel really heavy, but my body feels lighter."

"That's good, that's the energy that's been expended from your spirit. The heaviness of coming to such realizations is normal. I want you to just rest tonight. Eat a good dinner, and take care of yourself. Take a nice bath, okay?"

I nod my head as I wipe tears from my cheeks. "Okay, I will."

"And if for any reason you are not feeling right…please, don't hesitate to reach me. Or seek out Reimus. I know he may not be your favorite person at the time, but he is good."

The thought of talking to Reimus about anything other than small talk doesn't excite me. But I understand what Hecate is saying. "Okay, thank you very much. For being here for me through all of that."

"Of course, dear. Now, go get some rest, and I'll see you tomorrow. I promise tomorrow will be easier." She says as she rubs my shoulder before pulling me away from her. She's so friendly, not that I was expecting her to be cruel by any means. But the friendliness and compassion is not something I'm exactly used to.

As I wave goodbye to Hecate, I turn to walk out of the shop. When I do, I see the sun in the distance beginning to set.

Gods, I have been here for a while.

As I start walking the way back to the palace, I feel a distant fogginess that wasn't there earlier today. I can see faintly that there's much more people out now, but their voices seem drowned out. Like even though I'm right next to them, I can hardly make out what they are saying.

My focus lazily trains forward as I begin to see the Guardians Palace come into view. As I walk, I begin to become crowded with thoughts. Thoughts that reaffirm to me that I've been treated so unfairly, that it hasn't all just been in my head. I've gone the extra mile for my father, and have never seen the same effort in return. The weight of the realization crushes me, sinking into my bones.

Why couldn't I be good enough for him?

Why couldn't he see me like he sees Makaria?

Before I know it, I'm at the palace and walking through the main doors. My mind is lost in a fog, as I mindlessly walk myself to my room. As I pass the dining room, I can hear a chair scraping the ground until I hear footfalls coming from the room.

"Melinoë?"

I realize it's Reimus, and I want to respond to him but I just can't seem to find the strength to speak. Instead, I keep walking until I reach my room. Once my hand twists the door open, I walk inside and close the door behind me. Not bothering to even lock it.

I don't even care at this moment.

Walking into the room I plop myself onto the bed, with my chest meeting the bedsheets and my face turned away. I want to just lay here.

I hear a knock on the door. When I don't answer, I hear someone slowly twist it open. I know it's Reimus, but I don't bother telling him to get out. I'm finding I don't have the energy to even form words.

I hear him close the door behind him, and walk over to the bed. I hear him sit down in the seat that's next to the bedside table. My gaze is facing the chair, and I can see Reimus sitting in the chair, though I can't fully focus on him. His expression is wiped of any snarkiness, and instead looks pained. My gaze shifts to him propping a leg up, and I watch as he leans back in the chair. He doesn't speak a word, he just sits there and watches me.

As I fall deeper, and deeper, letting the fog pull me all the way under.

CHAPTER 24

Sometime later I wake up to the sound of a fire crackling. Realizing that at some point, Reimus must've lit a fire in my room while I was asleep. Suddenly I realize that I'm not the only one in my room right now.

I groggily open my eyes and find that Reimus is still sitting in the chair, though now he has a black journal in his hands. He's writing in it and when he hears me stir, his gaze finds mine. He closes the journal, and leans in. "Hungry?"

I nod my head sleepily. "Yes, but I can eat downstairs—"

"I will go fetch something." Reimus says as stands up and immediately walks out of the room. A short while later, Reimus returns with a bowl of vegetable soup, a smoked turkey and cheese sandwich, and some grapes. In one hand he also carries a glass of water.

"I hope this will suffice."

Handing the plate and water to me, I glance at Reimus. He must've thought since I slept through dinner that when I did wake up, I'd be hungry.

That's…unusually kind of him.

"Thank you."

Reimus nods his head and I fully expect him to leave my room. Instead, he takes a seat again in the chair next to my bed. Stretching his legs out in front of him, he folds his arms at his chest.

"You know, you don't need to be in here watching over me. I'm fine."

Reimus looks over at me with a gentle gaze. "I know you don't need me here, I get the impression that you can take care of yourself just fine. But if you don't mind, I'd like to stay."

Looking at Reimus a part of me wants to shoo him away, that I don't need the company. But I get the impression that he's not going to leave anytime soon. I take a bite into my sandwich before I try the soup. I grin after I take a spoonful of it, savoring the flavor. I'll have to remind myself to thank whoever made it later. Reimus goes back to writing in the same black journal, his serious yet thoughtful gaze trained into the pages.

"What are you writing in there?"

Reimus looks forward and for a split moment I swear he looked embarrassed. He closes the journal, and faces me. "I like to jot down thoughts. Poems from time to time."

This guy writes poetry? Yeah, I definitely never would've guessed that. I mean, he doesn't really strike me as the poet type, but to be fair, all I've done is give him a hard time since I got here. I really don't know this guy. "Poems about what?"

His jaw clenches ever so slightly, but still I notice.

"About life."

"Life? Well that's vague."

His mouth forms a half grin at my response. "Well, there are some things I do enjoy keeping to myself."

I don't feel inclined to ask further and I continue eating. As I make my way to my grapes, I plop each one in my mouth as I gaze openly at the room, staring at nothing. My mind feels blank, even after sleeping off the exhaustion that weighed on me mentally today.

I shake myself out of my mental fog and look over at Reimus who is carefully watching me. His gaze roams my face for a few moments before he stands up. He motions his hand for my now empty plate and cup, taking my dishes from my hands. His gaze meets mine once more.

"I know you say you are fine, but your eyes tell me otherwise."

Feeling disoriented from his strange comment, I blink a few times. "What?"

He watches me with an unreadable expression before standing up from the chair. "Let myself or Aven know if you need anything. Get some rest."

He turns to walk towards my bedroom door, pulling the door open as he walks out of my bedroom. He pulls the door behind him and I listen to his footsteps become more and more faint.

I pull the blankets up to my chin and curl myself into the midnight colored sheets. For a moment, I think back to earlier today with Hecate. How our first session together went, and how exhausted and numb I am as an after effect.

As I lie awake, I begin to re-experience the heaviness I once felt just hours ago. How the weight of it plaques my body into itself.

At some point, I manage to fall asleep again, letting the deep slumber temporarily whisk away my pain once more.

I awake again and the sunlight shining through my windows tells me it's morning. Probably late morning judging by how sunny it is already. I decide to lay in bed for a few moments before actually getting up.

If it were up to me, I would probably let myself lay in bed all day and sleep my burdens away. But I have to go see Hecate again today, and I don't want to take advantage of her generosity to train me.

Or teach me rather, I should say. I'm really hoping today is not like how it was yesterday. I don't know if I can energetically handle another day like that.

Forcing myself to crawl out of bed, I make my way over to utilize the bathroom. Once I finish, I walk over to my duffel bag and notice Aven took all of my clothing and had them cleaned. My heart pulls at the kind gesture. I pull on my baggy navy blue sweater, as well as some blue jeans from my duffel bag before I head downstairs.

When I approach the dining room, Reimus is sitting there drinking his morning coffee. He looks up towards me, his gaze watching me as I take my usual seat. "Did you sleep well?"

Well, someone is being awfully nice today.

"I did. You?"

"I slept decently."

I begin pouring myself some coffee into a mug. Taking a few sips, I set my mug down while I pile my plate with scrambled eggs, breakfast sausage, and a buttered english muffin. I begin digging in as I notice Reimus starts to fill his plate. I realize that everytime I come down here, he never has his plate filled until I've filled mine.

I finish off what's on my plate and sit back in my chair as I sip some of my coffee. I wonder to myself what this guy does all day, as 'Guardian of Vulir'. My curiosity overrides my desire for space for once.

"So what do you do all day? You know, as Guardian and all." I ask.

"Most days I simply check in with the village people. Make sure everything is in order. Sometimes Dimitri and I assist with Charon if there is trouble at the gate."

"What do you mean by trouble?"

Reimus takes a slow drink from his glass before he responds. "As in someone trying to enter who is not welcomed. Or in your case, someone who passed out trying to enter."

I roll my eyes in response and wonder why I even bothered to ask. "I hadn't eaten in a few days so *sorry* for my brief display of weakness." I say sarcastically.

Reimus watches me before he speaks a few moments later. "Why did you allow yourself to go days without food?"

I internally sink into myself at the reminder of the days following Eiran's death. How I felt magnetically stuck to his lifeless body as I mourned him. How I had even contemplated succumbing to starvation and let it end my suffering right there. Feeling like the minute I tell Reimus he will have something vulnerable against me, and I don't know him far well enough to be vulnerable with.

"I didn't pack enough." I lie smoothly.

"You mean you didn't plan *accordingly*?" He drawls.

"Whatever, it's none of your business anyway."

I bring my coffee back up to my lips and down the rest of it. Pushing myself out of my seat, I go to grab my plate when Reimus stops me.

"Leave them there."

"Why?" I ask as I furrow my brows.

"Because I will take care of them." He says calmly, his gaze meeting mine.

Does this guy think I'm incapable of cleaning up after myself? It's just one plate and one mug. Either he's trying to be an ass per usual, or he's insinuating because I had a bad day yesterday that I'm incapable of doing much. My ramping anger is no match for my common sense and over powers it in a swift remark.

"What is up with you?" I sneer.

Reimus watches me, his gaze perplexed. He tilts his head to the side as if he has no idea what I'm talking about.

I take that as my cue to continue. "First, you followed me into my room yesterday when I got home, and sat in that chair while I slept. Now you're telling me to leave my dirty dishes here? I'm not incompetent I can help myself. I had one bad day, it's not a big deal." I hiss through my teeth.

Reimus stares at me, blinking a few times as his expression simmers from confusion to understanding. He wipes his mouth with a napkin and sets it down.

"I can assure you that I do not find you incompetent, Melinoë."

Staring at Reimus, I thought he would for sure lash out and ask me why I'm being crazy. I thought he'd for sure ask me why am I being ungrateful. Now I feel like an ass that he's responding in the calmest manner possible. As these conflicting and disturbingly raw thoughts come up, I feel embarrassed at my reaction now. I'm acting like a damn lunatic.

"I thoroughly enjoy our bickering with one another, but after seeing how you walked through those doors last night, I thought you needed something different for a change. But if a bickering bastard is all you'd like from me, then I can be that for you."

My initial anger has tampered down and I'm able to look at things head on rather than through a lens of smoldering distrust. Fidgeting with my fingers in my lap, I avert my gaze forward. Shame begins to crowd my vision as I feel embarrassed for reacting in that way. I look up at Reimus who I should be grateful for even letting me stay here, even if I would much rather be someplace else. Biting back my usual retorts, I sigh.

"Thank you. I do appreciate you staying with me last night."

Reimus nods his head as he goes to grab his mug.

"This doesn't mean we're friends though. I still loathe you." I say as I stand up from my seat. I step away from the table, my chin lifted up as I glare at Reimus. I turn around and begin making my exit from the dining room.

"Whatever helps you, little spitfire."

My head whips around as I clench my jaw so tightly I nearly scrape my teeth. I watch as a wicked grin slowly grows on Reimus' lips and I instantly want to run a blade across it, severing it from his annoying face. I audibly exhale and curse under my breath as I turn back around, and tramp out of the room.

"See you for dinner."

I raise my hand and give him the middle finger, and I hear him bellow a deep laugh. I walk out of the dining room, feeling his gaze trained on my back the whole way out.

I meet with Hecate at her shop and before we begin, she checks in with me. I get people are trying to be nice but damn, I feel like I'm on suicide watch for gods sake.

"How are you feeling today?"

"I'm feeling okay. Not quite as heavy as yesterday." I say.

"Good. Did you rest?"

"Yes, I did." I say tiredly.

"Good, rest is very important while we really work through your shadow."

"What exactly do you mean by that? Working through my shadow?"

"Well, you see your shadow is the unconscious aspect of yourself that carries everything that you've repressed. Trauma, negative feelings/emotions, things you've grown to disown about yourself. The act of shadow work is simply bringing all of that up to the surface, recognizing it, and accepting it. Owning it."

The thought of bringing all of that up ensues a nervousness in me that's hard to ignore.

"Wouldn't you want to get rid of your shadow side? Why would you want to accept your trauma?"

"It's not about *accepting* it, but rather accepting that it is *there*. Because until you accept that what has happened, has happened, your shadow will demand to be heard. And shining a light on, and accepting the things you've repressed, means you accept yourself entirely. That you give yourself space to feel, entirely."

"Okay…" I say as my fingers play with a few strands of loose hair. "Is that why yesterday the first thing that came forward was about my father?"

"If that is one of your biggest traumatic experiences, then yes. That would explain it. Tell me, if you are comfortable. What did you see?"

"Well…" My voice trails off as I act like I'm trying to think of what I saw, knowing damn well I remember it vividly. I don't know why I feel so resistant to tell her, I doubt she would run and tell anyone what I say here. It's just not easy for me to trust others.

But I figured she's just trying to help me, so the least I can do is meet her halfway. "I saw my father back home. He was carrying a book I kept hidden, a book about psychic gifts. He found it and he got angry. He hit me."

Hecate watches and listens to me without interrupting me. I watch as her gaze stays trained on me.

"He said things to me like 'you're worthless' and I felt so angry, so hurt because I did everything for him and my sister. I felt…" I trail off, uncomfortable with the vulnerability I'm displaying.

"How does that make you feel? To do a lot for the people you love and receive very little in return?"

Tears start to well in my eyes as I try to hold back from crying. Clearing my throat I start again. When I open my mouth, Hecate cuts me off.

"Ah, I see."

Confused, I furrow my brows waiting for her to make sense and explain.

"You have a habit of that, don't you? That whenever you feel strong emotions coming on, your first instinct is to shove them down. When did that start?"

Baffled, I stammer over my response.

"I—I don't know. Since I was very young."

"I see. And was that around the age when you began taking the role of parent for your younger sister?"

"How did you—?"

Hecate gives a sympathetic smile as she takes a sip of some of her hot tea she brewed for us.

"You have a hard time allowing yourself to feel your emotions. So that tells me something happened to make you feel like you've been conditioned to think your emotions come last, while the needs of others always came first. Which makes me guess that you had to take care of your sister from a young age, conditioning you to that mentality."

Speechless, I process what Hecate is saying.

"Not only did you take on far too much as a child, but I am guessing your father not only didn't accept you as you are but also put your sister on a noticeable pedestal."

My breath hitches at Hecate's accuracy. "How can you know all of that?"

"I may be no therapist, but I have a knack for reading people, right down to their core."

Averting my gaze to the ground, I feel like I want to shrink into myself again. Hecate gently grabs my face and brings it back up to look at hers once again.

"Child, if there is one piece of advice I beg of you to learn now versus later, it's that *you matter*. And that there is *nothing* wrong with putting yourself first for a change."

Tears begin to slip down my cheeks as Hecate smiles gently at me.

"And the first way you can start by doing that, is by allowing yourself to feel your emotions. Give yourself permission to feel sadness, to feel anger. Give yourself permission to feel like you have been treated unfairly, and use those feelings you've long repressed to empower you to demand better for yourself."

At Hecate's words, I decided to stop fighting the tears back and I let myself cry once again, in her arms.

Feelings of shame rise within me for using this woman as an emotional dumping blanket, but I force myself to not resist what I'm feeling. I figured if she was truly uncomfortable with this, she would've made it known by now. For so long I've put myself on the back burner, making sure my family is taken care of at the cost of myself. Always making sure I appeased my father when he has rewarded me by treating me like I am a burden to him.

Then the one person who I have by my side, who loved me and treated me with *actual* respect dies and I feel like I can't blame anyone other than myself. I know Eiran would be displeased to know I blame myself for his death, but the darkness in me can't see it otherwise right now.

I miss the brush of his calloused fingertips as they would graze softly against my face. The feel of his full lips against mine, with the heat of his passion to fuel my craving for companionship. I miss him so fucking much I can't *breathe*.

I let myself feel it all. When I've cried what I could, I wipe my eyes dry.

"I'm sorry, I'm sure this is not what you envisioned our sessions to be like."

"Dear, this is all part of the process. I expected nothing different." Hecate says with a soft pained smile.

Feeling more at ease and less embarrassed, I relax more into the moment.

"And also, never apologize for needing someone to lean on. I know you've done much on your own for far too long, but there is nothing wrong with needing someone sometimes."

Feeling comforted by her words, I smile and nod my head in response.

"Okay, let's go ahead and continue then, shall we?" She asks when I nod again in response.

I've only been mentoring with Hecate for two days now, but I can already tell that I'm going to really grow to like working with her. She reminds me of my mother, with her compassion and with the strength she exudes. I begin to hope that through these mentoring sessions, I can hopefully grow to form a bond with Hecate that is something more than just a mentoring relationship.

Because other than Eiran, she's the only one who's made me feel seen and heard. Her compassion is contagious, and I think being around her is going to spark a motivation in me to want to become kinder to myself. I never realized how much I desperately deserve someone like that in my life.

I never realized how unfair I've possibly been towards myself, and truly how unfair I've let other people treat me. It's that same realization that both devastates and angers me.

After I get back to the palace, I head up to my room and where I change out of my clothes. Tossing the sweater and jeans to the side, I pull on some comfortable black leggings and a long sleeved shirt and head down to the dining room.

As I round the hallway, I can already smell the enticing smells of whatever it is that Aven is cooking up for us tonight. I wonder if he truly enjoys being a chef, or if he ever had something else in mind for his life.

Judging by how happy he always is, I doubt it.

Once I enter the dining room, Reimus is already seated per usual. As I walk closer to the table, I see Reimus glance up at me as Aven walks out with trays of food. Tonight he's made grilled seasoned chicken, green beans, homemade dinner rolls, and an assortment of cranberries and oranges. He goes back into the kitchen and comes back out with a bottle of wine.

Aven steps over to my seat and bends slightly at the waist. His smile is wide and I almost mimic his wide grin. "Melinoë?" He asks as he holds the wine out for me. I nod in response, and he fills my glass.

"Thank you." I say to Aven. In which he smiles even bigger in response before he nods his head and walks back to the kitchen. I take a sip and keep my glass positioned in my hand, as if it'll give me some type of distraction from Reimus just *staring* at me.

Gods, I really hope he cuts that shit out soon.

Setting my wine down I grab my plate as I glance at Reimus, before training my eyes on the grilled chicken. I begin forking a generous serving onto my plate. "Did you do that when you were young, too?"

Reimus takes a drink from his whiskey as he watches me. "Do what?"

"Creepily stare at people." I say.

Reimus chuckles as he sets his glass down. "Not until you."

A flutter to my heart jerks me from my coldness for a split second. Feeling caught off guard by his response, the ability to form words leaves me for a few moments. Until I shake myself back to reality and regain my composure again. "Well, cut it out. It's fucking weird." I scoff as I pile some cranberries and oranges onto my plate.

He laughs again, this time he smiles when he does. When he responds his voice deepens. "Staring at you makes you angry, and I enjoy seeing you angry with me."

I roll my eyes as I take another sip of my wine, which I will clearly need in order to deal with him tonight. I set my wine glass down and decide to ignore him for the rest of dinner.

Not even a few minutes after I've started to eat, Reimus interrupts the silence. Gods, how I wish he'd just let the silence linger.

"Are you finding mentoring with Hecate to be insightful?" He asks, as he finishes serving food onto his plate.

I look up from my plate and our eyes lock for a second. Reimus averts his gaze to his glass, taking a drink from it.

"Other than it being quite draining right now? Yes, I am enjoying being mentored by her." I say as I take another bite of the chicken.

"Draining how?" He asks as his brows lower.

I sigh gently. "Draining because we're doing a lot of shadow healing right now. Hecate says I need work on clearing out energetic *gunk* first, I guess. Supposedly after we've worked through my shadow, then mentoring will be much lighter."

"And have you ever done that before? Shadow work?" He asks. For a second I think he's actually interested in my answer, but I know that he's just being nice. Though when I look up, I'm surprised to see in his facial expression that he seems genuinely curious.

"Not really, no." I say as I try to ignore the look on Reimus' face right now. It's one thing for him to be an ass towards me, but a whole different story for him to actually show interest.

Reimus fixes his gaze suddenly on his plate of food. We both eat in silence for a short while, until I've finished eating and have drunk almost all of my glass of wine. Feeling a little chatty, I open my mouth to speak.

"So tell me something about you I don't know."

Reimus looks up at me, as he lowers his brows slightly. "I thought you loathed me?"

"I do. But I'm bored, and kind of want to know more about the strange man whose palace I'm staying in." I say as I twirl the remaining drops of wine left.

Reimus gazes at me as he takes a drink from his whiskey before he answers. It takes him a few moments to answer. "Only if you tell me something about yourself in return."

"Fine." I say as I down the remaining wine in my glass.

I watch as Reimus brings a hand up to his chin, and taps his pointer finger against it. He does this for an agonizingly long moment, until he raises his eyebrows. "That thing you do with mind manipulation? I'm impervious to that, along with most other magick."

I freeze internally at that fact. I chalked it up that day that I just haven't mastered the art of it enough for it to have affected him that day, but now that I know he's impenetrable to it, that leaves out my biggest defense weapon. "How?"

Reimus forms a grin on his face. "That is a secret for me to know, and you to, well, maybe one day I'll be kind enough to tell you."

Rolling my eyes, I should've expected no other response from him.

"Your turn." He reminds me.

Thinking to myself what I would be willing to tell this guy without getting too personal, it takes me a while to think of something I'm willing to share. But then, I decide on what that something will be.

"I have a sister back home."

Reimus watches me intently. "Are you two close?" He asks.

"Yes…and no." I say, kind of regretting bringing her up now.

"Do you miss her?" He asks.

"Yes, I do very much." I say as I wonder what she's up to right now. I wonder how she's coping with me being gone.

"Did you not trust her enough to bring her with you?" Reimus asks calmly.

I curl my fingers into my hands and see Reimus notice the action. I loosen my grip and take a deep breath in and out. "This was something I just had to do on my own."

"So you did travel here on your own?" He asks.

I begin to feel sadness and angst clog my throat. I lift my gaze up to Reimus and clear my throat as I change the subject. "Do you have friends or family here?"

Reimus visibly clenches his jaw and I regret asking now as I can tell I made him uncomfortable. Instead, he responds anyway. "I did."

Did? Oh…

"Sorry. I didn't mean to—"

"Don't apologize." He says, his initial tension slowly dissipates to ease. "They were massacred in battle, mostly. People don't always understand our kind—" Reimus cuts himself off almost as if he was going to say something that wasn't meant for my ears. Before he begins again, he clears his throat. "They just died a while ago."

For the first time since being here, this is the first time I feel like I could actually sympathize with Reimus. I lost my mother when I was young, and then losing Eiran turned my whole world upside down. I've felt like I've been on my own since a young age. But having lost your whole family and all of your friends? I can't even be spitefully cold to him with that. That's heartbreaking. "I'm so sorry for your loss"

"Thank you." He says as he downs the last of his whiskey. "Thankfully, I see them from time to time so I know they are never far."

"As in you can physically see them?" I curiously asked, my interest piqued.

"Sometimes, other times it's just through audible hearing. Or through an energetic knowing that they're around." He says.

"How long did it take you to master that? Seeing and hearing the dead?"

"I'm…actually not sure. I've been able to do it for as long as I can remember. I think it's a gift that's just been genetically ingrained into my family lineage."

"Wow, that's lucky. I'm still trying to get past hearing bits and pieces from the dead. It's getting better, but I still have a ways to go."

Reimus tilts his head slightly. "And the mind control, is that something you learned along the way?"

"That's something that just comes natural to me, like second nature. I don't have to really try to do it, I can just will it to happen."

Reimus watches me as he nods his head, a smirk growing on his face. "Interesting. And have you used it on anyone other than me?"

Thinking back to the few men I've used it on, I smile in response to the satisfaction I got from their terror. Reimus at the sight of my smile chuckles. "I'm going to take that as a yes."

"Only for those who truly deserved it." I say as I tilt my head.

"I'm assuming I'm included?" He asks, his grin not leaving his face.

I lower my head at him as my gaze adverts for a second. "For once, you would assume right."

Reimus laughs as I find myself huffing out a quick laugh. As I lay my head back into my seat, my mind jogs to something I wanted to do when I got here. Lifting my head up, I look over at Reimus.

"How do you guys send mail from here? You know, if most people don't even know about this place to begin with."

"Most of us have a raven that sends mail for us. This way we can still keep the secrecy of Vulir from those who may seek to wreak havoc here. Why?"

"If I write a letter for my sister, could you send it for me? I want her to know I'm alive and well."

Reimus gazes at me for a second before he responds. He nods. "I can do that."

I watch as Reimus looks around the room for a second, until he comes across a cabinet. He gets up from his seat, and walks over to it. When he opens it he shuffles around for a few moments, until he pulls out some old parchment paper and a quill. He walks over, handing me the items.

"Thank you." I say as he hands them to me.

Reimus watches me for a moment before he clears his throat. He takes a step back, as if to give me privacy while I write my letter. "You're welcome."

I flatten my lips and nod at him before I steer my gaze to the paper in front of me. It doesn't take me long to know what I want to write, but rather how I want to write it.

I drop my worries and just go ahead and write what comes to mind.

Makaria,

I am writing to let you know I am safe. I've made it to my destination, and will keep you updated along the way. I hope you are doing well, and are not too affected by my absence. I miss you.

Eiran is dead. I have no other way to say it, other than to be forward about it. I'm grieving the best I can. Please inform his roommates. When I am home, I can give a better explanation. I just wanted to at least let those closest to him know why he won't be coming back home..

Please take care of yourself, and write back. I love you.
- Melinoë

As I finish writing, I roll the paper up and seal it in a small cylinder container. I hold it in my hands for a moment longer, before handing it to Reimus. He takes it from my hands and nods his head.

"I'll send this first thing in the morning."

"Thank you." I say.

Reimus nods his head again, slipping the rolled up letter in his pocket. "Well I am heading off to my room for the night. If you need anything, I'm down the hallway. Otherwise, goodnight Melinoë."

Standing up from my seat I face Reimus now. We're standing only a few feet away from each other, and the smell of his cologne wafts towards my nose. It smells of notes of patchouli and sandalwood, and I find myself uncomfortable in the fact that I'm even allowing myself to notice. I take a step back from him, and force an awkward smile.

He stares at me for a brief moment longer, until he clears his throat, turns on his heels and walks out of the dining room.

CHAPTER 25

After I made my way back to my room, I decided to draw a bath for myself. After a long day, there's nothing else I would rather end my day with than a good hot soak in this clawfoot tub.

As the water fills, I shuck off my leggings and shirt and step into the tub. A soft exhale leaves my lips as I sink further into the hot water. Turning the water off, I sit back and put my arms on each side of the tub and close my eyes.

I let everything go as I relax into the water, my breathing slowing as the minutes pass. The silence around me fills my head, a nice change from the usual noise that tends to clutter my mind. I welcome the quiet like a visitor in my home.

"Meli."

My breath hitches as I'd recognize that voice anywhere. "Eiran?" I open my eyes, looking around to find him even though my chances of actually seeing him are low. At least until I get more acquainted with my gifts.

When I feel disappointed that I can't see him, a sadness evades me as I begin to feel heat along my right arm. My gaze shoots to my arm, and I know it's not the heat of the bath I'm feeling.

It's Eiran.

"I'm right here." I hear him say, clear as day through my mind.

Tears begin to well in my eyes as my initial reaction is to reach over and hug him, but I stop myself when I am reminded he's not physically here. Instead, I lean back into the tub once more and keep my gaze trained towards my right.

"I've been waiting to hear from you again." I say with a shaken smile on my face. I begin to feel comforted that Eiran is in my presence, like every worry I previously had has no effect on me while this moment lasts.

"I know. I tried to reach you a few times, but I had to wait for the right moment."

"I'm not sure what you mean by that?" I ask, confusion ridding my voice.

"In order for you to actually hear me, you have to be relaxed. Centered. Hearing a spirit is different from hearing the living, Meli. Like…the sound is only accessible when you're open to receive. Soon, it'll come much more naturally to you."

I take what Eiran is saying and don't argue with his words. My mind is usually a cluster fuck and takes a lot for it to shut up. That's why I love taking baths so much, and being out in nature. It's like they both give me the blueprint for quieting my mind.

I look at my arm, where I can still feel the heat of Eiran's energy. "Do you think I'll really get good at it?"

"I don't think. I know you will."

I smile at his words of encouragement and gods do I wish I could hug him right now. How I wish I could be wrapped up in his warm body, my head nestled against his chest. At the sad reminder that I'll never have that again, I begin to cry.

As I cry, I begin to feel Eiran's energy radiate from my arm to my shoulders, and down to my other arm. In a matter of a few seconds, I feel his energy gently pulsating along my arms and my shoulders, when I begin to feel something nestle against my neck—

I gasp as heat gently radiates against the right side of my neck and along my cheek. My breathing staggers as it—

It feels like a dull pressure is nestled against my cheek. I feel the energy pulsate suddenly, as if to bring awareness to it.

"Are you…"

"Holding you? Yes, I am."

I sit there nearly immobilized to the feeling of Eiran wrapping his arms around me and resting his head against my cheek. My eyes bulge as I begin to visualize in my mind's eye a picture of what's playing out before me. Eiran sitting behind me, his arms wrapped around me, and his head nestled against mine.

The confidence of what I'm experiencing is something I'm not sure if other people get to experience or not, but I sure hope everyone else can have the type of closure I'm experiencing right now.

I begin to relax into Eiran's energetic embrace, and I don't let my desire for wishing it to be more get in the way. I let gratitude wash over me as I embrace the bond we have.

That even in death, he still comes through for me.

I begin to talk with Eiran about how my journey has been since I've gotten here. I tell him about meeting Hecate, and how mentoring with her has been going so far. I tell him even about Reimus, and how much I loathe his presence. Yet how much I discreetly enjoy bickering with him all the same.

"I think you two are a lot more alike than you want to admit." Eiran says with a laugh.

I gasp playfully. "I am nothing like him."

"Yeah, you say that now. But you'll see eventually."

We exchange a laugh together, completely letting what Eiran said fly over my head as nothing else truly matters right now. All that matters is this moment, with Eiran.

I exhale as the smile begins to leave my face. Dread fills me as I know this moment can't last forever. I begin to panic when Eiran tries to soothe my anxiousness.

"I know it's not the same."

At those words, I begin to cry.

"But I will never be anywhere but with you. Because even in death, I have never left your side."

I wipe my eyes from the tears that escape. I take a deep breath in and exhale, training his voice to memory even though I know I'll hear from him again. I nod my head as I relish in the feel of his energy.

"I know. I love you."

"I will always love you. No matter what. I'll be back soon."

At the end of his words, I feel Eiran's energy slip away. Like a warm, heavy garment slipping off my body, exposing my skin to the sudden brisk air. I wrap my arms around myself as I rub my shoulders, self-soothing myself in his absence.

I know that I cannot be selfish and beg him to stay with me every moment of every day. I know this because I will never move on otherwise. I have to still live my life without waiting for him to visit me every night. I have to admit to myself that though I am blessed to be able to be gifted into feeling his energy, hearing his voice, that he is no longer alive. That he is, indeed, a spirit who has crossed over to the afterlife.

That he will regrettably never be able to be living again.

After a short while, when I feel the water begin to cool, I grab the lavender bar of soap and begin washing my hair and body. As I do, I think about all the things he might see that I'm not able to. Is he able to see Makaria? See how she's doing?

I wonder if he's able to see how my life plays out from here, if he can see how I'll mature into my gifts and into my power.

Once I've rinsed my hair and body, I pull the drain plug and listen to the sound of the water slowly circle down the drain. I stand up and grab the clean white towel I've laid out for myself. Wrapping my body in it, I step out of the tub and dry myself off. Wrapping my hair with the towel, I pull on a clean pair of emerald green pajama pants, realizing they match my eye color perfectly. I pull on a short sleeved shirt and walk out of the bathroom.

Unwrapping the towel from my hair, I grab my brush and begin brushing tangles out of my long black hair. After I do, I crawl my way into the silken midnight black sheets in my bed. Pulling the sheets up to my chin, I begin to relax into myself.

Shortly after, I drift off to sleep.

The next morning I decided to go out to the pastures and visit Alastor for a while before I headed into town to meet with Hecate.

When I stepped up to the pasture, Alastor was grazing as usual. Except this time I noticed him standing near another horse, and I'd be lying if I said I wasn't automatically happy to see he's socializing well with the other horses. And by other horses, I mean the only two other horses that reside here. Whom I can only guess both of which belong to Reimus and Dimitri.

Speaking of Dimitri, doesn't he live here? I know Reimus said that he's never here, but I thought by now I would've seen him around the palace.

As I unlock the gate, I step in the pasture. Alastor knickers at me as he walks towards me, the other horse following his lead. I give Alastor some much needed attention, as another horse approaches me. This one is like the polar opposite of Alastor. Her porcelain white mane and tail rests strikingly against her gray body.

"And who might you be?" I say as I hold my hand out for her.

"That would be Gizelle."

Spinning around, I see Reimus standing outside of the gate. I didn't hear anyone else out here, so his presence startled me. Today he's wearing black trouser pants, with a black short-sleeved shirt. If it were night rather than it being morning, I'd swear he would blend right into the night sky.

"Someone is jumpy today." He says with a smirk.

"Well considering a moment ago I saw no one else out here except for myself, your presence startled me." I say as I feel Gizelle nudge my hand. I begin to rub the bridge of her nose, a smile growing on my face.

"I usually come out here in the morning, to check on them."

"Oh." I say nonchalantly.

"But what's concerning is the fact that you did not see me when I was standing just inside the barn. You should probably seek medical attention about your eyesight, little spitfire."

I close my eyes and sigh audibly, not even bothering to look around because I just know that damn smirk on his face is going to thoroughly piss me off more. Instead, I take a deep breath in and exhale as I rub Gizelle's neck.

Reimus begins to unlock the gate, and steps inside of the pasture. When he does, Gizelle knickers at him and walks toward him. Immediately, nudging her nose into Reimus' hands. I watch him lovingly pet his horse, the sight strange to see as he's nothing but a sarcastic ass otherwise.

He must feel my gaze because he looks up at me. Feeling annoyed, I avert my gaze back to Alastor. I pretend like nothing happened by petting Alastor once more.

"He's a beautiful steed."

Looking back at Reimus, I notice he's now the one staring at me. Though he has horrible social skills, his stare is ever so intense that it makes my belly flutter. Shaking off the reaction, I turn my gaze back onto Alastor.

"Thank you."

I bend down to pick up a brush and begin grooming Alastor, trying my best to appear as though I'm preoccupied instead of becoming a flustered fool from a single man's gaze.

The same man I preach about loathing.

"So is she your horse?"

"Yes, she is. The other one is Arion and belongs to Dimitri."

"Oh." I say, looking over at the other horse who is walking towards Gizelle. Arion has a rich brown body, with a jet black mane and tail. He's a beautiful horse.

"Are you looking forward to Hecate mentoring you today?" Reimus asks, drawing my attention. I bend down to grab a body brush for Alastor.

"Yes, I am. Her sessions are intense to say the least. But nonetheless, I'm grateful to be learning under her."

Reimus falls silent for a few seconds, in which case I pause brushing Alastor to turn to look at him. He's gently gazing at me. After he meets my gaze, he forces a smile.

"You will learn much from her."

I force a smile and nod my head, as I turn my gaze back to Alastor. "Do many people get the opportunity to learn under her?"

"No. She is very selective of who she shares her teachings with. So she must see something special in you."

My memory jogs at Hecate mentioning that she knew my mother, and I know that's the only reason why she would feel inclined to mentor me. I don't mention that to Reimus though. I continue brushing Alastor as Reimus goes silent. I look over at him, and I notice Reimus staring at me again.

"What did I tell you about that staring shit?" I ask as my eyebrows raise at him

A grin grows on his face as he laughs. "When I can figure out a way to spare myself the unconscious effort of it, I'll let you know."

My gaze trains on him at his comment, and I watch Reimus turn around and head back to the palace. I watch him walk off as I take note of the way his shirt hugs his arms, and how his pants are like two long black voids against the shine of the morning sun.

I turn my gaze back to Alastor as I finish grooming him. I give him one last show of affection, and leave the pasture to put his grooming items away. Once I'm walking back to the palace, I roam the open landscape that they have here. It's just a ginormous stretch of green, grassy land. A few trees here and there, but no plants, shrubs, nothing.

I still highly believe they could spruce the place up a bit.

I head into the kitchen to grab myself something to eat before I head into the village. I walk through the dining room which is completely empty, fully thinking Reimus would be in here per usual at this time. As I make my way into the kitchen, my mouth gapes open.

Their kitchen is marvelous. There's a huge white and black marbled island that sits right in the middle of the room, surrounded by rows of sleek black cabinets. Etched into the glass are intricate designs that truly make the vintage cabinets all the more appealing. Plants hang sparingly throughout the room from the ceiling, along with a crystal chandelier that hangs from the center. White walls with traces of smokey gray filtered through them, and white tiled flooring.

No wonder why Aven always has a smile on his face. If I got to cook in a kitchen like this, I would be just as ecstatic.

Finding my way to the food pantry, I open it up and it is filled to the brim with foods such as canned goods and dried pasta. I gawk at all the food they have piled in here and am astonished there's *so* much for just two people that live here.

After a while of exploring my options, I end up pulling out some fresh bread before I head over to the fridge, where I find some eggs, shredded cheese, bacon and butter.

As I fry the bacon, I ponder over what my session with Hecate will be like today. Will she have me sitting in silence again? Or will we—

"I see you found the food just fine."

Gasping at the sudden interaction, I turn to see Reimus standing in the doorway. He's leaning against the door, with his arms crossed across his chest.

"Yes, I did." Turning back around focusing on my bacon. I hear Reimus stride over to me, and pull a stool out. I hear him settle himself into the seat, and I feel the gaze of his eyes on my back.

I'm going to gouge those eyes out one of these days.

Taking the bacon off the pan and setting them onto a napkin lined plate, I blot the excess grease off and let it sit there as I scramble my eggs. After I've cooked them in my pan, I transfer everything to a plate and turn around to walk over to the island to sit down.

I notice Reimus has a mug of coffee in one hand, and a newspaper in the other. He looks up at me and is gazing at me for a moment, before his gaze trains back onto the newspaper.

I take my plate and place it on the counter as I go to pull out the seat next to Reimus. I begin eating, praying that Reimus just reads his newspaper quietly, and lets me eat in peace. It's bad enough that he has a massive staring problem. When I finish, I sit back in my seat as I take a drink of coffee.

"You finished?"

Reimus gestures to my empty plate. Taken aback by his gesture, I hesitate for a moment. I'm so used to cleaning up after myself and my family. I nod my head and he takes my plate to the kitchen sink. He sets his newspaper and coffee down as he takes my plate and rinses it off in the sink. I never noticed before how muscular he is until now, how his arms hug his shirt. When he turns around, I avert my gaze to my coffee.

I loathe this man, why am I noticing his muscles? Rolling my eyes internally at myself, I finish off my coffee. Wanting to put as much distance between me and Reimus as possible. I begin to stand up when Reimus grabs my mug out of my hand, beating me to it.

"I got it." He says, calmly yet sternly. His gaze meets mine for a moment as time seems to stop.

I let go of my grip on my coffee mug as Reimus takes it out of my hand, walking it over to the sink. As he rinses it off, I stand up and out of my stool.

"You're still an ass." I say just to be spiteful for no apparent reason.

Reimus laughs deeply, and it makes the hairs on the back of my neck stand up. I've heard him chuckle and laugh here and there, but never a laugh this genuine. A sound that makes my belly flutter—

Nope. Not doing this.

I push my stool in as I walk out of the kitchen, the sound of Reimus laughing following me the whole way out.

CHAPTER 26

For the next few weeks, I mentor with Hecate. Each and every day I begin to find myself more and more eager to learn more from her. And each and every day do I find something else that I've bottled up for so long. But through all of the crying and energetic releasing I've been doing, she has stuck with me and has not made me feel shameful about it once.

It warms my heart as I begin to believe Hecate's warm words that I do matter. That I can accept myself without needing to overextend myself to others just to prove my worth.

In the same few weeks, I've also found myself spending more time with Reimus.

Though my annoyance for him still churns brightly, and any chance I get to bicker with him delights me, I can't not acknowledge how he's been there for me through this process of healing my grief and trauma. I've talked very little with him about it, the thought of being personal with him still mortifies me. Nonetheless, he's never pushed me to confide in him. Instead, he's simply just sat with me through it in silence.

I would be lying to myself if I said I haven't noticed him…differently these past few weeks. Notice how serious his face becomes when he writes in that damn journal. Or notice how he stares at me when he thinks I don't notice, how the thought of him gazing upon me makes my belly flutter in ways I wish it hadn't for him.

But I know exactly why I'm here, and I won't let a little bit of curiosity stray me from the whole purpose of being in Vulir.

"Yeah, good luck with that."

Pulling myself from my aimless thoughts as Nikolai interrupts me, I roll my eyes and sigh in response. "My self-discipline is stronger than I fear you give it credit for, Nikolai."

Nikolai chuckles in response, and then his energy slips away once again.

Since I've been working with Hecate, it seems like the more "energetic gunk" I've cleared out, the easier it's been to communicate with the spirits. And one spirit in particular that communicates with me often is Nikolai.

At first, I was baffled at how clearly I could hear him, and also how much stronger I could feel his presence. Though over time I began to get used to him intrusively, yet innocently popping in every now and then. He's not terrible company either, even if he's a sarcastic ass sometimes.

I chuckle at the thought, as I continue my walk over to the pasture. The grass is still damp from last night's rain shower, but nonetheless it's still a pleasant feeling against my bare feet. Nearing the pasture, Alastor raises his head in my direction. With some grooming tools in hand I reach the gate and enter the pasture.

As I groom Alastor and talk to him as I always do, I feel the sunlight peak through the clouds as it beams against my cheek. Looking up, I close my eyes and embrace the warmth against my face.

Warm weather is finally here.

"Enjoying the sunshine, I see."

Turning my head towards Reimus standing over at the gate, I share a smile. "Yes, I am."

Reimus gazes upon me for a few seconds before switching his gaze to my feet. "No shoes?"

Looking down at my feet, I wiggle my toes in the grass. "The thought of wearing them didn't interest me."

Reimus pulls his gaze back to me. "Well, you might want to wear shoes next time. You never know what you could end up stepping on out here."

I could understand if he was insinuating stepping on shit or piss, but the horses aren't usually in this pasture so it's pretty clean. Plus, they do a good job with keeping the pastures and the stalls clean here.

Instead, I'm sure he's insinuating I'm going to step on a broken piece of glass or something. Like it's broad daylight out here, I think I can see just fine where I'm walking.

"I'll be fine."

"Suit yourself." Reimus says as he turns around and walks back to the palace.

Shaking off his tone deaf remark, I finish grooming Alastor.

"You know, if you ever meet a lady horse, I hope you treat her better than that."

Alastor gives a huff and nudges his head at me.

"Hey, I'm just saying. I see the way you look at Gizelle."

Alastor looks at me as I give him a knowing look, he turns his head away and looks straight ahead.

"Uh huh. That's what I thought."

As I finish grooming Alastor, I give him a final rub on the bridge of his nose and walk out of the pasture. As I walk back to the barn to put the grooming supplies away, I feel the sun's warmth on my cheek as it peeks through the clouds once more.

After I put the grooming supplies away, I begin walking back to the palace. I figured if dinner is in a couple of hours, I might as well shower now before--

"Fuck!"

I hiss out as I'm immediately hopping on one foot, hovering the other one over the ground. My toes instinctively curl through the excruciating pain as I plop myself on my ass. Lifting my foot up, I look at the bottom of my foot.

"You've got to be fucking kidding me."

I stepped on a fucking burr, and it's embedded into my foot.

"I mean, he told you to put shoes on." Nikolai makes an appearance again as he bellows a sharp laugh.

"This is *not* funny." I seethe through my teeth as I hold my foot. I hear Nikolai laugh in response, and it begins to fade away.

"What's not funny?"

Turning my head around to once again, find Reimus standing behind me. I turn my head back around, rolling my eyes at the irony of it all.

This is just great.

Clenching my jaw, I force myself to speak. "It appears I have stepped on…a burr."

Reimus begins to walk into my view as he kneels down before me, a sly grin appearing on his face. "Is that so? Hm. It's almost as if—"

"Don't even say it." I seethe as I glare at him.

Reimus begins to tighten the corners of his lips, visibly holding back a laugh. A few seconds later, he loses the battle and begins to laugh. His smile glinting against the sunlight.

Rolling my eyes and feeling helpless, I close my eyes trying to tamper down my frustration. "If you just move out of my way, I will get—"

My eyes flash open as I feel Reimus' arms lift me up off the ground, cradling me as he stands up. I instantly try to push myself out of his hold, but his arms keep me locked into place.

"What are you doing? Put me down!" I bellow.

Reimus ignores me as he turns on his heels, and starts walking us back to the palace. He doesn't even look down at me as his gaze faces forward. Hating the fact I am this close in his proximity, I let a heavy exhale out as I shout again.

"Did you not hear me? Put me down!"

Reimus turns his gaze onto me, his expression looking ever so bored. "I heard you, *loud* and clear the first time. But my answer is no."

"*No?*" I scoff as I peer at him.

"Yes, that is what I just said." He says dully.

"Why?"

"Because right now I'm choosing to be more than just a sarcastic bastard to you." He says as a grin forms his lips.

We don't speak the rest of the time I'm held like this. Not when we enter back into the palace, not when we're winding down the hallway, and not when he enters the room I've been staying in since I've been here.

He walks us over to the bathroom, and sets me down on a stool near that bathtub. Turning his back, he shuffles through a cabinet. Feeling done with the silence stretching between us, I open my mouth to speak.

"What are you doing?"

He turns back around and walks over to me, where he kneels in front of me with a pair of tweezers, a new bar of soap, and a clean washcloth. "I am being helpful."

As he kneels in front of me, his eyes are trained on my foot as he brings it up towards him. He shifts my foot from side to side as he inspects it. The whole time feeling uncomfortable with the intimacy of...whatever this is. After inspecting my foot, Reimus locks eyes with me. "It's not too bad. Just a few thorns we need to pull out."

Mentally preparing myself for how much this is going to hurt, I flatten my lips and curtly nod. I begin to close my eyes, bracing myself for the pain. My breath begins to quicken as I inhale and exhale deeply. I begin to feel Reimus bring a hand to my ankle, his fingers slowly moving up my calf.

What is he doing?

Goosebumps begin to prick my leg as he moves his hand up slowly. His calloused fingers tracing my leg with a feather lightness, my back slightly arches in response and I hate myself for the unconscious reaction. My breath hitches and I immediately loathe the type of reaction he's eliciting from me right now—

"Fuck!"

Interrupting mid-thought Reimus uses the tweezers to pull out the first thorn. Clutching my hands into fists, I take a deep breath and release. My eyes shoot open as I glare at Reimus.

"You did that on purpose!"

"You were as tense as a wooden board, I had to distract you."

Meeting Reimus' gaze again, I notice the silver in his eyes begin to brighten ever-so-slightly. Enchanted by this, I don't even recognize that he's about to pull out the second thorn.

Hissing through the sting, I breathe through it.

"One more."

Nodding my head, I brace myself.

"Look at me."

Fixing my gaze back onto Reimus, I find myself steadying my breathing.

"We're almost done, just focus on me. Don't focus on the pain."

My gaze doesn't falter from Reimus as I watch him, trying to forget that he's about to yank out a third thorn out of my barefoot. He watches me intently, never looking down at his hands. His gaze stares so deep into mine it feels like he's crawling his way inside of me. It's…riveting and overwhelming at the same time.

Without a warning, Reimus pulls out the final thorn, his gaze never faltering from mine. This time, I either barely noticed the pain of it, or it genuinely didn't hurt as bad as the other two.

"See, not too bad."

My gaze still trained on Reimus, I begin to shake myself out of whatever trance I'm in and start to pull my foot away from him. His hand doesn't let off, and he pulls my foot back towards him.

"I need to clean it."

I sit there confused again by his generosity, and after a few seconds I finally nod in agreement.

As Reimus cleans my foot I notice he doesn't seem annoyed by it. As he lathers my foot with soap, my breathing begins to hitch as a sense of uncomfortably arises with me. Uncomfortable with the intimacy of whatever this is that's going on.

He even goes the extra mile to give my foot a massage and, my gods, does it feel good. Reimus has his hands firmly around my foot, as he rubs the sole of my foot with his thumbs. Working in circular motions, I revel in the relaxation it's bringing me. I close my eyes and release a soft moan in response.

Gods, I loathe this man but maybe we can be friends enough just so I can receive the benefits of this once in a while. I wonder if he's—

I notice now that he's stopped, and I open my eyes to find him staring at me. I furrow my brows as my frustration actually *wants* him to continue. "What?"

Clenching his jaw, he averts his gaze back to my foot. He takes a visible swallow and clears his throat. "Nothing. Almost done." He goes back to massaging my foot as he finishes cleaning the wound.

Confused by the sudden mood change, I don't have much in me to wonder why as I can't think of anything else other than how good this feels right now.

Reimus abruptly stops, and wipes my foot clean with a dry washcloth. Gently he sets my foot down, and begins to stand up. My gaze travels up his body as it meets his gaze, which now looks down at me. His expression looks pained, like he's annoyed but doesn't know what to do about it.

"It should be fine now. I will check on it later to assess for any infection."

Reimus gazes at me for a few seconds before he turns on his heels and walks out of the bathroom, and then out of my bedroom. I sit there on the stool and wonder what made him flee so suddenly. The thought itself stops me dead in my tracks that for once I'm not utterly relieved by his absence, but that I'm actually perplexed by it.

That thought alone sends me into a downward spiral of disorientation.

I loathe him.

I loathe him.

I loathe him.

I remind myself over and over yet the thought creates an upheaval of skepticism that's difficult to tune out. I take a deep breath in and shake my head as I sternly whisper to myself. "Remember the mission, Melinoë."

At that moment, the sound of Nikolai's soft laughter breaks the silence in the room.

"Oh, things are finally *about to get good around here."*

Later on when I make it down for dinner, I make a promise to myself that I won't act strange. That I won't let get in the way that something is...different in the way I feel about Reimus.

How so quickly I can go from loathing him, to actually tolerating him. I promised myself that I'll act like nothing is different, and continue to treat him the same as I have.

Once I enter the dining room, Reimus' gaze meets mine as I walk towards my seat. His hair is damp as some of it falls over his forehead, allowing me to assume he just showered. Tonight he's wearing a black short-sleeved shirt, and black trouser pants. I'm beginning to feel like that's the only color he wears.

As I take my seat, I keep my gaze trained forward on the food set out in front of me. Tonight Aven has made marinated steaks, mashed potatoes with chives, green beans and dinner rolls. As I begin to fill my plate, Aven comes out with a bottle of red wine, in which I happily accept a glass of. I watch as Aven pours wine into my glass, and I thank him in response. He smiles generously, before walking back into the kitchen.

Taking a big gulp of wine, I set my glass down and waste no time cutting up my steak. As I pick up my knife, I look over at Reimus who has begun to fill his plate now. I watch as the dark hair that falls in front of his forehead glistens from the light of the chandelier above us. After a moment, Reimus looks up at me before he looks at my knife I'm holding up right.

He grins in response. "Are you fantasizing about using that against me, little spitfire?"

My initial confusion clears as I realize I'm just staring at him as I hold my knife. Instead of admitting I was actually admiring him for a moment, I fix my gaze back onto my steak.

"Would that frighten you?" I ask, my voice steady.

"Actually, quite the opposite." He says and I look up to notice a wicked grin on his face. My breath hitches internally as I try to shake off the reaction that gave me. Training my gaze back onto my food, I cut a piece of steak up and before plopping it into my mouth with a fork. "You are a strange man."

"If strange is what gets your attention, then that is what I will be." He says with a grin.

Rolling my eyes, I continue eating. I take another big gulp of my wine as I commit to keeping my attention on my food.

If strange is what gets my attention? Then that's what he'll be?

He must be trying to make a mockery out of me, in which he will sorely be unsuccessful with. I continue eating as I savor the flavor that Aven has perfected with this steak. I take my cut up pieces of steak and scoop them into my mashed potatoes, savoring the flavors of both as I bite into them. I smile to myself in response to the deliciousness.

"Do you always do that?"

My smile quickly falters at the sound of Reimus' voice. I peer over at him. "Do what?"

"Play with your food like that." He says as his fork gestures to my plate.

I roll my eyes. "Do you ever just mind your own business?"

Reimus chuckles as he grabs his glass of whiskey. "Am I not allowed to know more about you?"

"Should I deem you worthy, then yes." I say with a wicked smile.

"And how will I earn the worthiness to know?" He asks as he takes a drink from his whiskey.

I ponder to myself for a few moments as I wonder how I'll respond to him. The answer doesn't take long to form as I grab my wine glass. My voice is steady but full of smoke when I answer. I feel Reimus' gaze bore into the side of my face as my gaze trains on my glass.

"Who said I wanted you to know anything about me?" I ask.

I look over at Reimus and he doesn't look puzzled at all. Instead, he looks far more intrigued than I was anticipating. In response, he takes another drink from his whiskey before setting it down again.

Aven appears out of the kitchen as he comes to collect mine and then Reimus' empty plates. He gestures if I would like more wine, which I kindly reject. He takes our plates to the kitchen, leaving me in a silent room with Reimus.

I watch as Reimus stands up with his whiskey glass. He slowly strides over to the credenza cart, where he tops the whiskey off in his glass. He turns around and walks slowly over to me. The look in his eyes causes me to freeze internally, and for my breath to quicken. As he approaches me, I worry that he will take the seat next to me. Instead, he sets his glass down while he stands to my right.

"I have never been more intrigued to know someone than when I met you." He says as he now stands behind me. His hands gently come to my hair and I jolt in response. He carefully bunches my hair, moving it over my left shoulder. I feel him lower his head on the other side near my neck, his hand slowly moving to gently wrap around the base of my neck. My breath hitches in response as heat begins to pool low, automatically hating myself for said reaction.

His lips brush against my neck as I exhale raggedly. "And I have never loathed myself more than I do now because of it." He says as he slightly tightens the grip on my neck, his voice teeters on the tone of smoke and despisement.

My breathing becomes labored at the feel of Reimus' breath dancing along my neck. I begin to wonder what's going to happen from here. If he's going to turn my head to kiss me, or will we just leave things here.

I find myself tormented at the fact that, though I preach up and down how much I loathe this man, right now I shamelessly fantasize about what he'll do to me.

And I too, *loathe* myself for feeling that way.

Reimus hovers his neck for another second, before he pulls away altogether. He grabs his whiskey and begins to walk out of the dining room. Before he leaves the room entirely, he turns his head to the side as his back faces me. "Get some rest."

He leaves the dining room, this time my gaze trained on him the whole way out.

319

CHAPTER 27

Everything is pitch dark. I look around and cannot find anything that can help me distinguish where I am.

Something feels wrong.

Off in the distance I see a dark figure that seems to be hovering over something. I try to walk towards it but my feet don't seem to want to cooperate. I look down at my legs, panicked that they won't respond to what my mind wants them to do. Then it hits me as I become familiar with this liminal space I'm in.

I'm dreaming.

"Don't worry...I'll take good care of you."

My gaze shoots up as I see the figure in the distance again, and recognize the voice is coming from it.

Who is this? What are they doing?

The energy in this space quickly becomes heavy, trickling a chill to run down my back. Though it's pitch dark in here, I can feel the energy around me.

I can feel the energy radiating off of this figure, and it is malicious.

Trying to get my feet to move forward so I can get closer, I successfully manage to get my legs to move though only a few feet.

The dark figure begins to lighten as I grow near it, and realize that with its broad shoulders and toned arms that it seems to be a man. But I'm unable to distinguish anything else about him as his back is turned towards me.

I try to peer over what he is looming over and–

It's a woman.

My entire body goes ice cold as I put it all together and realize why this man is looming over this woman. Frantic, I try to open my mouth to scream and become mobilized in fear when nothing comes out.

I have to help this woman before this predator does what I think he's about to do.

Trying my hardest to will everything I've got in me to help this woman, I fight against whatever energetic hold that's taken over me. As I fight against this invisible resistance, I watch as the man lowers himself over the woman.

No.

No, no this cannot happen. I *need* to help this woman.

As he lowers himself, I can see the woman is frozen in place. I don't see her try to fight her way out of it. It's like she's just accepted her fate.

Taking heavy deep breaths in and out, I grow increasingly frantic as no matter how hard I try, I can't get myself to move. Neither can I get myself to scream for help. I can't make anything out about the woman, except that she's lying on the dark, cold ground.

As I continuously fight against the hold I'm under, I begin to notice everything starts to fade away. I begin to feel myself forcefully being pulled away from what's about to happen.

No, no I need to help this woman! Somebody help!

Screaming in my mind as the words fail me to come out of my mouth, I watch everything around me begin to fade away. But before everything goes blank once more, I hear the man whisper one last sentence to the woman. It echoes around the void as if I can hear him speak in every direction.

"What a pretty thing you are."

In the next moment, I'm shooting up from my bed and my breathing is just as heavy as it was when I was dreaming just moments ago.

Sitting upright in my bed, I clutch my chest with one hand as my other holds me up. My breathing is heavy, and beads of sweat form over my forehead. I frantically look around the room and realize I'm in my room.

I'm awake.

I'm awake.

Repeating to myself numerous times until I begin to feel myself ground into reality. Forcing myself to slow my breathing until I get to a slower, steadier rhythm, I contemplate over the dream I just had.

I've never had such a traumatizing dream like that before. Why would I dream about something like that?

Once my breathing becomes more controlled, I climb out of bed and stand in place for a few seconds. Using the back of my palm to wipe the sweat from my forehead, I walk over to the window near my bed. I take in the rich blue and indigo colors that wash over the sky, which means the sun is about to rise soon. Walking over to the bathroom, I stand hovering over the sink.

It was just a dream.

I focus on taking one last big breath in, and one last slow release out. Unwilling to go back to sleep after what I just dreamt about, I decide that I might as well get a jump start on my day.

Turning on the hot water, I let the shower run as I shuck off my sweat-drenched clothes and stand under the constant fall of the shower water.

For a while I just stand there, noting how exhausted I feel right now. I usually don't get up quite this early, so that could explain why I feel so drained. Rubbing my eyes, I try to shake off the exhaustion I feel. I meet with Hecate today, but if I'm still feeling this tired, I may come home and take a nap afterwards.

Once I finish washing up, I step out of the shower and turn the water off. Wrapping a clean white towel over me, I embrace the softness of the material. I walk over to the mirror and quickly notice bags begin to form under my eyes, as my cheeks even look slightly sunken in.

Am I ill? This seems excessive for just a little bit of exhaustion.

Brushing out my tangled hair, I throw on some clean clothes and head downstairs to make myself some breakfast. When I get down to the kitchen, it's dead quiet. Not surprising though, as usually I don't meet Reimus down here until a few hours from now.

Walking over to the fridge, I pull out a carton of eggs, butter, and shredded cheddar cheese. After setting those down on the counter, I grab from the pantry a loaf of bread, and pop two pieces in the toaster.

After I finish cooking my scrambled eggs, I sprinkle some shredded cheese on top, topping my plate with my toast, and sit down at the kitchen island.

After I ate my breakfast, I remained seated in the stool for a few moments. Rubbing my eyes again, I begin to feel a dull pain form between my brows. I rub my temple as it begins to strengthen.

"What the fuck is going on?" I whisper to myself. The discomfort after a few moments begins to subside.

"Couldn't sleep?"

Looking over my shoulder to see Reimus walking into the kitchen, my breath hitches in my throat. Not only did he catch me off guard, but he's also wearing nothing but a pair of gray sweatpants that hang low on his waist. For a moment, I can't help but to find my gaze roaming his muscular figure, starting from his toned arms and chest, down to his abdomen, and lower—

Closing my eyes and shaking some self-control back into myself, I re-open my eyes and meet Reimus' gaze.

"Yeah, I had a bad dream. Couldn't go back to sleep."

Reimus walks over to me, but before he takes the seat next to me, he walks over to the coffee pot and pours himself a cup of coffee.

This man is simply just grabbing a cup of coffee, but gods does it feel like he's taunting me. After the altercation last night, my mind has felt frazzled about him. So much so, that I loathe myself for it. My gaze roams over his waist again, and this time when I meet his gaze once more, I find he has a grin plastered on his face.

"Look who's staring now." He says as he walks over to seat himself next to me. I force myself to get it the fuck together. Sitting myself up a little taller, I lift my chin slightly.

"Not nearly as much as I catch you staring at me."

Reimus laughs. "You're not wrong."

Rolling my eyes, I try to force down the smile that's forming. But when I feel like I'm about to be unsuccessful, I bring my mug to my lips and take a drink of my coffee.

"What was this dream about?"

Feeling an instant rush of crisp dread overfill me, I set my mug down as my gaze trains on my hands that hold it. "I don't want to talk about it."

I feel his stare on me as I stare at my mug. "Are you alright?"

When I don't answer, Reimus doesn't pester me to explain further. Instead, he grabs an unfinished piece of toast off of my plate and takes a big bite out of it. My head whips up to him as he chews on my piece of toast.

"Excuse you? Who said I was done with that?"

"Well, judging by how cold it is now, I'd assume you were."

Reimus gives me a grin as I roll my eyes.

Looking at Reimus as he polishes off my piece of toast, he takes another swig of his coffee. His gaze never leaves mine.

His hair is tousled from sleep, and the only clothing he's wearing is a pair of sweatpants that hang low off his hips. My breath hitches as temptation sparks within me, but another feeling that surges unfortunately is one that tends to override the other.

Distrust.

"Why do you want to know me?"

Reimus' gaze doesn't falter from mine, as he brings a hand up slowly to brush a loose strand of my still wet hair behind my ear. The touch of his fingers sends jolts through me that leave me feeling frazzled, and confused as this is definitely not normal behavior of him.

"Do you always doubt the intentions of others?"

Pulling myself from my roaming thoughts, my instant reaction is to pull away from his gaze and hide what I'm really thinking. But instead, I keep my gaze trained on him.

I lower my brows in a questioning gaze. "And you don't?"

Reimus' expression turns solemn as he tilts his head slightly. "Always."

Confusion causes my brows to furrow, in which case Reimus continues.

"I am always wary of who I put my trust in, but I also possess an abundance of good judgment."

"Really? And what does your judgment say of me?" I ask sarcastically.

Reimus gives me an innocent smile, as his gaze trails down my body. At first, I become flustered and irritated that he thinks right now is a good time to be looking at my body, but then his gaze meets mine again.

"I think you have been conditioned to do everything on your own. That your strength is unending, but also is your distrust in others."

I scoff as my anger quickly rises within me, but is soon overtaken by shame. It slithers its way up my chest and demands to pry itself out of my throat. Nonetheless, I remain controlled in my response. I have nothing to feel guilty about for how I chose to survive, and I need no explanation.

I clench my jaw slightly as I go to take another sip of my coffee. "You're not completely wrong in your judgment."

Reimus watches me as I begin to stand out of my seat to take my plate and mug to the sink. Reimus plants his hand firmly on mine, halting me from leaving my seat. My gaze goes to him as his irises churn wildly. I watch as the silver and blue dance together, never having seen anything like it before.

He moves my hand and grabs my plate for me, along with my mug. I nearly protest that I can do it myself, but his expression reads a sternness that tells me I won't win this argument. He stands up and walks my dishes to the sink. He turns around and walks towards me, his gaze menacing and causes me to shift in my seat.

He approaches me as he grabs my chin, holding my gaze up to his. My breath hitches in response. His gaze remains focused on mine, as if nothing else matters in this entire world then gazing into my eyes right now. Anticipation grows as I don't know what his reasoning is for this display of…whatever this is.

"Whatever it takes." Is all he says, before he lets go of my chin. His jaw ticks as he stares at me for a few seconds before he walks away.

"You know, a good night's rest will do wonders for you."

Sitting cross legged in front of Hecate, I can feel the grogginess seeping back into my bones.

"I did sleep. I am just tired for some reason today."

"Well, we have been working very hard the past few weeks clearing and releasing, maybe your body needs a break. Let's skip our session tomorrow, and resume the next. Deal?"

A yawn slips through my mouth as I nod my head. "Okay, deal."

"Good. You're making great progress anyway, I know your mother is very proud."

The grogginess vanishes at the mention of my mother. At the fact that she said *is* rather than *would be*.

"Does she communicate with you? Do you see her when you astral travel?" I ask.

"Sometimes, yes." She says with a soft smile.

"What does she say?"

"Mostly just gossip." Hecate says as she gives a wink. "But she also talks about you. She talks of how proud she is of you, and also how much she wishes she could be here to guide you. Help you feel less alone."

Emotion clogs my throat as I wonder what it would be like for my mother to still be here.

Speaking of mother, why hasn't Makaria written me back yet? I would think she would've gotten my letter by now. Maybe she hasn't gotten it yet? Or it got lost in…crow mail.

I really wonder how she's doing right now. I will have to ask Reimus about my letter later, and see if he can figure out if she received it or not.

"Will I ever be able to talk to her? I always thought that she was the first spirit I'd have open communication with. Am I doing anything wrong?"

Hecate grabs my hands and holds them in her own as a pained look splashes across her face. "No dear, you are not doing anything wrong. It will happen soon."

Feeling a little down, I nod through my doubt. I doubt that I'll ever be advanced enough to be able to communicate with my mother again. The doubt begins to overwhelm me as I begin to feel a heaviness of despair that rattles my body.

"Don't be so hard on yourself. I promise, you are making great progress. Be proud of yourself for all the hard work you've done so far."

Not feeling entirely confident in her words, even though I know we've done a lot of deep work over the past few weeks. A lot of shadow work, a lot of energy healing, and trauma healing. Although for some reason I just feel like it's not enough, even though I was feeling pretty confident about it leading up to today.

Ugh, what is up with me today?

"Thank you, Hecate. I appreciate your kindness more than you know."

"You're welcome, dear. Now before we finish for the day, are you sure everythings alright? Your energy feels…off today." She says with a look of concern on her face.

"Yeah, I'm fine. I just feel really exhausted today. I think when I get home I'm going to get some rest."

Hecate studies me intently, and for a few moments she doesn't look convinced. Then, her expression softens but still holds a curious look. "Okay, go get some rest. I'll see you in a couple of days."

Nodding with a smile, I get up and give Hecate a hug goodbye. Since I've worked with her regularly, we've begun to form a friendship that is outside of mentoring me. Sometimes I come in here and Hecate asks me about living with Reimus. I wonder if she can sense that there's something more going on, but for now I remain vague about it.

It's not that I don't trust her, but it's just that…I don't trust something long lasting could come out of this.

As I make my way back to the palace, the tiredness I feel begins to grow. As I make it to the palace, I walk straight up to my bedroom, closing the door behind me.

"Yeah, we are definitely taking a nap." I say to myself.

Shucking off my clothes, and changing into a nightgown, I pull back my covers and crawl into bed. The sun shines through the window, as it's still early in the day, but this tiredness has me thinking of nothing else but sleep right now.

So I decide to give my body what it's apparently craving, and I fall fast asleep.

I awake to feeling someone near me, but as I open my eyes I realize that I'm dreaming.

Looking around to see that I'm in my room, on my bed, in the same nightgown that I put on before falling asleep. Everything is hazy, yet clear enough for me to know that I'm in my room.

This is not a dream. I'm astral traveling.

"I've been waiting for this moment."

A cold sweat chills me down to my nerves as I remember that voice and realize who is in this room with me now.

The man who killed Eiran, is looming over my bed. And even though he's dead, his spirit feels ever-so-real in this moment right now.

Panicking, I begin to move myself up and immediately the man pushes me back down. I can feel the weight of his hands on me, the press of his fingers as they push me firmly down into my bed.

I can *feel* him.

Fighting against his hold he grips my throat, and suddenly I freeze as this man is about to strangle me.

"I told you I'd get my revenge, I just knew that I needed to wait. Wait for you to come more into your gifts, come more into your ability to astral travel. Then, I knew I'd be able to do what I'm about to do next."

My eyes bulge out as he grips my throat tighter. I bring my hands up to push his hands away, in which case he takes my hand and pins them up above me. Panic begins to ensue as he's somehow stronger than me even though he's a spirit.

How is this possible—

My mind begins to flash images of deja vu as I realize—

This was *my* dream.

The girl I dreamt of this happening to is *me*.

I had a vision of this happening, I was being warned about this.

Oh, gods. No.

This is actually happening.

My thoughts are interrupted as the man mumbles something to himself, before he lets go of my hands held above me. Instantly, I try to flail them down to attack this man but I can't move.

I can't move at all.

"That's the one good thing about being dead, my pretty. Is that witches over here talk, and talk about some pretty strong binding spells. I didn't think it would work but man, I was wrong." He says as his smile grows sinister, and I feel absolutely nauseous.

He uses his hands to then lift my nightgown, until it's brought up to my neck, exposing my breasts. I open my mouth to scream but the binding spell must've binded my mouth shut because I can't make out any sound. My breathing is ragged as panic doesn't even begin to cover what I'm feeling right now.

Dread.

Terror.

Helplessness.

I can't move or make any noises, and this man is about to—

I can't even wonder. I can't, I can't.

Tears begin to flood my eyes as I wonder why everything went so wrong. How everything in my life turned out the way it did.

Why me?

Haven't I suffered enough?

My mind begins to conjure up all the feelings until suddenly, my mind goes astray and I feel numb inside.

I realize the only thing I can do at this point is to just let it happen and get it over with. Because the helplessness that I feel suffocating my bones right now persuades me that I have no fight left in me, in this moment here.

That this man, is going to rape me, and I can't move to defend myself against it.

Tears pour from my eyes as I feel his calloused hands skim up my thighs, terror flooding me as he nears my underwear. His explorations halt, as he moves to unbutton his pants.

"Don't worry. I'll take good care of you."

My mind goes blank as I accept my vile fate.

He begins to pull his pants down, and I don't have to look down to know that his cock is freed from his pants. His hands move back to my underwear as he begins to pull them down—

In the next second, the weight of him hovering over me vanishes. It takes me a few seconds to realize it, since I've begun dissociating from this moment altogether, but I finally come back to the moment when I'm being jostled by someone.

"Meli! I'm here, it's okay. No one is going to hurt you. I promise you."

The sound is a male voice, one that I'd recognize anywhere. When I look up, I—

"Eiran?"

Suddenly, I'm able to talk again, and I instantly choke on a harsh cry.

"I'm right here, Meli. I'm right here with you."

I then feel Eiran pulling my underwear back up, and pulling my nightgown back down to cover myself. Once he does, he scoops me up into his arms and rocks me softly. Feeling the weight of him soothes me entirely and I begin to sob.

For the fact that this man just tried to rape me, even though he's dead. That my father never appreciated me, who never respected me. That I lost my greatest friend, my love.

Everytime I get into a funk, I always try to steer myself into remembering how far I've come. How much strength it takes to have endured what I have, and how things can be different for me.

But right now, the hole of depression is winning, and I can't get myself to pull out of it.

So I just cry, and cry.

Eiran kisses my forehead, still gently rocking me back and forth. *"I have never left you, I have been here watching you. I can't tell you how fucking brave you are, Meli. You are the strongest woman I have ever known. And I am so sorry that you have been treated so unfairly. I'm so, so sorry."*

My sobbing quickly turns into hysterical crying. I feel my body pulsating with grief, my body shaking as I cry into Eiran's arms. Not even the loving embrace of his arms can help me see the light in this moment.

And that thought alone mortifies me.

As Eiran rocks me, he quietly whispers how much he loves me, and how much he's proud of me. He continues this for a long time until I begin to calm down.

Eiran holds my head, and fixes my gaze onto him.

"That man will never hurt you again. I will never let him hurt you. You hear me?"

He places a hand over my heart, as tears freely fall from my eyes once more.

"Why do these things happen to me? Why can't things just be good for once?" I nearly plead with Eiran.

"My sweetheart. Life has not been fair for you. You deserve far better than what you've been given." He says as he kisses my forehead numerous times. *"But things are going to look better in time, please believe me."*

He pulls my gaze onto him.

"You meeting Reimus happened for a reason. You may not be ready yet, but you will see soon that he is the catalyst in more ways than one. I know you don't think that you deserve unconditional love, but he'll show you differently. You have always deserved the very best things this life can offer."

Feeling flabbergasted by his words, unwilling to believe him that Reimus cares for me in the way Eiran is making it seem. Instead, I brush past it.

"What about you? I feel guilty that we never really had a fair shot. I should've expressed my feelings for you sooner. I--"

"I always knew how you felt about me. But your path... Our paths crossed for a reason, but yours crossed with him for an entirely different one."

I furrow my brows in disbelief. *"For what reason then?"*

"So you could finally see what real love looks like."

Real love? Reimus and I *loathe* one another, we bicker with one another every chance we get. We have our moments of tolerance with one another, but...

He doesn't *love* me, let alone care for me. That's impossible.

"But you loved me? Why couldn't I have that with you?" I ask changing the subject, grief roiling through me.

"I do love you, my sweetheart. I always will. But you were never going to truly accept true love until you finally decided to leave Elzwin. You were never going to fully believe that you were deserving of love until you finally chose yourself, and you coming to Vulir was part of you finally doing just that. My purpose was to help get you to that point, and I couldn't be happier that I've been able to do that."

Wiping my eyes, I take in everything that Eiran is saying and I find myself speechless. Before I can respond, Eiran cuts me off.

"You're about to wake up, and when you do, Reimus is going to come rushing in here. Let him in Meli. Let him show you that through this treacherous life you've lived, good things are possible."

But I had a good thing with *Eiran*. What we had was *good*. Why couldn't I have kept that? I could ask myself that question a million times and I fear I will never truly understand. And maybe that is the whole point of this existence.

That certain things will happen and no amount of understanding it will make it easier to grasp.

"Why would he come flying in here?"

"Because you've been screaming in your sleep for the past few minutes now."

Confused how that can be possible when I'm indeed not screaming now. I realize that I don't have time to ask many questions, and just settle for what I really want to say to Eiran right now.

"How did you know…" I can't finish the sentence by asking Eiran how he knew what was happening.

"I told you, I've always been here. I will always protect you."

I stammer over my words as I try to wrap my mind around all of this. My eyes well with tears once more. As I'm about to form a sentence, Eiran cuts me off.

"Wake up, Meli. Let him in. And know that I will always love you, no matter what."

Eiran gives me a quick kiss and I savor the feel of it. In the next moment, I jolt awake.

Clutching my throat as it's sore and aches terribly, I begin to panic if I'm really awake or not. I feel the weight of hands on my shoulders and I shove them away from me, frantically fighting off whoever—

"Melinoë! It's me, it's Reimus!"

My wild gaze focuses as I realize I've been swatting at Reimus' hold on my shoulders. His expression looks worried as I swing my gaze to finally meet his.

I try to slow my ragged breathing down, but instead I burst out into a sob. I let myself fall into Reimus, and I sink into his embrace for a long time as I allow myself to painfully sob.

Reimus pulls one hand behind my head to try to calm my shaking, and he softly strokes my hair.

"You're okay. You're safe."

And for the first time since I've gotten here, I let go of my resistance.

CHAPTER 28

For quite a while, I remained in Reimus' arms as I sobbed. He didn't ask any questions, he just held me as I cried.

At some point, I must've exhausted myself into a slumber as I now wake up in my bed with the covers drawn over me. Even as I wake, I don't feel enticed to remove myself from this bed.

So I let myself drift back off to sleep.

When I awake a second time, I can feel someone else in the room with me. Instantly, I jerk upright clutching the blanket up to my neck. Looking over to my right, I see Reimus sitting in the chair next to my bed, with his journal in his lap. He meets my frantic gaze and remains still.

"My apologies if I frightened you. I just wanted to sit with you."

As my wild gaze begins to soften, I keep the covers still trained up to my neck.

Reimus begins to stand slowly. "I can give you some space if you'd feel more comfortable with that."

As I stare at him, unable to form words, he slowly nods his head and begins to walk towards the door. But this time, I'm not interested in him leaving.

"Wait."

Reimus lowers his hand from the doorknob, and slowly turns back around. His gaze is soft, calm as it meets mine.

"I would actually really like the company. I really don't want to be alone right now."

Reimus doesn't answer for a moment. He continues to watch me, until he begins his calm stride back over to the chair, where he sits once again.

Once Reimus sits back down, I lower myself back into the bed, facing towards him. The only thing I have any interest in doing at this moment is closing my eyes, and drifting off to sleep.

And so once again, I do just that.

When I wake up, the room is dark save for the glow of the fire that must've been lit sometime while I was sleeping. I see that Reimus is still sitting in the chair next to me, this time writing in his black journal. He must not sense yet that I'm awake again, and so instead I let myself admire this other side of him.

His jet black hair falls forward over his dark brow as he writes in his journal. I notice the seriousness dance with tenderness in his eyes, the glint of his eyes casting a glow from the firelight. His jaw seems rigid, but the rest of his body seems relaxed.

This is a sight of him I don't think I've ever seen before.

Suddenly, Reimus lifts his head towards me and meets my gaze. He gives a soft smile, as he closes his journal.

"Good evening."

"Hi." I say tiredly as I wipe my eyes. Almost as if on cue, my stomach gives a wild rumble. Reimus' eyes glance towards my belly, then they find me once more.

"I will find you something to eat."

I nod my head in agreement. Though the thought of being alone doesn't fill me with ease, I know that Reimus is near if I need him. Reimus stands and strides out of the bedroom door, where I hear him walk down the hallway.

After a short while, Reimus is back with a tray of food. As he kicks the door closed behind him with his foot, he walks over to me and sets the tray down on the nightstand next to the bed.

"I wasn't sure what you'd be in the mood for, so I had Aven whip you up a few different things."

Looking at the tray before me, I realize he's not exaggerating. I notice that he's brought me an array of different options such as tomato bisque soup, a grilled cheese sandwich, grilled chicken strips, a bowl of dried nuts, a bowl of grapes and cantaloupe, and a glass of water.

Looking at the different options he brought me, I suddenly feel emotional at the gesture. As I fight back tears, I meet his gaze. "Thank you."

He nods his head as he sits back down.

I begin with the soup and the grilled cheese, and when I finish that, I move onto the grapes and cantaloupe. I feel a little awkward at the silence as I'm just stuffing my face while Reimus just sits there not saying a word.

When I finish, I down half of the water before setting it back down. I sit up in bed until my back is flush with the headboard. Bringing the covers down to my waist, I realize my neck is tender. I move my hand to my neck and—

Fuck.

I wince at the soreness and hardly a moment after, I feel Reimus' hand wrap over mine. I look at him and chills run down my back. His gaze is menacing, and it's unlike me to be afraid of men. But Reimus' body language breeds rage, though I know it's not meant for me.

As he slowly moves his hand over mine, he meets my gaze almost as if to signify that he's about to move my hand. I haven't been able to take a look in the mirror yet, but this all happened while I was in the astral realm. There's no way that I have bruises on my neck.

Spirits can't actually hurt you…

Reimus gently moves my hand, and his eyes narrow to the skin beneath. Instantly, his eyes grow feral and his expression grows furious. His other hand goes to cup my face, bringing my gaze up to his. My breath hitches in response as his jaw clenches so damn tight that the veins in his neck bulge.

His cold gaze finds mine as his ice-blue irises churn brightly. "Who did this?"

He demands as I feel the brush of his thumb beneath my bottom lip. His gaze bores into mine, a stare that could slice right through someone's soul with how penetrating it is.

"It's a long story. A man was in my dreams—well, it wasn't a dream. I know I was astral traveling. He…"

As I trail off, Reimus' eyes grow dark. He averts his gaze and his jaw ticks, and it takes him several seconds before he's able to bring his gaze back to mine. He lowers his hand, and seats himself next to me on the bed. His gaze never leaves mine. "Tell me everything, and leave nothing out."

Feeling taken back by his sudden interest in me, I hesitate for a moment. But the look in his eyes right now tells me that he won't take no for an answer. Taking a deep breath in, and exhaling, I do just that. I tell him everything.

I tell him how I originally traveled here with another man, and how that man risked his life for me in the process. How I lost my best friend, and someone I loved. How I sought revenge on the man who killed him and butchered him to pieces, and then how that same man tried to rape me. I tell him every detail, and I watch as his expression ranges from deep sorrow, to rage.

After I unload everything onto him, I thought for sure I would have felt uncomfortable with unleashing so much personal information onto him. But instead, I felt a vast weight lift off my shoulders.

It felt…good to share myself like that with someone.

"Tell me what happened to the body."

I clear my throat and work on a swallow. "I left him there to rot."

Reimus clenches his jaw and immediately stands up. "Show me."

"What?"

Reimus shares a long glance with me. "If this man was able to attack you to this extent, in the astral realm, it usually means one thing."

Feeling worried by the seriousness in Reimus' tone, I avert my gaze to the floor. Fidgeting with my fingers, I move my gaze back to Reimus as he continues.

"It usually means that he's been siphoning your energy from you. He has energetically latched onto you."

"What? How—"

"Have you felt drained lately? Felt moody, low energy?" Reimus asks, interrupting me. His gaze is stern yet worrisome. Feeling confused by his questioning, my eyes widen as I realize.

The sudden tiredness I was feeling yesterday.

Oh, gods.

"Yes, I randomly felt extremely tired yesterday. I remember feeling like all I wanted to do was sleep. Ever since I had a dream of what was evidently about to happen to me."

Reimus watches me as his expression softens. "That wasn't a dream you had."

"What do you mean? Of course it was."

"Melinoë, what you had was a premonition."

Hecate said that my mother was known for her gift of sight, and having prophetic dreams. I must've inherited the same gift from my mother.

"I…had a premonition…" I repeat slowly.

Suddenly Reimus holds his hand out for me. "We must go."

I furrow my brows as I grab his hand. I stand myself right in front of him, and I can feel the energy of urgency leaking from him like wax dripping from a candle. "Go where?"

Without answering, he rushes over to my duffel bag and pulls out a sweater, leggings, socks, and grabs my boots that are on the ground. He brings everything over to me and hands them to me. His menacing gaze finds mine as it burrows itself into my soul.

"We're going to pay a bastard a visit."

It's been a half hour since Reimus and I saddled up onto Alastor. Since I don't remember how I got into Vulir, Reimus has been leading the way.

The journey isn't gentle either. I have Alastor going at a full gallop so not only is the ride bumpy and fast paced, but I also keep bumping up against Reimus the whole time. Reimus keeps his right arm firm around my waist to keep me flush against his body, so it only enables the friction more.

We reach a wide sky length awning made of gray brick. Standing in the center of it is a dark figure. I tense up in the saddle.

"It's okay, it's just Charon. The quickest way to the Sephyra Forest is past him."

My sudden nerves easing at the reassurance, I relax again into Reimus.

As we approach Charon, I begin to take note of him upclose. He's tall and wears a black robe that seems to evaporate at the ends. It's almost like his robe is made of…

"Shadows?" I ask softly. I gaze at the robe as the ends of it filter through the air and dissipate.

"He is a farrier of souls. Both for the living, and the deceased."

As we approach Charon, Reimus doesn't bother dismounting Alastor. Charon recognizes him instantly. His gaze sweeps over to me and he begins to gaze at me.

"Ah Melinoë, we meet again. I hope you are well." Charon says. As we approach him, I try to take note of his features, yet it's hard to do so with him encapsulated by the robe. I'm able to make out that he's quite pale, and his hair as white as the moonlight. It travels past his shoulders, and is unbound and messy. I passed out trying to get into Vulir, so I don't remember him.

I force a smile as I respond. "I am okay."

Charon nods at me with a gentle smile. He looks at Reimus once again. "Off to the Sephyra Forest?"

Confused by how he would know that, I turned my head around to look at Reimus.

"Charon knows and sees all."

"Oh." I say softly. Turning my gaze back to Charon, he sweeps his gaze to me again.

"Understand Melinoë, that what happened to you will not go unnoticed. That such actions will be dealt with as his soul departs to The Underworld."

My stomach drops at the declaration Charon makes. I find myself at a loss of how to respond to that, so for now I just flatten my lips and nod my head.

"We'll be back." Reimus says to Charon.

Charon nods his head, and opens the shield. Looking through it I can clearly see the Sephyra Forest. Without hesitation, Alastor gallops through it. We ride through the Sephyra Forest for some time, until I begin to see a familiar ducked off cave come into view.

I slow Alastor down to a walk, until we reach the corpses laying out in front of us. Their bodies tinged with an awful smell that would make me gag if I weren't reminded of why they lay there in the first place. I pull Alastor to a halt, as Reimus dismounts off, where I follow behind.

"This is the place?" Reimus asks quietly.

Forgetting that Reimus is even with me for a moment, I take in the sounds of the trees. The smell of the grass, and the sound of the water trickling down the stream. My gaze once more pins to the rotting corpses, and I slowly walk towards them. I hear Reimus follow behind me, not saying a word.

Once I had all three bodies in my immediate sight, I thought for sure I would turn around and find that the sight would be too much. Instead, I take it all in. Training this sight to memory that they are indeed dead and deserved their fate.

I approach the familiar face of the man who killed Eiran. The same man who attempted to assault me. I stand there as my fingers curl into my palms, hot rage beginning to cloak my face.

Reimus moves to my side, and I can see from the corner of my eye that he's not gazing at the body but at me. He gently reaches out for my hand, and I uncurl my fingers as he squeezes it, turning my attention towards him.

"From this day forth, you will never have to deal with this man again. I vow it."

I nod at his promise, as he gently releases my hand. He digs for something in his pocket, when he pulls out a small jar. He hands it to me as I look at him confused. "When it's time, put his ashes into this jar. We will take it back to Hecate. She'll know what to do with them."

Before I have a moment to ask him what he's talking about, he steps back a few steps from me. His gaze is still trained on me, as his back begins arching and his breathing begins to deepen.

"You're safe with me. That doesn't change. Remember that."

I furrow my brows not understanding why he'd need to remind me that. I open my mouth to ask him what the hell he's talking about until Reimus' body begins to morph into—

Oh, my gods.

Gasping, I jerk backwards and fall on my ass as I look up at the creature that now stands in Reimus' place. The shift, it all happened so fast. I open and close my eyes a few times, wondering if my gift of mind manipulation has begun to now infiltrate *my* mind this time. When I can clearly see that isn't the case, my fingers begin to tremble as I bring it shakily up to my mouth.

His skin the color of midnight and ash, rough and scaly all over. His onyx hued wings flex wide open as he stretches his neck out. My gaze tracks over his large figure, lowering to the sharp talons for claws the size of my hands. He glides his enormous tail along the forest floor, sharp ridges coastin along it and meeting at the blade-sharp end.

"Oh, my gods…"

He's a fucking drago.

Reimus lowers his head down towards me, a soft trilling noise emitting from his large jaw. He gently nudges my hand at my side, and I tentatively bring it up to him.

Staring into those eyes…those eyes that I'd recognize anywhere. I stammer over my words as I try to speak.

"You're Guardian of Vulir…"

He nods his head.

"And you protect the village, but I never asked *how* you protect the village. You said that there were others like you that were killed."

He nods his head again.

"I—"

My mind goes blank as I remember stories being told by my mother about the Draghi. My mother used to read stories about them to Makaria and I when we were younger. She must've been trying to tell me that they're not simply folktale stories.

They're *real*.

I bring my hand up as I lay it against the top of Reimus' head. He leans into my hand and I am at a loss for words with what I'm witnessing right now. This whole time I've been being a smart ass with a *drago*? A creature that can very well set me on fire?

Reimus halts my thoughts as he stalks over to the man's body, emitting a loud shrilling noise that is so loud I have to cover my ears. I shakily bring myself to my knees as I watch Reimus. I watch his severely long tail as it moves behind him. Those ridges after further examination appear to be barbed spikes that—unless noticed up close, camouflage into his skin. My gaze follows the spikes all the way to the tip of his tail and I can't help to find myself rather…intrigued by this side of him. My gaze finds him again and I realize he's watching me.

In the next second, he turns his gaze to the man laid before him, and he opens his mouth as fire erupts out. Fire incinerates the man and I stand there and I watch every second of it. I watch fire scorch the man until little by little, his body burns to nothing more than crisp ash. Heat wafts towards me and is nearly too hot for me to stand near, but I need to see the man dead.

I need to remember this moment, that he can no longer try to hurt me.

When Reimus is finished scorching this man, he looks over to me. His gaze flicks to the jar he gave me, and nods his head. Looking at the jar, now it makes sense. He wants me to put this man's ashes into this jar.

Grimacing at the fact that I have to touch a dead man's ashes, I decide that I'd rather do that than have to live another day knowing that this predator is still alive.

I approach the ashes, and kneel down to the ground. Scooping the ashes into the jar, I try to get all of it, but can't get every last bit. So I get as much as I'm able to fit in here. When I close the lid, I stand up and my gaze stays trained on the remaining ashes that I wasn't able to fit into the jar. I stare mindlessly at it, until I'm ready to turn around back towards Reimus. But before I do, I lift the jar up and stare at it as a smile grows on my face.

"Seems only one of us succeeded in seeking revenge." I say.

I turn around to find Reimus has shifted back into his human form and my breath seems to go nowhere. I tentatively walk towards him until I'm right in front of him, my gaze roaming his face.

This man hardly knows me, yet is willing to go through all of this trouble just for *me*?

Reimus reaches a hand up as he brushes a loose strand of hair back from my face. His eyes search mine. "That is the fate for anyone who lays a hand on you. That is a vow."

Reimus' eyes search mine for a few moments before he tentatively pulls his hand away, and begins to walk back towards Alastor. I watch him stride away from me, feeling conflicted with this moment.

Feeling conflicted with why this man would go to great lengths to ensure my safety like this, and also feeling conflicted with the sudden distance between us at this moment, and how I want to close that distance. As if Reimus could read my energy, he halts sharply in his steps.

His head swivels to peer off to the side, as if he saw something on the ground next to him. I watch as his fingers begin to curl into his palms, then relax again. Suddenly, he sharply turns on his heels and strides toward me. My breath goes nowhere at the look of determination evident on his face.

"Fuck it."

Those words are the only warning I get before Reimus pulls me flush against him, as his mouth clashes with mine.

Reimus has his hands wrapped under my chin as he kisses me, his fingers splayed underneath my jaw. The kiss is greedy, and I match his same hunger as my hands come up to his. I shamelessly lose myself in the moment, the kissing all consuming as if everything around me suddenly blurs out from existence.

I came to Vulir with the intention of just learning how to tap into my gifts. To learn how to better connect with myself. And through it, I met a man who I loathed from the very beginning. A man who annoys the living fuck out of me, and who I thoroughly enjoy bickering with.

But it's that same man who's willing to go to great lengths to prove his genuine care for me. A man who will sit with me as I process my grief, my pain without seeking anything in return for his generosity.

I've never had that and I'm absolutely terrified by it. Yet in this moment, I let all of my preconceived notions fall away and just give in. I give in to how our lips glide together like two souls in rhythm with one another, how his silken tongue clashes with mine. Lighting me up from the inside out. I give in to how his calloused fingers feel against my soft skin, how everything about this moment is wickedly backwards for us.

And instead of resisting or thinking too hard on it, I say fuck it too.

CHAPTER 29

My hand lays flat atop the dry soil as the wind gently blows my hair back from my face. My knees begin to ache from kneeling on the ground as my gaze is trained on the grave I dug once before.

I told Reimus I needed a few minutes before we headed back, in which he was more than understanding.

"Take your time." He'd said.

I spent a few more minutes at Eiran's grave. Once I've taken the time I needed to, I lift my hand from the soil and stand up. Turning to look at Reimus, I see he hasn't gone far, but has also given me some privacy.

A few feet away, he's standing by Alastor giving him some neck rubs. Alastor is, of course, enjoying every moment of it. As I approach them, Reimus looks up. He gives me a mournful gaze as his hand reaches out to graze my cheek. "Are you alright?"

I lean into the palm of his hand as I exhale. "I'm okay."

Reimus nods his head as he hands me Alastor's lead rope. I move to saddle myself up on Alastor, as Reimus saddles himself up right behind me.

"We can always come back. Anytime you want to visit." Reimus says as I feel him wrap an arm around my waist, pulling me closer to him.

I turn my head and nod in response. Then, I gently squeeze my heels and Alastor begins to trot.

By the time we make it back to the palace, it's completely dark outside. We make our way to the dining room, the whole time my mind is unable to think about anything else other than the fact that he is able to shift into a drago.

Also unable to focus on anything other than the moment we shared back there. How I can almost still taste his lips on mine.

Once we make it to the dining room I head to take a seat as Reimus heads to the credenza cart. I watch him grab two glasses and a bottle of whiskey and bring them over to the table. Setting the glasses down, he meets my gaze. "Would you like a drink?"

I nod in response, though I'm not much of a whiskey drinker. But after everything that's unfolded today, I will not reject a shot of whiskey.

I watch as Reimus pours a shot into my glass and slides it towards me. I grab it and without much thought, I down the amber liquid. Setting it down, I slide it back to Reimus, who without judgment, fills it again.

"I understand if you have questions." Reimus says, as he pours another shot before sliding me the glass once more.

For the whole ride back, my mind conjured up numerous questions to ask him. But now that we're face to face, I can only think of a few that I really want to ask. Taking the glass into my hand again, I grip my fingers against the grooves of the glass. Taking a breath in, I sip the whiskey before setting it back down again.

"How long have you been able to shift into a drago?"

Reimus takes the seat next to me. "I was born with the gift."

"And you can just shift on a whim? Does it hurt?"

Reimus gives a low chuckle. "No, it doesn't hurt. I can shift on a whim. But if I'm not careful, my anger can cause me to shift involuntarily. But that's rarely the case."

"Rarely? As in it *has* happened before?" I ask.

Reimus is quiet for a few moments before he responds. "It happened once."

Thinking about how angry he'd have to get in order to involuntarily shift into a drago, I wonder what triggered that. "What happened?"

Reimus doesn't answer for a while, and I begin to wonder if I pried too far into something personal. I begin to think of something else to ask, to ease the silence, but to my surprise he answers.

"People weren't always accepting of my lineage. The Draghi have been around for a millennium, but we have lived in secret most of our lives. To protect what was left of us."

I watch Reimus as his expression grows rigid, and it's enough to tell me that he has experienced great loss. For once, my heart doesn't dispel him but actually sympathizes with him. I watch as his jaw ticks before he continues.

"When war broke out years ago, I knew that my family would be in danger. I knew that I had to stay to protect my people, but that didn't mean my family had to suffer through the crossfire. I gave them coordinates to a safehouse, to stay at until the threat was gone and I could bring them back. Except, I was unaware that the safehouse had been infiltrated—" Reimus halts in his speech as his jaw ticks again. He averts his gaze off to the side, and I begin to feel sorrow for him.

"I'm so sorry." Is all I can manage to say as my heart actually breaks for him.

I suddenly realize that I feel something other than detest for Reimus and I wonder to myself how and when that happened. Yeah, we kissed in the Sephyra Forest earlier, but lust is not always correlated with like. You can think someone is hot but still loathe their very existence, not really *caring* for them. Yet what I feel now is…genuine empathy and care for him.

"It's just Dimitri and myself now. I should've scoped out the safehouse first. If I had, they'd still be here." Reimus says, bringing me back from my thoughts. I watch as Reimus internally torments himself on this, and it's evident that this is still something he fights with himself on. I frown at his self-inflicted shame, and understand how easy it is to shoulder the weight of a burden, and also the blame of it too.

"That was not your fault. You couldn't have known that the safehouse had been compromised." I say as I watch Reimus. His expression is still taught, but he loosens up slightly at my words.

He looks over at me, and his gaze roams my face for a moment before he nods curtly. "What else would you like to know?" He asks softly.

I realize he's trying to evade the subject, and as someone who is a master at doing that, I can only sympathize with him. "Tell me more about what it's like being able to shift into a drago."

Reimus is only quiet for a few seconds before he answers. "We have heightened senses, more potent than any human."

"As in…you can hear from miles away or something?"

Reimus forms a half smile at my question. "Something like that. We can also see far more than what the human eye can. Our sense of smell is…much stronger, too."

"Like you can see spirits?" I ask, my interest piqued.

"Yes. We can see energy, too. Such as a person's aura but it's deeper than that. I can't quite explain it much further than that. But it gives us the upper hand when reading people in cases that warrant it."

"What does mine look like?" I ask, feeling fascinated by this fact.

Reimus tilts his head at me. "Are you giving me permission to read your energy?"

Feeling hesitant now if I really want to know what he can see, I bite my bottom lip but I nod anyway.

Reimus studies me for a short while, as a half-grin forms his lips. "You have some blockages in your aura, but can be easily fixed with effort."

Well, blockages in my aura don't really surprise me. Hopefully since I've been mentoring with Hecate for some time now, that they're getting worked out.

"Overall, your energy is very…intriguing."

"Intriguing?" I ask, my brows raising slightly.

Reimus' grin grows deeper as he stares at me. "Yes, intriguing."

My mind has struggled to fully process everything that has occurred in the past twenty-four hours. Coming back to how Reimus looked in his drago form. From the length of his wing span, to the ashen scales that surface his whole body—

My mind redirects me back to when I passed out in front of the gate to Vulir. How I felt like I was floating, my body against a rough surface. When I awoke that day and realized I was very much alive, I thought it was just a dream…

"It was you."

When Reimus just watches me, waiting for me to reiterate, I continue. "That day I passed out at the gate. I remember momentarily coming back to consciousness, and feeling like I was floating. But it was you carrying me in your drago form, wasn't it?"

Reimus takes a drink of his whiskey, his eyes never straying away from mine. "That's correct."

"So, how did Alastor get back here then?"

"I had Dimitri bring him back on foot. Let's just say Alastor was very keen on staying by your side." Reimus chuckles to himself as he smiles. The light from the chandelier above casting a quick glint from his teeth.

For a moment I can't help but catch myself admiring his smile, and how handsome he actually is. How his eyes burn wildly when he stares at me, and the way his lips—

Remembering how it felt to kiss those lips I almost bring my fingers up to my mouth before Reimus shifts in his seat, his eyes glancing towards the dining room entrance.

"Speaking of having a heightened sense of hearing," Reimus says as he looks over towards the dining room door. I grow confused when I see no one there, and I look at Reimus as I furrow my brows. Though my confusion does not last long when I hear two sets of footsteps walking towards the dining room.

Peering my gaze towards the doorway to see who could be coming here, I sit and wait impatiently.

Until Hecate walks in with a man next to her. He's tall like Reimus, and muscularly built as well. His sleek medium brown hair parts in the middle, as it tapers on both sides. His hair hangs low enough that it brushes over his brows, similarly to how Reimus' does. His eyes are a bright golden honey, and they drastically stand out against his golden bronzed skin.

I watch as he and Hecate walk into the room, and approach our table. Reimus stands up, gently bringing me up with him with his hand. He looks over at me. "Melinoë, this is Dimitri."

My gaze moves to Dimitri as I take in the fact that not only am I meeting this other Guardian for the first time, but at the fact that he too, can shift into a drago. He meets my gaze and nods his head. "Pleasure to meet you."

"You as well." I say, unable to think of anything else to say to him. He smiles briefly before his attention is on Reimus. He goes to bring him in for a hug and it's clear to see that they are close friends. I'm sure being the last draghi, they must have really formed a bond with one another. My gaze fixates on Hecate when I feel her hand gently press my shoulder.

"Hecate, what are you doing here?"

Hecate watches me with an empathetic look on her face that tells me she knows about what happened last night. "I'm here for you, dear."

She embraces me into a big hug and I wrap my arms around her in response. When she pulls away, she finds my gaze.

"Come, there's some work that needs to be done."

Walking out of the dining room with Hecate, I turn to look at Reimus and Dimitri. Reimus gives me an approving nod, and I turn back around with Hecate's arm wrapped in mine. She takes me down the hallway to a room that I've never been in before.

I realize quickly that the room we're in is pretty empty. It's also nearly pitch dark in here, save for the windows that are filtering the moon light from outside.

"This room will have to do for now."

"I really appreciate you being here, but what's going on?"

Hecate leads us into the middle of the room. "Have you ever learned to shield, my dear?"

"No, I mean I've never even really heard of it. Except for when I was told there's a shield at the gates of Vulir. Why?"

As she stands in the middle of the room, I see the outline of her body turn to face me. I watch as she raises her arms, and flicks her fingers as fire lights up the room. I look all around me as torches are jutting from the walls, lit by Hecate's magic. I stare in wonderment as I begin to look around the room some more. I realize that the room we are standing in is a room tailored for rituals and spell casting. My gaze finds Hecate's again as the words escape me.

"Shielding is a defense mechanism." She says.

She moves from the middle and steps in front of me, folding her hands in front of her. "Shielding is a way for you to protect your energy, from those who…have malicious intent, or even from those who project their emotional wounds onto others. Think of your energy like a sponge. When our energy is very open and receptive to everything around us, it allows us to become receptive to new opportunities. However, it is also much more receptive in the energy of everyone and everything around us. And when we let just anyone or anything inhabit our energy, well then that's where people can begin to siphon our energy to their benefit. Whether they realize they are doing this or not. This is one way we give away our power."

Processing what she's saying, I begin to wonder if this has happened to me before. Then I wonder if this is why that man…

"Not shielding…is this why what happened to me last night…"

Hecate's gaze turns serious yet mournful as she watches me. "What happened to you was *not* your fault, and nobody could've known that he would've had access to magic like that. My intention is to not put blame on you for something that is far from your fault, dear."

Feelings of shame begin to shed away at her declaration. I nod my head in response and bite my inner lip. "Okay. So how do I shield?"

"I'm going to teach you." She says as she walks a few steps closer to me. "I want you to close your eyes, and focus on your body right now. Bring your immediate surroundings, including yourself into your mind's eye."

Closing my eyes, I take a few deep breaths in and out as I try to focus. I focus on what I'm wearing today, how the room around me looks and bring those into focus. After a few minutes, I begin to visualize myself.

"Good. Now, I want you to continue visualizing yourself, but now I want you to visualize a protective ring that wraps around you. I want you to imagine it as a reflective ring, so that whenever someone with ill intentions approaches you, their ill intent will only bounce back to them."

As I focus on bringing a ring around me, it takes me a few tries to get it. But once I do, I can feel the difference the moment I visualize it. I start it from my feet, and move it up my body, until it's covering my head. I visualize the ring until I feel my body feel increasingly lighter, yet more steady.

"Perfect. Now really sit with this shield. Get to know it."

I stand here for what feels like forever, consistently visualizing my shield. After a while, I feel Hecate place her hand on my shoulder.

"When you're ready, you may open your eyes."

Opening my eyes, I can't believe how much more steady I feel in myself. "Wow, I wasn't expecting to feel the difference that quickly."

"Well if this is the first time you've ever shielded, then that doesn't surprise me." She says with a soft laugh. "Now, you'll want to keep up on this. Every day. It will really make a difference."

I nod my head in agreement.

"Now, before I head out to get started on the rest of the ritual, I want to do one more thing with you. If you don't mind."

Feeling unsure of where this is going, but trusting her anyway, I slowly nod my head.

"I would like to teach you a bit of magic. Specifically protection magic."

"You mean like casting spells? I—-I don't know if I have it in me to successfully do that. I've never practiced witchcraft before."

Hecate smiles. "I think that you are capable of a lot more than you let yourself believe."

Feeling slightly uncomfortable yet grateful for her positive reinforcements, I say nothing and let her finish. I nod my head as I wait for her next instruction.

"We will just start with the basics. It's good to know protection work as a beginner witch."

"Beginner witch? What makes you think I am a witch?"

"You take after your mother, child. And I've seen what your power will do some day."

My breath hitches as I realize she's insinuating she's seen visions of what I am in the future. Curiosity rings me as I wonder what exactly she's seen, but maybe that's for another day that I can ask about that.

"You have far greater power than you know, and it would be a disservice to yourself to let all that go just because you're afraid of what you're capable of."

She is right, though. I don't want to sit on the sidelines and let my life pass me by as I live a life that I don't want for myself. That's why I came here in the first place. I know that if I want the life I want to live, I know I have to make some changes. Regardless of how terrifying the change is.

Besides, it would be interesting to know what kind of power I wield.

Taking a deep breath in, and exhaling out, I lift my chin and straighten my shoulders. "Okay, I'm ready."

Hecate smiles and we get right to work.

I mainly just watch and listen to what Hecate is saying, as she explains how to perform the protection working. She only has a few items with her. A black candle, a few cloves of garlic, some herbs, and a necklace.

The necklace is simple, yet beautiful. At the center of it is a shiny black crystal, in which she tells me the crystal is obsidian, which is a powerful protective crystal.

As I watch her perform the spell, I listen to her chant to herself as she places the necklace around the black candle. She says that she's charging the necklace, that it will serve as a protective talisman for me, and to wear it for its protection.

It takes hours for the candle to burn all the way down, and by that point I am starving to say the least. But, I don't complain as I am grateful that Hecate is going out of her way to share her knowledge with me, and teach me.

Once she's cleaned up the remaining items, she hands me the necklace.

"Wear it always, my dear. It will protect you."

Nodding as I let her put the necklace on me, I immediately feel the charge of energy from it. Placing my hand on the crystal, I can physically feel the energy emanating off of it. Shocked, my gaze looks to Hecate.

"Wow, I…I can *feel* the protective energy."

"It's a wild feeling, huh? Shocked me the first time too." She says smiling, as she pulls me in for a hug. With her head close to my ear, she speaks softly. "Your mother is so very proud of you, Melinoë."

Tears well in my eyes, as I hug Hecate a little tighter. When she lets me go, she nods and begins to walk out of the room when I stop her.

"Hecate?"

She turns around, her gaze on me. "Yes, dear?"

"What exactly are you going to do with his ashes?"

Hecate gazes at me for a few moments, in which I see a flash of sinful delight fill her face as she answers, "He will never be free, not ever again." She says before she leaves the room entirely.

My hand coming up to my necklace again, I feel the energy surge beneath my fingertips once more. I don't think I'll ever get used to this. Excitement begins to unfurl within me at how much I've grown into my gifts thus far, and how much I'm thrilled to be learning from Hecate.

Walking out of the room and into the dining room, I see Reimus and Dimitri are not in here. Judging by how dark the sky is becoming now from the nearby window, I'd say it's past dinner time. Looking at the table, I see that a plate of food has been left out for me.

I walk over to it, unsure how long it's been sitting out. I take my hand and lightly pat the sliced chicken breast, realizing that it's still warm. Reimus must've known I was finishing up with Hecate and set this out for me. Something akin to appreciation floors me, as my throat clogs with emotion.

Since I was young I've always put my family before me. I've always made sure they were taken care of, even if it meant at the expense of putting myself last. So though this may seem like a small gesture on Reimus' part, it's a lot deeper than that for me.

It's been only a few months that I've been here now, and I realize that I've never felt more safe and at home than I do when I'm here. I've never felt more like a human being and less like a maid than when I've been here. I've never been expected to be anyone other than who I am since I've been here, even when I've given Reimus a hard time. He's never quelled my fire, but has instead fueled it.

As I pull out the chair to sit down and eat what Reimus has left out for me, I realize the hunger I feel has nothing to do with food at this moment. Up until recently I've thought of Reimus as nothing more than a bothersome, but now…

I'm not so sure that's entirely true.

I push the chair back in and stride out of the dining room. As I make my way up the stairs, and down the hallway, all I can think to myself is how and when things got to this point. That aside from bantering with Reimus, I also want to feel the brush of his lips against mine again. I want to feel much more.

As I make my way down the hallway, I can hear low voices coming from Reimus' room. I'd recognize Reimus' voice anywhere, and I can only guess the other one is Dimitri's.

As I make my way to the door, I see that it's closed almost all the way shut, save for a sliver of a crack that shows the glow of a fireplace going. As I push open the door, I see Reimus and Dimitri standing near the fire, each with a glass of whiskey in their hands. Reimus locks eyes with me instantly, as Dimitri's gaze follows. I stride in and though I haven't had the chance to truly meet with Dimitri yet, I have other things on my mind at the moment.

My gaze swivels to Dimitri's, my voice is low and stern when I speak. "You were just leaving."

Confusion flashes across Dimitri's face for a moment, before he looks at Reimus who has his gaze locked onto me. He watches me intently for a few seconds, noticing the heat in my stare. He takes a drink from his whiskey before he speaks to Dimitri.

"Leave us." He says, his eyes still trained on me. His gaze feels like it's piercing into my soul, causing me to breathe in deeply. Dimitri doesn't waste time by standing around, he takes his glass with him and leaves the room, closing the door behind him.

Reimus turns to set his glass down on the nightstand near his bed, which I realize now is almost identical to the one in my room. My gaze looks over to the bathroom adjoining his bedroom and notice instead of a clawfoot tub, he has a large whirlpool up against the far wall, nestled against an array of windows. My gaze roams over to the double wrought iron door that I can only assume leads out to a large balcony. I walk over towards it as Reimus watches me. I push the doors open, feeling the fine detail press against my finger tips. I look out to see his balcony looks over the whole village.

My gaze turns up and my breath hitches as I am instantly amazed at how clearly the stars shine in the night sky above. As I stare admirably at the night sky, I feel Reimus approach behind me. I turn my gaze to him and it's like the first time I'm seeing him.

The way his grin curves into his sharp jaw, how those midnight black strands fall in front of his forehead. My gaze trails down until I notice below his neck is a scar. I find myself walking towards him, until I'm right in front of him. I raise my hand as I gently place it on his scar, noticing how his body tenses up in response. I look up at him who's watching me with an intensity I can't ignore.

"What is this from?" I ask, my voice hushed.

Reimus brings a hand up and cups it over mine. As he watches me, I feel the heat from his skin evaporate through my palm, and it causes me to breathe deeply.

"Someone tried to sever out my heart."

I gasp at his words and my brows furrow as I wonder why someone would do that to him. Beginning to realize that my reaction is because...I care about Reimus.

"Though they were unsuccessful, of course." He adds, with a grin formed to his lips.

Feeling lost in this moment, I feel like I have no other choice than to just let it guide me without resistance. I can always fight with Reimus tomorrow.

Tonight, I want to do much more than just fight.

"What did they get in return for their attempt?" I ask, a wicked grin forming my lips.

Reimus is silent as he watches me for a few seconds. He tilts his head slightly. "I think you can guess what their fate was." He says, his voice full of sinister smoke.

We stand there for a few moments, my hand wrapped into his as our bodies are only an inch apart. As I watch Reimus, I find myself beginning to feel inclined to put distance between us. Out of sheer habit, I try to pull away from him, but his hold on my hand remains. His other hand comes up to brush my cheek, causing my breath to hitch. His fingers splay out on the side of my chin as his thumb guides my chin up to meet his gaze. He lowers his head slightly until his lips are right above mine. I can nearly taste the whiskey from his lips, feel the words as they brush up against mine.

"Tell me," He begins as he lowers his head until his lips are next to my ear. "Did you come to my room tonight to fight with me, Melinoë?"

His breath grazes my neck, causing goosebumps to prick my skin. My breathing quickens as I notice now he's taken a step closer into me, resulting in my breasts to bump into his chest with each passing inhale.

"Would that surprise you if I said no?" I ask, steadying my voice.

"It wouldn't surprise me as it would possibly upset me. I do love it when you're angry with me, that fire of yours is…all-consuming." He says as he lowers his head further until his lips brush lower against my neck. Heat begins to pool low as I grow frustrated as Reimus moves his hand from my chin, slowly down my body. His hand stops over my breasts, causing me to gasp at the contact. His thumb begins to circle over a hardened peak through my shirt, causing my back to arch into him as I moan softly. He smiles against my neck as his hand moves lower until it's right at my waistband. My pussy begins to ache as I breathe through my rising need.

"Though I wonder if I can wring that same fire from you in other ways. Such as with my cock filling you, while you take all of me." He says as his hand moves under my waistband, lower until he's cupping my pussy. I moan softly as I writhe against his hand, my frustration growing until I roll my eyes and huff out an audible exhale.

"Then why don't you find out instead of wasting time talking about it—"

That's all I manage to say before Reimus suddenly lifts his hand out of my pants, and hauls me up onto him with my legs wrapped around his waist. He holds me up with one arm as he brings the other one to grab the back of my neck as he brings me into focus. I gasp at how quickly everything just happened, and Reimus only grins as I stare at him. His grin wicked, menacing.

"Ah, there's that fire I was talking about." He says as he begins to walk us back into the bedroom, his hands coming around my ass until he deposits me onto the bed. As I lay on my back, my legs lay open as Reimus stands in front of me, pulling me flush against him. I feel his hard cock press against my pussy and I shamelessly writhe against him, wanting far more than what he's teasing me with.

Reimus clenches his jaw as he watches me, his gaze ravenous as his grin deepens. He takes a step back as he slowly begins to remove my leggings. As he removes them, he tosses them to the ground before his gaze is on me once more. He lifts a leg up, as it bends at his shoulder. His head leans in as he kisses my calf, causing my anticipation to rage within me. He meets my gaze. "Patience, little spitfire."

He lowers my leg as his hands move to my underwear. He slowly trails them down my thighs, and down my calves until he's tossing those onto the ground as well. He lowers himself down to the ground until he's eye level with my pussy. His hands come up to open my hips as he pushes my legs back, fully exposing myself. I watch him lower his mouth as his tongue flicks out, tasting me. I cry softly in response as my hands grip the sheets beneath me.

"All I ask tonight," He begins as he flicks his tongue again, causing me to jerk against him. "Is that you give me that same fire you show me when you argue with me. As I taste you,"

Tongue flick.

"As I fuck you."

Tongue flick.

"Until your fire is the only music my ears have ever been graced to hear."

With that, Reimus' mouth is on me as he *devours* me. His tongue laps in between my pussy, wringing soft cries from my lips. I instantly writhe against his mouth as his tongue descends into my pussy. I cry noises of pleasure at how his silken tongue feels, how I want to feel more. Need to feel more.

His tongue moves to my clit and I gasp in response. His tongue laps around my clit and the pressure builds tremendously. I instinctively move my hands to his head as I grind against him. I feel Reimus grin as my fingers slightly curl inward into his hair. As the pressure builds I feel Reimus move a finger inside of me, my cries intensifying. He works his finger in and out of me as I can't help the cries that pour from my lips. The pressure builds until I feel myself about to climax, and I feel Reimus sliding through my wetness.

My climax reaches as I'm hit with an overwhelming orgasm that crashes throughout my body. I cry as I ride my orgasm, Reimus not letting off with his tongue or his finger until I've finished.

I look down at Reimus at his glossy lips, as he hovers over me and brings his finger up to my mouth. I shamelessly take his finger into my mouth and taste myself while he watches me.

"Now you are on both of our lips." He says as he removes his finger and pushes me further up the bed when he steps back. His hands go to his shirt as he pulls it off and tosses it to the floor. His hands go to his pants then as he pulls them down his legs, shucking them off his legs and to the floor. My gaze goes straight to his cock and gods, he's *huge*. I watch as his hand goes to his cock, and all I can think about is how he would feel inside of me.

I begin to sit up as I bring my hands to my shirt, slowly bringing it up and I relish in the way he's watching me right now. Like he has absolutely nowhere else to be as his heated, undivided attention remains on me. As I sit completely naked before him, his gaze tracks over my body greedily. He grins as his eyes darken, and I don't think he's blinked even once. As if he's mentally saving this moment for him to remember later on.

He descends upon me, his muscular body hovering over mine. I gasp at the feel of his cock teasing my entrance and I shift myself so I can feel more. But Reimus doesn't move, he stays put. His jaw ticks as his body twitches.

"Gods, you're so fucking wet." He seethes through his teeth.

I begin to wrap my arms around him, pulling him closer but he stays locked in place. He sheathes his cock slowly, and stops. The fullness is already filling me as I moan.

"How does this feel?" He asks, his voice low.

"Good." I say in a breathy voice.

Reimus grins as he sinks deeper into me, but still not fully yet. I moan at the fullness I'm beginning to feel, but it's still not enough.

"And how about this?" His words full of wicked delight.

My impatience is crying for him to just thrust into me fully. I roll my eyes as my need to have him inside me is overwhelming me. His hand comes up to my chin as he jerks my gaze back onto him.

"The next time you roll those pretty eyes at me, it will be because the orgasm that I wring from your body is too much to handle."

I gasp at his words and I grow wetter at his admission. Reimus exhales deeply as he feels my growing desire. He begins to sheath himself deeper.

"Say please."

Annoyance and confusion clouds my lustful mind. "What? Just give me—"

"I want to hear you say 'please, Reimus'."

Frustration crowding out my senses, I let out a ragged exhale. At this point, he's only halfway inside of me, and the need to know how he feels fully sheathed makes me feral. "Please, Reimus."

"Please, what?" As he begins to sheath himself just a little deeper, wringing a soft cry from my lips.

"Please, fuck me Reimus."

"Good girl." He says, and that's all I get before he thrusts himself deeply.

He begins thrusting in and out of me *hard* and the fullness of him is the only thing I can concentrate on. He pistons in and out of me, and after a moment Reimus' mouth comes crashing into mine.

His tongue prods my mouth to open, in which I meet his same greediness. Our tongues clash together as he thrusts into me, causing cries to wring from my lips. Reimus lifts his mouth from mine as his gaze moves to his cock as it moves in and out of me. His gaze meets mine once again. "Such a good girl. Look at you, taking all of me."

As we move around the bed, Reimus brings a hand around my head as the tension in me begins to build. My cries become louder as I feel myself about to orgasm once again.

"That's it. Let my cock wring cries of pleasure from those pretty lips." Reimus says as he grinds into me. I move my hips against his and nothing about this is gentle. As my pussy clenches up, I scream as my orgasm ricochettes through my body. I hear Reimus curse as he pistons in and out of me, until I feel him come inside of me shortly after. We both greedily ride out our orgasms as I hear Reimus whimper through his release. The sound of his pleasure only intensifies my orgasm.

As our bodies slack and begin to fall limp, Reimus pulls out of me as he stands up. I watch him walk over to the bathroom, and grab a hand towel. He comes over to me, and begins cleaning me up. Only once he's finished does he bring the towel to himself, and cleans himself. Tossing the towel in a nearby laundry hamper, he moves to lay next to me. He grabs the blanket and pulls it over my body, as he pulls me flush against his chest.

I listen to the sound of both of our hearts racing, as the silence stretches between us. After a few minutes, I turn around to face Reimus. His gaze meets mine, as I feel a whole lot of…everything right now. Feeling rather sated with the sex, but also wondering how he will think this will change things from here.

Reimus brings a hand up to my cheek, as he brushes away a loose strand of hair. His fingers brush through my hair as he gazes at me longfully.

"You do not need to feel bad if this was just an impulsive interaction." He says softly.

Feeling jarred by his words, my brows furrow. I begin to think to myself what this man has been through for him to be so okay with being used for sex, and I wonder to myself once again at what point did I start caring so deeply for a man I swore I despised.

As my gaze roams his, I feel this is one of those times where I can't make my point across by being a sarcastic asshole.

"It wasn't an impulsive move. Not for me at least." I say, as sleep begins to pull on me.

Reimus watches me intently for a few seconds before he lifts my chin up. "My intentions with you are the furthest thing from impulsive. You are not nothing to me. In fact, I'm certain you are absolutely everything."

My breath hitches as I feel words can't express what I feel or want to convey, so instead I use my lips. I kiss him softly as I map his lips to mine. Reimus meets my kiss as it grows far more passionate from there.

And once more I do not worry, and instead just give in.

CHAPTER 30

When I awake in the morning I find myself tangled between Reimus, the both of us still naked from last night. I lay on top of him, his hand resting over my thigh as I have one leg hooked over him. His head is turned towards me as my arm lays atop his chest. His head rests along the top of my head, and I can feel his breath warming the top of my head.

The way we're sleeping on one another is far more intimate than what I'm used to. I swore I wouldn't resist this, though I can't help that the closeness of it begins to cause an unfamiliar sensation to creep into my bones, leaving me crawling out of my skin.

Vulnerability.

My mind begins to race over my worrying thoughts as I think about how I can get myself out of this bed. I'm not ashamed of what we shared last night, though the way that my body reacts to Reimus terrifies me. The way he wrung pleasurable cries from my lips, the way he felt when he moved inside of me, it was…a sexual encounter I've never experienced before. Though I knew it was a move I made because I *wanted* to experience that with Reimus, I know that the avoidance in me can't experience that again with him. Because the thought of being that close with him—

It just can never happen again.

Stirring myself slowly from Reimus, I manage to remove myself from our entanglement. As I walk to the bathroom, I close the door as quietly as I'm able to.

Once I've finished using the restroom, I open the door to see that he hasn't moved. Feeling successful, I walk over to where my clothes are lying on the ground. Quietly, I pull them over my body until I'm fully clothed again. I walk slowly over to the bedroom door, placing my hand on the nob. Turning it slowly, I look back over to Reimus who's still sleeping.

Pulling the door open enough for me to slip through, I slither my body through the opening, and close the door behind me. I begin walking down the hallway to my room to get ready for the day.

As I walk, flashbacks to the way his fingers felt against my skin resurface. It's like I can still *feel* the way his lips felt against mine. I instinctively place my fingers against my lips, craving to train the sensation to memory. Though instead, I pull my fingers away from my lips and raggedly exhale the desires away.

It can never happen again.

As I sit with Hecate my mind can't seem to concentrate. All I keep thinking about is how things have escalated between Reimus and I. Biting my inner lip, I think of all the possible ways that this can't work out between us.

I'm supposed to be going back home, and reuniting with my sister. I'm supposed to be going back home so I can resume my boring life as a fly on a wall in my own home. But now, the thought of going back home actually breaks a vast part of me. Terrifying me because it's not supposed to cause me to feel that way.

How am I supposed to go back home and live with my father who doesn't accept me for who I am, who gets physically violent with me.

When I could stay here and…

No. That's not a possibility. I've only known Reimus for a short amount of time, and getting close to him like that is not even a question. The deal was that I stayed here until I learned my gifts, and to return home once I found what I sought.

Besides, my sister still hasn't written back to me. So I have to go home and check in with her anyway—

"Are you listening?"

Hecate says pulling me from my train of thoughts. I meet her gaze and nod.

"Yes, I'm sorry. I'm listening."

Hecate gives me a knowing look. "You know that I'm psychic, and have mastered the art of reading energy, and yours my dear, is all over the place right now. Have you been grounding and shielding?"

I exhale raggedly. "Yes, I have. I'm sorry, I just am a little overwhelmed with my thoughts. I promise I'll be more present."

Hecate tilts her head slightly, as she smiles. "Okay, give me the tea."

Confused, I furrow my brows. "What?"

"You heard me, give me the tea. What's got you so frazzled?"

I hesitate for a few moments. Hecate has mentored me, yes, but has also treated me like a friend since I've been here. I don't have many of those back home, so her company has been...really heartwarming. I'm used to keeping everything to myself, so opening myself up to her causes me to hesitate. But, I know that I'm worth more than handling everything on my own.

I deserve to have trusted friends who I can confide in. Who I can laugh and be vulnerable with. I deserve more than just being alone. And gods, do I really want to tell her about Reimus and I. So, fuck it.

I tell her everything from the moment I got here, and first met Reimus. I tell her about how life is very different for me back home, how I'm not used to being so...close with men like I have been the past few days. I tell her about last night and this morning, and her face lights up with astonishment as she laughs.

"Oh, this is good. I am so glad that I pried into this." She says as she laughs, and I find myself laughing as well.

After we finished laughing, she clears her throat with a smile still on her face. She reaches a hand out to me and places it over mine. "Now this, this is what I want to see more out of you. Your energy now, versus a few minutes ago is significantly different. You let all that worrying get to you, when you have absolutely nothing to be worried about."

"But I'm supposed to go back home, and if I'm already beginning to feel the way that I do now, I just…I don't know. I can't stay here."

Hecate furrows her brows as her head tilts slightly. "Why's that?"

"Well…for an obvious reason. I haven't heard back from my sister yet, so I have to go back home and check on her. I have to make sure our father is actually taking care of her. I have to–"

"Stop." Hecate says sternly.

I watch as her expression goes from amusement to serious in an instant, and I just know that she's about to tell me something that I *need* to hear, versus what I *want* to hear.

"Everything that you just said just now sounds like things you think you *should* do. But not one of those sounded like things you actually *want* to do. Why are you still living your life for other people?"

Feeling at a loss for words, I stumble over what to say next until I settle on making out a few words.

"I—I don't know."

Hecate takes a deep breath in, and out again. "Dear, let me ask you. What do *you* want to do? Take everything out of the equation right now. Pretend for a moment that you aren't actively taking on the parental role for your sister for a moment. Take out the conditioned mentality that you have to put everyone else above yourself."

I pause, thinking. My gaze adverts to the side as I ponder.

Hecate sternly, yet calmly repeats herself in my silence. "What do *you* want to do, dear?"

For a few moments, I think about what I want my life to look like. If I knew my sister was well taken care of, what would I decide to do?

Would I go back home?

Would I stay here?

I let myself ponder over how I've felt since I've been here, regardless of everything that's happened. I think about how it feels to lay in bed with Reimus, to even share my anger with him. How he lights me up from the inside out, and I have never met someone who encourages that fire within me before. How it feels to be surrounded by people who see *me*.

I bring my gaze back to Hecate, as sureness seeps into my tone. "I want to stay here. I don't want to go home—" I catch myself and stop as I realize, the only way Elzwin has felt like home was with Eiran by my side. But now that he's no longer alive, I'm not sure what's really keeping me there anymore.

I love my sister dearly, and I want nothing more than for her to be happy and have a far better life than what I was dealt. But I can't let myself play parent to a child that is not my own. I can't let myself be surrounded by a father who abuses me, who treats me like nothing when I deserve to be treated like a human being.

If I go back home, that's exactly the type of life I'll be subjecting myself to.

And I…

I focus on Hecate. "I want to make a home out of Vulir. I want to feel like I'm part of a community, surrounded by others who value and respect me. I want to lay in bed next to the man that I'm beginning to care for and not crawl out of my skin with resistance towards him because of it. I don't want to feel bad that I'm choosing myself this time. I want—"

My words end on a choke as tears fill my eyes. "I want to be happy! I want to be *loved*. For fucks sake, I want to be seen! And this time, nobody takes that away from me." I say as my voice ends on a rough pitch.

Hecate watches me as she begins to softly clap her hands, a smile tugging wide on her face. "Now *that*, is the Melinoë I have been looking for. *That* is your power rising."

She brings me in for a hug and I embrace the supportive companionship she's shown me. I smile into the hug and cherish this moment as I finally feel like I have people on my side.

She pulls away, her hands on my shoulders as she meets my gaze. "When I first met you, you were broken inside. Your energy was like a dark cloud hanging over you, begging to be tended to. And now, you're taking that pain and alchemizing it. And *that* is true feminine power."

My heart swells because gods, her support and encouragement has lifted me to new levels and I couldn't be more grateful for having met this amazing woman.

A woman I get to call a friend.

"You're shifting, my dear. You're tapping into that hidden power of yours, and you're feeding it exactly what it's been demanding."

"Which is what?" I ask.

"Who you were always *meant* to be."

My throat works on a swallow as I have felt a little different since I've been here, but still feel like my old self. Yet, I do agree that my mindset is changing, and that is something I can be grateful about.

"Well, I think with all of the progress you've been making, we don't need to see each other every day. We can meet twice a week instead. That is, unless you want to stop by and say hi. I won't be opposed to the company." She says with a wink.

I smile in response. "Thank you, sincerely. For taking time out of your days to mentor me, and…for being a friend to me." I lean in for another hug before I stand up.

Before I walk out of Hecate's shop, I turn around and face her. "And, I think I will stop in sometime. Who else am I going to tell my dirty tea to?" I say with a wink, and Hecate smirks.

"Oh, I will never not be open to hearing it. Have a *good* night, dear." She says as we both laugh.

I walk out of the shop and begin my walk back to the palace. As I walk back, I feel a distinct lightness to myself that I haven't felt in a long time. Not since my mother was alive.

As I walk, I wonder to myself what Reimus is doing right now. If he's even home or not, yet a part of me hopes that he is. I'm sick of resisting shit that I actually want. And one thing I do want is to work through my fear of real connection. It took me *years* to finally decide to give Eiran a chance, and when I did he was taken from me. I never thought I would let myself grow close to another man after losing Eiran, but with Reimus I can't help the magnetic pull that entices me to know more about him.

Once I reach the palace, I walk down the hallway as it's quiet. I waste no time looking for him as I know that if I don't say what's on my mind right now, I will most likely bury it deep within me for it to never reach my lips.

As I walk to the dining room, I see Reimus sitting down with a glass of whiskey with his black journal closed on the table. As soon as I walk through the door, I stride over to Reimus who peers his gaze up at me instantly. Once I approach his table, I find myself losing everything I was just training myself to say moments ago in my head.

"Something on your mind, little spitfire?" He asks nonchalantly as he takes a drink from his whiskey.

"Yes, there is *something* on my mind. I—" My sentence ends abruptly when I begin to feel nervous about what I'm going to say. It's an incredibly odd feeling when I have never found myself nervous in the presence of a man before. As I avert my gaze and pace back and forth, I hear Reimus scoot his chair back as he approaches me, leaning up against the table. He doesn't rush me, he doesn't use snarky comments to pry. Instead, he waits for me to pull myself together before I speak again.

My gaze now trains on him as I watch his expression smooth out. I can't gauge what he's thinking, as his expression is unreadable for me. But in the best way I can describe it, it appears he's simply making space for me at this moment.

Which is something I've never really been given.

Shoving my remaining resistance down and exhaling audibly, I finally speak. "You are like a parasite." I begin as I work up my courage.

"Ouch." He says as he shakes his head, his brows raised.

"Let me finish," I snap, reeling myself back as I try to tamper down my emotions—

No, you know what. Fuck it. I'm airing it all out.

"This isn't normal for me. I'm not someone who gets involved, I'm someone who stands off on the sidelines while I watch everyone live the lives they could possibly dream of. I'm the maid, the servant in my family—" My sentence ends on a choke as I can't bring myself to look at Reimus, not yet. "My father shows his love by using the silent treatment, and when I rebel against him, he rewards me with *strangling* me."

My breathing ramps up as I try to quell my breathing to slow down. "I loathe the thought of even being with a man in the type of capacity we were last night. The only man I ever let myself be like that with was Eiran, who *died* for me. Because I let him come with me! And I lost the only man who *ever* showed me love."

Tears begin to flow from my eyes and instead of resisting them, I let them flow freely. "It took me *years* to finally say 'Okay, I'll finally let myself have more. He's earned it at the very least.' and when I did he died. *For me* out of all people! I—I am used to being on my own. I've accepted the fact that maybe I will just need to fend for myself, that that's the life that's destined for me. Because surely no one in my life has ever shown me that it's possible otherwise."

I pause as I finally peer my gaze to Reimus who is watching me intently. His expression is both solemn, and remorseful. He does not interrupt, and remains silent as I unleash my innermost feelings, drudged up from the very pit of my soul.

"But then I met you and I *loathed* you from the minute I arrived. Gods, did you get under my fucking skin. You crawled your way under me, seeped into my very bones and now I *can't* get *rid* of you. You are a parasite that I loathe myself for letting in, almost as much as how I don't actually loathe you at all. And I am *terrified* of that truth. But I am more terrified that you will try to show me genuine connection and I will resist you for it. For I don't know anything other than being on my own and being invisible."

Reimus studies me for quite some time before he calmly walks over to his black journal. He picks it up, and flips through a few pages before landing on one. I furrow my brows as confusion arises. "What are you doing—-"

Reimus interrupts me as he clears his throat, his gaze never turning away from the pages that lay in his hands. He takes a breath in, and exhales as he speaks. His tone is both calm and stern.

"Today was another day since she has been here. She graces me with the brash of her anger, as well as the scorch of her fire. I find myself shamelessly at the mercy of both, and I loathe myself for it.

In every way imaginable, I have secluded myself from the idea of love. But it is her light that suddenly has begun to evaporate every protective wall I've ever placed. How just a gaze into her emerald eyes causes my inner foundation to splinter at the seams. How the touch of her warm skin ensues a hunger within me that not even starvation could compare to. She is the reason I've begun to question myself. Not because I loathe her existence, but for the detrimental fact that I have never been this weak, nor this starved for another's touch or presence. Until her.

She has made it clear of her dislike of me, yet I am still magnetized to her anyway. How I would willingly follow her through any of life's challenges, and shoulder those burdens as my very own. How I cannot decide what kind of fool that makes me. The kind who's wickedly pathetic, or blindly loyal. Nonetheless, the truth remains the same. That I am a man who has never been one to beg. But for her, I fear I would willingly fall to my knees and plead to the gods if I ever had to. For receiving the brunt of her dislike is far better than receiving nothing at all."

Reimus closes the journal before he sets it back down on the table, his ocean blue and silver eyes piercing into mine. My entire body freezes into place as my mind stammers over what he just read to me.

I never knew he was writing about *me* in that journal. My mind is overwhelmed with words expressed about me, I can't seem to think clearly. Reimus steps away from the table and steps up to me, causing my breath to go nowhere. His hand gently lifts my chin, my gaze unable to stray from his.

"You may not think you are deserving of genuinity, but I will live my life proving to you that you are worth far more. Because in my world, it is *all* about *you*. Need to unleash your anger with me? I'm here to fuel it. Need your own space for a day? It is yours. I will make it my life's mission to prove to you that there is one person in this existence who wants *nothing* more than to put you on a gods-damn pedestal. Even if it takes me until my final breath."

Tears prick my eyes as I process everything Reimus is saying. I've never, ever had someone speak to me so devotionally like this. With the admiration glowing wildly in his eyes, the seriousness etched into his jaw. There is nothing about this moment that tells me he's being untrue to me.

And that…terrifies me.

Reimus brings a thumb up to my cheek as he gently wipes a tear from my blushed cheek. He tilts his head as he studies me, his voice hoarse as it fills with ice. "I would lay this entire village to flames if anyone even *spoke* about hurting you. Your retribution is my will, and I will *gladly* serve it to anyone."

The fine hairs along my arms raise and a chill runs down my spine at Reimus' tone. My gaze lowers as he narrows his head slightly. I begin to wonder just how alike we really are to one another, and how maybe that can be a good thing. I wonder to myself what it would be like to finally be the one who experiences what it's truly like to be cared for.

To be genuinely worshipped and praised by someone rather than belittled. To be respected, to be honored. The thought of him making these promises to me fills me with an insatiable sudden need that heats my blood. It pulsates and envelops throughout my entire body, fighting against any feelings of uneasiness way back down into the shadows to deal with later.

"You would do anything for me?" I ask as I step out of Reimus' reach, my lips brushing across his when I do. I walk slowly along the table as I feel a surge of foreign energy course through my body. Energy that feels like absolute power, and I have no intention of squandering it at this moment.

I can feel Reimus' heated stare bore into my back as I take in the energy that's coursing through my blood right now. I revel in it, and I delight it into my veins.

"You will spend the rest of your days understanding what it means to be treated like a goddess, and never again as a nuisance. I vow it." He promises firmly.

As I slowly turn back around, I gaze upon Reimus. Heat erodes my skin as I observe him. His midnight black hair hangs loosely in front of his forehead, as the silver in his eyes churn wildly. I lift my chin as a lustful smile plasters my face, a wicked desire filling my veins. Without second guessing myself, I speak with a sensual fluidity.

"Kneel."

Without hesitation, Reimus kneels onto the ground before me. As he looks up at me, his eyes turn into heated pools of silver, and a wicked grin forms his lips. It only ignites the fire within me that much more.

As I gaze upon him, I find something spark within me at his show of submission. Something awakens within that no longer desires to be at the mercy of others' abuse, no longer desires to live my life for the sake of just existing. In the short amount of time being around Reimus, he's unleashed a part of me that I buried long, long ago. A part of me that felt shame for using my voice, and for allowing the fire within to ignite me. A part of me that I dimmed down and as a result, shrunk myself to avoid altogether.

I understand now what Eiran meant. That he's been the catalyst to not only allowing me to unleash that fire, but for me to *own* it as well. Even through my bickering and cold remarks, he's never quelled my fire, but instead further coaxed it out of me. That even though I am flawed and don't trust easily, that even though I push people away, he's never judged me or begged me to change.

He's always accepted me for exactly who I am. And that realization breaks my soul wide open in a deeply cathartic kind of way.

Reimus' voice is low and smooth like honey when he speaks. "Does the sight of me kneeling before you intrigue you, little spitfire?"

I slowly begin to walk towards Reimus, taking in the sight of his willing submission. I circle around him as I feel this new side of myself take over. A side that's been demanding attention from me.

So, I gladly give in to it.

"I think I'd be far more intrigued at the sound of you begging for me."

I come to stand directly in front of him now, and I move close enough to him where his face is mere inches away from my pussy. With my left hand, I reach for his jaw and guide his gaze to mine. I stare down as power drips over my body and my voice, coaxing my desires to be unfurled. I gaze down at him, watching the hunger dance brightly in his eyes.

"Only then, when you're whimpering for release will I give you what you want." I say, my voice sounding nothing like what I'm used to. In the next second, I bend down to slowly pull my pants down to the floor. I keep my gaze locked onto his the whole time, and I watch Reimus' jaw tick with anticipation. It only makes me move even slower as I revel in his anxiousness.

"You said you will show me what it means to be treated like a goddess?" I say as I straighten to pull my shirt off, tossing it onto the floor. I watch as Reimus' gaze moves to my breasts, and his breathing is noticeably heavier. I bring my hand to his cheek, my thumb sweeping across his soft lips as his breath dances across my thumb. I slide my thumb inside his mouth and his heated gaze bores into mine as he greedily sucks it, eliciting a thrill inside of me. I feel the glide of his silken tongue as I pull my thumb free. "Then show me."

And in the very next moment, he wastes no time proving to me he meant what he promised.

CHAPTER 31

"Fuck."

Reimus hisses, his body subtly trembles as his hands wrap themselves into my unbound hair. We've managed to make our way from the dining room, to the hallway, and back to his bedroom. It's been hours and the sex only lightens up for a short reprieve, before we're back to satisfying one another once more.

My tongue makes good work as I swirl it around the tip of Reimus' cock, my hand working him with my mouth. I ravish in the little jerks that his body makes and it only amplifies when I moan against his cock. I hear him moan softly and I know he's getting close, but I'm not ready for him to finish just yet.

Sliding my mouth off his cock, I sit upright as I watch as his heated gaze snaps to mine. His breathing is ragged and his body tenses as I climb over him, and press my pussy against his cock. I slowly slide it up and down his cock, without actually letting him enter me. I watch as his jaw ticks ferociously, and I almost fear he'll break his jaw.

"I want to hear you beg." I say, my voice husky.

Reimus glares at me as he presses his lips inward under his teeth as I slide along him. I hear him groan as his hands come up to my hips, his fingers gripping into my skin. I'm fully aware that I'm torturing him with my teasing, but there's something about him being anxious for me that really gets me off.

"Please." He says through his teeth as he exhales audibly.

"Please what?" I ask, as my hand goes to wrap around his cock. I lower my head slightly as I spit on the tip, and move my thumb over it, gliding it around his cock as I slowly work him. I watch as his gaze fixates on my hand and he begins to softly whimper.

"*Please* let me inside of you. I *need* to feel your pretty pussy around my cock." He says as he trembles slightly.

In the next second, I move my hand as I begin slowly grinding against him as he helps move my hips. A groan gets trapped in his throat as he clenches his jaw, his frustration evident and I fucking love it. I finally lower myself on his cock slowly, a deep exhale leaving his lips as he fills me entirely.

"As you wish." I say, and that's all the warning he gets before I'm grinding into him.

My head leans back as I revel in the feel of him moving in and out of me, causing me to moan loudly. I feel his hand come up to the back of my neck as he brings me down flush against him, before he flips us over. Now lying on my back, Reimus hovers over me and his gaze is *feral*.

He grinds against me hard and deep, wringing cries from my lips. My legs wrap around his waist as he plunges into me over and over again. I bring his face down to mine as our lips crash into each other. Our tongues lapping against one another as Reimus fucks me. It's all too much, and not enough at the same time.

As the pressure in me builds, I begin to cry into Reimus' mouth. He lifts his mouth free from mine as he flips me onto my stomach. His hand comes under my ass and I feel his fingers slip over my pussy.

"Gods, you're so wet for me."

I moan in response. In the next second, Reimus has his hands on my hips as he's bringing my ass up, my knees bent into the bed. He brings an arm underneath me and brings my back flush against his chest until my hands are supporting me up.

I shiver as I feel Reimus lower his head against my neck, as his tongue grazes my skin. I feel him move his cock at my entrance, but he doesn't fill me yet.

"All of this wetness belongs to me. And I'll incinerate *anyone* who dares to take what's mine."

I gasp as Reimus thrusts inside of me, filling me completely. One of his hands comes to my neck, as he turns my face towards him. The other goes to my clit as he begins circling it with his finger. He grinds into me deeply and I can't control the cries that leave my lips.

"That's right, little spitfire. Tell me how much you love this cock."

As he fucks me I meet his same feverish need as I meet his same thrusts. His hand holding my neck keeps me locked into place as he watches me come undone. The pleasure that rolls through my body is unending, and I find myself rolling my eyes to the back of my head. In which Reimus only fucks me faster, causing my pussy to clench up as my orgasm greets me. I scream as I ride my orgasm, as Reimus lowers his head to my neck.

"Such a fucking good girl." He says gruffly as I feel his body begin to tense up. He pistons into me as I feel him come inside of me. We both ferally ride our orgasms together, as I hear Reimus moan into my ear. His moan causes electricity to course through my body.

Reimus lets go of his hold of me as I limp to the bed. He pulls out of me as I hear him breathe heavily as he stands up from the bed. I hear him walk to the bathroom, and walk back to the bed a few seconds later.

Reimus comes back with a towel, and wipes me clean, then himself next. Tossing the towel into the laundry hamper, he lays down next to me.

We don't say much for a while as we catch our breaths. But after a while, Reimus brings me into him and wraps his arms around me. I nuzzle my head onto his chest and we lay there for a long time.

Reimus brings a hand up as he interlocks it into mine. His thumb gently sweeps my skin and I feel myself relax in a way I've never felt before. I physically feel myself sink into this moment, into the awareness that what I have with Reimus is different and…I deserve this.

No more worrying about how this could turn into a disaster, or how I thought I had all of these preconceived demands that I thought I *had* to uphold. Right now, I'm exactly where I *want* to be.

I'm finally choosing what makes sense to *me*.

Taking a deep breath in and out, I close my eyes and let myself drift off to a deep sleep.

Knowing confidently that I am safe, where I am right now.

The next day I decide to spend the day in the village getting to know the local shops and what Vulir has to offer. Since I've spent so much of my time here mentoring with Hecate, now that I see her less each week I have more opportunities to see what Vulir is really about.

As I walk out of the Guardian's Palace, I become engulfed by the warmth of the sun's rays as they beam upon me. Next to me Reimus is swatting a bee away, and I can't help but to laugh.

"What? He won't leave me *be*." He grins as he lowers his head closer to me. "Get it?"

Rolling my eyes, I smirk at him. When I asked Reimus to show me more of Vulir, he was more than pleased to oblige. As we walk down towards the village, I take in the hustle and bustle of people that are out today. Reimus catches my gaze and grins.

"People are preparing for the summer solstice, so it's much busier today than it normally would be."

My thoughts fixate on the fact that I've been here for two months now. And suddenly, I'm now fixated on the fact that I still haven't heard from my sister yet.

My smile transforms into a frown.

"What troubles you?" Reimus instantly asks, drawing my attention.

"It's just that I haven't heard from my sister, and I sent her that letter almost two months ago. I just worry that she either didn't receive it, or that something is wrong."

Reimus quietly studies me for a few moments before he responds. "What can I do to ease your worry?"

I nearly melt at his effort to bring a sense of comfort into my life. Thinking over what I need, I realize what I want is to stay here. To begin building a life here in Vulir. But if I don't know that my sister is well, I won't find rest here until I do.

I look up at Reimus as he softly gazes at me. "I think I need to go back home. I need to make sure everything is okay before I can pick up roots here."

Reimus visibly tries to fight a smile but loses anyway. Confused, I tilt my head as my brows furrow.

"I apologize, I see your angst about your sister. But I cannot help but to grin at the fact that you do indeed wish to pick up roots here."

My heart swells as I see the visible excitement in Reimus' face. My eyes become glassy as tears fight to stream down, when Reimus brushes a tear that slips out.

"Are these tears for sadness or happiness?" Reimus calmly asks.

"Happiness." I say back, a smile forming.

"Good. Those are the only tears I wish to see from you." Reimus says, as he lowers his hand from my cheek. "Unless of course they're tears of pleasure. I will happily take those as well."

My breath hitches and I'm instantly reminded of our last twenty-four hours. How passionate the sex has been, how I've laid so closely with Reimus in his bed.

Everything feels like it's falling into place.

We continue walking until we reach the village, and the first shop we go into is a cafe. Inside there are small round tables along the wall, with the wall opposite of it a clerk that stands behind a counter of baked goods such as cookies, muffins, pastries, and donuts.

I decide on a blueberry muffin, and we take a seat at one of the tables. After that we walk down the sidewalk and he tells me about each shop and who owns it. He gives me a little history of the village as we head to a big building that is separate from the strip of shops.

"What's this place?" I ask.

Reimus smiles at me, as he opens the door. We walk inside down a short hallway, where we enter another door. Inside there are probably dozens of rooms, most with their doors open but some closed. I see as one woman walks out of one room and walks into another, with her child trailing behind her.

"This is The Sanctuary, also known as our women's shelter. We have three levels, and are hoping to expand to another building in the near future. But for now, everyone seems to be comfortable here."

My mouth gapes open as I walk slowly ahead. As I pass by a closed door, I realize that this one has decorations outside of it. Taped on the door are pictures that look like they're drawn from a child, and my heart sings. I look back at Reimus.

"We also give foster children a safe place to stay here as well, as you can see." Reimus points to the door.

I begin to wonder to myself how many children live here? How many children that do not have families to come home to?

Tears prick my eyes once more as I wipe them away, and continue walking forward. As we do, another woman comes out of her room with a hamper of clothing on her waist. When she sees us, she smiles. "Hi! Are you just checking in?"

I smile awkwardly. "No, I'm just trying to get more familiar with Vulir. I'm Melinoë."

The woman, still smiling, drops her laundry basket and brings me in for a hug. She gently squeezes me and the friendliness throws me off guard for a second. She pulls away and meets my gaze. "Nice to meet you, and welcome to Vulir! I'm Nefeli. You've come to a really respectable village, and hope that you enjoy yourself here. Has he taken you to The Garden yet?" She says as she nudges her head towards Reimus.

"No, not yet. But I'm sure we can go there next." I say winking at Reimus.

They have a garden? My excitement just roiled inside of me.

"Well, today is a great day to see it." She says as she picks the basket up once more, holding it up to her hip. "Well, this laundry ain't going to do itself. It was a pleasure to meet you, Melinoë." She says.

"It was a pleasure to meet you as well, thank you."

Nefeli turns around and walks down, every so often greeting some of the other women walking around.

"Wow, she's…"

"Chatty?" Reimus says.

I look at Reimus as I roll my eyes. I face forward once again. "She seems lively, like…the thought of being in a shelter doesn't bother her the slightest. Look at the way that all these women greet each other, say hello in passing by. They all seem…like they're a part of this warm family. It's…beautiful." I say as my admiration grows for a system that seems to be working very well here.

Reimus pulls me in for a kiss on my forehead. When he pulls away, he nudges at a door at the other end of the room. "Follow me."

I follow Reimus as he takes me through the door and outside to—

Oh, my gods.

"This is The Garden."

My mouth once again gapes open as I take in the beautiful array of flowers, shrubs, and greenery. For a few seconds, I can't seem to get my feet to move from where I'm standing, until Reimus guides me forward.

In front of me is a huge circular walkway that wraps around an enclosed greenhouse. I nearly run towards it as I come up to the all glass enclosure and find a few forest green tables and chairs spread out. At one table there's a woman sitting down, with her legs propped up on the table as she reads a book. I don't want to come off as creepy by staring at her, so I avert my gaze.

Around the ceiling of the greenhouse are various vines that drape around like hung curtains. I gaze to find there is an easel with various amounts of paint in the holder.

"This is incredible." I say in complete awe.

I walk back out of the greenhouse and completely forget I'm with Reimus for a moment, and follow the trail. I wonder to myself where it will take me as I find it leads to a small body of water. It's too big to call it a pond, but it's not quite large enough to characterize it as a lake. But nonetheless, the water looks impeccably clean.

I walk over to it, and am greeted with ducks coming out of the water. I walk slowly up to them so as not to spook them, and kneel down towards them. They walk right up to me, and I hold my hand out to pet them.

Turning around, I see Reimus gazing at me.

"Animals are just drawn to me, have been since I was little."

"Okay but…these ducks are known to nip at people. Most people can't even get this close to them without them trying to nip them."

Turning back around, I watch the duck as he looks at me. He doesn't seem grumpy in the least, and I continue to pet him. After a few moments, I stand back up and walk over to Reimus as the duck waddles back into the water.

My gaze roams his face as I can't wrap my head around what I'm witnessing here.

"I don't think you understand that this…this is amazing. Your village…does so much for its people."

Reimus slowly strides up to me, as his hand cups my cheek. "Providing a safe shelter for women and children who seek refuge, is one of the very least things that we can do, and will continue to do for our people."

I nuzzle my face into his palm as I smile.

"How about we stop at one more place before we head home for dinner."

As I nod my head, I realize something. "You just said home."

Reimus looks slightly perplexed at my comment. But then understanding takes form. He brings me in for a kiss and releases me. "Yes, that is if you wish it to be your home."

I smile. "I do."

Reimus smiles and we walk out of The Sanctuary. We walk down near the strip of shops once more before we head into a flower boutique. We walk in and there's a man standing behind the counter, trimming a bouquet of roses. He looks up and smiles as he meets our gazes.

"Hello! What can I get for you?"

"Whatever she would like, please." Reimus says.

I suddenly feel like a small child just entering a toy shop as I look around at the wonderful flowers that line this shop. But as I take in all of the beauty, I settle on the one flower that I admire most.

"A dozen black baccara roses, please."

The man nods his head enthusiastically.

Once the man gathers the roses, he hands them to me as Reimus pays for them. The man looks confused when Reimus gives him too much money. He tries to hand it back to Reimus, but he shakes his hand.

"Keep it. I insist." He says with a grin.

The man's expression grows humble as he nods his head and thanks him.

As we walk out of the shop, I keep putting my nose in the roses and a smile lights up my face.

"They're beautiful." I say.

"Not nearly as beautiful as you." Reimius says.

We're embracing this intimate moment together when suddenly a scream pierces the air. It sends chills over my entire body as Reimus instantly guards me, unknowing where the scream is coming from and why. When I find a woman laying over a man, I immediately run towards them.

Reimus is in front of me as we run across the street to the woman kneeling over the man. He doesn't look so good. He's pale and his eyes are hardly able to stay open. I drop the roses and kneel beside her, unsure what is drawing me to do so but I don't second guess it either way.

"What's happened?" I ask, trying to reel in my panic.

"H–he hasn't been feeling good for some time now. My h–husband, oh gods. The doctor suggested bed rest for him but nothing seems to work. And now–" Her voice ends on a sob as she peers over at her husband.

Suddenly, I begin to feel an overwhelming vibration take over my body. It feels like I'm pulsating and I begin to heave over as I can't contain it.

Reimus is by my side in an instant, worry etched into his tone. "Melinoë, what's wrong?"

"I don't know—-"

Suddenly, the vibration becomes vocalized and I feel it distinguish itself to my arm, and notice that something is touching my arm. I look up and see the man standing before me.

Except it's not his physical body standing, but his soul.

My eyes widen as I have never seen a tangible spirit before, other than in my dreams. He stands there, with a hand on my arm as I watch him begin to kneel next to his wife. He watches me with a calm expression, too calm for someone who's dying at my feet.

He looks at me. *"Please, tell her I'm okay. I'm not in pain anymore, and I will watch over her every single day."*

I am frozen still as I watch this spirit speak to me clear as day. Reimus nudges me gently.

"Melinoë, are you hurt? What's wrong?" His voice begins to sound panicked.

I can't bring myself to answer as I continue to gaze at this man. The man speaks again. *"Tell her I love her, more than all the galaxies in the universe. She'll believe you then."*

After a few moments, I shakily nod my head as I train my gaze onto the woman. She's still kneeling over her husband as I clear my throat.

"He says he loves you, more than all the galaxies in the universe. That he's going to be okay."

As if someone just poured ice cold water over her, her entire body freezes. She slowly peers her gaze from her husband and eyes me with a wild gaze. "What did you just say?"

I repeat myself to the woman.

"How did you know that? How did—"

Only then does understanding and remorse begin to flood her. She begins to sob as understanding that her husband is dead plaques over her body. She falls into me and I catch her, holding her as she sobs. I shed a few tears with her as I hold her in my arms.

"He says he will watch over you, and that he's not in pain anymore. He loves you very much."

I look up at Reimus whose gaze is pinned to mine, shock and also admiration gleaming from his eyes.

The woman pulls herself away from me, and grasps my hands into hers. "Thank you. As long as I know he's not in pain anymore, I can begin to grieve."

She lets go of my hands as I notice people are surrounding us now, everyone mute as they watch the interaction between us. She is helped to her feet by a woman nearby, who talks to her gently.

Reimus helps me up onto my shaky legs and just gazes at me. He leans in to give me a kiss on the cheek. "You gave that woman closure today. I hope you realize that. That's not an ordinary thing, Melinoë."

I fix my gaze over to the woman, and nod my head. She notices me and gives a mournful smile, as she gazes upon her husband once more.

Who just died in her arms.

Who I just talked to and saw.

I look back at Reimus as the words to speak slip from me. "I—that's never happened to me before."

Lost in a daze, I turn around to grab my flowers that I tossed on the ground when we ran over here. I take them as I begin to feel a weight of immense fatigue rush over my body. Beginning to sway, I fall into Reimus as he catches me. Without a word, Reimus picks me up and carries me the whole way home, with my black baccara roses in hand.

"I've got you."

And at some point, I fell asleep in his arms on the walk back home.

CHAPTER 32

When I awake I hear whispers coming from outside my bedroom door, with one distinct voice that I can make out on.

"It's imperative that I see her as soon as she wakes. Everything will make sense once I'm able to speak with her." Hecate says softly.

"Tell me what's going on." Reimus says, the worry seeping from his hushed tone.

Why is Hecate here? What does she have to talk to me about?

As I open my eyes, I notice how alert my body feels. I no longer feel sleep deprived as I did when I fainted into Reimus earlier today.

As I extend my legs and arms, I turn my head to the side as I wake my body up. As if on cue, Reimus walks into the room and locks eyes with me.

"You're awake." He says as relief visibly washes over him. He strides over to me as he leans over to give me a kiss. "How are you feeling?"

Confused why he looks so relieved that I'm awake, I shrug my shoulders. "I feel fine now. I think I was just tired and fell asleep."

At Reimus' stern and worried look, I can tell from his expression that I've been asleep a lot longer than I think I've been. I tilt my head to the side. "Just how long have I been asleep for?"

Reimus clenches his jaw and then immediately relaxes so as to not worry me, yet it's too late for that. "You've been asleep for two days."

My body feels frozen with disbelief and worry, as I shake my head. "Two days? How is that possible? Why was I asleep for so long? I—"

Hecate walks into the bedroom and comes closer into view. She keeps her hands folded in front of her waist. Her expression is calm, but it's obvious she's forcing herself to appear calm so as to not cause me more worry.

Under the surface, I can see that she shares the same worry as Reimus does.

"Are you well enough to stand up?" She asks.

Confused by her urgency, I begin to pull the covers away from me as I stand up. I'm wearing a black satin robe, and can tell now that I've sweat myself through it.

My nose scrunches as I smell myself. Gods, why was I sweating so hard? As I stand there and nod at Hecate, she nods back.

"Good. Get yourself washed up, and meet me downstairs when you're ready. We have much to discuss." She says as she turns on her heels and walks out.

I look at Reimus with confusion. "What's going on? Why is she here?"

Reimus looks at me. "I don't know. Yesterday she stopped by asking for you, when I told her what happened she said she already knew. That it was important she talked to you."

Panic begins to flow through my body as I begin to overanalyze what she would need to talk to me about. Suddenly, I begin to feel like a child again, getting ready to be scolded by my father by all of the ways that I'm not doing enough. I begin to fidget with my fingers as I can intuitively feel that something is not right.

Reimus guides my gaze back to him as I didn't even realize it shifted to the floor. Looking at him, he watches me. "Let's just worry about one thing at a time, okay?"

When I nod in approval, he begins to usher me to the bathroom. I watch as he leans over to turn the faucet on for the bathtub, and I begin to feel self conscious.

I stink.

"Thank you, but I can take it from here. Besides, I smell awful."

Reimus comes up to me, and holds my face in his hands softly. He gives me a half smile. "Well, yes. You do smell." He begins as I roll my eyes. He smiles in response before he continues. "But trust that a little stench won't deter me from taking care of you. So please, let me help you."

As my heart swells, I nod my head.

The same heart with barbed wires surrounding it that Reimus proves time and time again, is capable of being set free. He gives me a gentle kiss, and then he opens my robe before dismantling it down to the floor. I watch as his expression doesn't turn heated at the sight of my naked body this time.

This time, his expression is full of tenderness.

As Reimus guides me into the bath my legs prick at the wonderful hot water that greets them. I gasp in response, before giving a long exhale.

"Too hot?" He asks.

"No, it's perfect." I say with a smile as I lower myself into the bathtub.

Reimus grabs two bars of soap in hand, and sets them down on the cart next to the bathtub. He begins to take off his clothing.

"Wait, you're getting in here too?" I ask.

Reimus looks confused as his hands pause on untying his sweatpants. "How else did you think I was going to bathe you?"

As he takes his sweatpants off, I stare shamelessly at his naked body. It's beautiful.

He catches my gaze and smirks. "Careful, my little spitfire. Keep looking at me like that and I'm not sure I'll be able to hold myself back."

He goes to stand behind me as he steps into the tub, lowering himself until he seats himself behind me. I instantly feel the harsh brush of his legs rub against my soft skin as he pulls me closer to him. I feel Reimus's hands gently brushing back my hair with his fingers, as he begins to lather my hair with the soap. He massages my scalp and does this for more than a few minutes, taking his time with it.

My body becomes limp as my arms rests on each side of the tub. I close my eyes as I let him lather and massage me. After he rinses my hair, I relax against him as his hands massage and lather my body now. His hands start from my shoulders, and work their way down. Once they make their way to my breasts, I arch my back into Reimus.

"What are you doing?" I ask breathlessly.

"Taking care of you." He says, his voice low.

His fingers begin circling my nipples, and it takes everything in me to remain quiet. I could only imagine the embarrassment if Hecate were to hear me.

His fingers trace my nipples as I squirm against him, ushering quiet moans from my lips. I feel Reimus lower his head and nip at my neck, wringing a gasp from me. Reimus moves his fingers down slowly, until his fingers trail over my pussy. My breathing becomes heavy as I grind myself forward, wanting desperately to feel his fingers inside of me.

"Hmm, you like when my fingers touch you, don't you?" He asks, his voice low and heavy.

I manage a breathy response. "Yes."

Reimus begins to trail his fingers down to my clit, and I nearly buck at the contact. This man has been taking his ever-loving-time with me, and now I'm frantic with need.

I go to wrap my hand around Reimus' cock when he grabs my wrist, placing it back over the side of the tub. His hand stays there, locking me into place.

"I appreciate the offer," Reimus says with his head still against my neck, where he begins trailing his tongue. I gasp in response. "But this time, I want this to be all about you. So you're going to let me finger you, and take it like the good girl you are. Understood?"

My back arches into Reimus as I try to resist his hold, wanting to touch him so badly. I nod my head as my breathing becomes heavy.

Reimus immediately thrusts a finger inside of me, as his thumb now circles my clit. Reimus is still kissing and licking my neck, his other hand holding my arm in place so I can't move it.

It's all so…intoxicating and I fucking love it.

As Reimus works me I grind into his hand, feeling his mouth form a grin against my neck.

"Tell me, do you love the feel of my finger inside of you?" Reimus says in a low husky voice.

"Y–yes." I hiss out.

"Yes, what?"

"Yes, I love it when you finger me." My sentence ends with a pleasurable cry as Reimus fingers me faster.

"I think you can take more."

When I open my mouth to protest, I feel Reimus sink another finger inside of me. I cry with pleasure as he works me with two fingers, stretching me deliciously.

I grind harder against him as I feel the pressure building inside of me. At this point, I can't contain the cries that are coming from my mouth and dear gods, I just hope Hecate can't hear any of this.

Reimus lets go of my arm. "Keep them both here, or we'll start this all over again. Understood?"

As I nod fervently, Reimus grabs my throat and his mouth is on me. His mouth devours mine as his tongue greedily laps against mine. With his hand still on my throat, his other hand fingers me and I cry into his mouth. He grins in response but doesn't let up.

I grind against his hand harder as water splashes around in the bathtub. I cry into Reimus's mouth as I feel pleasure everywhere in my body, all encompassing. Then my orgasm hits and I ride the wave, savoring every single second of it.

Before my orgasm finishes, Reimus lifts his mouth off of mine as he digs his mouth near my ear. "I want to hear you."

As if on cue, I scream as the last of my orgasm roils violently through me, sending my body limp against him. Reimus removes his hand, and leans over each side of me as he gently kisses each of my breasts, wringing a soft cry from my lips.

"If I could choose the last song I hear before my life fades from this existence, it would be to the sound of your sweet cries as I wring them from your lips."

Reimus kisses my mouth before he continues to lather soap over the rest of my body.

As I lay against Reimus' chest, I allow myself to ravish in the sweet bliss of this feeling. The closeness I feel with him, the level of care he's exuding for me.

Because I know that when I go downstairs, I'll very likely walk into something that will tilt my world from its axis completely.

A knowing that I feel deep in my bones.

Nerves begin to fill me as I wonder what Hecate needs to talk to me about. My hand trembles as I brush my hair when Reimus comes up to me, steadying my hand.

"Whatever it is, we will go through it. Together." He says with a gentle look in his eyes. I meet his gaze and anxiously nod my head.

Reimus and I head down the hallway to the dining room where Hecate is standing, waiting for us. I look at her expression and if she was able to hear me at all, she doesn't show any sign of it now. I walk over to her, and begin to pull up a seat.

"No need. You may want to stand for this."

Feeling worry course through my body, I move away from the chair and stand directly across from Hecate. "What is going on, Hecate."

I demand rather than ask, because now I'm fully worried. Hecate stands so still, that if she weren't speaking I would've guessed her to be stunned in place. But then she moves two steps towards me, as her gaze fixes to Reimus who stands directly behind me.

She takes an audible breath in, and exhales before she speaks. "Do you remember when I told you that you are far more powerful than you realize?"

Unsure of where this is going, I nod curtly.

"That over the years, your power has been demanding attention. As if ignoring it could no longer be an option. Do you remember me saying that?"

I nod again slowly.

"That is because I have not been entirely truthful towards you about something."

Feeling my body freeze in place, I stand there watching her intently.

"You come from a powerful bloodline, Melinoë." Hecate says, her voice remaining calm.

"Bloodline?" I ask.

"You are more than just someone who can see and communicate with the dead."

When she doesn't elaborate, I wave my hand to suggest that she continue.

Her gaze remains trained on me as she continues. "When you helped that woman yesterday, you felt a surge of energy, yes?"

I nod my head.

"And as I understand it, that was the first time you saw a spirit. Not in your dreams, or in the astral realm. But in physical tangible form. Correct?"

Nodding my head, still not following.

She takes a few steps forward towards me, as I track her movements. She lowers her head slightly, still meeting my gaze. "That is because you are not mortal."

My eyebrows furrow as disbelief gathers throughout my body. "I'm sorry…what?"

I feel Reimus stiffen behind me. "That's impossible." He demands.

Suddenly, the ability to form words again strikes as my gaze hardens on Hecate. "Okay, now I know you're lying. There's no way I'm not mortal. I think I would know if I weren't—"

"You would not have known, not until recently as your powers have lied dormant your whole life. This is one reason why I was adamant about mentoring you. I knew what you were long before you decided to come to Vulir." Hecate says.

My breathing begins to quicken as panic and disbelief begin to flood my nervous system. I feel Reimus put his hands on my shoulders, trying to keep me steady. Once I've brought my breathing to a more natural state, I respond.

"I'm…immortal?" I ask shakily.

"That is correct."

"How do we know you aren't lying?" Reimus demands from behind me. I can feel his grip tighten slightly on my shoulder.

In the next moment I see Reimus' head whip towards the door as we hear footsteps come down the hallway. He grabs me, and stands in front of me as he faces towards the door, his gaze shooting over to Hecate as he seethes through his teeth. "Who's in my palace, Hecate."

Hecate says nothing as she visibly looks like she's bracing herself for whoever is about to emerge through those doors. As the footsteps approach the door, I see Reimus tense up. But once the footsteps enter the door, I watch as Reimus' back freezes in place. I push myself out from behind him and stumble in my steps when I see her. My hands come up to my mouth as I force a hysterical cry back down my throat. My hands begin to tremble as I take in the woman walking towards me.

My shaky gaze takes in the resemblance that I've always admired about her, because I am the spitting image of her. Midnight black hair with piercing emerald green eyes.

"M–mom?" I gasp.

I instantly burst into tears as I rush toward her and before I can hug her I fall to my knees in front of her. I sob hysterically into my hands as my *living* mother kneels down before me. She pulls me in and she hugs me tightly as my face nuzzles against her shoulder.

"My sweet child, I am here. I am so, so sorry for everything. This is never how I wanted things, you need to believe me." Persephone says, grief racking her voice.

I sob harder at her words as she brings me in and holds me, rocking me like I'm a child all over again. My mother is holding me in her arms, after all these years thinking she was dead.

After I'm able to compose myself, my overwhelming sorrow and relief that my mother is alive, is suddenly transfixed to a wholly different emotion.

Anger.

I shoot straight up onto my feet, as I now loom over my mother.

"Why!" I roar.

She begins to stand, with an expression on her face that tells me she fully expected this kind of reaction.

"You are supposed to be dead. How are you here? Why did you leave us? I had to do everything on my own--" My voice cuts out on another choked sob.

My mother grabs my elbows, training her gaze on me. "Melinoë, what I'm about to share with you is going to be a lot. But I want you to know the truth. Are you sure you are ready to go down this path of truth?"

My wild gaze finds hers as I don't understand why she would ask me something like that. The truth? What more truth is there possibly to share other than the fact that my mother is *alive*.

I tentatively nod my head as my mother guides me to sit down, as she seats herself next to me. My gaze meets Reimus as I watch him stand behind me. His presence is a wash of comfort over this confounding situation.

My mothers gaze turns worrisome as her fingers visibly shake. She takes a long inhale before she speaks. "When I met your father, it was long, long before Elzwin was even a village." She begins, and my brows furrow how that's even possible. She continues before I have a chance to ask.

"You are not mortal, Melinoë. And that is because your biological father and I are neither mortal."

I shake my head in confusion as I train on a word she said.

Biological? Why would she say that—

"Your father has certain gifts. Just as I have certain gifts. One of those gifts being manipulation. He's able to shapeshift himself into different people, different forms…"

She trails off as I cannot look at anything else but my mother right now.

"Your father Sebastian…his real name is Zeus. He is the King of all gods, of the sky and thunder."

Shock roils through me at my mothers confession. My father is…not even human? Not only that, but he's a *King* of all the gods? My gaze falters for a few moments before training on my mother again. "W–why didn't I know this? Does Makaria know this?"

"She does not. I'm afraid Zeus went to desperate measures to make sure she didn't."

My gaze bores into my mothers. "What do you mean by desperate measures?" I hiss through my teeth, anger rising within me.

My mother watches me with a sadness to her eyes I've never witnessed before. "Zeus had a compulsion spell put on your sister long ago. A spell that would coerce her to share any news of my whereabouts with him, and to also let him know of any developments with your gifts…" She says, trailing off once again.

My mind no longer feels frazzled and instead is flooding with rage that our father—no, Zeus, would place a compulsion spell on a *child*, just for his sick gain.

No longer able to remain seated, I stand up from my chair and take a few steps back. Pacing in place, my hands begin to tremble at my side as Reimus moves closer to me. I feel him next to me, but I can't match his gaze right now. I can't think of anything other than the fact that my sweet-souled sister has been manipulated by Zeus this whole time.

Breathing heavily, I train my gaze back to my mother. "Why would he do that to her?"

"If there is one thing Zeus craves most, it is power, no matter what it costs him." My mother says as she slowly steps out of her seat to stand across from me.

My mind clusters together memories of a man who treated me poorly, who was supposed to be a father figure to us but proved otherwise. As that thought finds me, my mind trains on something else.

"So…he knew you weren't dead? He lied to Makaria and I?" I ask, my voice beginning to tremble.

My mother watches me for a few moments, before she answers. "That is correct."

Jerking my head to the side as if I'd been slapped, my anger is winning the best of me as I am losing the ability to keep it tampered down. Clenching my fists into my hands, I keep my gaze trained on the floor. "Why?" I seethe.

I look over at my mother who takes a long inhale in before releasing again. She watches me for a moment, her expression as if to ask me if I'm sure I want to know more. When I don't back down, she speaks. "Zeus used his ability to shapeshift for…other nefarious reasons. One of which to procreate with me…"

My brows raise as my hand comes up to meet my trembling lips. "No."

I watch as a tear trails down my mothers cheek, and my knees nearly buckle right then and there.

"Zeus shapeshifted himself to appear as my husband. That is…how all of my children were conceived."

As I put the pieces together, I'm absolutely sick to my stomach. My mother doesn't need to elaborate any further. Bile rises in my throat and it takes great effort to tamper it down. My breathing becomes ragged at what my mother is sharing with me right now. The bite of despair is so potent in my lungs I'm afraid they'll collapse right in my chest.

"And when I threatened Zeus that I would go to great lengths to bring my children home, he shapeshifted himself to appear human, and has been hiding you three in Elzwin under powerful cloaking magick since. He thought if he told you I was dead, that you would never go looking for answers on me. But he knew that wouldn't have been enough. That there needed to be something monumental to happen for it to truly become believable."

My gaze finds hers, and I am shaking with rage. "No."

Persephone meets my gaze. "Zeus issued the mass burning in Elzwin, and used that to feed to you and your sister the lie that that was how I died."

Feeling overwhelmed with all of the lies and secrecy being confided to me, my knees sink hard against the floor. Everything was a lie. My father was a lie. My mother dying was a lie. As those thoughts flood me, I can only ask my mother one question that I'm not sure I truly want the answer to.

"Was…I a mistake?" I say. My lips quiver as I break into a sob. Reimus is instantly kneeling on the ground with me as his hand caresses my hair back from my face. I suddenly feel my mother kneel in front of me as her shaky hands bring mine to hers. I meet her gaze as tears flow from her eyes.

"*No*, my child. None of my children were a mistake. You *must* believe that. I *need* you to believe that." She says as she squeezes my hands. My mother watches me as tears fall from her eyes.

My mind goes numb as numerous things run through my mind. My mother was violated by a man that I've called my father my whole life, who's not even mortal. She's also not mortal.

Everything leads me back to how I was created, and an overwhelming feeling in the pit of my stomach fills me. I begin to cry as I feel the burdening weight of unfairness dampen over me.

My mind comes back to what she said just a second ago, and my tears halt in their tracks. "Wait--you said your husband earlier?"

She slowly nods her head. "The man who should've been your father, Melinoë."

My brows furrow, trying my hardest to keep up with all of the information I'm gaining right now. "Who is he?"

She stares at me for a while before she answers. "My husband is Hades, King of the Underworld."

My eyes bulge at the title. *King of the Underworld*? I gasp as my body tenses at the knowledge that if she's married to Hades, then that means…

My eyes meet hers as understanding sinks in. She continues. "Melinoë, I am Queen of The Underworld."

I gasp as my hand goes to my chest as surprise seeps in. She's married to *King* Hades? She's *Queen* of The Underworld? I—

"So is that where you've been this whole time? In the Underworld?"

"Yes, my child. But I have watched you through the astral realm, as Hades has as well. Who do you think sent Alastor to you?"

My mind hyper fixates on how I met Alastor. How I saw him in an adoption ad in the market one day, and felt so called to know the horse more. That I couldn't explain why I felt so called to befriend him…

"You sent Alastor? Why?" I ask, shock flooding my tone.

"I did not send him, Hades did. He is, after all, one of Hades' horses. He sent him to you to protect you. To watch over you."

My eyes bulge at the fact that Hades, *King* of the *Underworld*, who also happens to be my mothers *husband*, sent one of his horses to protect *me*. It explains why I've always felt so connected to Alastor, and how he came to me at a pivotal point in my life.

As I try my best to compile everything I've learned in the past thirty minutes, I find it hard to form words anymore. As I kneel in silence, I feel my mother guide my chin up to hers.

"I knew your soul was going to guide you to Vulir eventually. So while I waited, I watched you through the astral realm. I watched you go through so much on your own. I watched you become a victim to abuse. I watched you cry and it all deliberately *broke* me. I need you to understand this was never the way I wanted things to happen. But now you are here with me. And soon, we will bring your sister home."

Tears begin to stream down my cheeks as my mother sheds tears of her own. My feelings become tangled together as I don't know what is appropriate to feel right now. Everything is melted together in one erupting pot within me. Until all I begin to feel is unending rage. Rage that extends to far beyond how Zeus treated me, but how Zeus treated my mother. How he put a compulsion spell on a child just to sate his need for power. My fists begin to clench inwards as I feel my blood turning into molten lava.

I feel Reimus tense as him, my mother and Hecate all watch me. The energy begins to shift in the air as my mother stands up, backing away. I don't even bother to look at them. As my breathing deepens, I quell all of the power rushing through me and I unfurl it.

My only goal in this existence was to make sure Makaria didn't fall victim to Zeus' abuse, that I'd willingly shoulder the abuse as long as it meant that she was treated better.

But she's been a victim all along.

Fury ignites me as understanding sinks in. My sister cannot live this life, not like I have. I will go back for my sister, and I will undo the compulsion that's been put onto her.

I stand up and look over at my mother. "Who really am I?"

My mother watches me. "You are The Goddess of Ghosts and Nightmares, Melinoë. You are essentially, a Guardian of the dead."

At my mothers declaration of who I was born to be, understanding begins to take shape at how I'm so easily able to invoke fear into the minds of others, and drive them insane. At this declaration of who I'm destined to be, I curve a smile as rage fills my bones.

Rage for how I want nothing more than to see Zeus burn to the ground. Rage for how unfairly he has treated me, my mother, and now my sister. How greatly I want him to pay for it.

Opening and closing my hands at my sides, I can't focus on anything other than the fury crowding my sight. The intense energy coursing through my veins causes me to begin laughing maniacally. My gaze fixes to Reimus, who's watching me intently. His gaze pierces into mine, and I know confidently that he will fuel my fire if that is what I wish.

I smile wickedly at him, my voice full of sinister smoke. "Then nightmares are exactly what I'll give them."

AUTHORS NOTE

To *you*, thank you. For hitting add to cart, for deciding to take the time to read A Fate of Shadows and Fire, I am forever grateful for you. This story is something so personal to me for many reasons. One of which is that I love all things mythology and occult studies. I have always been one that has been very closely tied with the spiritual sense of life (and I've had my *very* fair share of spirit interactions). It was important for me to retell a story of a lesser known goddess that I, well, never hear people talk about. I felt it was only right to share some of Melinoë's story.

Another is that I felt myself relating to Melinoë in so many ways. Writing her story has been both healing and empowering for me and I am already scheming what the next novel will foretell for our badass, banter-queen FMC.

When my vision for AFOSAF first came to me in January 2024, I felt I had no other choice but to put it all onto paper. Everything was flowing so effortlessly out of me and even though at the time I worked two jobs (& even three for a few weeks—yikes talk about fucking exhausted!) I knew writing this story was right.

Not for the potential that this could maybe sell a decent amount of copies, or maybe it would lead to other successful novels that could really further my career. It felt right because I knew the messages in this novel would reach the people it needed to and *that* is why I write.

Because if I can even have just one single person read this, who potentially struggles with some of the themes in this book, but can walk away feeling empowered enough by Melinoë to unleash that very fire within themselves and demand better for themselves, than I will have succeeded in the real reason why I truly wrote this book. So once again, thank you. And if you are in the beginning chapters of this book, struggling to find your spark, I promise it's coming.

ABOUT THE AUTHOR

Michelle Rossa is the author of the Shadows and Fire series, and her work centers around Adult Romance and Fantasy. From writing poetry, to daydreaming fantasy worlds inside her head, Michelle has had a vast imagination since she was a child.

When she's not writing, she's most likely spending her time out in nature, snuggling with her cat Diva, or re-watching The Vampire Diaries for the millionth time. Outside of her passion for writing, she practices as a psychic medium and tarot reader. She is greatly passionate about all things astrology, the left hand path, occult studies, greek mythology, non-conformity to societal/gender standards, and advocating for women.